SPLASH

SPLASH

Val Corbett,
Joyce Hopkirk and
Eve Pollard

LONDON   NEW YORK   SYDNEY   TORONTO

Printed and bound in Great Britain by
Mackays of Chatham, PLC, Chatham, Kent

To our husbands and our children

ACKNOWLEDGEMENTS

With thanks to Lyn Thornton for research at the House of Commons, Marion Shirt, Linguistics Department, Leeds University, Tony van den Bergh, Maggie Goodman, Finnuala and Finbar McDonnell, Judy Wade, Debbie Pye, Brenda Porter, Patsy Baker, Russell Cox, Carl Bruin, our friends in national newspapers, magazines and television, the Longueville Manor Hotel, Jersey and Champneys of Tring, where some of this book was written.

Special thanks to our agent Carole Blake for her enthusiasm and support and to our publishers, particularly Marion Donaldson, Charles Nettleton, Elenore Lawson and Diane Rowley for the hatbox and the fun.

MAIN CHARACTERS

Katya Croft	Anchor, Morning TV
Joanna Glaister	Editor, *Women's View* magazine
Liz Waterhouse	Acting editor, *Sunday Chronicle*

THE SUNDAY CHRONICLE

Fergus Canefield	Proprietor
Charlie Mays	Editor
Tony Burns	Assistant editor (news)
Bob Howard	Number three
Nicola Wellesley	Fashion editor
Geoff Wilson	Picture editor
Andrew Cahill	Political editor
Roddy Hamlyn	Freelance Paparazzo
Peter MacLennan	Doorstepper
Barry Donlan	Reporter
Debbie Luckhurst	Reporter
Belinda	Newsroom slave

WOMEN'S VIEW MAGAZINE

Miss Angus	Editor's PA
Stephanie Ross	Deputy editor
'Upstairs'	Managing director

MORNING TELEVISION

Martin Pickard	Programme controller
Paul Hayes	Programme director
Alex Kyle	Political editor

HOUSE OF COMMONS

The Minister for Broadcasting	Katya's lover

| The Rt Hon. Edward Saunders MP PC QC | The Prime Minister |

OTHERS

David Linden	Liz's lover
The Hon. George Langford	Joanna's husband
Catherine, Lady Langford	Joanna's mother-in-law
Hugo Thomas	City businessman

Prologue

The image of the lovers would not go away.

A pair of tall Venetian mirrors in heavily engraved glass frames reflected their moving bodies on the bed. Sighs and whispers floated up above the silken canopy of the four-poster which dominated the entire room.

The couple were engrossed, fingertips lightly stroking inner thighs, delicately caressing the curve of a flushed-pink breast, tongue gently probing a nipple, both totally oblivious of the watchful eyes of the silent spectator.

The atmosphere was heavy, hot and sticky.

So it was in the car.

Ahead the road was damp and the steamed-up windscreen only seemed to reflect the perspiring, absorbed bodies on the bed instead of the Warwickshire landscape.

Click.

The swansong of summer mixed with the bosky squalls of autumn as the Range Rover drove towards the London motorway.

Click.

The left hand windscreen wiper was slightly askew so it clicked irritatingly at the end of each sweep like a metronome.

The driver's thoughts were still centred on the bed, where generations of the family had started and ended. But not like this, never like this.

Long, firm fingers held the leather-covered steering wheel as the car turned into the bend. Horse-chestnut branches wove a pattern where they met high across the narrow lane.

Click.

1

A silken head slowly trailed down the body and lips sucked and licked, moving down, down, down.

Click.

The car sped through the tiny hamlet, its windows almost level with the overhanging thatch. A whiff of 'Duc de Savoie', the last of the summer roses, wafted into the half-opened window.

Click.

The frenzied whimpering reached a concentrated silence. It brought a sharp intake of breath from the watcher.

'Oh, my darling, my darling. I love you . . . I love you.'

Click.

The very memory made the driver lose control momentarily and the vehicle began weaving and sliding as, rounding a tight bend, the brake was applied hard to miss a wayward sheep munching in the hedgerow. The car slewed off the road with a screech of scorched rubber and a spray of mud and wet leaves beneath its wheels, hurtling down a steep embankment into a gully, in a tangle of metal, smouldering engine and shards of glass, front wheels spinning.

Two red boxes embossed with their distinctive EIIR gold insignia slid forward, wedging themselves behind the front seats. Everything was silent except for the windscreen wipers still moving relentlessly back and forth.

Click . . . click . . .

Inside the mangled car, blood slowly slicked across the leather upholstery and dripped on to the blue canvas sports bag on the passenger seat.

The driver's confused thoughts ran out into a deepening void.

'Christ . . . I didn't do the bomb check . . .'

Click.

Chapter One

The phone burred softly.

'Are you in, miss?'

'Depends. Only if it's the Prime Minister,' said Katya, winking at Joanna.

As she reached forward for the phone, Katya was aware of a frankly appreciative masculine sniff from the chauffeur as her movements unleashed a cloud of Giorgio of Beverly Hills scent.

She settled herself deep into the leather seat of the Bentley Turbo Milane. Next to her, Joanna Glaister, who was nervously entering the second trimester of her pregnancy, felt unsettled as she thought of the long night ahead.

Katya and Joanna were both elegantly, if uncomfortably, encased in black evening dresses in that season's most fashionable shape: long, narrow and constricting at the breasts, waists and hips. As so often happened, the frocks were designed by a man who had little boys in mind.

Joanna had shoe-horned herself into a chenille sample borrowed for the night from the fashion cupboard of the magazine she edited, while Katya's sheath had been purchased for her by the wardrobe supervisor at the television station.

The phone crackled as Katya recognised the confident tones of their great friend, Liz Waterhouse, who was on her way to join them.

'Hi! You two feeling okay?'

'Hang on, I'll switch you on to the speaker so you can talk to us both.'

Liz's voice flooded the car. 'Katya, I've just had this Piscean flash that you're going to win the award, and have I ever been wrong?'

Joanna and Katya nodded vigorously and shouted, 'Yes!' into the microphone.

Their laughter merged with Liz's metallic chuckle.

'Toads. Katya, all I can say is, just start practising your acceptance speech.'

'Thanks.' Katya gave the smile which millions of TV viewers appreciated every day. 'Where are you?' she said.

'I'm over here . . . no, not there, I'm behind Trendy Bald in the Testarossa. On your left.'

Katya and Joanna turned in unison and spotted the top-of-the-line dark green Daimler belonging to the proprietor of the *Sunday Chronicle*. It had been passed on to the editor and was currently being used by Liz, who was acting editor in his absence.

Apart from hearing her, they could now see her, shaking a flurry of almost Pre-Raphaelite mahogany curls, gesticulating at Katya's cleavage through the car window.

'I've heard of figure hugging but I can see, even from here, that that top's ridiculous. How you going to keep it up? as the actress said to the bishop.'

Katya laughed. 'Strong chest muscles.' She had enhanced her rather small bosom with a push-you-up, push-you-together basque. Underwear which had cost almost as much as her outer wear. 'By the way, thanks for the loan of that gorgeous cloak.'

Joanna stroked the thick black velvet, admiring its exquisite embroidery. 'I must get one like this. It'd be great to hide the bump.'

'That wouldn't be a hint for an early Christmas present, would it?' asked Katya.

'Don't hold back, it's only about three grand,' boomed Liz.

'Bloody hell, then I'd better take good care of it tonight. I'd wear it now but our PR people want me to show a bit of cleavage so that I might make the front pages. I'll save it for a dramatic exit. And thanks for sending it round with your driver. Very flash. You're getting used to this editor business, aren't you?'

'Damn right, but any marks on that cloak and I'll never be able to borrow anything again. Hang on, my mobile's ringing.'

Liz broke off to answer it and Joanna chuckled. 'Only Liz would have two phones in her car.'

'I heard that,' Liz shouted. 'I didn't want to bring it but the lawyer insisted he had to keep in touch. The man we named in the splash today has been rushed to hospital. He may have taken an overdose. Got to go, 'bye.'

Liz's Daimler and the rented black Bentley were part of the capital's glitziest traffic jam, a metal flotilla crawling slowly down Park Lane.

The famous plane trees of Hyde Park, planted in Victorian times because of their tolerance of polluted air, rustled over a multimillion pounds' worth of hardware as Rolls-Royces, Porsches and the like laboriously snaked their way toward the Grosvenor House Hotel for the annual British Academy of Film and Television Awards ceremony, known as BAFTA, the UK equivalent of the Oscars. The guest list read like a *Who's Who* of the British TV, film and media industries.

Although all three of them had important jobs, it was Katya Croft who mattered to the public. In the past two years she had worked hard to get her programme to the top of the morning television ratings. Her pungent style had made her required viewing for politicians as well as the millions of viewers who demanded a bit more bite with their breakfast.

Publicity from Katya's television station put her age at twenty-eight but she was really four years older. Inside the company, unknown to her, she was known as Miss Rise and Shine by those in the control gallery. 'Rise' because male viewers lusted over her and it was suggested that about one million of them a day would watch her first thing in the morning and rise to the occasion. And 'Shine' because the female audience envied the halo of expensively sun-streaked hair and the blue eyes of their idol.

Her boss was delighted with the BAFTA nomination. It meant welcome publicity which should lead to higher viewing figures and, even more important, a reason to hike up the station's advertising rates. For Katya, winning the award would mean her agent could really dictate the terms of her next contract. More than money, she wanted some freedom to quit the studio sofa. She had to get out of the straitjacket of interviews that could never go on beyond four minutes twelve seconds, not to mention the tyranny of the 4 a.m. wake-up call.

The light drizzle on the artificial stone pavements in Park Lane, swept daily, glistened alongside a road packed with reined-in horse-power, now choked back to a snail's crawl.

Inside the stationary limo, Katya switched on the overhead ceiling light and anxiously scanned her face in her 1920s Stratton enamelled compact. Her high cheekbones needed nothing, not even a dusting of powder. But she re-examined her face to check that she didn't have the word 'guilt' stamped on her forehead.

For the hundredth time she wondered how she, who had made it a golden rule never to become involved with anyone married, had got herself into this mess.

For years she had watched other women destroy themselves in this way. Here she was, Morning TV's most popular presenter, lucky enough to appeal to both male and female viewers – 'no negatives', as the research company reported – and a betting certainty to pick up her first BAFTA award, yet she was petrified.

As always, Joanna was sensitive to Katya's moods. They had been friends for years and words were not always necessary. 'Don't be nervous, Katya.'

'I'm not really,' she lied. Joanna's sceptical expression told her she had not managed to fool her. If only it was just the bloody award, she thought. If only this affair was like all the others and I could talk to Joanna and Liz about it. But that was not possible. Would it ever be?

She was about to meet her lover in public for the first time; this was the real reason for her nervousness. The terror, and that was not an overstatement, was compounded because tonight, after an affair lasting eight months, she would also come face to face with the person they were both betraying. She prayed her on-camera training would not let her down.

Joanna was watching her carefully. 'If Barbara Daly had done my make-up, I wouldn't have changed lipstick three times between Chelsea and Mayfair,' she said, her elfin face suffused with concern. 'It's not the awards, is it? *He*'s going to be there. You've been torturing yourself for months. Go on, you know you'll tell me in the end, who is he?'

Katya hesitated. She would have given a great deal to be able to confide in Joanna but she let out a deep sigh and shook her sleek, blonde hair, a mixture of Daniel Galvin's Golden Ash and her own Polish ancestry.

'But I know him, don't I?' Joanna persisted, fishing for clues. 'He's famous, right? He's married . . . right?'

'I'm sorry, Jo, I just can't tell you. Not yet.'

'Okay, but if you change your mind, I'm here.'

Joanna was always there. That was the good thing about her and, for that matter, Liz. However hectic their lives, they always had time to talk, give vital advice or rush round to each other for a chat, to sort out problems, exchange gossip, and talk about what they were going to do when they 'grew up'. In the twelve years they had known each other Joanna, Liz and Katya had become as close as any sisters. Closer.

The three had shared everything in the beginning, jobs, flats, contacts, everything except men, encompassing a friendship that had at first surprised all of them. Though all three had what they called the 'curse' of ambition or drive, even overdrive, and more than a soupçon of egomania, without difficulty they had developed an ability to mesh with each other on several different levels.

When Joanna was organising a fashion shoot in Harrods for her magazine, she might find a pair of gossamer-fine tights which she knew would be an exact match for Katya's new Sonia Rykiel dress and would be as pleased as if she were buying them for herself.

When Liz was at a drinks party for the new American ambassador at Winfield House, in Regent's Park, it was Joanna she thought of after meeting the VIP visitor, the First Lady. Liz knew the President's wife had turned down interviews with every Fleet Street newspaper and supplement. The First Lady's press adviser was going for what she called the softer option and the longer read of a magazine feature. Liz paved the way for an exclusive interview for Joanna's magazine.

And Katya, because of her star status and beauty, was most able to attract eligible men. While fending some of them off, she was quick to introduce them to Liz and, before her marriage, to Joanna.

There was a discreet cough and the driver looked round apologetically. 'I'm afraid it's going to take us a few more minutes in this crowd, Miss Croft. But don't worry about the drizzle, I'll get you right to the front door.'

Theirs was the sixth car waiting in line to get to the red carpet. Under the canopy leading to the hotel entrance were dozens of photographers. Katya gave a nervous groan and Joanna patted her arm. 'You're looking gorgeous. Come on, relax. We're not curing cancer here, it's only a bloody award, for God's sake. Enjoy yourself.' She tugged ineffectually at the waist of her slinky-black dress. 'This is the very last time I can possibly get into this type of garment,' she said deprecatingly, trying to take Katya's mind off whatever was bothering her. 'The designer might have been proud of his sewing but he would have a heart attack if he could see these straining seams. I'm sure he never meant you to see each stitch,' she sighed. 'But it was either this or straight into the maternity gear and you know how superstitious I am about buying anything.'

Katya gave Joanna's tummy a friendly pat. 'I'm sure you're going to make it this time, Jo,' she said. 'You are feeling all right, aren't you?'

'It's rather stuffy in here. I'll be okay in a minute,' she said and nearly succeeded in convincing herself. Well, what was the point in worrying Katya on this particular night?

This was Joanna's fourth pregnancy, the three before having ended without a living child. Katya and Liz had been there for the baby born so young it was virtually a large clot of blood and the horrendous night when a perfectly formed minute baby boy was captured in the lavatory bowl and they did not know who to comfort first, Joanna or her husband George.

Joanna always wondered if the abortion in Mallorca had for ever damaged her chances of becoming a mother.

Tonight she had just returned from a trip to New York. Her doctor had reluctantly given permission on her patient's solemn promise that she would be there for only three days and would rest on her return. She had kept her promise diligently – apart from this BAFTA outing.

She adored Manhattan and had not wanted to cancel her annual trip. The fact that you needed sunglasses every day, summer and winter; the restaurants with their punctilious undergraduate waiters reeling off today's specials as if reciting a modern poem; the wide Fifth Avenue pavements with bookshops that stayed open late; the horses and carriages at the edges of Central Park; the excitement of the city was like a mixture of pethidine and the Four Seasons' onion tart. It gave a powerful high.

The get-togethers were mainly used to thrash out promotional material but they also provided a chance to monitor the staff world-wide, to see if any of the editors had grown sloppy or complacent.

So many British journalists had been hired in New York and now it seemed that girls who could speak English could work anywhere. Joanna had been tempted by an offer but, however much she enjoyed visiting the Big Apple, she felt her future lay in Britain with George and her friends.

Joanna had been the first of the trio to get married. Her wedding to George had taken place in the sixteenth-century church on the groom's family estate in Broad Chalke, in the heart of Wiltshire. Apart from making stunning-looking bridesmaids, her two friends had shielded her from her mother-in-law's obvious antagonism. Joanna never forgot the glacial look in her eyes when George told her they were going to be married. Those eyes had not become warmer over the years. The thought that her precious only child, the Honourable George Peregrine Langford, should walk down the aisle with a divorcée – the daughter of a bankrupt father and alcoholic mother from South Africa – still gave Catherine Langford difficulties. Why did George have to marry a foreigner when she had introduced him to so many suitable, and wealthy, English girls?

George was doing in-the-field training as part of a long-term commitment to an international charity – he wanted a job that made a contribution to society rather than to their bank balance. Joanna's cash-earning potential was considerably greater than his, but her job was not simply about money. For Joanna, as for Liz and Katya, it was about the buzz of being involved, of making things happen, of being a success through their own efforts in a highly competitive environment. This was one of the things that bound the three women together. And it was why they were all invited to prestigious events like this one.

Katya was still worried about Joanna, who was hugging her

stomach, looking pale. 'Shall I arrange for the driver to hang around in case you feel like going home early?'

'Thanks, that would make me feel better,' replied Joanna. 'You're quite right. The important bit at these events is the first part, when you can move around and make contacts. If I can do that, I'll feel I've done my job. After that we'll be stuck at a table. I'd like to see you get the award but if I don't feel well I'll go home and watch it on television.'

The car phone rang again and Liz's voice with its slight inflection of a Geordie accent said, 'We've just moved a whole four inches. I've lost sight of you, where are you now?'

Joanna shouted towards the mike, 'Just about to pull up outside the entrance. How's the man with the overdose?'

'Doesn't look like it was a serious attempt. How's our star?'

'Nervous. Hasn't stopped fiddling with her face since I got in. I'm surprised she didn't bring Barbara Daly as her date.'

'Don't worry, Katya, you'll walk it,' said Liz.

How bloody typical, thought Katya. This should be a brilliant evening. Her best friends were egging her on to win and all she wanted to do was duck for cover. Life was so shitty. You worked and worked and the one time you should be on top of the world, basking in the glory and enjoying it all, something always came along to make you feel miserable. Like love.

'Have you heard from George today?' asked Liz. 'When's he back?'

'Who knows? Next week maybe,' answered Joanna. 'The rat. He's never here when I really need him.'

Katya and Liz disregarded this, knowing she was as crazy about her husband now as the day they had clicked at the Diamond Day races four years ago. Although they had gone to Ascot with other people, she and George had left for an evening and, they later remarked, a lifetime together.

'I could criticise him if he was out enjoying the fleshpots. But no, I have to marry a saint. He's just got to Zaire and he says there's a terrible problem at one of the orphanages so he can't tell exactly when he'll be able to come home.'

'Hey, the traffic's moving at last,' Liz broke in. 'You two wait for me in the Ladies, okay? 'Bye.'

A mischievous smile flitted across Katya's face as she stared out of the window at a short, stout man steering a slim woman at least five inches taller along the red carpet. 'Look over there!' She pointed to the May–December couple. 'It's Tiger, my chairman,' she said gleefully, 'with Rosina, that brown-noser from our Press Office. Oh, I can't wait to tell them at the office. That's an MPP of at least seven.' Items of juicy gossip were known as 'Moments of Pure Pleasure' and rated on a sliding scale of one to ten. A ten was so rare they would drop everything to listen but a seven still rated high on the attention scale.

A few seconds later they finally drew up outside the hotel. The sky lit up as photographers' flashlights splattered a reflection on the rainy pavement. The paparazzi army rushed forward to surround the car.

Well used to this barrage, Katya coolly turned the cloak inside out to protect the velvet from the soft rain and tucked it over her arm. The hotel doorman pushed through the photographers towards the shiny Bentley and held a huge umbrella over her head as she manoeuvred her hair and then her décolletage carefully out of the car.

She took a deep breath. The dress was clinging like a second skin. No wonder the designer had told her to eat practically nothing for two days. She licked her lips to make them shine, mentally crossed her fingers and walked down the red carpet into the blinding flashes of light. She was still anxious about the meeting to come but she remembered the instruction she received when she first became a celebrity: 'Keep moving, keep smiling.'

'This way, Katya . . .'

'Lean forward, Katya!'

'Just one more . . .'

'Look to me, to me, Katya.'

It was a trick of photographers to use your name even though they had never met you.

'Here, Katya.'

The shutters clicked in unison as she turned and gave them a wave.

'Just one more, darlin'.'

'Turn round, lean over for me, Katya, over here.'

'Come on, Katya, show us those teeth . . .'

Whenever they shouted that, it always reminded her of the story of the Queen meeting her latest portrait painter. 'With or without teeth?' the monarch had asked him. The thought of Her Majesty without her dentures unsettled the artist; he did not realise it was royal shorthand for whether or not he wanted her to smile.

The photographers loved Katya because the camera loved her. Even in repose and looking serious her wide eyes and generous mouth appeared friendly. Her figure worked for her too and even though she was constantly trying to shed the extra eight pounds the TV cameras added, her neat body made attractive pictures.

She was always slightly insecure about one aspect of her body or another. At a time when even supermodels thought some part of them was not perfect Katya mirrored the discontent of the modern age. She had never been secure enough in her looks to rely on them.

Katya paused, waiting for Joanna who, unused to the limo life – she travelled to work in a five-year-old Ford Escort – was struggling uncomfortably out of the motor's deep leather seats.

Her exceptionally long, slim legs exiting from the car attracted the paparazzi and through the flashing bulbs and the motorised whir of the Leicas Joanna saw the photographers surging towards her, then heard a whooshing sound of lowered lenses when they realised she was not A Face.

Not only Cinderella, but the Ugly Duckling as well, thought Joanna. This was one time she really would like to have George to hide behind.

As always, Joanna was being hard on herself. Pregnant or not, she was a striking-looking woman. She had a tendency to under-estimate the impact of her thick, burnt-amber, bobbed hair, creamy, freckled skin and tiger-coloured eyes. Anyone looking at her could see she was important, a woman who appeared exactly as she was: a successful editor, each shaft of hair clipped to perfection by John Frieda, who returned calls from only a few clients. She was one of them.

Only those closest to her realised that behind that cool, confident composure lurked a little girl biting her nails.

Nowadays, Joanna felt she could only get herself together with the help of Sellotape, Araldite and Taylor Woodrow scaffolding. It was only the thought of making some useful contacts that had got her up, out and dressed in the full toot by five o'clock on a wet Sunday afternoon when she could have been watching the whole thing on telly with her feet up.

She had recently switched from the softer world of women's magazines to the harder, faster news operation of *Women's View*, a news-orientated magazine, the first of its kind. For the first time, it put her in competition with her friends. She was a rival at their level, ready to hustle for the same stories, which was why she felt the need to come to events like BAFTA.

The paparazzi spotted new prey coming up behind her, a famous Hollywood film star. As one, they turned from her to greet the new arrival, snapping away apparently at random.

The star and his wife, who was clinging on to his arm, gave the perfect picture of happiness LA-style. Only insiders understood that the marriage was a total sham and that he was conducting a long-standing romance with another equally famous Hollywood star. A male.

Joanna marvelled at their performance. If I knew the *News of the Screws* was waiting round every corner to catch me out and splash my life across the front page, she thought, I couldn't possibly smile like that.

As a showbiz writer a few years ago Joanna had spent a whole afternoon with the star and recalled the effect his sexuality had had on her. I was practically at meltdown, she remembered. How unfair that a homosexual should be created so attractive to women. Would he remember her? He had been great for sales when he had featured as her cover story the month before when, like Clint Eastwood, he was rumoured to be standing for Mayor in his town.

Just then the star caught her eye and gave her the lazy, slow smile that had earned him millions.

'I bet he does that to all the girls,' she muttered to Katya. 'And the boys.'

Liz watched her two friends disappear through the glass doors of the ballroom entrance as her driver steered the Daimler neatly between the two TV arc lamps.

For Liz, confronting the paps was always a moment of pure schizophrenia. Should she ignore them and stride out of the car manfully – no, womanfully! – like a newspaper editor (which she expected to be, please God)? Or slink past the photographers looking as feminine and glamorous as she could?

It's not fair, she complained to herself, not for the first time and probably not for the last. The editors of *The Times*, the *Telegraph* or the *Daily Express*, all male, don't have to suck in their guts and hope their hair doesn't frizzle in the damp air.

No, it was not fair, but Liz still held in her stomach muscles tightly as she paraded up the red carpet. It was quite difficult to walk elegantly wearing satin stilettos. And smile. And breathe in. All at the same time.

She was moving gingerly across to the entrance when an unknown photographer shouted at her, 'Hi, Liz, you still owe me for those Clinton pictures.'

Her smile froze. That would not give the paper a good name in front of all the other photographers. They would take their pictures elsewhere if they thought her paper was slow to pay.

Without missing a beat, she smiled at him. 'Take it up with the picture editor.' What a nerve these freelances had. Still, running into the acting editor was probably too good a chance for him to waste.

Liz operated on a seesaw of journalistic panic and good humour. Part of her success was due to an inherent pessimism. As she always expected the library not to have the right information, the reporter to miss the plane and the picture shoot not to work out, she was always ready with an alternative.

Half the time she enjoyed her fascinating and fulfilling job, even though it meant, as the years went by, many ruined evenings, missed dinners, hanging around Fleet Street pubs with 'the boys' and never finding the time to build a relationship. Now, as she found herself going to more and more peer-group weddings, she wondered if she would ever meet a man clever enough for her who would also want her. The tick of her biological clock was sometimes deafening.

Working a virtual sixteen-hour day in the cut-throat world of newspapers, she could not easily confide these fears to colleagues, so she relied more and more on her two soul sisters.

As she walked into the Grosvenor House's multi-mirrored cloak-room, she looked at herself critically. Six sequined black visions semaphored back at her. She pulled in those disobedient stomach muscles again. Not bad for Lizzie Waterhouse from the genteel Newcastle suburb of Jesmond Dene. A dull, windy district, all twitching net curtains and bills stuffed behind the mantelpiece clock. And not bad at all for someone who had been stuck in the office until midnight the previous night.

She had plastered the bags under her eyes with Guerlain's Teint-de-something-or-other concealer and blessed the day she had been persuaded by Joanna to buy this really expensive Catherine Walker number. It looked pretty good considering she was six pounds heavier than when she bought it three months ago. This time I must go on a proper diet, she promised herself, just as she did almost every week. When a woman reached forty, she always said, she had to decide what shape she wanted her body to be. Liz still had six years to go but she was no nearer making up her mind.

It was a constant battle between her love of eating and drinking and having a shape to be proud of. Not that she did not try. Like the others she had been bathed in mud, wrapped in seaweed, covered in hot wax and swaddled in warm mummy-like cloths. She had gone so far as to buy an exercise bicycle which she had used energetically for one week but was now just a handy place to hang the previous night's clothes.

Once, she and Joanna had tried to cut down their eating by hypnosis. They were side by side on one of Wimpole Street's finest sofas while the hypnotist told them over and over again, in a sonorous voice, that they would never, ever, ever overeat again.

'Except for Mars Bars,' said a sleepy voice at Liz's side.

The session had ended with them going home to a feast of bananas and cornflakes, the only food they had in their tiny flat.

Liz's desire to be slimmer was as strong as ever, but she was constantly lunching cabinet ministers, discreetly dining with minor royalty and, these days, attending three-course powerhouse breakfasts with captains and even majors of industry. When the world's best chefs were sticking their finest products under your nose and you were perpetually tired and under pressure, your willpower was filed under 'G' for Gone Away.

In the powder room, she took a look at the queue of glamorous women lining up to check in their coats. This bit was always a pain. Why didn't hotels double up the number of cloakroom attendants? And why didn't women remember it was worth leaving your coat in the car and freezing for a few minutes, rather than put up with this tedious waste of time? Either that or swathe yourself in a stole which you could simply hang over your chair.

It dawned on Liz how used she was getting to having a driver at her beck and call. Dangerous. Newspaper proprietors were notoriously fickle and unless Fergus Canefield officially offered her the editorship of the *Sunday Chronicle* she could be back on the buses. Well, back in taxis anyway.

Spotting Katya and Joanna, she pushed her way forward to join them. There was a sudden hush. Everyone in the line stiffened. The British hated queue-jumpers. Liz waved her Chanel bag in the air and smiled at Julie Walters, nodded at Esther Rantzen and addressed the crowd in general: 'Look, no coat, I'm just here to gossip.'

The line immediately relaxed and the buzz of conversation restarted.

She looked at her friends' amused faces as they surged forward for a communal hug. Onlookers would think they had not met for months. In truth, not a day went by without a call from one or another, or a week without them meeting up for some of the most inside, high-powered gossip in town.

'God,' exclaimed Joanna, catching sight of Liz's full sequined glory, 'a minor miracle. You didn't look like that when I saw you a couple of hours ago.'

'Who says prayer and Estée Lauder don't work?' Katya grinned.

The three friends surveyed the queue. Tonight was going to be a good one. Shoulder to shoulder, it was the best-looking line-up in London, wearing the winter's most fashionable colours. Black, deep black and deeper black. It was a gossip columnist's diary come to life. The Collinses were three-deep – Pauline, Jackie and Joan. So were the Redgrave clan, while major and minor film and TV stars, supermodels, media moguls' wives, mistresses and Significant Others wondered why no architect had worked out that women's loos should always contain twice as many cubicles as men's.

A guest wearing a Rifat Ozbek creation was waving at her. Liz smiled but could not place the face. Then she looked at the figure and remembered. It was Wendy Leigh, a big-time feature writer. As always, Liz couldn't help but give a quick glance at her thighs. How on earth had they held the weight of mega-tycoon Robert Maxwell when they were lovers?

'See you later,' she mouthed. She liked Wendy.

Her mobile penetrated the din. It was the newspaper's lawyer again and she listened intently through the buzz of conversation. Joanna and Katya grinned at each other. Liz was a phone freak and, though she pretended to sigh each time a call came through, anyone attempting to take it away from her was liable to get their hands severed.

'No, you can't get me later. They've banned phones inside. Because it's live on TV, that's why. I'll ring you in a couple of hours, okay?' Liz switched off the mobile and tucked it back into her bag.

At last Katya checked in the cloak and the three of them moved purposefully towards the mirrors for a little prink and primp.

'You both look sensational,' said Liz. 'How the hell did you fit into that?'

'Starvation will do it every time,' retorted Katya.

'I'm going to try that after I have the baby,' said Joanna. 'Perhaps when it's about sixteen.'

Talking about their weight was as natural as breathing so it was a while before Joanna and Liz noticed that Katya was staring at the back of a close-cropped blonde in a tailored lamé suit.

Katya was sure it was her.

When the blonde turned, it was the face of a complete stranger. Katya sagged with relief, then noticed her two friends looking at her. She had to be more careful.

'What's up?' asked Joanna.

'Nothing, nothing, I'm fine,' said Katya, escaping into the queue

17

for the loo, worried that her nerves were bringing out the blotches that always appeared when she was under extreme stress.

When she was gone, Joanna hissed to Liz, 'Did you see how she reacted when she saw that blonde? Maybe that's *his* wife. That's why she's been so twitchy all evening.'

'Hell,' replied Liz, with feeling, 'it's always the hardest thing, isn't it? Remember the state I was in when I was in the same room as Esmond's other-half? Couldn't lift my eyes up all evening. I was so self-conscious, I couldn't wait to get out. Never again.'

'He must be married, and he must be special for her to take such a chance,' reflected Joanna. 'She never usually goes near married men.'

'Who do you think it is?'

'Dunno. Must be important though. It's the first time she hasn't told us all the dots and commas. Somebody famous, I bet.'

A mixture of love, concern and curiosity made Joanna remark, 'Let's keep an eye on who she talks to.'

After a few minutes, Katya returned and fished in her bag for some putty-coloured cream. She could count on the fingers of one hand the times her blotches had been as bad. The night she met her father pacing the pavement as if, with ESP, he knew she had lost her virginity. The first interview for the job with Morning TV. On her way to her first date with the love of her life. Consultations with dermatologists the length of Harley Street had done nothing to help.

'Don't worry,' said Liz, watching her rapidly rubbing in the concealer. 'You know they'll start to fade as soon as you relax. Come on, we always say we never have enough fun, let's enjoy ourselves tonight. When was the last time we were all three tarted up to the eyebrows with plenty of Bollinger to see us okay?'

They paused to think for an instant then chorused, 'Last week.'

'That doesn't count,' objected Liz over their guffaws. 'I was nervous. I had to make a speech.'

'All you have to do here,' said Joanna turning to Katya, 'is to pick up the award, remember to smile and thank those who knew you when you were poor white trash.'

The svelte blonde in the severe lamé suit was walking towards them. Joanna thought, blimey, a showdown.

They stared at Katya intently but she appeared unperturbed and the blonde merely leaned over, took two tissues from the box and put them into her tiny black-beaded clutchbag. After an unhurried look at her perfect image, she walked away with a satisfied smile.

False alarm, thought Liz.

Joanna sat down heavily on the bench. 'I've just got to take the weight off my feet.' She looked up as two concerned faces peered down at her. 'Don't you think it's hot in here? I'll be better in the ballroom.'

She vowed to see her gynaecologist tomorrow. She loathed the fact that, for her, pregnancy was a problem; she wished she could float through the forty weeks like so many others. But when she didn't feel sick, she had backache; if she didn't have backache, she had tummy ache; if she didn't have tummy ache, she had heartburn, swollen ankles or puffy fingers. Radiant? Blossoming? Blooming? Leave it out!

George had made her promise she would take things easier this time. He was probably even more desperate to have this child than she was. Was she unwise to be here? If anything were to go wrong again, George would not find it easy to understand why she needed to go out to a crowded, noisy, hot, thoroughly unhealthy evening like this. But however much she tried to explain, George never understood her insecurity and the curse of ambition which drove her on.

She fluffed up her hair and the one-carat diamond circling her long tapering finger flashed. As it reflected the light it reminded her of George. She smiled fondly. Once again she thought how lucky she was to have found him.

Theirs had been an instant sex match. She found the sight of his long, lean frame and thick mop of brown curls arousing. For the first few months they spent very little time out of bed. But as the passion subsided she realised that, at long last, she had found an equal. He was not only as quick-witted and intelligent as she was but unflappable and solid. These were the qualities she appreciated because they were so unlike those of her father, who was hot tempered and unreliable as a result of his gambling addiction, or those of her first husband, who only enjoyed their relationship when they were rowing.

She observed her friends at the mirror, fiddling with odd strands of hair and rearranging shoulder straps, and thought, 'The times we've shared. How glossy we all look,' then realised she had said it out loud.

Liz wheeled round. 'Continuous maintenance, dearie.'

'Jo's right. We have changed,' said Katya. 'If you compare us with that photograph hanging in my loo taken on the balcony in Palma, we look completely different, except for our eyebrows.'

'And they've been plucked more than a Christmas turkey.'

'Remember when we all had boring hair?'

They smiled at the memory.

'And we were so hard up we had to share hair dye, handbags, even knickers?'

'What about my blue dress?' Katya said.

'Not the blue dress again,' the other two chimed.

Katya had splashed out a whole week's wages on the blue dress. On its third airing it had been punctured by Joanna who had used an old brooch with a blunt pin to restrain her more ample cleavage, producing two large unsightly holes which for ever had to be covered by an even bigger brooch, which successively made even more holes.

'How many years is it going to take for you to stop nagging on about that bloody dress?' asked Joanna.

'I want you all to know,' said Katya, 'that I bear you no grudge for that. I just remember, that's all.' She leaned forward with a sable blusher brush and lightly skirted over Joanna's cheekbones. 'Well, at least now you look healthy, even if you don't feel it.'

'I feel fine. Really.'

They suspected she was putting on an act.

'Don't rush, there's plenty of time,' said Liz.

'One good thing, I can't eat a lot tonight even if I wanted to. This dress is so tight, there's no room for food, baby and me.'

'Me, too,' said Liz. 'I'm too nervous to eat.'

Katya looked at her.

'Of course. The lunch tomorrow.'

Liz was meeting the Boss, Fergus Canefield, the multi-millionaire Canadian proprietor of the *Sunday Chronicle* who was rumoured to be rifling through Fleet Street's finest for a new editor. He was giving Liz a two-hour opportunity to persuade him she was the best man for the job.

'What do you think your chances are?' asked Joanna.

'Evens. I've been told he's the kind of man who mostly thinks of women as horizontal beings. At the moment he's taking a crash course in the fashion business.'

'You mean what's-her-face – Nicola Wellesley?' asked Katya.

'Yeah, he's crashing and she's coarse. Ha ha.' Liz's reply brought in Joanna.

'Don't be so pickey-pickey,' she said. 'That's ambition for you.'

'Ambition? Listen,' retorted Liz, 'I don't mind a female journalist making it to the top if she spends at least twenty-five per cent of her time on the words or the pictures. But this one's hardly ever in the office and relies on her old "contacts" to smooth her path. She gives all of us a bad name.'

Katya wrinkled her nose. 'The trouble is we're all irritated we've had to do it the hard way, with sweat and toil.'

Liz joined in the laughter. 'Huh, I would like to have been asked,' she said. 'What is it about millionaires that they don't think I've got what it takes?'

'Think of it, Liz, if you had millions, what would make you get out of bed in the mornings?'

'Oh, easy,' she answered. 'Believe me, I could spend it all by lunchtime on the first day. But then what would I do in the afternoon?'

A head popped round the powder room door. It was Morning TV's ferocious news desk secretary, Janine.

'Look out,' whispered Liz. 'Vlad the Impaler's on the war path.'

Janine was bristling with importance.

'Katya, HRH will be here in five minutes. They want us all to go to our tables – now.'

Royalty or not, Joanna did not dare leave the cloakroom at that moment. As an expert on miscarriages, she had a ghastly feeling

21

that something was on the move. Oh God, not again, she thought anxiously.

'Sorry,' she told her friends, 'I must go to the loo again.'

'You go on, Katya,' said Liz, detaching a loose sequin from her dazzling bodice. 'I'll wait here for Jo.'

'Are you sure there's nothing I can do?' asked Katya.

'No, really. Thanks, Katya. You go ahead. I'll see you later.'

Katya paused at the glass doors leading to the huge balcony bar, scanning the room in the hope of finding a familiar face. She smiled over the crowd at Shirley Conran. Now that cosmetic operation was a great success, well worth the four grand.

No one seemed to be moving to their tables. As always, Janine was panicking unnecessarily. Katya felt there was little chance of her bumping into her lover who, as a VIP guest, would be in a VVIP reception with the Princess Royal and the other BAFTA bigwigs. But right ahead of her was the one person she had spent much time dodging at the TV station.

Rosina Smith, Morning TV's head of public relations, gave one of her phoney smiles, flashing the results of £10,000 worth of bridge-work, dating from the time she had made a vain attempt to get a front-of-camera job.

'Katya, darling. My, I meant just a hint of cleavage, not a surfeit.' Without pausing for breath, she turned her back to smile at the rather debonair figure standing next to her. 'You do know Ian, don't you?'

Katya withstood the barb and looked up at the rather embar-rassed young man smiling awkwardly at her. 'Where would we all be without Rosina's constant support, we always say at Morning TV,' she said, flashing him her famous smile.

Like most men Katya tuned into, he was instantly smitten.

'Are you in this mad business, too?' she asked.

Towering over her, he pulled a wry face. 'Sort of.'

Rosina could not keep the note of triumph out of her voice. 'Darling, I thought you realised. This is Tiger's son.'

Oh my God, it just shows how uptight I am, thought Katya. I can't even remember what the chairman's son looks like. She was aching to get away and gatecrash the VVIP lounge. Now she would have to spend precious minutes making up for her goof.

She turned towards him with a look of professional enquiry. 'Yes, your father mentioned you were coming into the company. Which bit are you most interested in?'

Unfortunately the enthusiastic Ian was keen to tell her. He had been started off in accounts, he said. Five minutes later he was still happily discussing the cost effectiveness, or lack of it, of outside broadcasts.

Katya was desperate to get away. Trying to look over his shoulder without him noticing was not easy. Even for someone used to dealing with the studio director yelling in one ear, a monosyllabic guest, the moving autocue and the gesticulations of a floor manager, all at the same time.

The minutes were ticking by. Soon they would be called in to dinner and it would be too late to exchange even a few words with her lover. With dismay she realised nobody would come to her rescue while she looked as if she was successfully buttering up the boss's son.

A sudden murmur reverberated among the guests as the sound of the gavel ricocheted off the table.

'My lords, ladies and gentlemen,' the reassuring boom of the scarlet-coated toastmaster rang out over the clinking glasses, 'pray take your seats. Dinner is about to be served.'

Damn, thought Katya. Despairingly she looked around. Damn. Damn.

The stars, their publicists, agents, lawyers and other hangers-on were beginning to surge down the stairs to the biggest ballroom in London. Unwillingly, she was swept along with the throng of excited guests. When she reached her seat, she could not resist looking anxiously at the top table. It was still empty, apart from a cluster of waiters rearranging the place settings. One of them brushed by her table holding aloft two gilt chairs taken away from the top table. She felt the heat spreading across her chest and shoulders – the blotches were returning fivefold.

'What's going on over there?' she asked, turning towards the country's best-known newscaster, who was on her left.

'Haven't a clue, duckie.' He gave her a dimpled grin. 'Unless it's on autocue, I'm kept in the dark.' His usual bottle and a half of Laphroaig a day had not yet doused his renowned sense of humour.

Upstairs in the Ladies, waiting for Joanna, Liz was alone except for one of the world's sexiest film stars, who was yanking her wig forward, teasing the top and making a good job of disguising her lamentably thin hair, caused by years of studio wigs, bad diet, back combing and lacquer.

To Liz's astonishment, she pulled her skirt up to smooth her stay-up stockings, unconcerned by the fact that she was not wearing panties. How extraordinary, thought Liz, that she had so much hair in one place and so little in another. What would her readers give for a picture of this? She tried to pretend she was not staring and walked towards the cubicles.

'Joanna,' she called, 'are you all right in there?'

Behind the closed door, Joanna was willing herself to feel better. Was it not ironic, she mused, that you spent your twenties rushing to the loo hoping to see some reassuring red spots, and then in your thirties, when finally pregnant, rushing to check and praying you wouldn't see them?

'Won't be long,' she called, trying to sound cheery. She wanted to sit for a moment longer, resting her swollen ankles. Although she was not losing blood this time, she felt something was not quite right. Should she duck out and go back home to bed? I'm too twitchy, she said to herself. But if I feel like this in half an hour's time, I'll go home. Although that prospect appealed to her, it was great fun to be with Liz and Katya. Once the baby arrived, it was bound to happen less and less.

As she and Liz swept out of the powder room, she straightened her shoulders and patted her stomach. 'Come on, baby, let's mix with the stars.'

The eight hundred or so guests were standing behind their chairs, chatting. A few looked on interestedly at her slow progress down the stairs. Although she was embarrassed at being so late, Joanna did not dare hurry.

Liz, at her elbow, was already thinking about tomorrow and her next meal, lunch with the proprietor. It could be the most important of her career.

Passing Katya's table, they gave her a big thumbs-up but she seemed hardly aware of them. Her eyes were firmly pinned to the top of the stairs, waiting for the royal party to emerge, her lover among them.

Joanna at last found her seat. Across the ballroom a woman in a really advanced state of pregnancy was laughing, joking and sipping a glass of champagne. Joanna sighed enviously. Her gynaecologist, Dr Bischoff, had told her that a woman's womb was much like an apple orchard. She could always tell which woman would produce apples that summer, which next year and which never. And, according to the doctor, this was Joanna's time to bear fruit.

Waiting with the other guests for the VVIP party to emerge, Joanna, more than most of them, wished that protocol did not prevent her from sitting down before the Princess Royal. For the umpteenth time she asked herself why she was here.

Joanna liked the idea of feeling fulfilled as a domesticated spouse but she could not step off the career carousel. Other women were not driven to sweat until midnight thinking up cover lines for magazines, nor did they forgo family occasions because there was a crisis at the printers. Why did she?

Her friends were no different. If Liz's newspaper sent her on a story, she did not hesitate to put her personal life on hold. And Katya did not have to spend the hours she did in subterranean editing suites on pre-recorded interviews, she could have left it to the technical staff and director. But she needed to strive for just the right shots to produce the perfect three-minute interview. Few other front-of-camera people bothered with this time-consuming production process, matching the right shot to the right quote – however many times it took to run and re-run through the frames – even though few of her viewers would appreciate the difference between the director's cut and her own; but it was for this she was admired by her programme controller as well as the production crews.

The three of them were part of a growing army of females who were beginning to act like hunters, stalking the workplace jungle and hacking away at the undergrowth of the normal feminine territory of relationships, etiquette, community spirit and good neighbourliness. Liz and Katya's single state at their age was testimony to the fact that boy friends had unanimously decided not to stick around and share them with their jobs. Those they might have loved simply moved on to other, more accessible, women. Nonetheless the inner urge meant they could not change the way they behaved.

Nor did their enduring friendship change. Each year they celebrated with a special lunch the fortuitous set of circumstances that, twelve years before, had led to their meeting.

Chapter Two

Joanna Glaister had landed in Palma de Mallorca by an unhappy route, but for her unhappiness was a fairly normal state of affairs.

From the moment she was carried, as an eight-day-old newborn, into the imposing family home, things were never as they seemed. An outsider looking at the child wearing the hand-sewn, French cotton, embroidered infant's dress would have imagined that this little girl, growing up in an eight-bedroomed, white-gabled mansion in the Constantia wine-growing area of Cape Town, was truly blessed. They would have had no inkling of the sombre childhood to come.

Joanna's conception marked the last time her parents shared the same bedroom. In exchange for bribes from both sides of the family, the couple had cynically agreed to an arranged marriage which joined together two entirely opposing personalities and two parcels of adjacent, fertile vineyards. Overnight, the family became the biggest wine producers in the country.

The Glaisters' gracious home was the background to drunken arguments, physical violence and, worst of all, days upon days of sulky silences when, locked in hate, neither of her parents had any inclination to spend time with each other or their daughter.

Incredibly, in the midst of these affluent surroundings, money was always tight. Her mother spent her fortune, and then her overdraft, on cruises, drink, ever younger men and pioneer experiments with designer drugs. Ralph Glaister simply lost his inheritance on the turn of roulette wheels all around the world.

Like many children of unhappy marriages, Joanna endlessly dreamed she could somehow magically bind the three of them

27

happily together but this idealism was shattered when at the age of twenty she discovered the thefts.

Insecurity and thrift had always been Joanna's guiding influences because of the financial fecklessness of her parents. When she began to earn her own pay packet, it did not surprise her that her mother stole from her to pay for her 'hobbies'. But when she found out that Sarah Glaister was also pilfering from the purses and wallets of her friends and colleagues when they came to visit, it was too much.

Temporary escape from her turbulent home life came in the form of a junior reporter's job on one of the more liberal morning papers, the *Cape Times*. To avoid the war zone at home, she was soon volunteering to do fourteen-hour shifts. Her constant availability meant that the news editor gave her more to write and then, later, more important features and news stories to cover.

Joanna discovered with surprise that, although shy, she was extremely competitive. If she was not given the front-page stories or important features, she was disappointed. A keen student of those with more experience, she redoubled her efforts. The seeds of ambition had rarely been planted in such fertile soil.

Her intense drive to succeed in journalism combined with her misery at home urged her 'overseas', as South Africans called it, for the dream – Fleet Street. Ever since she had started in newspapers, Joanna had wanted to work on the best in the world, the British national press.

When she first arrived in the early eighties, all the rival newspaper groups were clustered within one square mile. Sharing the twenty-four-hour village were wire agencies, Reuters, Associated Press and the Press Association, provincial and foreign newspapers. Liberally scattered between them were even more vital ancillary services – pubs, wine bars, betting shops and late-night cafés, all safe havens for the shifting population of journalists, printers and van drivers.

Later, the newspapers spread across London. All that remained in Fleet Street were the façades of two buildings, both preserved for historic architectural reasons: the glass-fronted *Express* Building, always known as the 'Black Lubyanka' after the Moscow prison in which dissidents were tortured, and, next door, the *Telegraph* Building.

Foreign visitors were usually eager to see Buckingham Palace and the Tower of London but Joanna raced first to Fleet Street so she might have the chance to spot the writers behind the picture bylines, stored in her memory from the foreign editions she had read at home. It was only years later, when she met them, that she realised those photographs often bore little resemblance to the real thing. Most of them had been taken in unreal studio settings many years and even more gins and tonic ago.

Like thousands of young journalists before her, she trekked up and down Fleet Street, London EC4, looking for a job, however junior. She did not think about the millions of newspapers being churned out below her feet, being too busy gawking at places like Ye Olde Cheshire Cheese where, over 200 years before, Samuel Johnson had sampled the ale while gossiping with his cronies. The spit-and-sawdust eating house with several floors of secretive nooks and crannies had changed little over the years.

At the other end of the Street, Joanna read the plaque that commemorated the workplace of the distinguished thriller writer, Edgar Wallace: ' . . . to the world he gave his talents but to Fleet Street he gave his heart.'

As she strolled along the Street of Adventure, she scanned the name plates on the windows and doors housing the London bureaux of the world's newspapers, repeating their names like a mantra: *The Scotsman*, the *Liverpool Daily Echo*, the *Boston Globe*, the New York *Herald Tribune*, the *South China Morning Post*, the *Jamaican Gleaner*, the *Jerusalem Post* and *Pravda*. Surely, somewhere, there was a job for her?

A few days later she discovered why Fleet Street was equally well known as the Boulevard of Broken Dreams. British journalism was then a closed shop and without membership of the National Union of Journalists she could not get a job. Without a job, it was impossible to get the coveted NUJ card.

Catch-22.

Some editors, polite enough to grant her an audience, were cruel. 'If I sent you to Selfridges, you wouldn't know where it was, would you? Or even what it was,' said one disinterested chief sub-editor on the women's section of a top-selling daily.

'You'd only have to tell me once,' retorted Joanna, who then made sure she memorised the names of all the department stores in Greater London and beyond. But it was no good. Able to pick and choose from the *crème de la crème*, the editors of the best newspapers in the world did not feel the need for a young foreigner with no experience outside the small pond of Cape Town. She could not get anyone to give her a chance and her carefully saved bank balance was beginning to dip alarmingly.

What happened next was the result of her small-town lack of sophistication and a desperate need to be loved. The speed with which events happened she later attributed to her virginal state. Until she had left home, no man had touched her below the earlobe.

Until Neil.

Three weeks after Joanna's arrival in London, the girl in the bedsitter above hers invited her to supper. They were living in the Earls Court district of London, known as Kangaroo Valley because of its army of flat-sharing young 'colonials', particularly Australians and South Africans.

This was Joanna's first proper foray into London's social life. An hour before the supper, she dissected her wardrobe. Holding her clothes against the window in the clear light, she realised that nothing she owned that was suitable was completely clean. London grime, something totally unfamiliar to her, had permeated collars, cuffs and lapels. Pushing a despairing hand through her shiny cap of light-brown hair, she cursed her sluttishness. At home she'd been used to the constant attention of servants.

She arrived at the supper party wearing a white skimpy T-shirt which showed off the remains of her South African tan and her best pair of jeans. She was mortified when she saw the formal pearls and velvet of the Sloane Ranger guests but tried to cover her embarrassment by being true to her background and not holding back.

It worked. Her funny, artless comments and the amusing slant she put on her fruitless search for a job appealed to them, melting the famous British reserve.

Sitting round the rickety table, it was Dr Neil Creighton who laughed hardest. Fresh from his home in Aberdeen, he was about to start a high-powered job at a prestigious research laboratory. Before he left his cousin's flat, he made sure of Joanna's telephone number.

Two days later, at a corner table in a fashionable Chelsea bistro, Joanna found herself confessing to the clear-eyed amateur rugby player that, for her, the game was nearly up. Her money was running out and it seemed impossible to get a job in journalism. She would have to go home.

'Couldn't you try something else?'

'I don't want to do anything else,' she wailed.

Neil put down his glass of Beaujolais deliberately. For a long time over the flickering candle his dark blue eyes locked into her disconcerted gaze. It was such an intentional action, it made her feel there were only the two of them in the room.

At last he broke the silence.

'That's my trouble, too, I don't want anything else either.' He paused. 'I just want you.'

Her mouth went dry.

'Joanna, I know this sounds crazy but I want to marry you, as soon as possible.'

She was dumbfounded.

Neil's gaze did not waver as he waited for her to react. Time seemed to be frozen. Later, she could not remember whether it had taken seconds or minutes.

'Well?' he smiled. 'Will you?'

Joanna succumbed because he overwhelmed her with something she had rarely had, total attention and, caught up in the romance of it all, she found herself nodding. As she later told anyone who would listen, her decision was incredibly exciting. And very, very dumb.

Joanna might have had second thoughts had her parents shown any inclination to come over for her wedding. But they were too embroiled in the foreclosure of the mortgages of their house and vineyards to leave Cape Town. The bride-to-be decided that for once she was not going to wait for them.

The wedding took place a few weeks later. It was a great success. Unlike the marriage. That lasted less than a year. After the page-boys' hired Highland outfits had been returned and the wedding presents unpacked, they found they had virtually nothing in common except an interest in the game of rugby and a churning physical attraction. Horizontally they were a perfect union; vertically there were problems right from the start.

Neil liked the windows shut at night. Joanna felt suffocated unless they were open. He was alert in the morning, a lark; she came alive at night, the archetypal owl. She cared nothing about quantum physics, he knew about little else and described journalism as parasitical, not a 'proper job'. His party trick was to tell jokes in Latin and she tried, feebly, to match him in Afrikaans. Nobody laughed.

For Joanna, the most terrible part was that they started to have rows. With the fearful memory of the shouting matches at home in Constantia, she could not bear to think the same thing was happening to her marriage and despairingly tried to keep the peace. When they were rowing, Neil felt the marriage was alive. But when his wife genuflected to him and tried to placate him, he became bored.

Then he fell in love again.

The object of his affections was younger than Joanna. Twelve-year-old Glenfiddich malt whisky. After a surprisingly short time, this new fascination cancelled out their sex life completely. Their celibate marriage finally fizzled out when Neil, offered promotion with a transfer to San Diego, accepted without consulting Joanna. Though they both made vague sounds about her joining him once he was established, they realised this was a convenient way out. Since all her friends had warned her against a hasty marriage, she felt she could not tell anyone the real reason for the separation and so found herself completely alone in the flat surrounded by all the things they had chosen together.

Neil sent money from California to pay the rent but she needed more to live. She finally signed up with an agency as a temporary secretary. She convinced herself she would still get her big break in Fleet Street.

Her first job was fun. She worked for a famous novelist, a millionaire, whose hobby in life was to save the pennies, his pounds having already been taken care of by several international bestsellers. At first she was amused by the sight of a household name bending over his chopping board, Stanley knife in hand, splitting matches vertically so there would be double the number in the box.

One day she came in to find him standing on his desk, straining to reach the light fitting. When she asked him what on earth he was doing, he explained that dusting each bulb could elicit twenty-five per cent more light. This from a man who possessed every known electrical gadget including a heated lavatory seat, curtains that were programmed to close at the onset of dusk and a bath whose taps could be switched on to the right temperature and the right depth from the bed, not to mention a piped-in, code-controlled stereo system issuing music to match any mood.

Joanna's humour began to wane when he instructed her to grade the incoming mail. Not the letters, the envelopes. The ones that had been least mauled by the Post Office were designated for re-use, with labels. The rest were kept by the telephone in a wicker laundry basket to be recycled as notepads.

His other eccentricities began to annoy her. One of the house-keeper's regular tasks was to scrape up the fluff from the filter of the tumble drier to be saved until there was enough to stuff a cushion. Staff and regular guests were instructed to walk up the sides of the staircase to save wear and tear on the centre of the carpet.

After his permanent secretary returned from holiday, Joanna was relieved when the agency sent her to spend the rest of that grey summer working for a business consultant based in Half Moon Street, Mayfair.

This gentle man was so affected by the obvious unhappiness caused by her short-lived marriage that, when Neil wrote to ask for a divorce, he handed her triple her normal wages and said, 'You need a bit of sun. Try Mallorca. It's cheap and from here it's the nearest climate to Cape Town.'

The extra money had to go to a solicitor, but somehow she survived the rest of an unseasonally chilly August. For the first time in her life she felt a failure, a stranger in a cold, wet land. Unable to be completely honest, she avoided the few friends she and Neil had made as a couple and spent her days in a succession of unfulfilling jobs where her temporary status meant she did not really get to know anyone.

Joanna had to grow a hard shell to cope with the lascivious bosses who felt that a young, attractive woman should not be left alone, particularly at night. One employer, having tried and failed to bed her, fired her mid-week, so losing her two days' money.

The decision to move came when a letter with a South African postmark arrived. Lynette Checkley, her Constantia neighbour, was on her way 'overseas', inspired by Joanna's selectively truthful weekly letters to her old nanny. Lynette would find out in five minutes that Joanna's so-called interesting life was a sham. And if Lynette knew, so in a flash would the rest of Cape Town. It was the spur Joanna needed to escape from London and her mistakes. Remembering her previous employer's words, she went to a bucket shop dealing in cheap air fares and was wait-listed on a Godforsaken flight at 4 a.m. from Gatwick.

Joanna flew out to the island of Mallorca the day before Lynette was due to arrive from South Africa.

The city centre airport bus disgorged Joanna, clutching her father's battered pigskin holdall and her old typewriter, by the sea's edge in Palma.

She could feel the warmth of the early-morning sun on her back and across the road she could see the vast, breathtaking bay. She was charmed by the clinking noises from the rigging of boats of all sizes, from the native Mallorcan fishermen's *'llauds'* to the black-hulled, tinted-windowed, ocean-going toys of multi-millionaires.

Cape Town had taught her that living near the sea was expensive, so she climbed the narrow cobbled streets at the back of the medieval city to find a cheap base.

Having established herself at a small but comfortable pension, Joanna went to look for a British Council office. Although no world traveller, she understood from her colonial past that one might be found in many capital cities.

It took her an hour to find its shabby, unpainted office, ample proof that the stingy subsidy was not enough to keep up appearances. It did, however, have all the English-language newspapers in its reading room, including one magazine-sized newspaper, the *Mallorca News*, which Joanna saw from its back page was published in Palma.

The British Council receptionist told her the newspaper was produced on a shoestring by a local businessman who was always looking for English-speaking people who did not expect much money to help write and distribute it. Nobody stayed long.

Joanna begged a photostat of a map of that area of the city, jotted down the address and went to see Señor Eduardo Gonzalez, owner of the *Mallorca News*.

The newspaper office was certainly not what she expected. She walked past it twice before seeing a hand-drawn sign Sellotaped across a first-floor window.

Señor Gonzalez was about thirty-five, tall for a Spaniard, with the insouciant look of a successful man. In fact he was also the owner of the prosperous Garaje Pintar downstairs. But he had an attractive smile, and his English had been perfected at Cambridge. The Language School. Despite the heat, he wore a white linen jacket over black silk trousers and a matching open-necked silk shirt. Mr Cool.

It took only a few minutes to discover it was his Alfa Romeo concession for the island that brought in the money. The paper was a new idea, his entrepreneurial effort to take advantage of the increasing number of British tourists crowding into the island.

The paper had been up and running for only a few months and, more importantly from Joanna's point of view, the previous editor/sub-editor/reporter/bottle-washer and advertising rep had left a few days earlier. Señor Eduardo said smoothly, 'A how do you say it . . . personality clash.'

Later, Joanna discovered that the personality clash was with the proprietor's wife, who thought that her husband had been showing an undue amount of interest in the previous sub-editor/reporter/bottle-washer and advertising rep. From then on she insisted on vetting any new employee. Luckily Joanna passed the wife test with flying colours.

With hindsight, the three friends observed that not only were wives usually the last to know about their husbands' affairs, they always suspected the wrong women.

Felipe promised Joanna a week's trial, paying expenses only. If she worked out, he would talk money. 'A little money.'

Journalism at last. It was not exactly *The Times* of London but it would do.

Life on the *Mallorca News* did not remotely resemble even the *Cape Times*. Not only did Joanna have to find the stories, write them up, then design the pages, she also sold the advertising. Far from objecting to this, she was actually good at it and was exhilarated any time she clinched even a quarter page.

She learned the Spanish for ems, blocks, typefaces, wobs (white on black headlines), bots (black on tint) and the real meaning of *mañana* ('Come back next week – maybe').

Even the siesta system suited her. She cultivated a tan on the beach at lunchtime and returned to the office at 5 p.m. Working often till 11 p.m. meant she hardly noticed that she had made few friends and was not socialising.

The glorious weather did indeed remind her of the best bits of home, just as her Mayfair employer had promised. Joanna now enjoyed her life because it had a purpose. Her salary, though modest even by Spanish standards, paid for her rent and meals, and gradually she became part of the small expatriate population that was taken up by rich Catalonians and the international set.

At the end of her tenth week in Mallorca, Joanna realised she had not thought about Neil for days.

At the Morning TV table in the Grosvenor House Hotel Katya was receiving homage. A bear hug from Channel Four controller Michael Grade, a quick squeeze from Sir David Frost, a kiss on the cheek from Michael Douglas, a butterfly kiss from Michael Caine's wife, Shakira. Even Hugh Grant had taken the trouble to come over.

Some instinct made Katya look up at that moment. Across the sea of pink starched table linen and the terracotta of fading Côte d'Azur tans, she, Joanna and Liz made eye contact at precisely the same moment. It was the kind of uncanny coincidence that made them joke they were linked by a telepathic telephone.

Katya was smitten with angst. I should've gone back to check that Joanna was all right, she admonished herself. What a lousy friend I am, so caught up with my own problems.

For the thousandth time since it had all begun, she told herself that this affair was not right. She lifted her eyebrows at Joanna, who patted her tummy and gave her a thumbs-up.

The red-jacketed toastmaster shouted for attention. 'My lords, ladies and gentlemen, pray be upstanding for your president, Her Royal Highness the Princess Royal, accompanied by Lord Attenborough and Lady Attenborough.'

Katya, heart thumping, looked to the top of the stairs, beyond the peach Hartnell gown and Windsor diamonds, beyond the rotund muttonchops of a smiling Dickie Attenborough. Behind Lady Attenborough came two unknown BAFTA luminaries and their wives.

So where was her lover? Protocol dictated that you did not arrive after the royal guest or leave before, so where was Her Majesty's Minister of State for Broadcasting?

The top table descended the stairs, two by two in a mini-crocodile, to the traditional walk-time beat of the handclapping guests. With a fixed rictus grin, Katya moved her hands like a robot. What could have happened to keep the minister away from the industry's most important function of the year?

For a second, she allowed herself the luxury of thinking that her lover had stayed away because of her. If she did win a BAFTA award, there was no doubt about it, it would add to their difficulties. They might even have to pose together for a photograph and one did not have to be a politician to know that would not be wholly wise.

But Katya was a realist. Reluctantly, she had to admit to herself that no minister would stay away from a high-profile event like this because of a personal crisis. It had to be something devastating.

She must get a grip. This was her big night too. Her boss had made it quite clear how vital this prize was. It would show the industry's recognition for a TV station that had modelled itself on the best American morning programmes, offering a liberal sprinkling of politics and business news before the 8.05 a.m. watershed.

Katya and her colleagues had found it a hard slog at first, persuading the right calibre guests to appear. It was then a matter of adjusting the mix to raise the viewing figures and attracting a demographically correct audience rich and big enough to appeal to advertisers.

Her boss, Martin Pickard, Morning UK's programme controller, recognised her telltale blotches and leaned over with a friendly smile.

'Don't worry, Katya. It's not life or death – it's more serious than that.'

Katya hardly paid him attention. What could have happened? She could not help herself, she had to ask him.

'Do you know why the minister hasn't turned up?'

Martin shrugged and shook his head. His wife, never known to disguise her boredom for the sake of her husband's career, muttered, 'Probably got something better to do for the next seventeen hours.'

At the next table, Stuart Roberts, known to everyone as 'Robbo', waved cheerily to Liz, who gave him a broad smile. It was Robbo who had given her that pivotal first job in Fleet Street when he was news editor of the *Daily Graphic*. Since then he had become the risk-taking editor of the downmarket *Sunday Gazette*. He was always teasing her that if it wasn't for him she would not be where she was today. At their occasional lunches they never acknowledged that she had worked twice as hard as any of his other reporters, then or since.

Liz could remember every second of the day she had met Robbo.

On one of his regular over-nighters to London, William Batty, editor of the *Newcastle Evening Post*, did the time-honoured rounds of Fleet Street's well-used watering holes: the White Swan, known more usually as the Mucky Duck (frequented by journalists from the *Daily Mail*), Poppins (*Daily Express*), the Printer's Ink (*Daily Graphic*) and the White Hart (*Daily Mirror*), more commonly known as the Stab-in-the-back.

It was here on a typically busy Thursday night, just as the first editions were rolling, that he and the picture editor on the *Mirror* were joined by the news editor of the *Daily Graphic*, Stuart Roberts, Robbo.

Quietly, so no one could overhear, he said to Robbo, 'I've a girl on my paper who looks quite useful. She wants to come down here and I'd rather you had her than that sod Flinty,' indicating the tall moustachioed man at the bar. 'The *Mirror* wouldn't know what to do with her anyhow. Have a look at her, will you? Name's Liz Waterhouse.'

It had always been so easy for Liz. Other young reporters were as talented and would try for years to get to Fleet Street and still not make it. But Liz had a special nose for a story, an instinct that identified which were the stories worth hours of doorstepping and which were not, which local council meeting might spin into something interesting and which would not. In the newsroom, her record of good splashes for the *Newcastle Evening Post*, which also turned into page leads for the nationals, was unsurpassed.

Added to this, she was lucky. When she filled in for a reporter who was ill, it proved to be an extraordinary break. The story concerned a deranged husband who had in a jealous rage beheaded his wife and two young sons and was being sent for trial to the County Court. When the prosecuting counsel began outlining the grisly evidence, Liz felt so sick she had to leave and so missed most of the prosecution case. After the day's proceedings had ended, a veteran reporter on a rival paper, having heard it was her first court story, generously offered to share his notes, something nobody could remember him doing before.

This luck stuck with Liz throughout her career.

It helped that people remembered her. It was not that she was tall but a combination of five feet eight inches, good deportment and high heels made her stand head and shoulders over other women. And early on, Liz had gravitated towards suits. Not for her jeans or chainstore dresses, another thing which made her look different and rather more elegant than her peer group in the north of England.

At press conferences it was her questions that were usually picked up. Later she learned enough not to ask much in open sessions where answers to her carefully researched material would be picked up by the other journalists. Instead, she would waylay the speaker afterwards.

She was not pretty but when she was busy talking her angular features and surprisingly full lips and dark eyes became so vivacious that she could outshine the most beautiful woman in the room. And, in repose, her face had a quality which made people feel they could confide in her.

Liz had been pushed into journalism by her father, an insurance salesman who was frustrated in his own ambitions to be a professional man. Since her primary school he expected nothing less than excellence from her. He was miserly with his praise and she would try harder and harder to win his approval. It took years, but when she finally realised that, however successful she was at exams or her career, she could never, ever please him, something went out of their relationship. She perceived he was playing a mind game not really with her life but with himself, and it was unwinnable.

Liz's mother tried to fill the void but she was too nervous and too crushed. In any case, the family recognised where the power lay.

Later on Liz was in no doubt that the roots of her ambition stemmed from trying to impress an uncompromising father.

He tried the same technique with Liz's younger sister, Sarah, but she, having watched her sibling, decided the game was not worth playing. She avoided the worst consequences of her father's obsession by pretending she was far less intelligent than she was, got herself married to the wealthiest of the local lads at twenty and then tried to fulfil herself through her three demanding children.

When Liz leapfrogged from a small local paper to the region's largest daily, the top-selling *Newcastle Evening Post*, her father merely grunted it was a pity she could not have got on to what he thought of as a posher paper.

It was he who urged her on to London, but when she got there at the age of twenty-three, he constantly criticised the tabloid she had joined as a 'shitty' paper. Well, perhaps it was, but it was Fleet Street!

As Liz's career on a national began, so did her friendship with Katya Croft. In fact they were intertwined from the first day.

Liz was not easily daunted but the newsroom of the *Daily Graphic* was vast by comparison with the *Newcastle Evening Post*.

She paused inside the swing doors. A visiting stranger was no news at all in a big city newsroom and she had time to look around because absolutely nobody was bothered enough to notice her.

The room was a testament to management thrift. Rows of ancient wooden desks were lined up to form regimented lines. Many of the old-fashioned swivel chairs had turned their last circuit and were plugged with wedges of paper to stop them toppling. The high ceiling and walls were the colour of pale, singed tobacco which barely reflected the grey light filtering through windows misted over by decades of cigarette smoke. The nicotine stain spread all the way down to the maroon Wilton and nylon mixed-twist carpet which had given up its bounce years ago and was now a melange of walked-in pencil shavings, cigarette butts, chewing gum and carbon-paper grime.

The lighting continued the yellowing theme. Fluorescent tubes shone through glass with a pale amber tincture and at least one was on a constant flicker.

Liz pretended to be reading her letter of introduction as she slowly took it all in.

Serried piles of dusty back copies of morning papers, out-of-date news magazines, once-precious copies of exclusive stories and frayed cuttings which were due to have been returned to the library long ago were in piles across the floor. Some were tidy and neat and some were crumpled up, especially those circled round the industrial-sized rubbish bins, showing the lack of spatial skills among the staff. It would be another year before Fleet Street computerised itself and Liz could hear the loud clack of ancient typewriters and at regular intervals the resonant ping of the carriage return as another line of copy was finished.

She discovered later that at this time of day most of the journalists were occupied on the greatest fiction writing of the week: their expenses. Considerable ingenuity and penmanship could turn a meal with a friend into a three-course dinner at an expensive London restaurant with a celebrity with the explanation: 'background for future feature'.

Liz was surprised, and delighted, to see how many women there were scattered around the desks. An over-the-top redhead who could have been a mother or a grandmother, strolled over slowly and enquired, 'Are you this week's fodder?' The woman flicked her cigarette ash vaguely in the direction of the bin with a hand that had seen too much sun on Rimini beach.

Liz, taken aback by her unfriendly tone, was determined not to look intimidated. 'Stuart Roberts told me to come in.' She indicated her letter. 'I'm Liz Waterhouse from the *Newcastle Evening Post*.'

The woman was under-impressed. 'Sit over there till the news editor comes back from conference. Don't look so scared, you won't be asked to do anything yet.' Cigarette still in place, she strolled away then paused and nodded her head towards the corridor. 'The loo's that way if you want to throw up.'

Liz tried to settle down to read the papers for the third time that morning and was at page four of the *Guardian* before she realised her hands were shaking and she had not registered a single headline. Just then a corner door burst open and a tight knot of white shirts, ties and crumpled trousers unravelled into the room. It was men who now dominated the newsroom as they would throughout Liz's career.

A few seconds later another figure emerged. This one was smaller, rounder and older, and the only one wearing a jacket. Even from her far corner, Liz could see he had an air of authority.

Stuart Roberts, the news editor, walked over to what she imagined was the newsdesk and went into a huddle. She saw the glint of his steel-framed glasses as his face turned towards her.

'Hey you, Waterhouse, over here,' he bellowed.

She was pathetically grateful that he had remembered her name.

'This is going to be a change from Newcastle. Johnny Renato's in town and you're the lucky girl who's going to get an interview and ask him about his marriage plans, aren't you?'

She nodded nervously, and thought, Oh my God, why would Renato talk to me? Johnny Renato was a Hollywood singing and dancing sensation whose latest film was grossing a fortune as the number one movie in the States. He was in London for the royal premiere. The Renato publicity hype had been relentless. It included lookalike contests and competitions to win his trademark white suit, not to mention a trip to the place of his birth and the disco in the Bronx where the film was set.

'He's staying at the Dorchester.' The balding news editor picked up a pencil and stabbed it in the air, in time to his words, 'And listen, young lady, if you don't get that interview, you may as well get the first train back to Newcastle.'

In the taxi on the way to the hotel, his menacing words repeated themselves over and over as Liz tried to read the Renato cuttings, hurriedly photostatted in the library before she left the office. What could she say to make a film star want to confide in her?

Liz felt waves of panic rising as the taxi reached the steps and swing doors of the Dorchester Hotel and she saw hundreds of fans swarming round the entrance, as well as press photographers and reporters who were waving their passes.

The doorman registered Liz's black crepe suit and confident walk, and persuaded himself she was a guest. He parted the crowds to let her into the hotel. That suit had cost her almost a month's pay and thank God for it, she thought. The first hurdle over, she looked around the lobby. Now what? As she sat down on one of the opulent sofas, half hidden by a giant display of orchids, she ordered a coffee from a hovering waiter while she pondered what to do. Even from her interviews in the Station Hotel, Newcastle, she had learned that stars always stayed in the penthouse suite. Draining her coffee, she walked as confidently as she could, high heels clacking against the marble floor, to the lift. A tail-coated Dorchester employee looked at her quizzically, trying to work out what business she had in the hotel.

'Can I help you, madam?'

'No, thank you. I'm expected upstairs.' He stood aside as she brushed past him to push the lift button firmly.

Another hurdle jumped. Liz was starting to feel she might be able to make this job work.

The lift doors parted on the fifteenth floor and to her horror she saw about a dozen men smoking and lounging around in the lobby on two over-sized sofas, all apparently hunting the same quarry. They had been there for a long time judging by the number of empty cups and ashtrays overflowing with cigarette ends. For a moment Liz felt deflated. But she pushed her shoulders back, took a deep breath and marched towards the burly man standing with his back against the door, as if on guard.

'I have an appointment with Mr Renato at one o'clock.'

'Mr Renato ain't up yet. Name?'

'Oh? That's strange.' She put an authoritative tone in her voice. 'It was definitely fixed for one o'clock. I spoke to New York.'

'Right, right, but what's your name, lady?'

'Liz Waterhouse,' she said as brightly as she could manage.

'From where?'

This was the moment she had to come clean.

'Canefield Newspapers.'

The other reporters immediately began taking a great interest in this exchange. They shot out of their seats and shouted in a chorus, 'Which paper?'

The minder echoed them. 'Yes, miss, which paper?'

Liz gulped, wildly trying to think how she could wriggle out of this, but there was no way to avoid answering.

'The *Daily Graphic*.'

Loud guffaws came from the reporters. One jeered, 'After what your lot did to him last year? You've got a nerve.'

Six months ago the hardened showbiz editor had offended the star with a snidely written centre-spread splash about his very close relationship with his married leading lady.

'I don't know what you're talking about,' bluffed Liz, having glanced at the cutting in the taxi. 'I only started there this morning.' She turned to the minder. 'Can you let me in, please? I have a firm date.'

The minder gave her a long look, up and down. 'Lady, I admire your nerve, but if you don't get out of here now, I'll call hotel security.'

All the other reporters clapped and cheered. Liz took a deep breath and fired one last salvo. 'Give me your name. I'm not going to be treated like this. It was all arranged in New York and I'll contact them as soon as they wake up.' And with that she decided to exit with as much dignity as she could manage and marched to the lift with the reporters quietly jeering at her stiff back.

Back at the office, she gave the news editor an edited version of what had happened. 'Renato wasn't awake. I'll go back later.'

'You shouldn't have left!' he screamed over the noise of the newsroom. 'Didn't they teach you anything in Newcastle? You should have stayed and doorstepped him. We got a great story on him last year that way. What if he decides to go out shopping . . . or anything?'

Liz went scarlet. 'The minder told me he wasn't moving until he had to leave for the premiere this evening,' she lied.

'Never mind that shit, they always say that. Get your backside down there now and take this with you.' He handed her an invitation to the after-premiere party. 'Stick to him like glue and get that story. I don't want any excuses.'

Liz quickly discovered which was the star's stretch limo parked outside the Dorchester and, by judicious sliding of the wrought-iron table in the window seat of the coffee bar across the street, she spent the entire afternoon keeping an eye on that car. She made the occasional sortie to get through the security barrier but after her second warning from hotel staff she decided to abandon the tactic.

Just before 7 p.m. there was a series of blinding flashes as Renato bolted down the steps and into his car.

'Damn!' She grabbed her shoulder bag, ran out of the café and hailed a taxi. 'Follow that car,' she yelled.

The driver turned a weary head. 'Listen, lady, I'm too old for that movie stuff. Just tell me where you want to go.'

She shouted louder, 'I have to follow that stretch limo just going over the lights. It's Johnny Renato and I have to talk to him, I'm a newspaper reporter.'

'Okay,' answered the driver as he slowly pulled out into the traffic.

'Look, could you hurry? He's getting away.'

'All right, keep your hair on. He'll get stuck in the roadworks down Piccadilly.'

But he didn't and she arrived ten minutes after Renato had pushed his way through the screaming fans and was safely ensconced in the VIP suite of the Odeon, Leicester Square, where the guests were waiting for HRH The Princess Margaret to arrive for champagne before the premiere of the movie. By now Liz was near to tears. The news editor's words were reverberating in her head and she almost wished she had the guts to ask the taxi driver to take her back to Newcastle. She stood on the fringe of the excited crowd and cursed Stuart Roberts. What a cynical move it was to send her, a completely untried junior reporter, to try to get an interview with one of the most difficult and most sought-after stars in Hollywood.

With a pang, she realised everyone on the *Graphic* probably expected her to fail. This caused her to straighten her shoulders. She was damned if she was going to give up now. In her handbag lay her last chance – the precious invitation to the after-premiere dinner at the Lyceum Ballroom.

Liz hailed a taxi and asked to be taken to the ballroom. She did not know it was only a short walk away. The driver kept that information to himself.

Not for the last time in her career, Liz reflected there was no time for the niceties of life. You could be going to the smartest dinner in town, which this was, and not have a chance to shower or dress up. You could never relax because you were always so full of terror and the fear of failure. You could never eat at the right time and, more important, hardly ever drink. Enjoying yourself was out of the question.

In the Ladies at the Lyceum she did her best, combed her hair, redid her face and layered on more perfume, preparing herself for the Renato party and the battle to come.

Katya Croft was looking forward to an evening of total pleasure at the very same party.

Her editor was the official *Viva* Magazine representative there but Katya was at a table back against the wall, so there was no fear of bumping into her.

As assistant beauty editor of *Viva*, she was attending the function through the good offices of a friend in public relations organising the event. He had been granted an additional ticket because his account executive hoped for an editorial favour from the beauty department at *Viva* in a few months' time when a client launched a new perfume specifically aimed at the youth market.

Unlike the *Daily Graphic*, *Viva* had a solid reputation. It sold 300,000 copies a month and, such was the enthusiasm for the magazine, it was estimated that each copy was shared by at least four other teenaged readers, inching the readership to over one million. Any adolescent who thought of herself as smart, sophisticated and well dressed would never feel the month was complete without her *Viva*. The magazine was friendly, it was accurate and was copied throughout the world. More importantly, *Viva* was non-threatening and, as such, was courted by advertisers and the publicists of Hollywood stars.

With the party in mind, Katya had paid a visit to *Viva*'s fashion department that afternoon. Two photo sessions were in progress in the downstairs studio, one going horribly wrong, the celebrity model having called off the shoot only an hour before. The place looked like a large untidy toy room, except the toys were dresses, belts, shoes and blouses. This did not deter Katya, who stepped over assorted bags full of costume jewellery, boxes of shoes, fashion specs and several hats lined up in rows on the carpet. In front of the crowd, she stripped unselfconsciously to her underwear and began sorting through several outfits. The fashion junior looked across and sighed. If only she could get into sample sizes.

'Is this slinky little black number me or will Johnny Renato notice me more in this flamenco red? Or,' taking another outfit out, 'maybe I should match him in white?'

The fashion editor, admiring Katya's slender silhouette, screamed over a jumble of accessories, 'Don't even think of that Caroline Charles number, you'll muck it up.'

'Well, could I borrow the red shoes?'

'Yes, if you promise to wear them only indoors. The soles are taped.'

Katya lifted up the shoes to examine neat lines of tape protecting the soles so they could be returned to the shop, the tape taken off, and sold to an unsuspecting customer.

'Okay, I'll stick to the black. But what about some pearls?' Her hands dived into the bag of jewellery and pulled out long strings of pearls in all colours and sizes.

Katya was not obsessed with clothes but she had long appreciated the impact of the right outfit at those places where the right people would recognise it for what it was. And it was useful to be noticed.

Clutching her choice for the evening, a little black satin number, she returned to her own department and opened her well-stocked beauty cupboard to choose her party look.

Already she had enough lipsticks to last a lifetime, but she selected yet another – the latest entrant from Dior, supposed to be so moist it made lips irresistible. She might wear the subtle French gold shadow by St Laurent – she would see after she had her bath. Ah ... She sniffed at some Floris Lily of the Valley scented soap. She was looking forward to tonight.

Katya's job was fun. Sometimes she thought she should be paying *Viva* instead of getting a salary. Cosmetic manufacturers would beg her to have the leading make-up artists road-test their new range on her face. And who else would be paid to jet off to the South of France to try a new perfume just outside Grasse? Or be sent to test the new champagne vintages at the Berkeley in Knightsbridge? Not to mention having to spend a week of sheer luxury at the most famous health resort in Europe, Champneys. There, massaged and pampered, she would write articles reporting their valuable advice on body conservation, which she herself would follow for a couple of weeks before she reverted to her usual lifestyle, promising herself a return visit to become inspired again.

It was dirty work but someone had to do it.

Of course, there were snags.

Katya was one of the first beauty writers to realise you did not have to drop your intelligence quotient to write about beauty matters. And the first to realise women were as interested in the scientific properties of cosmetics as in buying a dream with the packaging.

She had been two years in the job and was beginning to find it repetitive. The first year she could write about sun-screening products and find it interesting. She had no scientific background but she was fascinated, and made her readers so, by the laboratories and paraphernalia of the pharmaceutical world that lay behind the cosmetics industry.

She was still interested in her second year but with the approach of her third year she was beginning to think it was about time to move on and up. Perhaps it was because she was a little bored with her career that she took Mike Stanway so seriously.

She had met him at Trumpets club in rather bizarre circumstances.

A wig manufacturer had taken over the Regent Street club for the night to prove that his false creations never came unstuck, even when subjected to the most athletic behaviour. The long-limbed cabaret dancers he hired to wear them did cartwheels, splits and breathtaking backflips without a hairpin coming adrift.

Katya and the other beauty editors had become blasé at the huge amounts of money manufacturers paid out to convince them to write a couple of paragraphs, the wig manufacturer being the latest example.

Apart from hiring one of the most expensive clubs in London, he was offering endless bottles of champagne and bountiful dollops of caviar as well as a superb dinner. Katya worked out there could not have been much change from £20,000 for the evening. She had the misfortune to sit next to Mr Wig who thought it was his mission in life to boast about every aspect of his business, claiming that his wigs were made from hair straight from the shorn heads of Italian nuns. Katya realised there were not enough nuns in the world for that. Like other manufacturers, his wigs were probably made in Taiwan from best nylon.

By the end of the first course, Katya had a surfeit of information on the nuns, the plaits, the number of knots per inch and the interweave. The only way of escape was to the Ladies. As she crossed the sofa-lined lobby, she was conscious of the intense stare from the tall, rangy maître d' she had noticed towering over her as he oversaw the serving of champagne cocktails earlier.

He came over. 'I know you're a journalist. Rod Stewart's in tonight and between marriages.' He winked. 'Would you like to meet him?'

Oh no, a toss-up between Mr Wig and Rod Stewart.

Katya nodded.

'He'll be here in half an hour. That's his table over there.' He pointed to one out of sight of the wig party. 'Let me get you a glass of champagne while you wait.'

Katya assumed that this was his job, to introduce useful people to each other, but he was attentive. His repartee was amusing and she began laughing out loud at some of his anecdotes about the insiders at Trumpets. But Mike Stanway was also careful to ask her questions, about her job, the magazine and her family. He was unlike most of the men she had met before. Used to mixing with the rich luminaries of the showbiz world, he was not over-impressed with the flamboyant lifestyles other people seemed to find so awesome. Katya found herself in a rather unusual state for her, relaxing with a strange man.

He put a hand on her arm. 'Ah, I think Rod Stewart's arrived. Will you stay and talk to me afterwards?'

Katya had no time to reply before the star arrived with two athletic-looking minders who, having delivered him safely, were asked to wait in the car.

He turned to Mike, thanked him for keeping his table, then added with a mischievous look at Katya that he hoped Mike had not been too bored waiting. The two men then launched into an animated discussion of the football game on television the night before between Tottenham Hotspur and Manchester United.

Katya interrupted the flow by commenting that it had been a pity Spurs had played too deep in defence. Rod stopped in mid-sentence. Both men stared at her.

'Blimey, mate,' said Rod. 'A blonde and a football fan. If she's also a nymphomaniac, she's the girl for me.' It was said with such a deprecating grin that it was impossible for Katya not to smile. She marvelled that once again her bluff had not been called. She knew nothing at all about football; she had just happened to store a remark picked up from a commentator in a match postmortem after last night's television news. She was blessed with a useful facility for picking up stray pieces of knowledge and using them in the right context, making her appear far more knowledgeable than she really was.

The millionaire rock star invited her to share a bottle of Krug. She surprised herself by turning him down.

Why did I do that? she thought as Mike accompanied her back to Mr Wig, the tedious entrepreneur.

'How about having a coffee with me after the club closes?' Mike whispered in her ear.

Yes, that was it. She would much prefer to have coffee with Mike than Krug with an attractive pop star.

Katya was in such a good mood, she dumbfounded Mr Wig by rewarding him with her most dazzling smile.

The evening wore on and one by one her colleagues drifted homewards. 'Need a lift, Katya?' she was asked but as she smilingly refused each offer she began to feel uneasy. Should she have agreed to wait for Mike? He had not caught her eye once since she had sat down and she wondered if she was making a fool of herself. She grew increasingly self-conscious.

When even Mr Wig took his leave, Katya decided to hide for a while in the Ladies. As she walked across the lobby, she felt as if everyone was looking at her and each step was an effort. In the cloakroom mirror, she saw a pale, unsmiling, unsure face, quite different from the start of the evening. She made a decision. 'Right, I'll go back to the table and if he doesn't appear in five minutes, I'll leave.'

She still lived with her parents and it was a measure of their control over her life that she felt she had to get home by the curfew they imposed, 2 a.m.

Katya was born at Queen Charlotte's Hospital in the Goldhawk Road in London but as far as her upbringing was concerned it could have been central Warsaw. Her Polish father, who had changed his name from Kroczynski when he came to live in England, was both strict and possessive and even now he and her English mother liked knowing their daughter's every movement.

As she came out of the Ladies, she saw with great relief that Mike had positioned himself at the foot of the stairs, obviously determined to waylay her if she tried to leave the club.

'I'm glad you're still here. I was worried you'd gone, ditched me for Rolex-man.'

Katya was rather disarmed by his apparent vulnerability and found herself agreeing to the euphemistic cup of coffee back at his place. But first she had to phone her parents.

Even at 1.30 a.m. the receiver was picked up immediately by her worried father. 'Are you all right?'

'Of course. I'm with Liza, the girl I've talked about, from *Vogue*, and Lucy, who's beauty editor at *Harpers*. They're going to a party and they want me to go with them.'

'At this time of the morning?' His voice was rising, a sign she recognised so well. It meant he was about to explode. 'But you have to go to work in a few hours.'

'So do they. Look, Dad, I'll stay with one of them. Stop worrying, I'll be fine. I'll phone you when I get to work.'

It was the first lie. It was just the beginning.

Physically, Katya was not a virgin but she knew little about sex and nothing at all about lovemaking.

Although she regarded herself as an accomplished flirt, she usually dodged situations where she ended up in bed with anyone. But it seemed so effortless with Mike. He was obviously very practised. Until then she had avoided men she thought seemed too sexually experienced. This did not seem to matter now.

He was an enthusiastic and skilled lover but at first she felt unmoved by his caresses. All she was conscious of was his abrasive chin against the sensitive skin of her breasts as his mouth and tongue sucked and circled her nipples. When his body juddered to orgasm, Katya inwardly sighed with relief that it was over because now he would turn over and go to sleep. But then she heard him whisper, 'How near were you?'

When she made no reply, his tongue started snaking its way from her shoulder across to her breasts, down the centre of her flat belly towards her navel. Her breath began to quicken and she put her hand on his thick, silky hair, unsure whether or not she wanted him to continue. But as his tongue burrowed deep inside her, she felt her back arch.

Part of her still wanted him to stop. She had never lost control of herself with a man before but she could not find the strength or the willpower to resist the unexpected wave upon wave of excitement his insistent tongue and fingers were bringing to her body. The intensity of the waves reached such a crescendo, Katya held her breath and kept absolutely still, tensing her legs and thrusting her pelvis towards the ceiling as a slow-release explosion took over all her senses.

It was Katya's first orgasm and for a second or two she had no idea where she was. She was brought back to earth by his triumphant voice. 'You're my little darling now, aren't you? Aren't you?' he whispered more insistently. 'Katya, Katya, Katya. Do you want me to do it again?'

She gave him a slow, sensuous smile and stayed silent.

'I can't get enough of you. Look what you've done to me.' And he guided her hand downwards.

They made love throughout what remained of the night. Again Mike's tongue repeated its erotic exploration. He was accomplished enough as a lover to know just how much pleasure to give her and when.

Later, when she was analysing Mike's influence over her, she could never really understand why such a transitory feeling, however intense, should exert such power.

The next day, Katya had yet another serious quarrel with her parents. Their barrage of questions about the night before drove her to distraction. And she was forced into more lies to explain why she had not come home. On the one hand she was financially independent, working on *Viva*, a lively, outgoing magazine, and on the other hand she was expected home for dinner every night or had to ring up and apologise for not being there, and then there was the irksome task of getting home by a predetermined time.

She understood why her parents wanted her to live that way. They had had their share of turbulence when her father, an immigrant from Poland and, worse, an unemployed musician, wished to marry her mother, the daughter of a bishop who used most unreligious language in his fierce opposition to the match. So Katya hoped that they would be understanding when she eventually told them that she had a special boyfriend. She had been building up to telling them after weeks of evasion and of explaining her absence by introducing a host of fictitious colleagues at work.

She decided to bring Mike home to meet them when her mother had phoned the office to be told that Katya was off ill that day.

After an edgy dinner, at which her father bombarded Mike with questions, they were convinced he would never make their daughter happy. Katya's parents made it clear they did not want their only daughter to marry a nightclub maître d'.

'The only person you think is good enough for me is Prince Charles,' she had shouted, after Mike had gone home.

'No, no, *malenka*,' admonished her father in his husky mid-European accent, 'but what sort of life would it be sitting at home with your babies, waiting for that man to come home from his night-clubbing?'

Her parents pretended not to understand that the club was a business like any other. The discussions were getting more heated . . . and more frequent.

When, a few weeks later, she told them she was considering giving up her job and going with Mike to Mallorca, they were appalled and spent many evenings trying to dissuade her. Katya found the strength for once to survive their emotional onslaught and when they saw how determined she was they had to settle for a promise that at least she would not marry him. Or live with him.

'I know a girl who has an empty room in her flat,' she told them. Another lie.

But problems with parents and boyfriend were put aside that night in the excitement of preparing for the biggest party in town . . .

Liz was stuck at the back of the ballroom, behind a mirrored pillar, adjacent to the kitchen. The position told her everything she needed to know about what they thought of her newspaper and its show-biz correspondent.

She was sitting with eight women and two men who she later realised were totally uninterested in the female gender. Her chair was squashed between the two men on her right and a tall, immaculate blonde on her left. The woman obviously worked for a fashion magazine. Looking like that, she could never be a news reporter.

Liz was very conscious that she had had no time to freshen up and she was worried that the tobacco smoke from the taxi and the nervous tension of waiting at the Dorchester – the stench of hard work – would collide with the potpourri of jasmine-scented bath water, essential oil of patchouli and Givenchy Insensé assaulting her nostrils from both sides.

The mannered, well-tailored man on her right was every bit as faultless as the beauty on her left. In fact, in the eyelash stakes, it would have been hard to choose which was the more curled and mascaraed.

The blonde's place card read 'Katya Croft, *Viva* Magazine'. Other cards announced representatives from *Time Out*, *Woman's Own*, *TV Times*, *Woman's Journal* and *Good Housekeeping*. Liz was disappointed that her first day in Fleet Street was in the company of magazine journalists instead of in what she thought was her rightful place with reporters from the *Daily Mirror*, *Daily Express* and *Daily Mail*. She had been hoping to meet a kindred spirit who might work close to her in Fleet Street. Instead she was with people whom hard news reporters described disparagingly as the 'strawberry jam correspondents'. Liz later found out that the news guys were quite wrong.

The blonde from *Viva* looked at her place card. 'Peter Earling, *Daily Graphic*' it stated.

'What did you have to do to him to get here?' she asked Liz.

'At this moment, I'd much rather he was here than me,' Liz replied with a smile.

'Why? I know a lot of people who'd kill for an invitation to this party.'

'Oh, I'm not here to enjoy myself,' said Liz firmly. 'If I don't get to Johnny Renato, I'm finished, and I've only been on the *Graphic* for a day.'

'You've got to be joking.'

'My news editor isn't. He's told me to go back to Newcastle if I don't get the interview.'

'Isn't he just winding you up? He must be.' She put out a hand. 'I'm Katya Croft, hello.'

'The late Liz Waterhouse. Hi.'

They both laughed.

'Have a drink, for goodness sake,' suggested Katya. 'You look as if you need it.'

'Okay, but only if I can have it in a syringe, straight into the vein.' It was a favourite saying of Liz's. 'I'll need binoculars to see Johnny Renato from here, never mind getting to talk to him.'

'This might help your eyesight,' said Katya, pouring a glass.

As they looked around the cavernous ballroom, minor showbiz

and TV personalities, editors, their wives, mistresses and assorted other hacks were attempting to gyrate à la Renato to the soundtrack of the film.

It was an era when the publicity and public relations budgets almost overtook the cost of the movie. The Lyceum was decorated to look like the Bronx disco where the action of the film took place. Liz could hardly believe she could see so many top editors in the same room. They looked older, greyer and fatter than the photographs she had seen over the years in the *UK Press Gazette.*

'It's a long time since any of them could squeeze into a white suit,' she muttered to Katya and they smiled conspiratorially.

Four hundred couverts of lamb – two slices per head, steeped in over-cooked glutinous sauce – soggy carrot batons and over-boiled new potatoes came and went. Katya, who was a health freak long before it became fashionable, knew mass catering should come with a health warning so while she steamed her face in the bath, her indulgent mother had prepared a nutritious salad. She hardly ate, merely pushing her food around the plate. As did Liz, whose tension-packed stomach would have none of it.

The Renato party came into the ballroom to a burst of applause and excitement. As Liz saw her prey, her skin began to prickle. Katya was looking for her friend Caroline Neville, the top PR queen who had been brought in by Twentieth Century-Fox to mastermind the film launch. When she spotted the distinctive silver wispy bob of her friend, she gracefully glided in a wide sweep through the tables to reach her. She was standing next to Renato.

'You look marvellous, darling.' Caroline was delighted to see Katya, giving her a social air kiss, her lips just missing each cheek.

'St Laurent, Dior and none of it paid for, thank God,' said Katya. Caroline, being a beauty PR, understood the truth behind the designer make-up and clothes that covered every inch of every beauty editor.

There was a tap on Caroline's shoulder. 'Introduce me to your friend.' It was the same minder who had been guarding the star all day and had been so peremptory with Liz at the Dorchester. The gorilla smiled at Katya. 'Why don't you join Johnny for a drink?'

he said. 'He loves meeting the locals.'

Yeah, but only if they're tall, willowy and pretty stunning, thought Caroline.

The gorilla guided Katya to a table packed with Twentieth Century-Fox suits, animatedly discussing how much the movie would gross that week Stateside. One of them reluctantly got up to make room for her. Liz watched from the other side of the ballroom with a mixture of admiration and envy. It was make or break time. If Katya could do it, so could she.

It did not take her long to push her way through to Katya's table. As she was leaning over to say something to her new friend, her arm was grasped rather too firmly. She was edged away and the gorilla blocked her view.

'I think we met this morning, lady. You're the one from the *Daily Graphic*. And the answer's still the same.'

'Look, it's my first day on the *Graphic*.'

'Oh yeah?' He looked at her in disbelief.

'Really. And they're going to send me back to Newcastle if I don't get just a few words with Johnny.'

The gorilla gave her another of his long, lingering looks, his eyes travelling from head to toe. She had a smidgen of hope.

'Lady, maybe you'd be better off there.'

Liz retired hurt to her corner, the adrenaline evaporated. She felt deflated, a failure. I suppose if I had worn a scooped neckline I could be sitting with Renato by now, she thought sourly. She considered leaving and secreting herself in the penthouse of the Dorchester and was picking up her bag to leave when Katya came bouncing back to her table extremely pleased with herself.

'Right, I've got some really good stuff you can use.'

Liz was surprised. 'Don't you want it for your own magazine?'

'No,' replied Katya. 'We're working three months in advance and by then we'll be on another personality. Teenagers are very fickle, you know. He told me a heap of stuff about his diet and his weight-lifting. I know where he gets his clothes and what kind of aftershave he uses and he did all the dancing sequences himself and, best of all, he's desperate to get married and have babies.'

'Oh, Katya, thanks very much, but the *Daily Graphic* really wants to know why he was sharing a bungalow at the Bel-Air Hotel with Julia Ryder last weekend.'

'Oops, I didn't ask him that.'

'Well, thank you for try— Oh, he's leaving.' Liz was panic-stricken. 'Please, try again. Get him before he goes out.'

Without a word, Katya was off again, weaving in and out through the chairs like a slalom racer. Liz saw her catch hold of Renato's sleeve and watched as his dark head bent towards her upturned face. They stayed like that for some seconds then the heads parted and Renato and his henchmen moved off.

Katya returned covered in smiles. 'I've got it, I've got it.'

'Ssh, don't say a word,' pleaded Liz. 'Come over here.'

A reporter from the *Daily Mail* rushed up and shouted at Katya, 'What was he saying to you?'

Liz gripped Katya's arm and hissed, 'Tell him nothing. Let's go and have a real meal. Have you ever tried the *Daily Graphic* canteen?'

Katya shook her head.

'Neither have I, but it can't be as bad as the one at the *Newcastle Evening Post.*'

It was. Every bit. Their friendship was cemented, not in blood, but in bacon butties. And an exclusive page lead in the following day's *Graphic*.

Chapter Three

Katya's parents failed to stop her when she finally announced she wanted to follow Mike Stanway to Palma, where he was now manager of Tito's nightclub, the result of a recommendation from a millionaire member of Trumpets.

Mike phoned Katya daily telling her how wonderful the island was and, although she had done her best to dissuade him from leaving London, he did make her feel that staying in her magazine job was dull compared with the adventures she could have in the sun. These were frankly dirty phone calls where Mike described all the things he was missing and all the things he was planning to do to her. She could tell by the escalating number of calls that his patience was wearing thin and his sex drive was in top gear. If she didn't go over there, his tongue would be working its magic on some other girl. Another woman might have been able to respond on the phone with equal fervour to keep him turned on to her. But Katya was too inhibited to match his erotic talk. While he was able to produce orgasms for her by taking her step-by-step from foreplay to climax, she found it embarrassing to do the same for him.

Perhaps if she had met someone else her life might have taken a different turn. But all the men attracted to her seemed unexciting after Mike.

This, her increasing boredom with her job and the continuous claustrophobic atmosphere at home made up her mind. After the next row with her parents, she handed in her resignation to a surprised and regretful editor and booked a one-way plane ticket to Mallorca.

An hour after her flight landed, she was in Mike's bed. He was voracious. He had missed her. Over the next few weeks he insisted on their making love in the sea, on the beach, on boats, in the shower, in a beautifully preserved, wrought-iron lift in one of Palma's most luxurious buildings on their way to dinner, on his balcony and, once, behind the back of an imperturbable driver in a horse-drawn carriage.

Mike had always enjoyed an experimental and active sex life. He was used to holding women in his sexual thrall and assumed that Katya, like all his girls before her, would be happy to satisfy his every sexual whim. But as the weeks wore on, to the surprise of them both he became more enthusiastic about her and she became more and more detached from him.

Mike enjoyed women and was genuinely interested in what they wore, their food fads and aspects of their lives that most men were completely blind to. He loved the fact that he saw them after they had spent hours perfecting their looks, combed and mussed to within an inch of their lives.

The trouble was that Mike's view of women had been overly coloured by the sort that went to chic nightclubs like Tito's. He imagined that Katya would want nothing better than to spend her days aiming to make herself perfect for him. The fact that it might be boring to spend her waking hours worrying about nothing more serious than a broken nail and making no more weighty decision than which top to wear, never occurred to him, as it did not to most of Tito's female clientele.

Mike loved being at work, alert and watchful, when richer, smarter people were at play. It made him feel powerful that men with millions would jump off their yachts to seek him out. Mike was a great fixer. Within weeks of arriving he could arrange a mooring in the harbour, the August lease on a villa that never seemed to come on to the market and introductions to useful contacts, business or otherwise. Especially otherwise.

He was thrilled that he and Katya had all the time in the world for lovemaking, that she did not have to go home but could stay all night. He persuaded her to be there, bathed, scented and ready for him whenever he could return for sex. But Katya, who wandered around the apartment, sometimes for hours, in underwear and high heels waiting for these high-voltage sessions, gradually realised he was becoming her jailer. Just as her parents had been.

She had no job, limited money and no friends or family on the island. But, far from making her cling to Mike, the absence of all these ties made her less dependent, not more. She missed the gossipy lunches, the outings to the cinema and the shared confidences of Liz, who had over the preceding few months become her best friend. Weekly phone calls, she found, were small compensation. As they were both on a limited budget, their conversations had to be concise. It was very unsatisfactory.

What she hardly dared admit to herself was that, even though she had found it all so exciting on the phone, sex on demand was just that, demanding. In London, there had been a certain frisson in making rushed and furtive love when she should have been at work or at home. Now she had thrown off these shackles, their new, open relationship was less thrilling.

Her sense of unease grew when she discovered huge differences between them. She found it mattered that Mike never read anything more demanding than music magazines. And she hated herself for caring so much that Mike's love notes were littered with spelling mistakes. At first she tried to make light of it but gradually it turned her off him.

He loved the superficial and was keen to acquire the right labels, but paced impatiently outside while she visited Palma Cathedral and its medieval ramparts or stayed at home while she travelled to Robert Graves's shrine in Deya.

Apprehensive about Katya's growing indifference to his love-making, Mike tried harder and harder to rediscover her orgasms. The more he tried, the more elusive they were. Katya refused to discuss it but his ego could not cope with failure.

The other thing he could not cope with was the unwelcome visit of Mr and Mrs Croft. After weeks of anguished phone calls they had decided to come and see for themselves what their daughter was doing. She had only forty-eight hours' notice of their arrival, during which all evidence of Mike's existence had to be cleared out of the apartment. He was amazed and resentful at how determined Katya was to protect her parents from the truth. She gave him an ultimatum: either he stayed at the nightclub or she would move out permanently. It was his first glimpse of how frightened she was of her parents. And how resolute she could be.

Liz helped fortify that resolution. They spoke to each other every week and, when Liz realised how bored Katya was, she began suggesting features Katya could write for the *Daily Graphic* from Mallorca. 'Our foreign guy says there's a terrific girl running a little local English newspaper in Palma. Probably a tuppeny-ha'penny affair but it might be worth going to have a chat to see if you can get some work. Her name's Joanna Glaister.'

Liz had nagged her about this girl so many times that when Katya's mother started asking her how she was paying for the expensive apartment, the name Joanna Glaister and the *Mallorca News* popped out like hot bread from a toaster. And when, after seven tense and strained days, her parents returned home, Katya decided she had better try and make the lie come true.

Two days later she turned up at the paper's small, humid office above a garage, looking as if she was auditioning for a magazine cover shot rather than a junior job.

Fierce words were emanating from a tawny-skinned young woman sitting with her feet on the desk shouting into the receiver in a strange, guttural tongue. A sheaf of inky proofs had smudged her otherwise pristine white trousers.

'What language was that?' asked Katya when at last there was a moment's silence.

'Afrikaans. It's what we talk back home. I hope you didn't understand any of it. I was just, uh, sharing my feelings with an old friend who's done some photographs for me and who's missed this week's deadline.'

'No, I didn't get any of it, not a word, but if you're busy I'll come back another day.'

'Well, I thought I'd be finished by now but losing those pictures has made us even later. You must be Katya Croft. I'm Joanna Glaister, hello.' She held out a slender hand. 'Your note said you could sub, so maybe you could help. I'm having trouble getting these stories to fit and these pages were supposed to be at the printers,' Joanna looked at her watch, 'an hour ago.'

Katya realised her interview was over when she was handed two pencils and an Anglo-Spanish sub-editing style book. A couple of hours later, she who had only ever written or subbed beauty and fashion pieces for teenagers was busily editing down reports sent in by local correspondents. She found herself rewriting the inquest on the sudden death of a Preston man while swimming with his grandchild, the results of the wet T-shirt competition in Santa Ponsa and the latest nuisance antics caused by the annual go-slow of the French air traffic controllers.

For Katya and Joanna this was the start of a highly successful working partnership. The *Mallorca News* began to thrive. Tourism from Britain was up by fifty per cent and more Brits were buying homes on the island. Readership improved and so did advertisement revenue.

Katya's salary was minute but she found herself staying longer in the office, often turning up late at the flat for lunch, sex and siesta. It led to rows, with Mike asking why she was wasting her time earning a pittance.

But she became absorbed in the job. Her weeks of total dependence on a man made her realise that the dream that some women had, of a life of ease where the only effort was concentrated on beautifying their bodies, was ultimately unsatisfying, often leading to low self-esteem.

She felt she was lucky to learn this lesson so early. She would never live her life entirely through a man again.

So, with her growing absorption in the job, plus the offer of a share in Joanna's apartment, Katya found the motivation to break with Mike. After his hours of pleading with her to stay, it still hurt when she discovered how quickly he found a beautiful replacement. Cynically she wondered just how much Mike had loved her and it made her distrustful of those who would follow in his path.

A few months later, a sad and subdued Liz arrived on the island. Until now she had resisted Katya's earlier attempts to persuade her to come over for a holiday, but circumstances had changed. Within the last nightmare eight weeks her mother had died and the *Daily Graphic* had closed down, leaving her jobless. She had phoned

Katya every day and Katya had tried to raise her friend's crushed spirits by listening and consoling.

'The best thing you could do,' she told Liz, 'is to leave everything behind you and come over here for a while. Just until you get over the worst. What do you say?'

Liz did not need much persuading. It was a pale, overweight and puffy Liz who stood holding on to a hand rail at the airport, waiting to be collected. When Joanna was introduced to Liz, her first thought was how different she looked from the picture of the vibrant, thrusting personality Katya had described.

In the days that followed, Liz floated round the flat unwilling and seemingly unable to be coaxed out of her depression. Joanna, ever sensitive to other people's distress, tried making Liz feel welcome in her apartment, preparing appetising meals, buying flowers for her room and gently persuading her to talk.

Ten days after Liz's arrival, the other two came home after work to find a bottle of champagne chilling in the fridge. Liz said she wanted to talk about everything that had happened. It had all been bottled up. But what she most needed to make sense of was what had led to her mother's death.

Haltingly, Liz revealed that her mother had not died of natural causes as Katya had assumed. Susan Waterhouse had committed suicide. Katya tried, unsuccessfully, to hide her shock – Liz had given no hint of this in their frequent phone calls. Now, she tried to describe her guilt at being so preoccupied with her career that she had been unable to prevent her mother taking her own ife. Step by painful step she tried to imagine her mother's last thoughts before she swallowed the cocktail of alcohol and sleeping tablets, prescribed by a sympathetic doctor to overcome insomnia.

Susan Waterhouse had long lost the beauty that had attracted Liz's father twenty-six years before. He had been responsible for destroying not only her looks but her spirit. Drummed it out of her with his bullying, his nagging and his meanness. By rights, she should have been relieved when he died of a heart attack in the casualty ward of Newcastle's Royal Infirmary.

Liz and her younger sister Sarah tried hard to remember happy moments from their childhood so they could feel sorrow at the passing of their sixty-year-old father. But it was difficult. Their overriding memory of him was as a sitting-room dictator. One of their daily tasks had been to report on the exact set of his face as he drove into the garage after work. If he was in a black mood the television was immediately turned off, school books were whipped out and the atmosphere became quiet and tense. Dinner was eaten in silence lest they sparked off a sudden and violent explosion. Despite all these precautions, any little thing, like no salt on the table, would provoke a rage where one or other of them ended up with a beating. He ruled by fear and the repressive atmosphere hung heavily over their pebbledash home whether he was in or out.

After the funeral, Liz and her mother had their happiest few weeks ever, planning Life without Father. With enthusiasm, Susan Waterhouse made plans to sell the family home and buy a small flat near Liz in London. For the first time she had the freedom to help at least one of her daughters. She planned to take over Liz's domestic chores but she would live in a separate flat. She was anxious not to be in the way but she was going to devote her life with love, not fear, to her unmarried daughter.

Liz had never seen her mother smile so much – until the will was read. The first shock was that the family home which they believed had long been paid for had a huge mortgage. The second and greater shock was that the money this had raised had gone to another woman who also called herself Mrs Alec Waterhouse. It was through the building society lawyer that Susan Waterhouse found out that, for twenty-four years out of the twenty-six of her married life, her husband had been living a lie. Only an hour's drive away, he had embarked on another relationship and had fathered two other daughters. What was even worse, she found out later that, unlike her own family, this other one had been happy. To this 'wife' and these two daughters, the bully had become a gentle man.

Susan never recovered from the shock. She had never felt such a failure. How had another woman managed to make her husband loving, caring and kind? And even harder to bear, a doting father?

In Joanna's flat, Liz started to sob. 'Mum had convinced me she was okay. That's what I'll never forgive myself for. Maybe I just wanted to believe it.'

Joanna and Katya listened attentively, without interrupting.

'I go over and over it again in my mind. Maybe I was too easily fooled. After my father died, we spent every weekend together. Either I went up there or she came down. And we used to talk on the phone for ages at least a couple of times a week. She was getting to know me as an adult and I thought it was wonderful. Why I didn't see any signs of the torment she must have been going through I'll never know.

'The stupid thing is I was in on the night she killed herself, you know. I could so easily have been out on a job. That night I phoned and phoned and I could not understand why there was no answer.' Liz twisted and untwisted her fingers.

'Since . . . what happened . . . I've been trying to understand what was going on in her mind. She told me she didn't enjoy going out any more in case she bumped into the other woman or the daughters. I told her she was silly . . . silly.' Her hands were still tangling and untangling. 'That's why she was looking forward to leaving the area and coming down to London. My sister and I thought she was getting over it. Even the grief counsellor thought she was doing okay. And all the time she wasn't. Of course,' Liz said ruefully, 'she'd had a lifetime of hiding her feelings. She'd become good at it.'

After that long night, Liz's mood swings became less frequent. She seemed less bleak. Joanna and Katya began to hope that she would recover.

They were wrong. Like her mother, Liz was clever at disguising her emotions.

She began to help them out with the paper. They were puzzled that she would be asleep by 9 p.m. and at first Katya and Joanna teased her that she was having her siestas too late in the day. But when she had to be dragged out of bed at 9 a.m. and still complained of tiredness they became concerned.

At the office Liz found it more and more difficult to concentrate, losing all motivation, which made it all the harder to leave her bedroom. She would spend the time either pacing up and down or, as the others discovered a few days later, sitting on her bed rocking backwards and forwards, sobbing quietly. The bouts of weeping sometimes continued for hours and, in between, Liz would talk of the pain and guilt at not having helped her mother when she most needed it. She could not, would not, forgive herself.

Joanna and Katya felt distressed and inadequate. During the black days and nights, they did not know how to comfort her. They spent all their non-working hours with her, but they were unable to reach her or penetrate her despair and hopelessness. However hard they tried to persuade her, Liz adamantly refused to seek medical help. But when her loud sobbing every night evolved into panic attacks, Joanna was galvanised into taking the initiative. Over-riding Liz's screams that she should shut the fuck up and get out of her life, Joanna called a doctor.

Nestled in the cliffs on the eastern side of the island, the white-washed clinic for nervous diseases was a tranquil and effective haven.

Liz could not recollect much about the first few days and was not fully clear how she had got there. She did not remember the car journey hunched in the corner of the back seat, wrapped in a blanket. Nor did she have any memory of Joanna beside her, holding her hand, while Katya struggled to control the car through curving mountain roads on one of Mallorca's stormiest nights.

Once she was inside the clinic's thick walls, the undisturbed peace of the place helped her regain some equilibrium. Regular intensive sessions with a highly perceptive psychiatrist made some sense of her inner turmoil. But it was the constant support, the gossip, the laughs, funny gifts and regular visits from her friends that really effected the cure.

After only six weeks of treatment the doctors agreed Liz was well enough to go home. More importantly, so did she. Her swift progress delighted the psychiatrist though he told her he was not entirely surprised. 'You reminded me of a railway train shunted into a siding, All you needed was a little push to get you back on the right track,' he told her.

The psychiatrist's little push. And a runaway heiress.

The millionaire's daughter who left her grand home in Britain to live with a penniless waiter was the talk of the island. And the story persuaded Liz that she could make a living out of journalism in Mallorca.

Lucy Briggs-Norton was a love-struck fifteen-year-old who had run away from her mock-Tudor home in the exclusive St George's Hill area of Weybridge to live with Pedro Llorat, a waiter she had met on holiday the summer before.

Lucy was immediately dubbed the 'Princess' when the press obtained a photograph of her playing the role of Princess Minnehaha in the Benenden production of *Hiawatha*, a favourite play of the school since the Princess Royal had been a pupil.

Authorities around Europe were searching for Lucy. Her worried parents had alerted the British consul and the Spanish police had informed Interpol.

Liz was not the only journalist on Mallorca with an interest in 'Pedro and the Princess', as the story came to be known. Tony Burns, the resourceful chief reporter on the *Sunday Chronicle*, read about them in his continental edition of the *Daily Express* while sunning himself on the beach on the last day of his holiday in Calvia.

Unused to coping with a wife, a toddler and a baby on a twenty-four-hours-a-day, seven-days-a-week basis, he had found the last fortnight rather restricting. A few days in the sun working on this story, on his own of course, would be a real holiday. The tale would strike a chord in Middle England and, as his editor just happened to have fifteen-year-old twin girls, he might go for it.

Tony's first task was to make the news editor realise what a bargain of a story he could get with Tony already on the island. He spent a useful half-hour on the phone while his wife was packing.

Once he had safely stowed his family on to the package tour bus in the early hours, Tony lost no time in booking himself into a top hotel in Palma and renting a BMW convertible. He decided he was at least a day ahead of the pack and went down to the swimming pool.

The picture the British press painted of the Princess, a young, innocent girl barely out of her gymslip being lured away by a fortune hunter, was in no way accurate. The reality, as Liz discovered from Pedro's family, was that the girl had been a wild child. Pedro was neither her first waiter nor her first lover.

The couple had run away to Palma when Lucy's father stopped her allowance because he disapproved of Pedro following Lucy to England. Mr Briggs-Norton had long decided that he had not become a self-made millionaire for his daughter to shack up with a Spanish waiter or 'waster' as the family, unfairly, called him.

It took Liz two days to find them and as they were down to their last 1,000-peseta note it was not difficult for her to persuade the runaways to sell their story to a British Sunday newspaper.

Tony, meanwhile, was under instructions to pay top dollar for the story. He had rightly surmised that his editor was more than interested. Liz, too, had the same impression. Of all the papers she had approached on behalf of the runaway couple, the *Sunday Chronicle* was the most keen. They suggested she discuss terms with their chief reporter who, luckily, was on the spot. Liz did a quick interview with Lucy and Pedro and carefully arranged for Joanna to guard them at their Palma apartment, so as to keep the couple's location secret. If any reporter, including Tony himself, got to the couple, the *Mallorca News* would be cut out of the picture.

Liz enjoyed this newspaper skirmish. To the outside world, this was cheque-book journalism. In the ignorance of youth, Liz thought there was a great deal of hypocrisy surrounding it. Unless the story would positively harm some innocent person, she did not see why newspapers were different from any other buying and selling trade. Later she would come to change her mind.

Having made sure the couple was safely hidden, she went to the bar at La Residencia, a short drive north from the capital, to meet Tony Burns.

He towered five inches above her, with a body that already showed it was succumbing to the excesses allowed by a generous expense account. Nevertheless, he was a striking-looking man. The Roman nose, broken as the result of an encounter with a prop forward at his minor public school, had been reset badly, giving him an air of toughness. With his full lips and lazy grin, Tony was a powerful mixture of impudence and assurance.

It had been some time since Liz had met a man who was plugged into the same wavelength and on the same current. They were both enthusiastic and quick-minded and she was rather regretful when, speedily, the deal was done with the young couple.

It was to be a two-part feature, with Pedro and the Princess telling their side of their love affair in the first week of the paper. Cleverly, Liz had suggested an unusual twist. If she could persuade Lucy to return home, without Pedro, her father would agree to recount his side of the story for the second issue. Liz also persuaded the grateful father to allow the pair to write to each other. If after two years they still felt the same way, he would reconsider Pedro as a suitor.

The Princess, Pedro and the two reporters, Liz and Tony, booked into a small hotel for the debriefing session and Liz, to Tony's admiration, managed to filch Lucy's passport and hide it under her mattress, just in case she changed her mind about staying around. It was the start of Liz's successful foray into the world of freelance journalism, selling stories about the British in Mallorca to the newspapers in Britain.

Of the three of them, Joanna was the most gifted writer so she was detailed to work with Tony for the newspaper, but Liz still had a job to do as she had to contact the women's magazines fast to sell second serialisation rights.

Tony had to return first thing on Saturday morning to be back at the paper on press day. Before leaving Palma he phoned Liz several times and left her in no doubt of his keen interest in her, both professionally and personally. But all three of them had long ago decided that married men were definitely off limits, so Liz did no more than have dinner with him. After all, this was a week to celebrate.

The next couple of months on the island were hectic and even included a police raid.

The girls shared a third-floor flat in Palma and were in the habit of dropping the front door key over the balcony to the constant stream of visitors from Britain and South Africa. Usually they were young men, friends and sometimes friends of friends, travelling the globe and popping in for a free meal, but occasionally there would be men of their fathers' age, relatives or business acquaintances arriving with a message or parcel from home.

The strict Catholic couple living on the ground floor, who had never exchanged one word with the girls, came to the conclusion that the three were practising the world's oldest profession. In Spain prostitution was a criminal offence, so the police were summoned. They raided the flat in the early hours, hoping to catch the girls at their work.

What the police found were three weary journalists putting together the last pages of the *Mallorca News*, which was in danger of missing its deadline.

Even the police saw the funny side of it when the three girls explained in their now-fluent Spanish that their job left them so little energy that they were too tired to run up and down the stairs to let their visitors in. The only legacy of the police visit was a succession of garlic-soaked Spanish dishes cooked for them by the mortified couple downstairs.

For all of them it was freedom. They pledged to dance at every disco on the island. They were young, unattached and effervescent but it was Katya's pale, blonde beauty which attracted most attention. She surprised herself at the speed with which she despatched each ardent suitor. One-night stands became her speciality and she rarely allowed a man a second night in her bed.

Liz, too, had her share of sexual success but for her the language barrier was more of problem than for Katya or Joanna. And she discovered that, though there were many men available, few attracted her.

Although Joanna enjoyed flirting, she was still too numb from the failure of her short-lived marriage to consider any sexual escapade and took vicarious pleasure in hearing about the antics of her friends. She was enjoying a bantering flirtation in the office with her proprietor, Eduardo Gonzalez, but it was strictly hands off.

In spite of their hectic night life, the paper prospered.

With *Willings Press Guide* as her Bible, and with the blessing of

Eduardo, who was offered a percentage share of the earnings, Liz learned they could make even more money out of a story by ringing the appropriate British provincial newspaper with the offer of a possible news feature that would be of special interest to their area.

Because of Liz's inside knowledge about how to handle rival news desks, Joanna and Katya were learning how to make a story more saleable and this was starting to make them extra money. Eduardo Gonzalez was so pleased that he designated a part of his share of the takings to buying another telephone.

All three of them were making great contacts but, more importantly, their friendship was growing in strength.

At first they noticed the small things. They were all a little unpunctual. They were all untidy in different ways. Joanna's bedroom seemed neat until you opened the cupboards and drawers. All Liz's handbags were a disgrace as she never threw anything away, including string. And Katya's make-up was such a jumble that no one would ever think she had once made her living out of telling her readers how to look well groomed. They all had grasshopper minds so that they could jump from subject to subject and still keep up with each other. And there was rarely a time when one of them was not using a safety pin somewhere about her person.

Their idol was the veteran journalist Katharine Whitehorn whose *Slut's Handbook*, published at the beginning of her career, had given them some valuable hints. Like using a black felt-tipped pen to cover up holes in black tights or throwing cushions to close a door if you were too bone idle to get up and shut it.

They were never bored for a minute in each other's company. From the beginning there had been an instant recognition despite their coming from different parts of the world and from different backgrounds. It was uncanny and they often marvelled how closely they mirrored each other.

Joanna's panic-stricken screams in the early evening shocked her friends.

It had started. At the makeshift clinic that morning, the Dutch midwife had warned Joanna that by the time she went into labour, after another eight hours, she and her minder would be long gone to another site in the medieval quarter of the city.

The baby that would have the mixed blood of the Gonzalezes and the Glaisters started its path down the birth canal induced thirty-two weeks too soon.

The timing of the male sperm meeting the female egg five days after Joanna's period was an appalling piece of bad luck for all of them. Joanna had not made love since arriving in Mallorca ten months before and Eduardo had only recently succeeded in convincing his wife that he was completely faithful. He and Joanna had spent months skirting around one another. Joanna had flirted with him but she had no intention of ending up like her predecessor who had been fired by Señora Gonzalez because she had become too close to the boss. In any case, she was still mourning the death of her marriage.

Despite her best instincts, she succumbed to him on the day she received the legal papers giving notice of her divorce absolute.

Joanna was alone in the office with Eduardo and, seeing how depressed she was, he insisted on taking her down the road to a little tapas bar overlooking the sea.

Two hours and two flacons of Sangria later, she responded to his gentle suggestion that they drive up to the top of the hill to see the lights around the bay. In the darkened car, it was only a small step to finding solace in the comfort of his arms. She relaxed, enjoying the smell and feel of him.

Separately, they had wondered for weeks what it would be like to make love. For Joanna the reality could never be as good as the fantasy. But she needed comfort.

A few days later she had come to her senses and ended the sexual side of their affair. Then she missed her period.

In Catholic Spain abortions were illegal and the only way she could get one was by the back-street route. It had taken Eduardo over a week to track down the Dutch midwife who had made it a crusade to help women on the island get rid of unwanted pregnancies, so much so that if someone could not afford her modest fee she would offer her services free. But those services were the most basic and they were quick. The midwife made it clear at the outset that she could never wait with the patient or leave a forwarding address, even if she thought there might be complications. Local doctors would sometimes have to deal with the consequences of her work, which in the main they would do without comment or phoning the police. These women had suffered enough already.

The room in which Joanna found herself early that morning was tiny and devoid of any furniture. In the middle of the floor lay a far-from-clean mattress. But on it, Katya and Liz noted with relief, was a small pile of clean starched sheets.

The brusque midwife was in a rush to get Joanna in and out as quickly as possible and her thick-set minder kept watch by the door with Katya and Liz in case there were any inquisitive strangers on the landing.

The woman unwrapped a grey, woollen blanket to reveal a canister containing an antiseptic carbolic mixture, some rubber tubing and other antique-looking instruments. Joanna's terrified eyes watched her as she spread a sheet on the mattress and asked her to lie down, legs spread.

What a lot of heartache, thought Joanna, for just a few minutes of hurried lovemaking which had done nothing to assuage her emotional needs.

'This won't hurt but you must expect labour to be painful because it is induced, it is early and it is your first. It is your first?' asked the midwife in her perfect English.

Joanna nodded. 'And the last.'

'Sure, sure,' replied the midwife.

Outside, the minder told Katya and Liz, 'Make certain you put a waterproof on her bed tonight. If her temperature goes up above a hundred and one degrees Fahrenheit, give her these antibiotics. If her temperature does not drop within a couple of hours, you must, without delay, call a doctor.'

Her friends were conscious that Joanna would have to be extremely ill before she would agree to that.

By the time the minder had finished speaking, the carbolic mixture had been flushed into Joanna's uterus. Later, just as for a woman going into normal full-term labour, the uterine muscles would contract, and the foetus would be rejected.

Two hours after labour had started, Joanna was sobbing uncontrollably. Katya and Liz kept up a steady trek to and from the bathroom with flannels wrapped round ice cubes to try to cool and calm her down. Nothing seemed to help.

The contractions were as strong as for a normal labour with waves of terrible pain but without the joyous arrival of a baby which blanked out the memory of childbirth pangs for most mothers; the only reason, Joanna would say later, that the world was not populated with only children.

But Joanna had no baby at the end of it to relieve her pain and loss. She would never forget that traumatic experience. Nor could she continue to work for Eduardo Gonzalez. The only comfort from the whole hideous episode was that it brought the three friends even closer together. And when Joanna said she would like to try her luck in British journalism again, this time with a National Union of Journalists card which Liz had helped organise, the other two decided to join her.

Liz expressed enthusiasm about her re-entry to mainstream journalism and Katya, too, tired of sun, sea but most especially of unloving sex, also readily agreed to leave. They gave a stunned Señor Gonzalez a month to find replacements.

It was a typically grey drizzly day when they landed. Coats wrapped closely round their shivering bodies, they asked each other whether returning to London had been such a great idea. But when their taxi turned into the Strand, past the Law Courts and into Fleet Street, they felt a surge of exhilaration. They were back at the centre of their world.

Chapter Four

At their table, Joanna and Liz were still watching Katya. Eventually, surely, her eyes would stray and give them a clue to the mystery lover. Their interest was ninety per cent nosiness and ten per cent concern.

'She keeps staring at the top table,' said Liz. 'I can't believe it's any of that lot, they're all married or otherwise inclined.'

'Maybe it's Dickie.'

'Don't be ridiculous. He and Sheila are joined at the hip. Don't worry. We'll get it out of her soon enough. She's never been able to keep a secret from us.'

The sharp-eared journalist sitting on Liz's left was all attention. 'What are you two going on about?' he asked.

Tony Burns had reappeared in their lives when Liz had joined the *Sunday Chronicle* three years before.

'Nothing, nothing,' she remarked airily. 'Nothing you'd understand, anyway.'

He was quite different from the man who had chatted her up all those years ago in Mallorca.

Tony, now assistant editor (news), had been on the *Chronicle* for years. He was well acquainted with all the Suits and was adept at keeping up relationships, politicking, playing golf, entertaining and drinking in the all-male bonding process so prevalent in Fleet Street. He wore the confidence of a man who was definitely going to make it. Physically, he had overcome his early tendency to run to fat by investing in the product – expensive haircuts, hand-tailored suits, workouts on alternate days, regular massage and, even, the occasional manicure.

When Liz had first arrived back from Mallorca he had been friendly enough to use his introductions to land her job on the *Daily Mail*, then had been genuinely pleased when she had joined the *Sunday Chronicle* in a lower position. But watching her overtake him on the paper had made him increasingly bitter.

Working closely with him at the *Chronicle* had totally changed Liz's original opinion of him. He regarded her now as a rival and treated her with hostility, his personality totally at odds with the one he had presented in Palma. But Liz had to allow him one thing. At least he took her seriously, unlike the editor who had elevated her to deputy editor mainly because he could not envisage a woman challenging him for the top job.

As assistant editor (features), Liz had become used to Tony playing dirty and undermining her whenever he could do so. And he was not overly concerned with the truth when he did it either. If he ever found out anything that could be used against her, he would not hesitate. It was bad enough when they were neck and neck in the mouse race, as they called it in the office, but since her promotion above him eighteen months earlier, to deputy editor, matters had gone from very bad to much worse.

There were many occasions when he could make mischief. He had recently spent an evening with her boss at one of those ritual blokeish occasions at Wembley Football Stadium. She could just hear him telling the chairman how she had been stitched up by the smart northern football agents who had squeezed £15,000 out of her for a column by a footballer who had disappointingly spent all season on the substitute benches.

Another editor would have told Liz it was just one of those gambles which sometimes came off and sometimes did not. In future, she would pay less attention to recommendations from Tony's crony, the sports supremo, and more to reports of groin strains from her contacts in television before being so generous with her contracts.

Liz saw Tony's watchful wife monitoring her husband's furtive eyes, which were at that moment doing guard duty on Liz's rarely bared cleavage. She was tempted to lean over and say: 'Look, dear, he's not interested in them – they're just something to blame for why I'm higher up the ladder than he is.' She gave the wife a warm smile and thought for the hundredth time that she was far better than he deserved.

She turned to talk to one of Hollywood's finest. What a great story he had to tell. If only she could persuade him to reveal that he and a gerbil were on more than nodding acquaintance. But then, how could you put that into a family newspaper? She was, as always, irritated with herself. Here I am, in the right place to be, sitting next to the man voted Mr Body and all I'm worrying about is how to fit unnatural practices into next week's paper. Why couldn't she occasionally enjoy something without looking for story angles?

The fact that Joanna and Katya were both in love made her feel envious. Once again, at a glamorous event, she was sitting next to a stranger and, not for the first time, she thought what hard work it was making small talk with people you did not know and did not want to know.

It had been ages since she had had anyone special in her life. Usually, the men she found attractive found her intimidating. And the ones who fawned over her, bored her. These days, she found the job filled up more and more of the empty space. And she had become adept at parcelling out small talk with strangers though it was still an effort.

The Hollywood star leaned over and said: 'Lemme tell you about my latest diet, it's really fabulous . . .'

Oh God.

The meal was interminable. Katya couldn't bring herself to eat more than a mouthful of anything. Logic told her that the minister was unlikely to arrive now but, like anyone in love, there was only one face she wanted to see.

Her daydream was interrupted by the toastmaster.

'Your Royal Highness, my lords, ladies and gentlemen, the broadcast will commence in ten minutes.'

This was the signal for a major table-hopping exercise and a rush to the loo. Producers smarmed up to money men; presenters floated past important directors, and directors tried to catch the eye of producers, while money men idly looked around for next season's bimbo, those who were not still smarting from the aftermath of one of the usual kiss-and-tell stories in the tabloids.

It had been a vintage few months for the 'red-tops', which was what insiders called the downmarket tabloids, the ones with red mastheads. The score of sex scandals so far included one US presidential candidate, a British princess and three senior government politicians including, their biggest scalp, the Minister for Health.

Joanna decided she had better stay put. She watched in awe as Liz worked the room, kissing this one, arranging an interview with that one, slipping a business card to another. What an operator. Nevertheless she always had to defend Liz from the editors in her magazine group. They treated her not as a pioneer in the male world but as someone who had forgotten she was a woman and did not fight for their cause. Liz did what was good for circulation whether or not it promoted feminism. She would not subscribe to politically correct theories. More women in top jobs was her aim but they had to compete on equal terms.

Sometimes Joanna felt envious of her friend. Perhaps she should have gone down the same road. Newspapers were seen to be far more exciting, were more instant and were better paid than magazines. But then, how would she cope with being a rival to Liz – and the editors, all male? She shuddered. No. Not that. George would not be too thrilled with the longer hours, either. It was easier this way.

In the outside broadcast truck, known as the scanner, parked discreetly near the back entrance to the Grosvenor, the orders were calmly given.

Inside the ballroom, those instructions came through the earpieces of the outside broadcast crew. Cameras aloft, they snaked through the tables, taking up their positions, crouching beside the nominees whose faces would be used over the opening credits of the live TV marathon. In the scanner, they focused on the six contenders for the major award categories.

'Camera one, cue Julia Roberts; camera two, stand by for Kenneth Branagh; camera three, Anthony Hopkins; camera four, David Frost; camera five, Julie Goodyear; and camera six, Katya Croft. Okay, stand by.'

Nick Arkwright, the director in the scanner, asked irritably, 'Why is Katya what's-her-name giving us the back of her head? Are we missing anything on that staircase? Don't these morning television people know what a camera's for? Number six camera, Andy, when I cue you, get that bitch to give us a big smile – from the waist up, get me?' He turned to his PA. 'I said we should've gone for Selina Scott.'

Andy, on camera six, felt more comfortable in jeans and anorak on the finishing line at Sandown Park race course than in his hired dinner jacket. Crouching at Katya's side waiting for his cue, he gave thanks for the lightweight Sony Betacam on his shoulder. It was a job like any other. Last month it had been Rwanda. Not so different from this place, he thought. Hermetically sealed. No news coming in, no news getting out – and just as bloody hot.

Inside the scanner, the producer shouted, 'Hang on, there's something going on at the top table. Dickie's about to spout.'

'Fuck,' screamed Nick. 'Doesn't he know there's only two minutes to air? What's going on?'

Dickie Attenborough, surprisingly agile for someone in his seventies, leapt on to the stage. 'Your Royal Highness, my lords, ladies and gentlemen . . .'

Outside in the scanner, Nick's PA Melissa tapped out, 'One minute to air.'

Downstairs, the mellifluous tones continued, 'There's been a car accident and I'm afraid it means the Minister of State for Broadcasting is not able to be with us tonight.'

'Fifty-three seconds to air.'

Katya stopped breathing. She felt as if her lungs had been punctured. A crash? How serious was it? She had to get to a phone.

'The details are still unclear, I'm afraid, but . . .'

'Forty seconds.'

' . . . I'm sure I am speaking for all the guests here tonight . . .'

'Get off, you boring old fart,' howled Nick.

Melissa was calm. 'Thirty-five seconds.'

' . . . when I say our prayers and our thoughts are with the whole family. But I'm perfectly sure the minister would want us to get on and celebrate this, the twenty-third BAFTA ceremony, a night so important for our industry . . .'

'Twenty seconds.'

'... I know all of you here will give your usual warm support to all the nominees present tonight.'

Number six camera, as instructed, never wavered from Katya's face and in the scanner Nick looked at the row of five smiling faces on the bank of screens above his head – and one face frozen in horror.

'What's the matter with that fucking Katya?'

Melissa looked up momentarily from her stopwatch. 'Three seconds.'

One thing an Oscar-winning director knew about was timing. Richard Attenborough announced, 'And now, our host for the evening, Michael Aspel.'

'We're on, Katya!' hissed Andy frantically, 'Smile, for God's sake.'

'Cut to camera six.'

The red light on her camera came on. Katya's instinct was to push it away, but habit made her respond. Another deep breath and she bared her teeth. It was an automatic reflex though you could hardly call it a smile as she fought to gain control of her face muscles. Liz and Joanna saw Katya's face on the giant monitors around the room. What the hell was the matter with her? Liz raised her eyebrows at Joanna, who gave a baffled shrug.

Upstairs, Nick looked at Katya's strained expression and turned to Melissa. 'Bloody prima donna.'

A uniformed police constable was measuring the skid marks where the crashed Range Rover was being attached to the tow bar of the recovery truck. But it was a plainclothes sergeant from Special Branch who was shaking off the glass from the blue canvas sports bag with its splatters of blood.

He dragged it out. It had obviously been left behind in the race to get the driver to hospital. He unzipped the top and looked inside the bag. It contained a few personal belongings and wrapped inside a pair of pyjamas was an unlabelled video.

After the lab boys were finished with the stuff, he would drop the bag into the hospital.

The moment of Katya's victory was completely spoiled. The news of the accident had so overwhelmed her that when she was announced as winner of the BAFTA Television News Personality of the Year there was little emotion left for elation or even triumph. Onlookers misunderstood her detachment. Her coolness made her look even more like a winner, as if the award were her right.

'She looks stunned and so she should be,' sneered a broadcaster from a rival station, irked that once more he had been passed over.

Seconds after the broadcast was over, Katya Croft and all the other category winners were shepherded from the ballroom to the interview room upstairs.

Katya did a quick piece for her own station. It would just be a soundbite for the news bulletins; they would use it in the early hours until she arrived to make a live appearance at 8.15 a.m. For once, she was to be the guest.

In the interview room, deadlines were king. Like a parcel, she and the other winners were passed from the newspapers first to other television stations and then to radio.

Knowing the routine, the reporters grouped themselves so the interviews could be done as fast as possible. For journalists, it was quite orderly.

Katya was desperate to escape and find out what had happened to her lover but the fastest way to get out was to co-operate fully. Only later, when she saw the cuttings, did she realise that in her headlong rush to leave she had been too gushy, talked too much, smiled too much, showing acres of pink gum instead of, as usual, restricting her smile to her perfect white teeth.

As the interviews went on and on and every journalist asked the same three main questions – How do you feel? What's your future? Who are you going to marry? – she longed to shout at all of them, 'Leave me alone, let me get out of here.' But she restrained herself.

She always remembered what Cecil Parkinson (now Lord) had ruefully told her after the party conference when he had announced his resignation: 'When you give an announcement to the newspapers at midnight, there's only one place for it to go.' It was midnight now and Cecil was right. Her picture would go on the front page.

At last it was all over. Joanna had been taken home by Liz long ago and the photographers had piled away their equipment while the writers drifted to the bar.

Like most performers, Katya had become an adrenaline junkie. Although she was filled with dread, her brain was in overdrive. On auto-pilot she headed towards the Park Lane exit of the hotel.

The first thing she had done was to ask about the car crash and the reporter's words were reverberating in her ears: 'He's hurt badly, she's all right, we think. Actually, we're not sure she was even in the car.' How could she find out exactly what had happened? Should she ring her own newsdesk? But a midnight phone call from Katya Croft was so unheard of as to be memorable and that might be dangerous later. And if she pretended to be somebody else, they would give her the brush-off. It was their job to disseminate information via the TV and they gave short shrift to enquiries on the telephone. As she was not a member of the family, a call to the hospital posed the same problem.

The one place where she felt the phones were secure was their mews hideaway. It was only yesterday afternoon but it seemed years ago that she and her lover had explored each other's bodies hour after ecstatic hour.

She was a few yards from the revolving doors when she realised it would be unwise to ask the driver to go to the mews. Since her affair had started, Katya had become good at covering her tracks. She decided to leave the driver there. He would get the overtime and she would phone from the mews and tell him to go home.

She quickly changed direction and made for the back entrance in South Audley Street. The cloak. Damn. She had almost forgotten it. There it was, the last garment left in the cloakroom, its pink ticket pinned to the collar. Even the attendant had gone.

Inside the anonymous black London taxi, she buried her chin in the voluptuous velvet cloak, hiding her well-known face from the driver. 'The end of the mews will do,' she called out to him as a few minutes later they arrived at the back of Buckingham Palace. Without speaking, she reached forward and pushed ten pounds through the inner glass window, overtipping him by at least two hundred per cent.

The driver sensed there was something familiar about his passenger, but when she climbed out she drew the cloak even closer round her slim body and within two steps had disappeared into the cobbled mews.

Katya walked along the mews as fast as she could on tiptoe, careful not to get her four-inch heels stuck between the uneven, shiny cobbles. Roland Mews was a horse-shoe shaped street of Georgian houses over garages, previously the stables and servants' quarters of seventeenth-century gentry, now a chic and expensive cul-de-sac much loved by foreigners passing through London on short-term contracts for banks, embassies or brokerage houses.

No. 16 was, like the rest of the houses, in complete darkness. For a minute she considered turning tail and going home, but she had to see if there was a message for her on the answering machine. She scrabbled in her small handbag for the key and moved quickly towards the front door.

Flash!

The mews was momentarily illuminated by a harsh, vivid light.

Terror.

Katya ran full pelt down the little street, the cloak billowing out behind her. She was ungainly over the cobbles but when she reached the asphalt of the slip road she made up speed.

'Shit.' The photographer in pursuit slipped on the wet stones and fell heavily.

Katya rushed into Lower Belgrave Road where the proximity of Victoria Station meant that even in the early hours there were always plenty of taxis for hire.

She could barely give the driver her home address and wondered what the noise was. Shuddering, she realised it was convulsive sobs struggling out of her windpipe. Oh God, she thought. If only she had not been so selfish, so needy, this could have been avoided.

Chapter Five

A couple of hours later Katya had never looked better. The screen was full of happy images of her as she ascended the stage to accept her award. However much they speeded up the film or wound it back and slowed it down, she looked nothing less than radiant. No sign of her inner turmoil. She had switched into professional mode. She made it easy for them to cut a twenty-second walk down to three.

'We've had enough of that, let's get some words. You're only interested because you're looking at her tits.'

Hunched over the online machine with its small monitor and console of endless buttons were two people on the dog-end shift in one of the eight Morning TV edit suites.

Twenty-four-year-old Terry Blackener, junior tape editor, defended himself. 'Well, they don't often come out. Although I'm told—'

'Move on to time code 0056, where she's kissing William Hurt,' instructed the producer, a bleary-eyed toughie called Fiona Taylor. 'Yeah, that's good, we'll have some of that.'

Terry moved the knobs anti-clockwise. 'Anyway, Bill says she was a real goer at TV Southern.'

'I heard that too. But she's Mission Impossible now, at least to the likes of you . . . Oh yes, there's another quote friend unquote, Liz Waterhouse.'

On screen, a smiling Liz and Katya did the fresh-air kiss.

'Do we note any flesh touching flesh here?' asked Fiona. 'No, we don't. They pretend to be such good pals but you can't tell me two women like that are popping over borrowing cups of sugar from each other.'

Like so many women, Fiona, who had several close girl friends in the business herself, had been brainwashed into thinking that higher up the ladder these kinds of friendships ceased to exist. It did not occur to her that Liz knew that Katya could not do TV interviews and a photo call with a great big lipstick smudge on her cheek from a friendly kiss.

'Anyway,' said Terry, moving along, 'we've got better than that – Dawn French comes up in a second.' He fiddled with the knobs. 'Look, here's the bit where Katya says thank you and gives us all a mensh. Better keep that in.'

In this way, Fiona and Terry worked for another hour. By the time Katya made her appearance in the studio, the fruits of their work, all forty seconds of it, would have been shown four times every half-hour tagged on to the end of the news.

The award winner had spent a tearful, worried night and it showed.

Katya had finally fallen asleep in the early hours and clambered out of bed, eyes still closed, following her usual ten-minute get-up-and-get-out routine – a peremptory brush of her teeth and into her Babygro-style floppy track suit with flat ballerina shoes, dishevelled hair and no make-up.

This was fine for four in the morning when she had only a few lorries on the road for company, but in her distracted state she had forgotten that today was different. At 7.30 a.m. her television station was full of fans and photographers, and through the glass swing doors she saw to her horror the managing director waiting in reception with three dozen long-stemmed pink roses.

Her only defence was a pair of huge, black Jackie O sunglasses. Even with these, the girls on the reception desk, used to her early-morning appearance, remarked to each other that they had never seen her look this rough.

Normally, she would be sent the script by courier the night before, but today was not normal. She was swapping roles and was taking her place on the sofa as a guest in the later part of the show, the soft strand reserved for so-called women's interest subjects.

Katya went straight into make-up. One look at Brenda's expression when she removed the shielding specs found her saying, 'Sorry, we had a bit of a celebration.'

It was the first lie of the day.

Katya made a silent vow. If she got through this, she would never look forward to anything again. It was never worth it. What was it someone had once said? 'Be sure you know what you want, for you might get it.'

She settled back, waiting for Brenda to work her witchcraft. Bags, blotches and blemishes were banished by the skilful use of many pots of tinted cream, layered on very thinly with a trowel-like brush. Brenda could 'reveal' cheekbones, contours and luminosity that did not exist, creating an illusion by blending and shading up to ten colours that to the naked eye would all look the same. Cracked, dry lips became lush Hollywood pouts. Bloodshot eyes were disguised in seconds with eye drops that contained blue vegetable dye only available in France. Make-up girls cajoled model friends to bring back supplies from Paris. Cosmetic toothpaste whitened less than perfect teeth. Lank hair was spritzed with instant gleamer, which often made it even greasier but for the few minutes of the broadcast gave it the appearance of being bouncy, shiny and healthy.

Appearing on the box was the art of the unnatural looking natural. Politicians who pretended to scorn artifice made sure they remembered to sit on the hems of their jackets so that they would not ride up and the camera then had a nice clean line of neck and powerful shoulders.

It wasn't life. It was television.

Katya, who was blessed with good looks, still gave daily thanks for the miracle worked in this mirrored temple of make-believe. If only everyone had a Brenda, she thought as she quickly put on a suit and high heels in her office. She was ready to face the lens.

Katya surveyed the colourful backdrop of the studio and stood silently behind the cameras, waiting for her cue while Steve and Lisa did the business. Normally Katya, totally at home in this studio, would by 5.55 a.m. have taken her seat automatically at centre stage where the lighting and the setting were arranged to show her at her best and where for three hours a day, five days a week, she was most comfortable. Her den, her lair. But this morning she was a guest rather than the presenter and the floor manager led her to the side of the sofa.

It was the wrong side for her. Like anyone trained for the cameras,

Katya was aware that everyone's face has one side more attractive than the other. Her professional self-awareness would normally have steered her instinctively to the side that would show her off more favourably. Today she was too preoccupied.

The minute she sat, the director in the gallery above remarked, 'Lisa's affairette with the floor manager seems to have paid off. Can it be an accident that he's put Katya on her wrong side? God, she looks fucking awful this morning.'

'Brenda's already warned me she tied one on last night,' said the vision mixer.

'Let's move her over.'

Katya had already been miked up and, like a zombie, she waited while they disconnected it all and moved her to the other side.

'She still looks rough,' said the director.

'Yeah, I've said it before, they never spend enough time lighting that guest spot properly,' said Brenda from make-up. They were both well aware that lighting could make a beauty look like a dog and vice versa.

'Why do you think your precious Katya looks so good every morning?' muttered the vision mixer under her breath.

'Let's get some blondes and redheads in during the ad break,' said the director, referring to the nicknames given to the various lights.

Katya was enveloped in her own misery. She could not concentrate on anything. The sounds and the calls around her were the noises she was used to but they did not penetrate. She was in it but not of it, alarmed about the effect the flashgun in the mews would have on her life and fearful of its consequences. The news about the accident involving the minister's car had been broadcast repeatedly throughout the night with the same standby phrase: 'critical but stable'. She felt she had heard every bulletin.

In Morning TV's glaringly bright studio, meant to resemble a suburban home, a commercial break was coming up and Steve read the menu off autocue: 'After the news, how to cope with a teenager on drugs; botanist David Bellamy will be popping in to tell you all about the jungle plants you may have in your own garden – and we'll meet our very own BAFTA winner, Katya Croft. Join us then . . .'

During the break, lighting staff went into a frenzy of activity relighting Katya. While they were getting it right, Steve, her co-anchor and security blanket, leaned over and gave her hand a squeeze. 'Wonderful, darling.'

'Congratulations, Katya sweetie,' breathed Lisa. 'We're all so very pleased for you.'

'Thanks. It's odd to be in freefall with no ear mike.' Katya had been an hour and a half away from her phone. She had to ask, 'What's the news on the Thomas car crash, Steve?'

'Oh yes, you were there last night. Hang on, I'll ask the gallery.' Steve gesticulated into the camera, pointing to his earphone. 'What's the latest on the Thomas accident?' he asked, straight into camera. 'Was it a bomb?' He listened while Katya watched his face intently as he echoed the words being relayed to him from the gallery. 'We don't know yet. Going to be a statement about it later. Okay, thanks.'

Katya was anxious to know more and opened her mouth to ask but both presenters put their fingers to their lips for silence. They pointed upwards to the control box, where that day's editor was briefing them on what was to happen after the news. Katya remembered how many times she had done this to guests. Now she realised how rude and irritating it was. If you did not have an earpiece you were excluded. No wonder so many people felt their trip to the TV studio was so difficult. It taught her a lesson for the future.

Once she left this sofa and the studio she was determined to speak to her lover. She could not return to the mews but however guarded, however coded the call, she had to make it. With a bit of luck she could be out of here in ten minutes.

It was just five seconds to the end of the break. While straightening his tie, Steve smiled at Katya. 'Guess what, Bellamy's late. He can get through a bloody jungle but he's not so good in SW5 so we might have to go on a bit longer. Okay?'

Steve could not understand why Katya sagged. He thought to himself, Hmmn, wonder who she was with last night? Hasn't mentioned a bloke for ages. Must be new, wonder who he is?

Katya could not concentrate on the interview. It all seemed so unimportant when she was dying inside. That damned photographer. How much of her face had been showing? It was Liz and

Joanna she usually turned to during panics but she could not involve them in this. God, what a bloody mess.

To Liz, watching on her bedside television set, Katya came over as though she had not a care in the world. Whatever had got to her last night at BAFTA – perhaps a quarrel with the mystery lover – had obviously been sorted out. She looked wonderful.

Liz's room was in total darkness. Three years ago, when she first moved into this maisonette near Joanna and George's small house, she had often been bothered by feature writers phoning her from all over the world at all times of the night. Sleep proved so elusive that Joanna suggested blackout material to line the striped Sanderson curtains so that she would not be kept awake by light outside as well. They worked brilliantly.

Though Liz spent little time in the two-bedroomed, two-bathroomed apartment, she had not stinted herself. The kitchen was a limed oak dream, used mostly as a backdrop to Indian and Chinese takeaways. It included a television, a fax and two telephones.

A comfortable white-walled sitting room had two large Chesterfield sofas and two large wicker baskets crammed with magazines. Huge shelves were piled with books and videos that Liz would one day get around to looking at. The walls were covered with framed cartoons, old photographs from her parents' house, lithographs and pictures that had caught her eye on her travels. Occasional tables, some kept level with a wedge of newspaper, held more books and silver-framed photographs.

This sitting room led off into a tidy dining area which remained in that condition through lack of use. The spare bedroom. had been turned into a dressing room filled from floor to ceiling with specialist cupboards and drawers so that her large wardrobe could be filed in unruly though colour-coded order.

Liz stretched and threw back the ivory cotton-covered duvet. Normally she would still be asleep on a Monday but she had to dress to impress today. Since waking up she had already had three imaginary conversations with her proprietor. He would say this and she would have some witty response ready – if only she could think of one.

Last night she and her friends had worked out that Fergus had not requested a meeting to give her the sack. Breakfasts were for sackings. For a hard-hearted boss, it got the whole dirty business out of the way early in the day. As she showered, she recalled a former colleague who had been taken to a sumptuous kedgeree and Buck's Fizz breakfast at Claridge's. While the proprietor waited for the bill, the editor was told his job was 'not working out'. His desk was cleared by noon and another name plate, already printed, was fixed to the door.

Lunches were a little more promising. What Liz had never worked through was what was going to happen at the end of it. There was no use speculating. One way or another, by three o'clock she would know.

Katya de-miked after her interview, left the studio hurriedly and was rushing through the foyer when the managing director ran down the stairs calling her name.

'Oh no, we're not letting you go so easily,' he said, putting an arm round her shoulders. 'And we're not going to congratulate you with just our little family. Come on, let's go in to breakfast and do it for the crew – they're as pleased as we all are about the award.'

Katya could barely bring herself to be polite. She had to get out. But there was no escape.

The managing director had never been one of her fans since she had ousted his mistress for the coveted heavyweight interviewing slot but since then he had reluctantly had to admit that her probing technique had elicited several major scoops which had made the station required viewing for politicians and other opinion-formers. And beating the BBC's top talent as best presenter was bloody good for the station. He would take an ad in the trade press. That would grind their noses in it.

They walked into the canteen to cheers and a mixture of waving champagne glasses and plastic coffee cups. It was a spontaneous plaudit from the 'little people', as he called them.

The all-night cafeteria served huge breakfasts free to cabinet ministers, stars and all the other sofa guests. It had become a major draw with interviewees and was renowned for its traditional fare.

Eggs to order and three sorts of bacon, thick Cumberland pork sausages, heavy black pudding, flat, wide, grilled mushrooms, fried Guernsey tomatoes, Heinz's best baked beans and thick triangles of white bread with crusts on, all enrobed in a thin layer of frying oil, were constantly on tap. Not for nothing was it known as Cholesterol Alley.

There were healthier but less attractive alternatives like Arbroath smokies and kippers, kedgeree, every known cereal, plus the *specialité de la maison*, a sunflower seed concoction that had been devised after five-times-a-night-lover Ralph Halpern was seen to have a dish of them on his desk. These were especially popular with the camera crews.

It was the modern equivalent of the chafing dishes on the groaning sideboards of stately homes. Employees used to joke that guests put up with getting up so early and taking a few sharp knocks from their TV interview just for the breakfast.

Champagne bottles in silver buckets were at Katya's table, ready chilled. She thought she would retch if she had to eat or drink. She would be stuck there for fifteen minutes at the very least and cursed herself that she could not enjoy the moment.

The usual long list of messages was waiting on Joanna's desk, the first, timed at 8.35 a.m., from the managing director and typed by the meticulous woman she privately referred to as 'Mother'.

Miss Angus – nobody but Joanna remembered her first name, Evangeline – had been allocated to Joanna on her first executive job as assistant features editor. It was an unlikely combination, the fast-thinking, naturally bright journalist and the slower-paced, methodical Scot fifteen years her senior. But it worked because each appreciated the other's qualities; Joanna had the freedom to concentrate on the creative part of her job, knowing the office admin and her diary were in safe hands.

When the new managing director wanted to ease out all the 'fossils', as he called them, Joanna reminded him that Miss Angus had an encyclopedic knowledge of *Women's View*, its readership, contents and personnel. 'She's indispensable,' she went on firmly, determined to get her way. Though his eyes started to glaze over, she pointed out that Miss Angus was the only person in the office who never forgot a single request in a busy day.

He did not give her time to tell him it was Miss Angus who dealt with the hundreds of readers who rang in with obscure requests, as well as giving invaluable help to the ever-changing staff, some of whom, incredibly, had never read the magazine before joining the company.

'Well, if she means so much to your efficiency, leave it with me and I'll give it some thought.' His clipped New York accent often made him sound more authoritative and decisive than he was.

Joanna had heard no more about it so Miss Angus stayed, albeit in limbo. It was an unsatisfactory state of affairs, like all her dealings with the latest American MD. Top of his class at Harvard Business School, he was at the lower end in sensitivity, personality and charm. As Liz said succinctly after the press launch of Joanna's new-look magazine at which the MD was at his charmless best: 'Devastating looks, pity he's had the charisma bypass.'

Miss Angus arranged the messages on Joanna's desk. They were neatly typed in order of what she considered their priority. She was usually right. But it was not typing and shorthand skills that Joanna valued in her PA. It was her discretion and, above all, her loyalty. Unlike others in the company, she did not seek to curry favour with the managing director by offering information about Joanna's movements or gossiping with the rest of the staff, or grumbling about her work load with the other secretaries. Miss Angus was a spare, compact, neat woman with a weakness for handmade shoes and her cat, a British Blue. She was one of those women so organised that her purse was always in the front zipper section of her handbag, copper coins in one section, silver in another.

All editors in the group were required to give a copy of their diary engagements to the managing director. Miss Angus so objected to this intrusive and odious request that without Joanna's knowledge she would doctor the diary. She often amused herself thinking the MD must believe that the editor of *Women's View* led an extremely dull life.

Clickety-click. Clickety-click.

She would recognise the sound of Joanna's darting footsteps

anywhere. The door was flung open. Another characteristic of Joanna's was that she could never do things quietly, she always hurled herself into everything. She gave a twirl, showing off her new fire-engine red Donna Karan wool coat. It was the sort of glamorous classic that seduced British journalists in New York since there it cost half the London price.

'Before you say anything, Angus, I know this colour's crazy but I couldn't resist it. I got it in a sale, it was the only thing I bought and it'll cover the bump.'

'It looks warm, at any rate.'

They both smiled. Joanna always tried to fool herself by dismissing any extravagance as a bargain.

Joanna waved a beautiful package in front of her PA's face, so professionally wrapped Miss Angus presumed Joanna's hands had had nothing to do with it. Indeed, the ribbons proclaimed it was from Bergdorf Goodman. Inside was an exquisite sable-haired clothes brush destined for Prince Panthro of Havoc, the most pampered cat in Britain.

'Oh, he'll love that, thank you.'

'Hey, guess who I sat next to at the Four Seasons? Only the love of my life, apart from George, of course. Andy Garcia. You should never see these idols eat, the magic goes.' Joanna did not pause for breath.

'Pity, he speaks very well of you.' Miss Angus loved living vicariously through Joanna's encounters with Hollywood stars.

'Any important messages?'

'Afraid so. Upstairs wants you, urgently.'

'Ah. I bet I know what that's about.'

Joanna flung the coat over the cream sofa which matched everything else in the room. The rug positioned on the beige-coloured floorboards was just a shade darker, setting off the rag-rolled parchment-coloured walls. The linen blinds were a shade of buff and the ceiling was painted a deep pearl. Three giant alabaster vases held interesting leaves in all shades of green, the only colour in the room, apart from covers from every issue of the magazine that lined one wall.

'I think I might have made a boo-boo in New York. The chairman and the deputy took me out to dinner at Twenty-One and I probably was a bit too enthusiastic about what I wanted to do with next year's promotional budget.'

'What do you mean?' Miss Angus was uneasy.

Joanna gnawed at her cuticle nervously and nodded her head towards the ceiling, indicating the MD upstairs.

'You know how he hates me to talk about anything important Over There? Well, I did. I let it drop that we weren't perhaps being as creative with the promotional budget as we could be.'

Joanna had been frustrated that they had no way of taking advantage of some of the exclusive news stories she had managed to unearth. She had put up good ideas for their major TV and advertising promotion and had been surprised when the MD was curmudgeonly about them.

'That story about the tribe that were made to hand over their sons at eighteen months to army crèches made headlines all over the world. Could we promote it? No. And that spread about the saint who's been helping slum kids and who has ten million quid in her Swiss bank account? No promos for that either.'

Miss Angus was used to being Joanna's sounding board.

'Do you know, I found Upstairs hadn't told New York anything about those stories until after we were on the street? And when I briefed the chairman, I could see from the way he exchanged looks with his deputy that he was irritated. The chairman gets upset if he doesn't know every dot and comma and he's made it quite clear he's in total charge of the European operations, whatever Upstairs may pretend.'

Miss Angus reported that the MD had been on the phone to New York on Friday nearly all afternoon and well into the evening. 'I suppose that must've had something to do with you.'

'Oh God, this is going to be trouble, just when I don't need it. Angus, how am I going to get out of this one?' Joanna pulled a face. 'They're the biggest stories we've ever had. How could he expect me not to talk about them?'

The sage was rational, as always. 'That's not what would infuriate him. It would be that you dared to discuss promotional plans without him being involved. He's paranoid about anyone having access to the real power without going through him.'

The two looked at each other reflectively.

'I think,' said Miss Angus, 'your best bet is to own up, be frank and apologise for having the discussion without him.'

'Why should I? I was only doing my job. I don't want to apologise.'

'Yes, but what do you want to achieve here? Do you want your promotional budget to go through or not?'

Joanna sighed. But she knew Miss Angus to be a tactician of the highest order.

'I've always found saying sorry disarms even tough nuts like this one,' Miss Angus assured her.

'It'll kill me,' Joanna muttered. 'The real trouble is he wants me out, doesn't he? I'm the only editor who doesn't say "Yes, sir, no sir, three bags full, sir" to everything he suggests.

'I'd love to ask Liz's advice now,' she added. 'She's had a lot of experience with those shits at the newspaper but she's having her first lunch alone with her Big Boss so I can't bother her.'

Joanna glanced at her watch. She knew that Katya, not so political but a friendly voice, was not free either. She would be at the TV studio.

It was characteristic of all three women that for all their polish, designer clothing and important careers, they were still full of self-doubt. During their confessional sessions, usually around Joanna's kitchen table, they admitted they were always expecting to be 'found out'.

None of the three had gone to journalism school or college. They had learned on the job. As Liz used to explain, 'A lot of what we do is by instinct, coupled with experience but I couldn't even start to explain that to somebody starting out.'

Because much of their skill was based on intuition, they reflected that it would all come to an end one day. There would be that knock on the door and the No-Talent Police would bellow, 'Time's up. You con artists have been found out.' They all agreed they would immediately throw up their hands, plead guilty and be grateful it had taken them so long.

'Ah well,' Joanna took a deep breath, 'I'd better go and get this over with. Kick some ass, as the Americans would say.' She reached in her handbag for the spray of Must by Cartier and squirted it behind her ears, smoothing it into the back of her neck. She was barely aware she was doing it. It was certainly not done for the MD's benefit but an automatic reflex, another layer in her armoury to be used when she was getting ready for battle.

Chapter Six

From its secret hiding place, Liz took the key of the editor's coveted cloakroom. Though she had never used it before, she had been told where Charlie Mays kept it.

If the huge newsroom had been crowded and full of people doing their daily work she would not have felt so guilty. But the silence added its own mystery to the breaking down of one of the last all-male bastions – the editor's private cloakroom.

No woman, except the cleaner, had ever stepped in here, Liz thought as she unlocked the door. No woman had ever been editor of a *Chronicle* newspaper, Sunday or daily, able to push her views which, by geographical accident on this island, would reach all corners of the realm on the same day.

Inside the cloakroom she looked at the mahogany fittings and dark green walls and thought how masculine it all was. Every free after-shave the beauty department had grasped over the last ten years to offer to the dapper fifty-six-year-old editor had been lined up in serried ranks on the shelves, some well past their sell-by date to judge from the strange green colour of their contents and the grime on the bottle necks. Liz noted with a wry smile that some of the manufacturers had gone out of business.

The mirror was badly lit. Well, if you spent too long at the tables in the Garrick, Reform and the Coach and Horses, not to mention El Vino's, you wouldn't enjoy the view either.

She prinked her hair – even though she had spent that morning, her precious Monday morning off, at Michaeljohn where she had sat between two queens, from Greece and Jordan, and wondered if her photograph in the glossies would ever be as pretty as theirs.

She preened into the mirror again. If only she was a stone lighter and a couple of inches taller . . . She sighed. But the new Armani suit had not been an indulgence, despite the sharp intake of breath she had taken when the assistant added up the bill. It was worth every pound for its flattering cut which subtly understated her curves.

She wanted to present herself as someone who appeared in charge without being a female man. The jacket came in for critical examination. Buttoned up to the top might give the impression of being uptight. Unbuttoned, she could send out the wrong signals. She wanted to avoid any notion that it was an invitation to the dance.

The proprietor, tall and a little overweight, was attractive to many women, or so he thought, mistaking a well-stocked share portfolio for sexual allure.

She left her buttons as the designer intended, firmly closed to preserve the line.

Today's lunch was important. Astrologer Patric Walker always said life was what was happening while you were sitting around making other plans. But here she was, about to go to a pivotal meeting. No doubt about it.

Ten minutes to one. Time to make her way upstairs. Still feeling guilty, she stowed the key back in its secret hiding place – not that Charlie, sunning himself in Palm Beach, would be needing it – and began walking purposefully through the newsroom to the lift.

The place was still eerily quiet. She sucked in her stomach and flipped her Chanel bag on to her shoulder. Maybe she had read it wrongly. Perhaps it was demotion or even the sack. Crazier things had happened. A former colleague had been fired from the deputy editorship just twenty-four hours after a drunken evening with his new editor. Worse than that, when he came in early to clear his desk, his successor, who had a reputation as a nice guy, had tipped the entire contents of his desk into cardboard boxes and put them out into the corridor.

A crackle of paper hissed behind her. She looked round, startled. She had thought she was on her own. But Belinda, the newsroom slave, had not gone out to lunch yet and had obviously been watching her determined march towards the elevator to take her to the penthouse.

'Oh, hello, Belinda. You doing Mondays now?'

'No, Tony just asked me to do today. He thought we would get a lot of calls on that killer nurse splash.'

'Have we?'

'No more than usual.'

Killer nurse, my foot, thought Liz. Tony just wants to know what's going on with my lunch today. It had been rumoured that the editor's farewell dinner was scheduled for a month's time. The job was up for grabs and Tony Burns wanted it. If only he put as much work into the paper as he did into knowing my every move, our circulation figures would be flying even higher, she thought acidly.

Tony was convinced that Liz had only leapfrogged over him in seniority because Charlie had always assumed Fergus Canefield would never give a woman an editorship. The longer he had no obvious successor as his deputy, the longer his reign would last.

Charlie had cunningly worked out that this was a winner all ways. It paid lip service to female equality, which earned him Brownie points. He had noticed that when representatives from all the corners of the far-flung Canefield empire met at their annual get-together there were so few women among the British contingent that it upset the politically correct Americans and Canadians. So in one simple stroke he sorted out Fergus's British problems – though not the ethnic minority ones. Liz's appointment as deputy editor also paid tribute to comparative youth in a middle-aged industry. Being older than his proprietor, Charlie thought appointing someone so young was no bad thing either.

This was only the second time Liz had been to the ninth floor. The first was that memorable day eighteen months ago when she had been offered the post of deputy editor. Then she had been whisked in and out of the proprietor's office in five minutes.

Although Liz had been to far more imposing offices in the course of her job, she couldn't help feeling nervous now. The lift door opened and she surrendered herself to the ninth-floor experience.

This was a universe away from the floors below. There the carpet was nylon and wool twist, here it was Aubusson. Downstairs there were tables of steel interlocking units, here was Chippendale, Hepplewhite and lacquered consoles shipped in from Tsingtao. Instead of aluminium-grey filing cabinets, here there were antique armoires made of chestnut from Calvados. All evidence of the twentieth century was well hidden. Where there was harsh 100-watt strip lighting, here were pleated silk lamp shades and recessed pearlised spotlights, not to mention the odd crystal chandelier.

Ah, the famous Whistler painting had been removed. She remembered the proprietor saying it was going to New York. He was buying the apartment above his in Trump Tower and planned to cut away the floor so that the six-foot-high painting could be given the display space he thought it justified. That was what billionaires did when their possessions did not quite fit.

The butler waved her along the director's corridor to the chairman's lobby. A round walnut table with inlaid ivory on ball claw feet sat on an elegant plinth. On this table the latest copies of all the group's publications, worldwide, barely fitted. Behind it was a huge marble fireplace which, Liz had heard, had been imported piece by piece from Siena. When she asked why it was so big, the butler jokingly reminded her of the size of the Santa Claus who would be using it soon.

It was a mild October day but a coal fire topped with apple wood was sending out an unsubtle message of affluence in the middle of this skyscraper. Liz could only wonder at the number of air vents and chimneys that had had to be installed to make this one-upmanship work.

She tried to mask her increasing nervousness. She had had no more than a cryptic message that her proprietor wanted her to have lunch today. For the umpteenth time she wondered when the Suits would ever remember that Monday was her day off. But still, when the proprietor called, you were not busy doing something else. She comforted herself. Trouble was never for lunch. If she was being used to charm an advertising agent or client, surely they would have given her the background hymn sheets. And as far as she could gather, she was the only guest. It must be about the editorship. Was the lunch a victory or a consolation prize? No, he would not waste his time on losers. Would he?

Fergus Canefield was a robust Canadian whose grandfather had made his fortune by starting newspapers in the towns that sprang up along the new railway lines over there. These were quickly followed by a string of complementary radio stations.

Fergus himself had lived in Britain for fifteen years but you couldn't see the join. Liz's recall of Fergus Canefield's face, apart from a few office functions, was mostly in the linotype dots of newspaper photographs. As she waited she remembered the pictures on the wall of his inner sanctum from her art books – Sotheby's had taken care of that. Image maker Gordon Reece had taken care of the provincial Canadian twang, after his successful work with Margaret Thatcher and after her with Princess Diana.

Youngish, rich and with a largely absentee wife, Fergus Canefield was *numero uno* in the international gossip charts and not least in his own office. Stories about his private life abounded. In addition to his family home in Canada he was rumoured to have women installed in each of his three elegant houses, in Hong Kong, Cap Ferrat and Trump Tower, New York, but nobody had ever seen a photograph or put a name to any of them. The one and only Mrs Canefield was reluctant to leave the marital mansion in Toronto, although her three children were ensconced in British boarding schools. Apart from her regular visits to Gordonstoun, Benenden and the Dragon School, and a brief foray to their mansion in the south of France, she felt obliged to stay close to her prized pedigree huskies, which were winning trophies all over the North American continent.

The truth was she had taken refuge in dog breeding because for many years her marriage had been celibate. It upset them both but after they had decided that two sons and a daughter were enough, Fergus had become impotent.

After a few months Mrs Canefield perceived he was not impotent with everyone. On one of her trips to Britain, she paid an unexpected trip to the office. When she was introduced to his new secretary, who looked exactly as she had done fifteen years earlier, she was absolutely certain he was being unfaithful. Her suspicions were confirmed when checking the family answering machine. She discovered that it had recorded an entire conversation between boss and secretary. It had not been business they were discussing but what she was planning to do to him at the next meeting in the boardroom: 'I'm going to hide under your side of the table and suck you off very, very slowly,' said the woman's voice. Mrs Canefield had never heard her husband giggle before.

Though the affair was long over, it was that same secretary who glided over the marble floor, smiled and ushered Liz through huge double doors into the chairman's private office. She was in the Presence.

Fergus was standing in the corner, wielding the phone. He did not turn round but gestured behind his back, 'Sit down, sit down.'

She lowered herself gingerly on to the frail-looking Louis Quatorze silk chair (how awful if it collapsed under her!) and studied him. He was much taller and bigger than average, around six feet three inches she thought, with a head of greying hair slightly balding on the crown. Then there was his famous killer smile. If she had been on a more personal footing with him, she would have advised him to change the Himmler-style specs for friendlier-looking frames.

Fergus's desk was awash with papers, contracts, faxes and three phones. They reminded her of the story of a former prime minister who was showing a friend of hers around No. 10. In the Cabinet Room he pointed out two telephones, one black, the other red. 'One is a direct line to the White House, the other is to the Kremlin,' explained the then Premier jovially, 'but I forget which is which.'

Next to Fergus's phones was a console with a direct connection to the Stock Exchange. Three televisions were on, one on Sky News with the sound turned off, the others mutely showing CNN and a BBC2 arts programme.

Even when he stood still there was energy and movement about Fergus. It was clear his mind was in three different places, talking French, motioning her towards a chair, catching the butler's eye. A few minutes later it became apparent the telepathy had worked. The butler came in bearing a silver tray and two Baccarat flutes of pale-cream bubbly liquid.

Liz decided a sip might help.

Fergus moved swiftly to the chair opposite her, speaking this time on yet another phone, while altering letters to someone else in yet another language. He was speaking in French, which she understood – well, he was discussing figures and Liz recognised big numbers. What was he buying next? The City abounded with rumours about his European ventures. His eyes flicked from one TV set to the other while his left hand pressed the button on the console. He was checking the constantly changing figures spread across the screen.

'*Attend!*' He pronounced it the French way.

Putting down the phone he shouted to his PA, 'Bring me the Bourse file and see if you can get Jacques on the other line.' At the end of this flurry, he turned to Liz and gave her what she privately thought of as his Citizen Kane/Orson Welles devious smile. What was he up to?

He reached out a large, tanned hand. Liz was unsure whether to stand up and take the outstretched palm or lean over and stay seated. But he was on to the next thing.

'Do you approve of the champagne? It's from my own vineyard. Now,' without waiting for her to reply, 'let's eat.'

She was amused. Maybe his personal secret service had told him she didn't just like champagne, she loved it. Was today a reason to celebrate or did he drink champagne at every lunch meeting? He gave her another wide dimpled smile before taking a sip.

'Here's to a profitable lunch.'

Profitable for whom? she thought as she dutifully raised her glass.

She was not altogether certain this man was ready to appoint a woman as editor of one of his newspapers. But he was not the kind who would take the trouble to give you lunch so you would not leave his employ if you were disappointed. Shall I just smile or try to say something clever? Liz was irritated that she could not think of anything. This was a strange sensation for her. Usually she was mistress of the situation.

The decision whether or not to make conversation was taken from her when yet another secretary came in with two letters to be signed. While Fergus was doing this, the telephone let out a beep and he picked up the receiver. Liz was beginning to get rattled, feeling as if she were part of the furniture. Her chair was set back from the desk and she unwittingly crossed and recrossed her legs, a mixture of nervous response and needing a reaction from him.

To steady these unaccountable nerves, she began to look searchingly round the room, trying not to appear as if she was listening to his discussion. She need not have worried. Judging by his demeanour, she was as interesting to him as a doorstop. Liz was gazing at the cluster of silver-framed pictures of his children taken at various ages when he leapt up, put on his jacket and strode halfway across the room.

'Right, let's have lunch, shall we?'

Liz fumbled hastily for her bag, put down her glass and wondered momentarily whether to take the champagne with her.

He saw her hesitation. 'Leave that, Henry will bring it in.'

In a second his tall figure was through the mirrored doors which slid open to reveal a tiny but immaculate dining room. Liz marvelled at its perfection. It was painted sky blue and white, with three walls of floor-to-ceiling clear glass. It gave her the impression she was floating, part of the sky. The table was laid for two, with starched white Irish linen, the points making perfect triangles at the edges of the table. Two huge Regency mirrors were hanging on the one solid wall, reflecting the view, with the City in the foreground. Trained on this view, in the corner, was a magnificent brass tele-scope. The tripod was Victorian but the Zeiss lens had been made in East Germany by a master craftsman only three months before. It was rumoured that Fergus could see who was on which floor in over-looked buildings doing what deals with which people. Nobody went so far as to suggest that he could lip read but they did not discount it.

For the hundredth time Liz wondered what this lunch meant and whether he would ever get to the point. It was true that Charlie was getting on but his twentieth anniversary had been marked by a riotous celebration, not a farewell one. Gossip that the veteran editor of the *Sunday Telegraph* had been seen in the building aboun-ded. Liz knew, because Fergus had made sure she did, that another possible contender, Jim Davis of the *Herald*, had sat in exactly the same chair a few weeks ago.

All this activity was meant to convey that nothing could be taken for granted and although the *Sunday Chronicle* was doing well, it was still lagging 200,000 copies behind the *Sunday Gazette*, its nearest competitor.

Fergus Canefield was discussing with the butler how he would like his beef.

I hate doing deals over lunch, Liz thought. I hate making one of the biggest decisions of my life over food. Since biblical days, she mused, breaking bread had been a symbol of friendship, hospitality and goodwill. Now it had been corrupted and reduced to 'doing lunch', which meant using it for business. In the main, friendship was the last thing on anyone's mind.

There was a frightening array of glasses and eating utensils on the table. Liz had eaten countless elaborate meals but she felt uncharacteristically nervous and was terrified of knocking over a glass or using the butter knife for the entrée. Fergus had reduced her to Lizzie from Newcastle.

The strong sunlight on the glass made the atmosphere close but nothing would make her take off her jacket and reveal that the skirt buttons were straining. She was so nervous she found herself saying yes to a hot roll when she never ate bread after breakfast. She felt worse when Fergus waved the bread basket away.

She left the roll untouched.

The vegetable terrine arrived and Liz wondered if he would ever get away from the small talk to the real nub of the meeting. Would he wait for coffee or would he be clear from the beginning?

'What do you think I should do about Charlie?'

It was the question she had feared, although she had never expected him to be quite so direct.

She felt she should be loyal. 'He's a great editor,' she parried.

'Yes, yes, I know. He's done some terrific splashes lately. The former Chancellor of the Exchequer and his mistress, that gold bond scandal, the babies for sale in South America. Wonderful stuff.' Fergus helped himself to another small portion of terrine. 'But the best one,' he went on, 'was about the Defence Minister's son joining a strange cult in the West Country. He's such a wimp, that man. Who wants a defence minister who can't even keep his son out of trouble?'

Liz forced a smile. 'I worked with his son and he's the wimp, not his father.'

'Oh, so you helped with that one, did you?'

Liz felt her face flushing. 'I think I've been quite helpful on all of those exclusives.' She hated herself for boasting but could not let Charlie get away with claiming all the credit.

Fergus brought his eyebrows together as his eyes narrowed. He put down his fork and for the first time really examined her. She decided to stare him out.

'Do you know the ex-Chancellor too, or did you go to university with his mistress?'

She smiled, breathed deeply and replied more tartly than she meant to. 'I don't think his mistress went to university. But I got the story because I've known his Parliamentary Private Secretary for several years and, although he didn't exactly tip me off, I knew him well enough to realise how frustrated he was working for that man. That made us take a closer look at his boss.'

He was silent for a second. 'Well, that's what's clever about Charlie. He chose you.'

Liz could not stifle her laugh.

Though Fergus acknowledged and joined in with her amusement, his restless mind had already moved on to another topic. 'It's this government we have to get rid of now. They hate me and I hate them. They're bad for business and bad for this country. We have to play fair but these stories show just how lazy they are. After only three and a half years in power, they're putting themselves first and the country on the back burner.'

He then told her a couple of anecdotes gleaned from inside the cabinet, alas, she thought, unprintable, about the American president's wife. This was his world, dining regularly with cabinet ministers, world opinion-formers or millionaires whose share dealings could, and often did, rock countries' currencies.

Mischievously he asked, 'Liz, what do you think of your opposition, Tony Burns? Good, isn't he? And I rather like the cut of Jim Davis's jib, don't you? Though I wonder if he's too old to be starting with another newspaper.'

What do I say? she thought. They're wonderful? They're terrible? I'm better than them? She forced herself to smile. 'Both are good journalists but are they what the *Sunday Chronicle* needs right now?'

He smiled back, nodding, as if pleased with the answer.

The *Sunday Chronicle* mattered a great deal to Fergus. It was the first British paper he had bought and it was his milch cow: ninety-six pages of newspaper plus review, Scottish and financial sections and a fat colour magazine poured huge amounts of cash into his business each week. The advertisement rates were the best in Fleet Street. Meanwhile he had sold off the print works and negotiated the best printing deals he could in a variety of locations all over the country.

Fergus Canefield did not have to worry about presses, printers and their maintenance; even the journalists were mostly working on short-term contracts. But he paid top dollar and if you wanted to get noticed, the *Sunday Chronicle* was the paper to be on. Other papers might have a higher circulation, but his paper had the profile advertisers drooled over.

'I hate all this,' Fergus confessed after what seemed like a long silence. 'People think proprietors love choosing editors. But I feel it's like standing at the roulette table. Charlie was in position when I bought the paper but I know he can't go on for ever.' He gave her a piercing look. 'The men won't like working with a woman editor.'

Her heart plunged.

'On the other hand I believe the women readers will like it and we'll get a lot of publicity.'

Liz's heart started to thump uncomfortably.

'But is that enough?' he went on. 'It's great front-page splashes we need, not just a personality. That's why I wanted to have lunch with you today. Charlie's going to be away for at least two more weeks. I told him he needed a rest.' Charlie was an editor so insecure that, wherever he was in the world, he flew home on a Saturday to edit the paper. Liz had never really stood in for him. He must have been really upset being told to take a holiday. 'So why don't you see what you can do while he's off and we'll talk again at the end of the month? If you do well, who knows, I might want to consider some more dramatic changes. Perhaps someone else can edit the Sunday and give you a chance at the *Daily Chronicle*. Anything's possible.'

The daily? Liz caught her breath and managed to nod, she hoped, with enthusiasm rather than panic. Harry Chambers, the editor of the *Daily Chronicle*, was drinking heavily, she'd heard. But never had a woman been given the chance to edit a national daily. It was not possible, was it? God, no. She would think about the daily later.

'Is everybody helping you down there?'

She smiled weakly, and nodded. What else could she do, even though she knew that while they were talking, Belinda on the newsroom six floors below would be checking her stopwatch and reporting back to Tony exactly how long the lunch was lasting?

'So you've got two clear weeks, young lady. Then we'll see if we can make some history.'

Her mind froze. Thankfully the butler caused a diversion as he poured coffee into the delicate Minton cups. Fergus threw back his chair. The meal was at an end and they both stood up.

Say something, you silly bitch, she admonished herself. Mentally he was already on the move.

'I've been giving some thought to how we can make sport better.'

Fergus turned and looked at her hard.

Encouraged, she went on, 'We intend making our journalists work twice. They'll file their match reports as normal, but they'll also file a commentary that goes straight on the tapes and can be heard on the Hotline number. Readers can dial their own choice of match and have a full commentary on the game. That way, our sports reporters will gradually become stars . . .' She gabbled on, not knowing whether this interested him or not. 'I think this ought to push up our circulation and we'll make money on the phone calls and maybe advertising will at last be attracted to the sports pages.'

A short silence.

'So, you know about sport, do you?'

'I've learned more than I ever intended,' she replied, without thinking.

He laughed. 'Hmmn. Let me know what the phone people say the profit might be.'

It was enough. She was elated.

His mind darted about and as they moved back into his office they touched on a raft of subjects, mainly politics. Liz told him that the hot gossip in Annie's Bar at the House of Commons was about the Home Secretary and the gaffes he made almost every time he opened his mouth, and not only in public. The politician's latest ridiculous pronouncements had been picked up by the 'red-tops'. The Annie's Bar chat had him spending too much time there as well as in the Strangers Bar downstairs and revealing far too much to backbenchers.

Fergus chuckled. 'The Prime Minister has assured me personally there are to be no changes at the Home Office. Which means,' he continued, 'there certainly will be some changes, probably a reshuffle of the whole pack of cards, including all the jokers.' He permitted himself a wry smile.

'I heard someone say politics is a dog's life, usually without benefit of the RSPCA,' Liz replied.

'Doesn't prevent them all snarling to grab each other's jobs,' Fergus replied. 'I heard that clever deputy of the Home Secretary's, Davina Thomas, might be due for promotion but the PM will have to sack that man first.'

He smiled and sat down behind his desk. She was dismissed.

It was still only ten minutes past two as Liz rushed out of the building, light-headed with euphoria. Unbelievably, she felt hungry. She had drunk a lot but eaten only a forkful of smoked salmon and vegetable terrine and two mouthfuls of the delicious beef. She looked up to the third floor. Yes, there was Belinda, Tony Burns's spy, watching the pavement and moving out of sight as soon as Liz spotted her.

Lately, she had been disturbed about something else. Whenever she was in the room, Tony often turned the conversation towards possible stories where those involved had neuroses or their minds were playing tricks or they were subject to anxiety attacks. Once he actually mentioned a 'great clinic somewhere in Mallorca that treated celebrities for mental breakdowns. Might be worth a story . . .'

It could not be a coincidence. Somehow he must have found out about what had happened to her on the island. The danger was he would not hesitate to use this information when the time was right. She would have to be on her guard.

Liz walked into a strange sandwich bar a few streets away from the *Chronicle* building. She was in no mood to bump into colleagues on the dailies who spent their lunchtimes buzzing in and out of the pubs and snack bars around the building. She ordered a large cappuccino and a sausage sandwich. Then she went slowly, word for word, over the conversation with Fergus.

Had she really understood him? Would he really consider her for editor of the *Daily Chronicle*, one of the most successful newspapers in the world? What was the circulation? Nudging three million a day. Christ.

Liz felt overwhelmingly tired as the adrenaline ebbed away. Perhaps he was only teasing her by dangling the daily in front of her. How many other people was he seeing for lunch? She would make it her business to find out if Jim Davis was on the list, and anyone else.

But he did feel a woman editor would please female readers. And people were always saying the *Chronicle* needed more of those. Maybe it was going to happen after all. It just depended on the next two weeks.

The thought galvanised her. She wolfed down the rest of the huge sausage sandwich and leapt into a cab, heading for her Filofax at home in Fulham. She had to ring all her contacts to get some stories moving.

Above all, she had to tell Joanna and Katya. She wanted to see their faces when they heard about the possibility of her getting the daily paper.

Chapter Seven

Katya was searching for aspirin, Anadin, Nurofen – anything. Why wasn't she more of a hypochondriac, then she would have all this stuff in her cupboard?

The sickly smell of forced winter jasmine filled the room, making her head ache even more. Flowers and congratulations had been arriving all morning. Among them bouquets, posies and elaborate plants sent by Aussie TV tycoon Bruce Gyngell in Sydney ('I knew you had it in you,' he wrote on his card), and one from Alexander Lestor, part owner of her television station.

The answering machine was full of messages from well-wishing colleagues and friends. Many were from newspapers requesting interviews but the only one she really wanted was not on the tape.

After changing into her faded old grey track suit, Katya had hardly moved since she came in from the television studios. Too listless to take off her make-up, she stretched out on the sofa, half asleep, waiting for that call. Surely it would come? A few words, however brief, just some contact. Why didn't the bloody thing ring?

Think about something else, she admonished herself, like the interview later in the week with the Prime Minister. She felt anxious about it. Get your mind round some interesting questions, Katya.

No good. It was hard to concentrate on anything else. What was happening at the hospital?

Her body jerked upright as the phone rang twice before the mechanism switched on the answering machine. In the pause that followed while her message went out, she waited tensely to find out who was calling. But she did not recognise the hurried voice asking for an interview. Damn.

She did not dare go out in case the call did come. Already she had tried the hospital three times but they had instructions, they said, not to put anyone through to that extension.

The receiver rang again, shrilly. It was Joanna, and Katya's shoulders slumped as she picked up the receiver.

'You sound as if you did too much celebrating last night.' Her friend was buoyant and cheerful.

'Not exactly.' Katya summoned all her expertise to disguise her disappointment.

'I'm dying to hear everything,' went on Joanna. 'Liz is coming round for an early supper tomorrow. Can you make it?'

Katya felt nauseous at the thought of food. 'I'll try.' She could not bring herself to tell Joanna the real reason for not wanting to leave the phone, then chided herself for forgetting, momentarily, that today Joanna was going to see her gynaecologist. 'Do you think you'll get a ticking off from Dr Bischoff? Apart from going out last night, have you been good?' she asked, with real concern.

'If you want to find out, you'll have to come round,' teased Joanna. 'It'll just be the three of us and you don't have to dress up.'

'I'll try, promise. Can I let you know later?'

'I'd really like you to come,' insisted Joanna before Katya said goodbye.

What a relief it would be to tell Jo and Liz about her affair. She was bad at keeping secrets anyway and totally unused to lying to them but she doubted if either of them would understand this madness. How could she even start to explain it?

They were the only two people in the world who could comprehend what the fame business had done to her life. And unlike most of the 'civilians' they met, her two friends were good sounding boards, able to evaluate how she ought to react to the intense media attention and speculation about her every move, particularly her love life. For Katya, an only child, they were her substitute family. She found her father too dominating and old fashioned, her mother too eager to please him to be a friend. Liz and Joanna had become her surrogate sisters. Liz would surely know what to do about the photographer who had taken her picture in the mews. But how to explain it to her without going into details? She could not. And if her friends knew the whole story, would they still remain her friends?

Katya Croft, just named Britain's top TV news personality, sat by the phone and wept.

An hour later, on the other side of town, in what used to be the ballroom of 55 Harley Street, Joanna was lying on an examination couch that would have been recognisable to Florence Nightingale. She was flat on her back, legs apart, while the white-coated woman gently felt deep inside her.

Completely relaxed in the hands of the doctor she knew and trusted, Joanna allowed her mind to wander to recent developments at work and to her latest tussle with her managing director, when she had had to restrain herself from marching out of the building.

A stickler for hierarchical protocol, he had been furious when told by New York that she had dared to discuss the magazine's promotional budget with the chairman, something and someone he considered his personal territory.

'Don't you dare go above my head again,' he had shouted. 'Anything you have a problem with, you talk to me about it.'

He would not accept her explanation that she had simply answered a direct question. He accused her of disloyalty and, worse, of being naive. 'Surely you realise they were on a fishing expedition to prove how extravagant we are over here? So when your precious editorial budget is cut, you'll know who to blame.'

That was an outrageous suggestion and he knew it. But it had not been a moment for rational argument and she wondered if there ever would be such a moment.

The sound of Harley Street traffic interrupted her thoughts. Examination over, the doctor stripped off her surgical gloves and said, 'You can put your knees down now. Well, so far, everything's progressing quite normally.' The kindly, weatherbeaten face of Dr Rosa Bischoff beamed with pleasure.

'So far?' Joanna asked anxiously.

'Now, now, no need to look for hidden meanings,' admonished the doctor. 'This one's coming along fine, though with your history

117

we'd be silly to take things for granted. And from now on you're going to be sensible, aren't you?'

'I have been already.' Joanna thought of all the invitations she had turned down in New York.

'Well, you know what I think,' Dr Bischoff told her. 'If I've said it to you once, I've said it countless times. You'll have to put your feet up and give up work. Just for a few months.'

Joanna sighed. The doctor did not understand, no medical person would. Only women like Katya and Liz knew what it was like to have a personal drive so powerful that it transcended almost everything else. Joanna did give her pregnancy priority, but choices were often difficult.

Why, when she was so happily married, was she so reluctant to give up the editorship of *Women's View*, even temporarily? What was it inside her that thrust her on so hard, kept her striving when common sense dictated it was foolhardy?

Yes, the money was important, they could not really make do with less. But she could earn nearly as much if she was a freelance writer. That was not the answer. She very much wanted this baby but she also needed everything her career gave her.

She had tried staying at home during her second pregnancy but she resented the repetitious drudgery and the lonely life away from the camaraderie of her office. When that pregnancy, too, ended in miscarriage she had felt cheated. The thought of being pitched back into that lonely and unsatisfying life again always made her nervous. If she gave up her career, who would she be?

The endless insecurity of her childhood, the need for money, status and a useful role in society affected her just as strongly now as they had all those years ago. She had struggled for success, worked hard for it and at last she had reached the pinnacle of her chosen field. It was difficult to give it all up.

George had the natural confidence engendered by old money and his confirmed status in British society as the son of an aristocratic family. His uncle, the Earl, had a title dating back to the seventeenth century. With this background, George accepted all he had as his right, even the small trust fund from his father's estate. He just could not understand Joanna's vulnerability. And his mother, Lady Langford, still considered her 'strange'. She would only approve of her daughter-in-law if she became a Sloane Ranger homebody with 'an heir and a spare'.

Joanna took nothing for granted, not money, not ancestors, not background. Her relationship with her father and Neil had taught her not to rely either financially or emotionally on any man. This attitude gave her an independence which George admired and which she did not want to abandon.

She had been through this in her mind a hundred times before but still had not come up with a solution that would suit both herself and George.

George's mother was a sprightly, bird-like seventy-two-year-old widow who had been left well provided for. George had not. For everyday life to continue with the comforts of a car and the occasional holiday, she and George needed her salary. How she envied the Langfords their capacity never to worry about money.

Joanna sighed. Dr Bischoff misunderstood and tried to reassure her. 'Come on, you're over the first three months. Your Concorde trip to New York hasn't caused any harm that I can find, nor that fright you had last night. So try and be positive.' She smiled over her half-moon specs. 'This little girl seems nice and secure to me.'

'A girl?'

'Well, I can't be a hundred per cent accurate at this stage but I've never been wrong so far. Now,' she warned, 'no more trips to New York. And far more rest. When I hear footsteps going like little hammers on the pavement past my window, I always know it's you. So that's a start, just slow down, will you?'

Joanna had told Dr Bischoff about the abortion in the backstreets of Mallorca. She often mused how her life would have changed if she had kept that child. He or she would have been twelve by now. She would probably not be married to George and she certainly would not have been able to give her job as many hours as she had done these last few years.

As Joanna dressed behind the screen, she suddenly felt the need to talk to her husband, to hear his gentle reassuring voice over that terrible crackling line from Kinshasa. But the phones from the children's home where he was working seemed to be permanently out of order and the fax worked only spasmodically. He would come home at once if she asked him but there had been so many false alarms in the past. Anyway, she did not want to put herself into a situation where he was sure to insist she went to stay with his mother.

The idea appalled Joanna. Catherine Langford's world revolved round several houses in the most exclusive areas of Britain. But they had fraying carpets, albeit priceless ones; large, unfriendly kitchens so untouched by time and motion studies that it was necessary to walk a mile to boil an egg. They were full of chipped enamel pans but had covetable flagstoned floors worn to a warm patina. The draughty hallways, cold enough to be the perfect temperature for the ancestral portraits painted by the Old Masters, chilled the blood. Joanna liked comfort, convenience and central heating. She could never really relax at family gatherings. No matter what expensive outfit she had nabbed from the fashion department, she always felt different from George's family. Her hands were too large, she walked . . . differently, her laugh seemed, to her ears, too loud and she had once worn a straw hat for an early spring meeting. A well-meaning distant cousin of George's had taken her aside and whispered, 'We never wear straw, my dear, not until June.'

Joanna shuddered. Stay with Catherine Langford? Not bloody likely.

Katya, drifting into a half-sleep at four o'clock that afternoon, was awake in a second as the phone rang. This time, after her message, she recognised her lover's voice.

She grabbed at the receiver. 'Don't ring off. I'm here. Wait, wait. I'll switch off the machine.'

The tone was cold. 'I can't talk now. It's too difficult. Don't try to call me again. I'm at the hospital. Thank God the children weren't in the car. Take care of yourself.'

The line went dead.

The call was completed without Katya having said a word. Sobbing, she replaced the receiver.

There was a click and a whirr as the government's counterintelligence unit in Cheltenham continued its work.

'Okay, that seems fine. Now let's get a few copies made of that video. I know one or two people who should see it. And make sure it's put back in the bag just as it was before you deliver it to the hospital.'

'Check.'

Katya paced the mahogany parquet floors of her flat. The interior decoration had been planned by the set designer at her TV studio. Every light, every piece of furniture had been chosen with one aim. To make Katya look perfect.

Flat 33, Broadwick Mansions, Cale Street in the most fashionable part of London's trendy Chelsea was also practical and comfortable with the tidy lushness usually found only in five-star hotels. Katya, educated by the professional designer, had an eye for just what decor touches were right and for how long. This year's topiary bushes on the table and in the hall replaced round tables with long quilted covers and the antique lace over-cloths of last year.

She had discovered that the secret of achieving a really clean flat was to let slip to her daily, Mrs Boon, that Prince Andrew or some other dignitary was coming to visit. The list of dinner guests over the years had become more and more extraordinary. Luckily Mrs Boon did not check that the head of the United Nations was in New York on the night he was supposed to be at dinner in Broadwick Mansions with Terry and Helen Wogan and Emma Thompson and Kenneth Branagh.

Usually Katya enjoyed being at home but now the flat felt like a prison. She made herself a third cup of black Café Haag in the thin Limoges cup and sipped it tentatively. She was tense, tired and terrified. Would that bloody photographer sell the picture he had snatched? Surely they would not be able to see anything in it, and if they did, how could they recognise her? And when would the love of her life phone again?

How stupid she was to have put everything at risk. It had been foolish to go to the mews. She could visualise the headline: 'THE MINISTER AND THE TV STAR'. It would trumpet a hot, hot story.

Sometimes she felt it was a miracle the press did not already know about them since the love affair had been conducted right under their noses. And she shuddered, thinking of how the news would affect her parents and what it would do to their relationship, which was tense at the best of times. If only they had something else in their lives. Katya curled up on the pale pink Knole sofa and gazed fixedly through the rain-splattered window. Was it only eight months since she and her lover, the Rt Hon. Minister for Broadcasting, Davina Thomas MP, had met? Could her life have changed so much in that time?

That day had started mundanely enough. After her usual 6.30–9 a.m. stint on Morning TV, Katya had been assigned to a press briefing at the Home Office in Queen Anne's Gate.

She was a mite resentful because, unusually, there was no camera crew free to go with her. That meant the item was less likely to make the news bulletins.

Her astute news editor had persuaded her. 'You're always going on about doing something more significant. This is a good way to earn your stripes. Going to political press briefings and conferences like this will help you get closer to the sods.'

She knew he was right, but without a camera crew ministers were usually not interested in talking to a TV reporter.

The Right Honourable Davina Thomas, MP, was Her Majesty's Minister of State at the Home Office, responsible for the broadcasting portfolio. It was obvious to the parliamentary press pack why this high-flier was one of only a few women to reach such an eminent rank in the government. Her skilful, and successful, campaign to persuade the Prime Minister to switch the broadcasting portfolio from the Heritage Department back to the more influential Home Office had, according to the prevailing wisdom inside Westminster, marked her out for even higher office.

She was an impressive sight. She was taller than Katya's five feet nine inches. Katya wondered idly who had cut her stylish blonde crop. And that navy wool crepe suit had obviously come from somewhere smart but safe and British like Aquascutum. From the top of her sleek hair to the tips of her Manolo Blahnik shoes,

Davina Thomas exuded style. But not so much that it would frighten the horses or make a fashion page in the tabloids.

Flanked by her civil servants, she was authoritative, cool and imposing as she briefed the dozen or so journalists in the oak-panelled committee room, outlining the government's plans for amendments to the new Criminal Compensation Act. She nearly made them sound exciting. She had been a successful barrister before entering Parliament. Indeed, Katya knew she had done a stint earlier on *The Times* in their legal department. The staff there had been impressed by her ability to say 'yes' to problems.

Katya was somewhat embarrassed to find after a few minutes that the minister appeared to be addressing her alone. She rationalised that the constant eye contact with her was probably part of Davina's courtroom technique, to fasten on to one juror while making a speech. That must be it. She was trying to impress a television reporter enough to get herself a slot on the box. What was more discomfiting was Katya's own response to the gaze of those steady, pale grey eyes. They were almost hypnotic. She experienced an overwhelming surge of physical attraction to the woman commanding all their attention.

Katya felt completely bewildered by this reaction, a mixture of apprehension and excitement. It was an emotion entirely new to her. She could not begin to understand it. What on earth was happening to her?

She was not altogether surprised when, later that afternoon, there was a telephone call from Davina's Private Parliamentary Secretary inviting her to lunch with the minister a few days later. Almost in a trance, she found herself cancelling a long-arranged date to make herself available.

Davina Thomas had taken the risk of asking Katya to lunch because as she watched her during the press briefing she realised that the old magic was working on the younger woman. Whether she could use this to soften her up to become a political acolyte or for something more Davina did not yet know. But she had done this skilful seduction before and the banquettes in the Savoy Grill Room were perfect for it. She knew she could touch Katya's hand, arm or knee, as a little test, without anyone seeing.

Katya was already seated when she arrived.

'I think this is going to be a memorable friendship,' Davina said, after ordering two glasses of perfectly chilled champagne. 'Let's start the way we mean to go on, shall we?' And she continued to take control, suggesting the food and ordering a bottle of expensive wine.

Knowing politicians rarely paid for meals, Katya volunteered, 'This is on Morning TV.'

Davina laughed. 'Fine. Better than on the taxpayer.'

Katya watched with amusement as captains of industry ordered food that they could eat at home. They treated the eminent Savoy Hotel with its five-star restaurant like the office canteen, ordering pea soup, Lancashire hotpot and heavy but comforting puddings like spotted dick. Liz had told her that two well-known editors of national dailies only ever requested that day's fish catch with chips. Swallowed down with champagne, naturally.

Katya and Da ⋅⋅aded indiscreet political gossip and exchanged views and opinions on a range of subjects, perfectly relaxed in each other's company. Davina had a fund of funny stories from her door-knocking days during past elections, many with a sexual innuendo about them, and they were soon laughing together like old friends.

Katya liked the way Davina listened to her opinions, quite a change for a politician, she thought. But she was conscious of a subtext which she had not yet decoded.

When she had lunch with Liz and Joanna, they often tasted food from each other's plates. Natural curiosity, they maintained, meant they had to sample three dishes from the menu instead of just one. Davina had the same habit but something about it was, somehow, quite sensual.

'Do try this,' she said, 'it's wonderful how it slides down your throat,' and, 'Aren't these asparagus the most luscious you've ever tasted?' She kept passing her own spoon and fork for Katya to put into her mouth.

Completely foreign to both their natures, they ordered pudding, to prolong the meal.

Every now and then, as if to emphasise a point, Davina would touch Katya's hand or arm, leaving her fingers a second longer than was necessary. Katya could hardly credit the effect they had on her. Why was it that the bit of skin where Davina had put her hand seemed to burn minutes afterwards? And why did she long for it to happen again? It did not occur to her to touch Davina's hand even tentatively.

Later, Katya wondered if she had imagined the whole episode; not the meal, but Davina's magnetic effect on her.

That evening, Katya had a long-standing engagement, a drinks party at a new art gallery in Cork Street with Roger Wynne-Jones, a television drama director whom she had known for a couple of years. After a mini-affair, their relationship had switched to one of Star and reliable 'walker'. When he was not busy bedding every other blonde on television, Roger rather liked being seen with her at West End premieres and sporting events like Wimbledon, Royal Ascot and charity dinners. These were occasions for which Katya's name was on the A list of celebrity guests. The advantage for Katya was that she would have an escort who knew that she usually needed to leave midway through an evening function to go to bed. Alone. But this evening, worried by the sensations she had felt during lunch, she decided to break the habit. To Roger's delight, she invited him back. She had felt sexually turned on all afternoon.

During Roger's frantic lovemaking, Katya wondered why oral and penetrative sex with Roger, who always made sure she enjoyed herself, was much less exciting than the few seconds of mere arm-touching with Davina at lunch.

'Can't you go more gently?' she whispered to him.

But even when he did, it was still not gentle enough. She began imagining a lighter touch, a smoother skin . . . and worried even more.

For Roger, this sensuous Katya was such an unexpected bonus after months of a pleasant but platonic relationship that it was hard to stop him wanting to continue for hours.

Katya was as good an actress as any female and did not want to hurt him. But by the time she had persuaded him that the intimacies they had shared that evening were more than enough, he began to suspect that she was simply using his body.

Katya disliked herself for doing it and vowed she would never go to bed with Roger again even if it meant she would have to find another walker.

The following day she received a thank-you note from Davina. 'It's so rare to encounter someone on one's own wavelength. I feel I've met someone special. And you understood, so well, the role of women in political life, I'd really like to talk to you about this again – we've only scratched the surface! Don't let's be polite and wait the usual three months. Why don't we meet again next week?'

Katya was thankful that she and not her secretary had opened the envelope. To her it was so much more than a bread-and-butter letter.

Davina's office phoned the next day. The minister could not manage another lunch for a couple of months but would Katya like to come to a drinks party the following Wednesday at the Home Office for a group from the European Broadcasting Union who were visiting Britain to look at satellite television?

The Home Office was in Queen Anne's Gate, an ugly 1960s concrete block totally out of keeping with the handsome Georgian houses that flanked it. For security purposes, the entire interior of the building was divided into colour-coded sections. Appropriately enough, all the ministerial offices were in the Grey zone. But at least the office of the Minister for Broadcasting was spacious, with good quality modern furniture. Paintings on the wall had been borrowed from the thousands stored at the National Gallery or the Tate, one of the perks of the job. Floor-to-ceiling windows overlooked St James's Park and during wintertime the bare trees allowed the minister to see the majestic view of Buckingham Palace.

The minister's sixty guests sipped warm white wine and manoeuvred to get their share of the sparse supply of canapés. Katya was not interested in either. Confused and excited, she was conscious of only one person in the noisy throng. Although she made a deliberate effort to avoid looking at Davina Thomas, they still, from time to time, would lock in eye contact. When that happened, Katya's body seemed to crackle as if a flash of electricity had passed through it. The feeling was so intense she knew it had to be reciprocated.

She was not surprised when, even before most of the guests had left, the minister quietly asked her to stay behind and invited her to 'continue the discussion', as she put it, at her home.

'Hugo and I bought this place when we first came to London,' Davina told Katya, opening the small fridge which contained little except bottles of Sancerre, Chablis, Laurent Perrier champagne and mineral water. 'Then we needed somewhere bigger so we bought a house in Lord North Street and it's perfect in many ways, especially for entertaining,' Davina went on. 'But when I need to be on my own, I come here to Roland Mews. It's my little bolt hole.'

She handed Katya a generous glass of ice-cold Sancerre and moved towards the large sofa, gesturing Katya towards it while she placed herself in the armchair opposite. Katya repressed an absurd feeling of disappointment.

They talked about the party, the future of television and Katya's interview that morning with the American vice-president. But as the bottle emptied, in the subdued lighting of the galleried living room, under Davina's gently persistent questioning about her private life, it seemed natural for Katya to confide thoughts, secrets she had never even shared with Joanna and Liz. She talked about how she had had many affairs but now found sex boring after the chase. And since becoming really famous even the result of the chase was a foregone conclusion. To her surprise she found herself telling the politician of her growing distaste for men and their penetrative bodies. This meant that her sex life, she told an attentive Davina, was virtually nonexistent. On the rare occasions she did go to bed with one of the men who constantly propositioned her, she ended up shuddering at his bristly jaws, his oppressive weight and the total lack of excitement he aroused in her.

Davina moved over to the sofa where Katya was sitting, put her arms round her and started rocking her soothingly, like a child. Katya felt as though a warm blanket had been wrapped round her. She did not need to pretend any more.

'Oh my darling, my darling,' Davina punctuated the words with soft kisses down Katya's temple and cheek, 'you've been so hurt and so alone . . .'

The soft, warm mouth and the smoothness of the skin against

hers brought Katya a delicious wave of pleasure which nearly over-whelmed her. For a brief moment she relaxed into the sensuous embrace before pulling away abruptly.

'This is all new,' she whispered. 'I've never admitted, even to myself, that I was . . . like this.'

Davina pushed her gently aside on the velvet-covered sofa. 'Then we mustn't go on. I don't want to persuade you to do anything that would make you unhappy.'

'I know you won't make me unhappy,' Katya found herself saying.

Davina moved back towards her. She slowly traced a circle round and across Katya's breast with a gentle finger and felt the nipple harden under her touch.

Katya shrank back again. 'I haven't done this before . . . I'm not sure . . .'

'I'm sorry,' murmured Davina, pulling her hand away instantly.

There was an imperceptible pause, then Katya said quietly, 'Don't be sorry.' Without haste, she began to undo the gilt buttons on her black fitted jacket and, gazing into Davina's mesmeric grey eyes, she slipped off the narrow straps of her silk teddy. 'Don't take your hand away, it feels so right.'

Since Mallorca, Katya had had a succession of short affairs with men where the chat-up and hunt had always been more exciting than the Deed, which she privately thought of as a hop, a skip and a jump.

After Mike Stanway in Mallorca, her affairs usually meant sex once or twice before she manoeuvred her partners from the seas of passion into the dry dock of platonic friendship.

Once when she, Joanna and Liz were discussing why no man lasted in her life, she had confessed, 'Men never seem to realise that I always lose interest in the sex pretty soon, sometimes unfortu-nately right in the middle of a session.'

Liz couldn't resist it. 'Oh, it takes a long time for men to notice they're poking a sack. They'll even do it to a pound of raw liver. Remember Portnoy?' That had set them off in a fit of raucous giggles.

Katya had always felt she did not really start to grow up until her friendship with Liz and Joanna.

She and Liz had been somewhat apprehensive when Joanna announced she was marrying George Langford, selfishly fearing it would affect their friendship. Happily, George was an easygoing personality. With typical English rectitude, he had made sure never to intrude. He seemed to understand instinctively that Joanna needed time with her friends. For their part, they gave him their highest honour. They dubbed him an honorary woman.

Katya discussed her close circle with Davina.

'That's worked because George is a man,' said Davina perceptively. 'But I'm afraid you'll have to accept that if you tell them about me, it will change your friendship.'

They would never understand.

And why tell them now if the affair was not going to last? Only a few days ago she and Davina had been planning holidays together. But Katya felt instinctively that Davina would sacrifice her rather than face the appalling publicity their relationship would generate.

She could not put off indefinitely telling Joanna and Liz what a mess she was in. And why.

Oh God. This was no good, she had to get some sleep . .

A few minutes later, Katya hovered in that dreamlike state half-way between oblivion and reality. She had, at long last, blanked out the events of the last forty-eight hours, after endlessly replaying them, like a video, in her mind.

Her reverie came to an abrupt halt as, to her astonishment, she found her body being pulled back to consciousness as wave upon wave of sexual excitement coursed through her frame. What was happening? My God, she was having an orgasm.

Did this happen to other women? Perhaps this was what people meant when they said they were kept in a state of perpetual sexual frenzy. Sexual arousal had not been in Katya's mind at all. Her last remembered thoughts were of the paparazzo and what the hell he was doing with her photograph. What was her body doing to her? Had she, in her dreamlike state, been thinking of Davina, as she did most of the time when she was awake?

Orgasms were once lonely, isolated things she did for herself.

Even with Mike they were rare and only with the help of his hands or tongue. With Davina, they were continuous and now it seemed she could have one solely due to her subconscious.

Katya found that her body reacted with surprising fervour to gentleness. She had often wondered why all the men who had ever made love to her seemed so heavy-handed. Davina's lightness of touch and softness of skin were sexually exciting.

It had been a wonderful discovery after years of secretly fearing she was frigid. She could shudder now at the memory of the ponderous limbs of men too much in awe of her beauty and her fame to concentrate on her arousal.

Under the duvet, she gave a last little shiver of pleasure and then, too soon, the feelings of dread returned. Their plans to have some kind of life together had all seemed so logical, so easy. During these past few months, after the turmoil of their initial meeting had subsided, Davina and Katya had both confessed to a great sense of peace, having made the decision to commit themselves to each other. Consequently, their lovemaking that Saturday afternoon had been all the more tender.

Afterwards Davina, quietly stroking Katya's hair, seemed to have no doubts about their relationship. She said she had been giving a great deal of thought to how they could spend more time with each other.

'Look, my marriage is a sham,' she told Katya. 'Hugo's no fool and he realises it even if we've never talked about it. Certainly we like each other and we don't want to do each other any harm. But I'm sure I'll be able to make him agree to a slightly different way of living.'

'What about your children?'

'Yes, the children.' Davina's voice was unusually tender. 'They're my only concern. I would never do anything to cause them harm but now they're at school I don't see so much of them. Of course I make a great of deal of effort to be with them at weekends and holidays. Hugo and I will have to spend the summers as a family. But apart from that, if the outside world is kept in ignorance, I don't see why Hugo and I can't discreetly live our own lives.'

'And you're sure he'll agree?'

'Yes. You see, we have a different arrangement to most couples. We live quite separately as it is. My work's to blame, I know, the hours. But Hugo's . . . not self-centred but self-absorbed. He has his business, his companies in the City, his golf and his precious club. I'm pretty sure that if I can convince him that his life isn't going to be interrupted or changed in any way, he won't care what I do. He might suspect there's someone else, but he'll think it's a man. It might give him the courage to have an affair. I've always thought he'd like to have one. But he'd want to keep it secret, even from himself.'

Katya shared her amusement and, though not convinced, for that moment she allowed Davina to persuade her.

'It'll be simpler than you think. On Saturdays, unless the children are around, I do my advice bureaux in the constituency and perhaps a couple of ministerial functions. Sometimes I don't get back home till late afternoon, by which time he's out riding. Then on Sundays he gets up before I wake to play golf with his cronies. And Sunday evenings, while he watches television, I wade through my wretched Red Boxes.' Davina laughed ruefully. 'Although we're quite relaxed with each other, I worked out we hadn't exchanged more than a few words the whole of last weekend.'

'But,' Katya countered, 'however discreet we are, how on earth can we manage it? You're pretty high-profile and the press pays a certain amount of attention to me, too.'

'Ha, we'll take a tip from the Royal Family. People think they're under scrutiny the whole time but almost all their activities are hidden from the public view. They have helicopters to whisk them away from any press pack.'

'Oh yes, let's get a Westland,' laughed Katya.

'What they have are safe houses,' continued Davina, 'dotted all over the country, for assignations or whatever.'

Katya had heard something about this. She had often shared drinks with the royal rat pack and had been told about a little bijou residence in London's Notting Hill Gate which Prince Charles was reputed to have used before his engagement. Safe houses looked no different from the houses next door. They were in neighbour-hoods with a shifting population, they did not have doormen or porters, they were registered in the names of companies and, above all, they were kept secret. Despite bribes from the media, there was still a code of silence, especially among the upper-middle classes and the minor aristocracy.

The idea of safe houses, so much more private than hotels with their waiters, desk clerks and house managers, gave Davina an idea. 'Why don't you think about buying a little place near my house in the country? You said yourself you're not making your money work for you.'

Katya, in thrall, nodded, pushing aside the fact that she had agreed to Joanna using any of her spare money to dabble on the Stock Market. In the six months they had been trading they had made such a small profit she did not think it worth continuing.

'It'd be a good investment and we could see each other at weekends,' continued Davina. 'Perhaps also take the girls away on holiday. Hugo only likes being in England so we could take them abroad. Wouldn't that be fun?'

But that was all before the car crash.

Chapter Eight

On the muzzy print, the woman in the cloak was unidentifiable. But it was only a small contact print, and in black and white, and the photographer hoped that a blow-up would reveal more.

Roddy Hamlyn was about to move along the contacts when something made him stop and look again. Funny, he had just the same sensation now as he had when he let off an opportunistic flash against the window of San Lorenzo's in London's Knightsbridge.

That hurried picture, dark and blurred at the edges, turned out to show Princess Diana gazing into the eyes of the new man in her life, the first since the break-up of her marriage.

Geoff Wilson, the *Sunday Chronicle*'s picture editor, had danced with delight when he saw the contact and had paid Roddy a five-figure sum for his paper's exclusive use of it. And Roddy's bank manager had done a similar jig later.

Roddy had the same feeling now about this picture. Maybe it was a lucky break to be doorstepping Tom Reeves's London house just at that moment. All he had hoped for was a picture of Tom and his wife coming home from a night out and, if he was lucky, Tom, notoriously short-tempered, would lash out at him. Nothing sold better than a candid shot of an angry star, capped teeth snarling at the lens.

The woman in this picture obviously did not want to be recognised. He was sure it couldn't be a wife, else why would she race off like that? But she had held a front door key in her hand and was moving toward the lock when his flash had frightened her off.

Roddy's instinct told him the picture was valuable.

The keen young sports writer approached the picture desk. 'Can you help out on this boxing match next week? The boss would like a picture of Lucky McDonnell in the ring with a lion.'

Geoff was used to odd requests. He saw himself as a miracle worker.

'What kind of lion, son?' His face betrayed no emotion. 'Stuffed or alive?'

'Don't mind really.'

Geoff turned to his assistant. 'Carl, get us a lion.'

'Where do I get a lion from? I can't go back to "ABC Animals". We didn't pay for the hippopotamus.'

'Why didn't we pay for the hippopotamus?'

'Because it ate the bloody duck,' replied Carl.

Geoff turned to the sports reporter. 'What sort of lion do you want, son?'

'Any old lion.'

At this, there was a commotion amongst the staff within earshot as they sang out, 'Any old lion. Any old lion. Any, any, any old lion.'

Geoff was still chuckling when Roddy came in and showed him his contact sheet.

'This may be something or nothing. I caught this woman going into the house Tom Reeves is renting, the one he uses while filming over here. It was after twelve on Sunday night. When the flash went off, the woman freaked out. She had just finished hunting in her bag for a key. What do you think?'

'Hmmn, his little London bit on the side maybe?' Geoff spotted Tony Burns, his assistant editor (news), out on the floor. 'Want to come and look at this? Taken after midnight the day before yesterday outside the house Tom Reeves is staying in.'

The paparazzo told Tony, 'The woman was shit scared when I let the flash off, scarpered faster than a rat up a tree.'

Tony Burns looked through his magnifying glass. 'Hard to tell who it is but we'll have a go. Has anyone else seen this?'

'No – after the Diana picture I promised Geoff I'd always come here first.'

Geoff smiled.

'Well, leave it with me. No point in bothering our dear acting editor till we know a bit more about this one. I'll put my boys on to it.' Tony had heard from Belinda that the proprietor had devoted a whole lunchtime to a one-to-one chat with Liz, and he was alarmed. He'd better play his cards closer to his chest than ever now, he thought. And maybe it was time to send a stringer to that clinic in Mallorca . . .

He brought his mind back into focus and looked round the newsroom. 'Somebody should go right now to Roland Mews,' he said, 'and take a snapper.'

Hearing this, the reporters in the newsroom hulked down behind their computers. Nobody wanted to stand outside in today's steady rain watching Tom Reeves's front door for hours. But at least only one team was needed because Roland Mews had just one exit.

All newsrooms had at least one doorstep king and Peter 'Mac' MacLennan was theirs. He was renowned for sitting up to eight hours in his car at a stake-out. What he did about his bladder remained one of Fleet Street's great mysteries. 'Trade secret,' he told those who enquired.

Mac was deeply busy writing the most important story of the week for him: a list of the expenses he had allegedly incurred the week before.

He had to stop, stuff all the blank receipts he had conned out of taxi drivers and restaurateurs into his desk drawer, and depart forthwith, with a photographer, to look over Roland Mews, London SW1.

After they had left, Tony scrutinised the picture again through his magnifying glass. 'Bloody awful contact. I mean, it could be anything under there, could be a gorilla. Get it blown up and come back to me.'

'The only thing we've got to go on is what she's wearing,' said Geoff.

'What is it? Some kind of blanket or cloak? Okay, Geoff, let's get the fashion girls in, see if they have any ideas for once. And I'll speak to Phil in showbiz, maybe they've heard some whispers.'

The hunt was on.

The print was pushed through the darkroom and blown up. By 2 p.m. it was on the picture editor's desk, but by then Geoff, one of the few on the paper confident enough these days to take late lunches, was in Simpson's-in-the-Strand tucking into rare roast beef and Yorkshire pudding, deep into the roguish Cabernet and deeper still into the machinations of *Sunday Chronicle* office politics.

On his return to the office at 3.30 p.m. he scribbled out a Post-it note, stuck it on to the print and told his secretary to put it on Nicola Wellesley's desk. The fashion editor was the person most likely to find out about the cloak.

Nicola was universally known in the business as the vainest woman in what was still called Fleet Street. This reputation had been reinforced when only a fortnight before, a colleague had proudly brought in her weeks-old first baby. The only comment Nicola made was when she put the child on her hip and asked the office, 'How do I look with a child? Does it suit me?'

Nicola was one of those working women who made no secret of how their sex lives had helped their career. In fact it could look to outsiders as if she bartered her perfect body for jobs. The whole office knew she was having an affair with the paper's proprietor Fergus Canefield. Nicola lost no opportunity to let Liz know, subtly, that she could and would make a detour to the top round her and all the other executives on the paper, if she needed to.

The latest nonsense had been last week, when she had gone over Liz's head to arrange a trip to see the Paris Collections. Liz had turned down the request because of budget constraints (planning a headline saying 'Non, non, non to Paris') but the last she saw of Nicola was her disappearing into Fergus's limousine en route to London Airport to join him on his Lear jet. Liz was only slightly mollified when she discovered later that Fergus did not know about Liz's ban and had only been manipulated by the thought of having thirty-six hours of Nicola non-stop in his suite in the Georges V hotel.

Nicola's rise to prominence had started under the reign of Charlie Mays. She had moved onwards and upwards since then but she still enjoyed the editor's protection. Office cynics thought it might have more to do with blackmail than sentiment. They still reminisced in the office about the sex in the shower story of three years earlier.

One busy evening, a torrent of warm, soapy water had cascaded on to the newsdesk through the ceiling. The flood was traced to the editor's bathroom. Eventually, an embarrassed Charlie came out after repeated pounding at the door. It did not take long to discover that there had been a naked woman cowering behind the shower curtain with him, then the paper's lowly second fashion assistant, Nicola Wellesley.

This was a rather more exotic venue for Charlie who, before Nicola – who was more geographically adventurous than he was – stuck to the large, leather Chesterfield in his locked office for his regular 'late editing' sessions.

At times, Liz felt almost sorry for Nicola. There was always a question mark over her talent because of her special patronage. She did occasionally produce some good work but she must have constantly asked herself whether she would have lasted in the job if she had to rely on ability alone.

To the men in the office, she was a perk you attained with seniority. In fact, because Nicola had achieved her present job through sexual patronage, Liz felt she was even more insecure about her talent. This sometimes made the fashion editor nervous and malicious.

But because of her past love affairs, she had unusual contacts and alliances all over the place. Nicola was dangerous because most of the men she had slept with were married and as she had stayed single she had a certain power because they felt she held all the cards.

'I feel uneasy about women like Nicola,' admitted Katya when she, Joanna and Liz were discussing her a few weeks before. 'In the long run, women will be judged by how they perform on the balance sheets not on the bed sheets.'

'Exactly,' added Liz. 'You wouldn't appoint a woman as editor just because she was a good fuck, would you?'

Katya laughed at that. 'Well, there're one or two top women I know in television who aren't averse to using the casting couch in reverse. In fact, there's a particularly pretty boy at our station who admits he got his first break by letting himself be seduced by his woman boss.'

'Ha,' said Liz, 'I'd be bloody thrilled to do that if only I remotely fancied anybody in my office. Anyway, I couldn't bear it if they only wanted my body to get a job.' They had all laughed.

'Don't be unfair,' said Joanna, 'they may really like cellulite.'

Tony Burns decided to brief a young female reporter, Debbie Luckhurst, to follow Peter MacLennan and dig around in the mews. Giving her a copy of the photograph, he instructed, 'I want you to find out who this is. You've got the job because of those languages you speak. Also you'll blend with those toffee-nosed tarts who live there. Ask around, see what Tom Reeves is up to. We think the woman in the picture might be his little bit on the side. And hang around. Someone who goes out at night's more likely to have seen her than the school-run lot. This job isn't on the news list,' he added. 'It's hush-hush so don't go blabbing about it to anyone. Anyone. Understand?' Debbie Luckhurst nodded. She wanted to keep her job secure so she operated on the premise that if she just did what she was told she would prosper.

Many stories did not make the news list, but the beginning of the week was used by a Sunday paper for sussing them out. Tony was a tough work horse. Some *Chronicle* staff spent Tuesday and Wednesday loafing about, usually in a pub. Not Tony.

In an attempt to find out for certain which house the woman in the cloak was trying to enter, he instructed another reporter, Alec Preston, to search for the owner of the house next to Tom Reeves's in case the star had a good alibi. They could be lucky. If the next-door occupant was also famous they would still have a great story.

Belinda, the newsroom slave, brought her boss a coffee, large and black.

'I've just had a call from a contact on the *Gazette* news desk. You'll love this one and I'm sure you'll be able to use it.'

He swivelled his chair towards her.

'Apparently, that creepy little editor of theirs came back after a boozy lunch and slapped down a wad of twenty-quid notes in front of his new deputy picture editor, who's a woman. And guess what he says to her? "How much for a blow job, kiddo?" '

Tony roared with laughter. 'The PC police will love this.'

The foreign editor interrupted. 'You haven't got time for all that cackling. I need to talk to you about the Washington story.'

'Oh, everyone's going to have that,' said Tony dismissively. 'We need something extra and if we look hard at this Tom Reeves story it could be our exclusive. Even if we don't get hold of the woman, we've got a good mystery splash and the picture to stand it up.'

This week was so important to her that Liz was leaving nothing to chance. At the first weekly editorial conference her antennae told her which of her colleagues were keen for her to make a success of the paper and, as importantly, which were not.

The frustrating thing was, thought Liz as she watched her number four gazing out of the window at the passing traffic, it was almost impossible to accuse anybody of not pulling their weight, even if they weren't.

This was the vital time for a Sunday newspaper. It was at this stage of the week that the clever and original ideas had to be developed.

Liz could not make some of her senior executives realise that Tuesday – which many of them still felt was the time for long lunches and doing their expenses – was the right day to think up and organise their stories. After Tuesday there would not be enough time to make those ideas bear fruit unless they had a lucky break. It was difficult to pull exclusives out of the air, especially with a staff that was only two-thirds the size of rivals.

The other problem was that, unlike many jobs, there was no end product until Sunday. As editor, you could not chastise someone for not producing the goods on Wednesday when they could argue there were still three days left to go.

Liz was grateful to those who were supporting her and putting up ideas, making intelligent suggestions, phoning contacts in this country and abroad for tips and news stories, pillaging foreign magazines for feature ideas to adapt or that exceptional photograph to buy or copy.

But how could you tell someone sitting at their desk for maybe ten hours a day that they were not working effectively, even though Liz felt some were not? The time-servers thought the paper owed them a living rather than the other way round and too many of them jerked into life only on Saturday morning. Too little, too late. Newspapers were all about hearts, minds and souls working flat out, otherwise they were only worthy of wrapping round fish and chips.

Now she was acting editor, Liz was certain Tony's acolytes were only going through the motions. If she asked them to do anything, she knew they would do it. But in their own way, at their own time and at their own unenthusiastic pace.

I'm going to put these five assistant editors, who are supposed to be my close collaborators, on the spot, thought Liz, otherwise we can wrestle with jelly all week. In any case, the fight was supposed to be with the other Sundays and not within the office. Liz had worked with most of these executives for the last three years. She had probably spent more time with them than their wives and she sensed they were all uneasy, to various degrees, at finding themselves working for a woman. In spite of the feminist movement, there were still few men in newspapers who were comfortable with women in charge.

Since Fergus had taken over the *Sunday Chronicle*, it had been transformed into an attractive tabloid providing glossy scandal that was acceptable in a family newspaper and had soon become the 'top of the bottoms', as it was known in the trade. Now, with a two-million circulation and four million readers, it was poised to take over from the *Sunday Herald* though Liz still felt Charlie published too many stories about World War II.

'We were beaten last week with that police story,' said Liz, looking at the news editor. 'What's the point of you pouring Laphroaig down the constabulary's throats night after night if they give the tip-off to another newspaper?' Without waiting for his excuses, Liz went on, 'And before somebody complains about the lack of reporters, why are our columnists writing better stuff for other papers and magazines than they are for us? It's lonely out there. Do any of you ring them up? Take them to lunch?'

'Yeah, I'm seeing Jeremy next week,' responded the features editor.

'But they need continuous tender loving care. You should be talking to them regularly. You know what it's like when you're working from home. It's easy to be wooed by the next journo on the phone. Their best ideas should be coming here. Why don't we get them in here for a think tank or something?'

Tony and his cronies kept darting looks at each other. I'm not going to be patronised by this lot, she told herself. I'm handing out baby stuff by comparison with some of the other editors they've worked for. Fleet Street abounded with stories that before morning conference at a certain highly competitive daily newspaper, one or two of the executives had been known to be physically sick. Of course they had been reporting to a male editor.

Liz looked at the chief sub. 'And why, when our best sub is already away on holiday, are you letting Jack have Saturday off?'

'Tony said it was all right.'

Liz looked at Tony at the end of the table and shook her head slightly. 'Real team spirit, Tony.'

She gazed round the conference table. 'The others are all on television promoting like mad this weekend and we're not. We've used up our budget till next month. So we've got to pull something out of the bag. We know the Home Secretary lurches from one disaster to another. How long is it since anyone spoke to his wife? What does she think of it all? For all we know, she may be the cause. And Tony, what's happened to that list of ideas I gave you last week? They seem to have dropped down a big, black hole.'

'I mentioned to Tony that whispers from party headquarters say they're looking for a mole,' the political editor Andrew Cahill chipped in. He loved being centre stage. Today it was all happening again. The government was in more trouble. 'I didn't raise it in conference until I could harden it up but there's a rumour that the sex scandal leaks have come from a woman.'

It had been a rough year for the government. There had been a flurry of minor sex scandals including the Scottish MP whose mistress, wired for sound by the *News of the World*, made him admit to his habit of wearing women's clothing at weekends; and the former minister caught in a *ménage à trois* with a mother and her daughter.

141

The government could only be defeated in the House of Commons by a vote of no confidence but another juicy exposé would certainly damage the prospects of their candidates in any by-election or the Euro-elections. And the British public had a notoriously long memory which did not augur well for their success at the next general election.

'Didn't our tip-off come from a woman?' asked Liz, giving Tony a hard look.

'Yes,' he said, 'and I'm sure we taped her. I asked Vera to keep it.'

Vera, the switchboard supervisor, taped every call coming into the newspaper. Each tape was ninety minutes long and if nothing significant was recorded it was re-used. This practice had started when the IRA began to leave coded messages with newspapers about bomb attacks.

'Vera is coming in later. I'll get her to dig it out,' Tony added.

'I'd like a progress report as soon as possible.' Liz paused. 'If that's not too much trouble.' The most annoying thing about Tony was that he never volunteered any more information than he absolutely had to. Under Charlie's regime he and she had both been assistant editors, Liz in charge of features, he news. Tony – and the rest of Fleet Street – was astounded when Charlie (or really, Fergus) put Liz in the deputy's chair.

When he had recovered from the shock, Tony had coped with it by arguing to himself that it was a clever move by Charlie who had always put his main effort into protecting his own position. The fact that Liz was acting editor did not make confirmation of the editor's position inevitable. The deputy editor rarely got the top job. There was still hope. Now Tony was more determined than ever to prove to Fergus that he, not Liz, was the best candidate to replace Charlie.

Nicola Wellesley was officially out on fashion appointments in deepest Knightsbridge but the clothes she was viewing were totally unsuitable in style, size, availability and price for the vast majority of *Sunday Chronicle* readers. They were, however, just the right kind of little numbers for dressing and undressing for a very private dinner with a multi-millionaire.

That was the great thing about expensive clothes, thought Nicola.

They did a lot of the work for you. With cheaper clothes, the body had to be held in or pulled up. But designer garments by Chanel, Versace, Valentino, Dior all knew just where to pull tight and where to ease off to make the best of a girl's figure. They held snugly above or just below the waist and around the sleeves and gave that perfect fit which flattered or flattened. That was what you were paying for – not that she ever did, of course.

So dedicated was Nicola to her work that she was not only looking at the clothes, she was actually inching her way into the sample sizes. Nobody was better at body enhancement than Antony Price, she decided, unzipping the strapless, tightly boned sheath. Hadn't broadcasting chief Janet Street-Porter once said: 'I call them result dresses. Because they get results.'

Nicola had gone from showroom to showroom all afternoon and weary PRs hoped the dresses she took away would not come back marked or stained. She and other fashion editors and assistants like her were adept at pretending they were intent on featuring the chosen garments. Occasionally, they did. But the PRs were not fooled. These outfits were going to be consumer-tested in the most exacting way. Only food and holiday editors entered into so much detailed checking with such enthusiasm.

This was why so many newspaper fashion pages featured clothes wildly out of the reach of most of its audience both geographically and financially. Fashion editors were paying the price of free loans in return for page space.

When Nicola had selected three or four dresses she personally liked she headed back to the office. She got back at five, carrying six designer carrier bags – she still could not decide what to wear tonight. Her desk was littered with phone messages, model profiles, a large bouquet of white roses sent by Moyses Stevens from a grateful fashion house, and the photo left by Geoff's secretary.

Seeing Tony at the sub-editors' desk, she made a great play of examining the blown-up print with a big eye glass. Tony watched as she picked up the phone to call her friend Amanda Deveraux on *Tatler*. Her encyclopedic knowledge of the collections was far more reliable than Nicola's own erratic filing system.

Good, thought Tony. She was getting on with it.

'Amanda darling? I've just tried on the Kenzo embroidered top and I thought it much more you than me. Have you seen it yet? Oh, you must. By the way, if you were me, would you go for the bottle-green Antony Price, the one Naomi looked so good in, or the gold Calvin Klein? No, not for the paper, for me. Hmmn, okay. Maybe you're right. Now, a bit of boring work. Who's done a black velvet cloak with embroidery round the edges?'

As Amanda rattled off names, Nicola wrote furiously – Jaeger, Frank Usher, Bruce Oldfield and Catherine Walker.

'Oh Gawd. Yes, I know the *Mail* did them last week. I'll tell you later. Thanks, you're a genius. See you at Benetton. 'Bye.'

A call to Jaeger brought the promise of two photographs of their cloaks for reference. Next on the list was Frank Usher but there was only an answering machine with a message from their doyenne of public relations, Shirley Young. She was at the factory looking at next season's fabrics.

Nicola glanced at the office clock. Five thirty-five. She would contact Oldfield tomorrow. God, only two hours before she met Fergus and so much to do. Crevasses to be creamed, curls to be teased, whiskery leg hair to be mown down, and she needed time and calm to apply, gingerly, a dab of depilatory cream to her nostril hair in case, looking down on her face, he was put off by a stray follicle.

Tonight, Nicola wanted to be perfect for Fergus.

Before locking the print in her desk drawer, she told Geoff, 'Surprise, surprise, it's this season's fashion cliché, a black velvet cloak. There are hundreds of them around now. Could be from anywhere, from C & A to Hartnell. And I bet the majority are made in Korea.' She fluffed up her pale platinum-tinted hair and pouted at herself in the mirror behind Geoff's head. 'It could be anyone under that. These cloaks hide a multitude of sins. They're ideal for pregnant women or those who just look pregnant. I'll try and help but it's a bad contact.'

Nicola flounced out of the office. No need to feel guilty about leaving so early. It was only Tuesday and there was a lot more work, of a different kind, to be done tonight.

Liz, however, did feel guilt at leaving the office so early on her

144

first day as acting editor but if she was having dinner with 'Cinderella' Katya, she had no option. Katya always had to be in bed by 9 p.m. so she could arrive at the TV station at dawn.

As Liz rushed out through the newsroom she noted, out of the side of her eye, Tony making a sweeping movement of his left arm to look ostentatiously at his watch.

Chapter Nine

The ice in the eighteenth-century crystal tumblers clinked gently as the tube raced by. Joanna's terraced cottage, freshly painted in John Oliver's Number 2, a pale 'greige', had been converted in 1879 from Lord Cadogan's stable but was rather too close to the London Underground's first overground stretch near Chelsea Football Club to be a truly des res.

Joanna now had almost no contact with her parents but still had never dared confess to anyone back home that she and George had paid close to quarter of a million pounds for what was merely the ex-bunkdown of stable lads. In Cape Town that sort of money would buy a sprawling, white-washed villa with swimming pool, overlooking the ocean at Llandudno.

But Joanna had fallen in love with the place at once, even though George had pointed out that it would be impossible to park outside their own front door on home game days. He was right, damn him.

Joanna's gaze wandered round her large yet cosy kitchen over-cluttered with inspired buys from local junk markets, bric-à-brac shops and even boot sales.

Katya and Liz were amazed at how their friend always picked out the one treasure from a maze of rubbish. The pair of Victorian brass wall lights was a particular triumph and Joanna still savoured the moment when the stall holder, misunderstanding her intake of breath when he asked for '£4 the pair', quickly reduced them to £3.

Pink was the highlighted colour in the room, along with the wood. At one end was a small sofa in white and pink cabbage rose fabric. Large pots, cheap and painted pink by George, were home for huge mop-headed hydrangeas which Joanna had cut and dried herself.

The light was fading behind the antique lace curtains as she started to lay the Jacobean oak table which dominated the room. It had been wrenched with great difficulty from George's acquisitive mother after an uncle had died. Joanna used to be taken aback by the way some members of the British aristocracy set such store by their inherited possessions. But she imagined now that she would find it difficult to part with her table. She crouched down to take out the Minton china plates and matching cruet set from the oak Welsh dresser. In the centre of the table she placed two brass candlesticks, another astute find from a ten-minute forage at a street market near her office.

On side plates she folded the white and pale pink *toile de Jouy* napkins, run up by Maud, the local sewing lady, from a fabric sample sent by Liberty's for a photographic shoot. Two white candles from her store in the freezer (she'd read in a piece she had commissioned for her own magazine that this made them burn more slowly) completed the look that had earned Joanna high praise from home decor stylists. She pressed the candles down, turned them firmly into place and put tiny white paper shades on special holders on top of them.

She gave a smile of pleasure as she took in the restful ambience it all created. She promised herself she would never take all this for granted. One of the things she liked most about her friends was that they responded to and appreciated the atmosphere as much as she did. They never forgot how life could have been and how lucky they all were.

Joanna knew there were still things that needed upgrading. But money was short. What expectations she and George had lay with an inheritance from George's elderly uncle, who even at this late stage could still have an heir, as George's mother never failed to point out.

George accepted that once the baby arrived he would have to get a job that paid real money. Easy to say, but what would he actually do? It was never talked about, but they were both aware that Joanna's earnings were more than double his and would be for some time to come.

This pretty artisan's cottage was too small for a live-in nanny and they would have to move somewhere with four bedrooms. They could buy a larger house out of London but then how would she cope with a baby and be at her desk in Mayfair by 9.30 a.m. having read all the papers and still look as if she had just stepped out of the pages of her magazine?

One of the things Joanna would have liked to renovate was the worn and frayed curtains, but George had pointed out they had been hanging in homes belonging to his family for well over 250 years. Secretly Joanna much preferred the new fabrics from Bennison that merely looked old. The fact that they were mostly over £70 a metre put her off only slightly. It was on the list for when she and George ever became rich. She felt more comfortable with those battered drapes when a colleague at work commented, 'The curtains at Balmoral are in a much worse state and they won't get rid of theirs, will they?'

They had both hooted with laughter. The monarch's parsimony was legendary. Liz had once shown her a photograph of the Prime Minister standing with the Queen in her private sitting room. In the cavernous opening of the room's huge ornate fireplace, a one-bar electric fire glowed.

The friends had had some of their best nights in Joanna's kitchen. Eating there had the advantage that she did not miss a word of the conversation even though it meant her pristine dining room remained largely untouched. The gossip, the talk, the shared intimacies – this was where they ironed out what was worrying them, the people who were bugging them, the office politics, the problems with particular jobs. Many hours were spent dreaming up 'Money Making Suggestions'. None of the ideas so far, like Money Making Suggestion Number 5,923, a fleet of mobile manicurists, had moved even into the first stages. But that did not stop them coming up with Money Making Suggestion Number 5,924.

Katya once said, 'If only we could make this table talk, we'd have a bestseller and then we'd make the loot that way.'

'Ah, we'd need it all to pay the libel lawyer,' intervened Liz.

Dabbling on the London Stock Exchange had proved equally unrewarding. She, Liz and Katya had formed a syndicate inspired by the stories of a tipster on the *Financial Times* whom they had met at a splendid dinner at the Worshipful Company of Fish-mongers' Hall in the City.

The motive was clear from the start; he wanted to bed Katya. But as Joanna was the keenest of the three to make extra income, he found, to his disappointment, that the syndicate had nominated her as their liaison. From time to time he would phone suggesting some hot tips and always enquire hopefully after Katya.

'Joanna? Westralian Nickel is a real goer. Put your baby's dowry on this one.'

She had invested the syndicate's money and also a sizeable chunk of her own, only to find, a few weeks later, that she was left with a handful of worthless share certificates.

Joanna sighed and began to prepare a salad. Her idiosyncratic way of making salads was famous among her circle. All she did was open the door of her fridge and throw the contents into a bowl. But that did not fully explain her success. When her guests tried to emulate the bizarre combinations of sweet and tangy ingredients, they failed. The ingredients were tossed together without any pretence at refinement in huge chunks and the parsley put in whole, while the garnish was expensive pine kernels and sun-dried tomatoes bought earlier at the trendy deli round the corner.

This may cost a bloody fortune but I'm tired, she rationalised without a pang of guilt. I deserve it.

The dressing combined fresh lemon juice, Balsamic vinegar, Ridleys Strong English Dograpper mustard ('also great for sinuses'), dribbles of walnut oil and several cloves of crushed garlic.

However, if one of her salads was an extra-special success, Joanna could never, ever duplicate it. That was the only disadvantage of her method.

The faint, pathetic whirr from the antique door bell signalled the arrival of Liz.

'I can't understand why you don't get that damn bell seen to. It's very pretty but I've been standing there trying to get a sound out of it for ages.' Liz was in full flow. 'It would drive me to drink,' she laughed, 'and speaking of that, where is it? Don't bother with a glass, I need a straight injection into the veins after the sort of day I've had.'

Waving the mint-green Fortnum and Mason bag she was carrying, she said gleefully, 'I like this editor lark. I took a tip from Charlie and sent the driver on a shopping expedition and told him to buy me his usual, which turned out to be a pretty decent vintage. Can you stick it in the freezer for a few minutes?' She plonked the bag down on the pine drainer. 'I remembered you're not drinking so I found some freshly squeezed peach and mango juice. Very good for the baby and almost as expensive as the champagne.'

Free of her shopping, she gave Joanna an enthusiastic hug. 'Now, important things first. What did Dr Bischoff say?'

'Not yet – and don't say a word about your lunch with Fergus till Katya gets here. I'm fresh out of syringes but try this.' Joanna passed her a glass of perfectly chilled Sauvignon.

'Jo, you'll never guess what I heard today about Maggie Webber. Remember last year I sent her off to interview that Brazilian writer, a really difficult bugger, and she didn't surface for two days, and then only to get clean knickers? Well, you know she got pregnant? I've just heard she got the Brazilian Embassy to translate a letter so she could write telling him about the child. But he turned up on her doorstep with his wife. Apparently he'd always thought he was sterile and now they want to adopt the kid. Maggie's going bananas.'

'Poor girl, what's she going to do?'

'Well, I've said she can work in our Paris bureau for a couple of months until the Brazilian blood cools.'

They chuckled and Liz foraged inside the Fortnum and Mason carrier bag.

'I hope you can eat some of this,' she said, flourishing a hefty loaf heavily studded with large walnuts.

'Oh, evil, but I love that stuff.' Joanna was already fishing out the bread knife.

'So do I, but I'm going to be good tonight, only one slice, I swear. Mind you, it'll be a fairly thick one. How long before we eat? Should we have a piece now?' Without waiting for an answer, she snatched the knife and started hacking at the bread.

'Right,' said Joanna, sitting down opposite her, elbows on table. 'What's the latest goss?'

Another bite of bread and Liz was off.

'The best story's from the GATT talks in Geneva. Apparently one of the foreign ministers had a schnapps too many but even in this state he remembered the protocol. He knew he had to ask the wife of his Ambassador to dance. So he goes up to this woman in a bright red dress and asks her onto the floor. And she says to him, "There are two reasons why I don't want to dance with you. The first is that you're in no fit state. And the second is that I happen to be the Archbishop of Montevideo." '

Joanna laughed. 'George'll love that.'

'Hadn't you better take the champagne out of the freezer now?' asked Liz. 'It might explode in there. We'll open it soon. Katya should be here any minute,' and Liz cut another 'tiny' piece of bread. 'Hey,' she went on almost without taking a breath, 'that Home Secretary seemed to be falling asleep on parade in today's picture. The PM has to get rid of him. He's proof that renouncing your title to get into the Commons isn't enough to make you a man of the people.'

One of Liz's great strengths was her instinct for what Middle England would regard as fair and just. It was what made her good editor material.

'Do you think the Prime Minister would promote Davina What's-her-name to number one?' asked Joanna.

'Nah,' said Liz decisively. 'She'll get one of the so-called feminine ministries, like Health or Heritage. Gentle, sympathetic, intuitive, you know the sort of departments they allow women to head.'

'I'm told Davina's a pretty good political operator,' Joanna said. 'Have you heard how her husband is after that crash?'

'Still in a bad way, I think. Do you remember that other MP who had to give up his seat because he lost part of his memory in a car smash?'

'I'd have thought that was a positive advantage at the Gas Works.'

Joanna finished mixing the salad and handed a teaspoon of the mixture to Liz to taste.

'Needs a tad more garlic. Listen, before Katya arrives, what do you think made her so nervous on Sunday night?'

'Seeing *him* of course,' replied Joanna. 'And remember how she looked at that woman in the loo? I reckon she thought that was his wife.'

'I sussed that out and in the interview room I'm told she seemed to be on automatic pilot although I thought she looked great on the television.'

'It's so strange she won't talk about it. Who could it be?'

'I don't know, but he's not making her happy, is he?'

'Yeah, but what's bugging me is, for the first time ever, she's not trusting us. I mean, why can't we be told who it is? She knows we'd never tell anyone, whoever it is. Heaven knows, we've kept enough secrets already, haven't we?'

'I assume he's married – not a good idea, but even so we're hardly going to be judge and jury.'

'Well, I think we ought to have it out with her. I hate to see her so mizz. I think we should try and get the old Katya back.'

Another feeble ring on the bell sent Joanna racing to the door. Katya was standing there, clutching a large bunch of pink daisies which were nearly squashed as they embraced.

Joanna was shocked to see Katya's pale, strained face, the grey half-moons under her eyes. Not many of Katya's adoring public would notice or criticise their idol's appearance but she did not look like someone who had just won a major BAFTA. Joanna hid her concern behind a Niagara of words. 'Thank you, only you could find daisies like these at this time of the year. They're lovely. Come in. You'll never believe it but Liz has actually managed to get here on time. It's a major miracle.'

Liz was opening the freezer door to rescue the champagne. Pleased to see Katya, she too instantly noticed the shadows under her eyes. 'Hello. What's the matter with you?' she asked. 'You look like shit.'

Despite her gloom, Katya grinned. 'Cut the flattery,' she responded, 'and open that bottle. I've had almost no sleep and these days it shows up quicker than it used to.'

One of the comforting things about their friendship was that they could rely on each other to tell the truth even if it was critical.

Liz opened the champagne in the way she had been taught by a maître du tastevin at the Ritz, delighted to share his skill with such an obviously appreciative pupil. She was turning the bottle under the cork so that not a drop of the expensive contents was wasted. 'Always a leetle burp, not a loud belch,' the maître had told her.

'I heard a great story today,' said Katya, making a determined effort to hide her misery. 'It just sums up the television business. One of our news reporters sneaked off with his mistress for a week to Italy. Of course he told his wife it was for a job but the wonderful thing was that, when he got back, his wife asked him to hand over his exes which, as you know, are pretty hefty when you're on location.' Katya chortled. 'He has a joint bank account so, get this, the mistress has to fork out for the exes which, of course, he had already spent on her. Then, later, when he began whingeing to his wife about how hard he worked and the long hours he had to do, she asked him for a share of his overtime. So the mistress had to cough up again!'

They all laughed at this story, then Joanna lifted her glass. 'I think we should toast the heroine of the hour. Here's to your well-deserved BAFTA, Katya, and well done.'

'No, no,' said Katya quickly, 'here's to something much more important. To the baby.'

'The baby and BAFTA.'

Three glasses clinked, as they had on so many occasions before and for an instant their world was warm, loving and safe.

'I have another toast,' Liz added. 'To friendship. Let nothing come between us, not men, not work, not money.'

This was a familiar salute, honed through the years of friendship. Since their early days on the newspaper in Mallorca, they had developed a support system which was the envy of many of their colleagues. They believed this friendship was partly responsible for the success they had enjoyed in their careers, for the pooled knowledge, experience and, sometimes, resources. This could vary from exchanging ex-directory telephone numbers of so-called ungetatable celebrities to survival services like the name of the dry-cleaner who would collect and deliver from the office or of the shiatsu masseuse who would come to your home or office any time to give you the upright, stress-relieving shoulder and neck workout which they decided was better than a facelift because there was no anaesthetic involved.

'Right,' said Liz. '*Now*, Jo, tell us what the doctor said.'

'Dr Bischoff said the baby was fine.' Joanna beamed broadly. 'She says there's absolutely no reason why I shouldn't carry to full term this time.'

'That's wonderful,' said Liz. 'George will be ecstatic.'

'And,' Joanna let out a little squeak of delight, 'she is pretty sure, in fact she's ninety-eight per cent certain, that it's a girl.'

'Terrific,' said Katya.

'That's the best news of the week,' said Liz. 'Don't forget, when you think of names, keep them short so that, when she grows up, she can have a nice big byline.'

'Or,' mused Katya, 'when her play gets to the West End or Broadway, there'll be a saving on neon. The Suits would appreciate that.'

Joanna said she would take these suggestions into consideration when discussing names with George. She was far too superstitious to think of them this far in advance.

'How can the doc be so sure it's a girl?' asked Liz.

'Apparently it's a combination of the shape of the cervix and the heartbeat rate. One hundred and forty beats per minute means it's a girl. It's slower if it's a boy.'

'That sounds like a good story,' cut in Liz. 'Remind me to take her phone number before I leave.'

Joanna and Katya exchanged looks and started to laugh. Liz could make a story out of anything and they teased her that she was ruthless enough to sacrifice her grandmother for a front-page headline. Liz had the journalist's technique of blurring her off-duty and on-duty interests. She had always had good judgement on whose stories she could repeat and whose she could not. Once or twice, she had sailed close to the wind but, so far, she had not come a cropper. And if a few famous people were wary of talking to her, the vast majority regarded her as a 'good egg'.

'I've been trying to phone George in Zaire all day,' Joanna went on, 'but I haven't managed to get hold of him yet. I know he'll be thrilled though his old bat of a mother never stops nagging that the family needs an heir. She's worried that if we don't hurry up, the Earl might get married again.'

'But I thought you told me he was sixty-five or something and a widower.'

'Yes, but she told me last week that he brought home some woman who looked young enough to be his granddaughter. Good breeding material obviously, if he can bring himself to do it.'

'Picasso was well over eighty when he fathered his last child,' Liz reminded them, 'and Charlie Chaplin was seventy-eight, so don't get the family crest on your notepaper yet.'

'Not to mention the odd things they can do in Harley Street now.'

They were teasing but they all knew that Joanna was much more concerned about carrying the baby than whether she would or would not have a handle to her name.

'Dr Bischoff actually wagged her finger at me today,' admitted Joanna. 'She says no more travelling, no more cocktail parties, in fact, no more going out of the office unless it's to come home to put my feet up. Nothing extra at all. I'm allowed to visit the office, make my phone calls, and do a little bit of organising. At lunchtimes I have to make sure I find somewhere quiet to put my feet up level with my waist.'

'Make your phone calls? Put your feet up?' Liz was incredulous. 'The doctor's a professional woman, doesn't she know how difficult that'll be?'

'Of course she does, but she doesn't know about Stephanie.'

Joanna's deputy editor, Stephanie Ross, was not yet twenty-six, a Roedean-educated achiever. Joanna had been delighted to appoint her, even though she was the daughter of the MD's best friend, because she found her exceptionally quick and creative. Blessed with the longest legs in the office, Stephanie had the kind of blonde hair that usually came out of bottles but in her case was natural.

'Can you imagine how that little opportunist would take advantage of me not being in the office? The MD's turned her against me. He's given her the impression that he can make my life so difficult that I'll leave and then he'll give her my job. But we know, don't we, that he'd never make Stephanie editor? She hasn't the right experience yet and she's a fool if she believes his hints. I'm going to have a confab with Miss Angus, she's extremely good at protecting my back.'

'And perhaps,' said Katya, 'it was a mistake to give that delightful

MD of yours the impression you would give birth behind the photo-copier and be back at your desk the same afternoon.'

Joanna had signed on as a patient with Dr Bischoff after writing a story about the doctor's work with pregnant women in native American reservations in Canada and her philosophy that western women's minds were responsible for the increasing complications of what was, after all, Nature's conveyor belt.

'That story about women in rice fields, taking a couple of hours off to have a baby, is not as apocryphal as you may think,' said Joanna. 'Dr B says it actually happens. But of course they have an extended family to help them. Can you see my ma-in-law helping me? Changing nappies? I don't suppose she even did that for George.'

There was an unusual second or so of silence as they pondered Joanna's dilemma.

'So how am I going to handle this?'

'Tricky,' said Katya. 'I can't think of many women in our business who've had really top jobs and had a young baby at the same time.'

'Ah, but don't forget our motto,' Liz said and chanted like a monk, 'We can have ever-rey-thing.'

'True,' said Katya. 'This might kill you but I think it could work. Send the conniving Stephanie to all those posh dos you can't get to. Tell her you want to give her more responsibility. It worked on me when I was at school.'

Joanna and Liz laughed, having heard the story of the most difficult girl in the class having a St Paul-like conversion when bribed with a prefect's badge.

Joanna applauded. 'You're right, it will kill me. But I think it's a great idea and she's so vain she won't suspect anything.'

'She's not as smart as you so she won't be able to make the most of the opportunities,' said Liz.

'The trouble with Stephanie,' said Joanna, 'is she's being manipulated by the bloody MD. She'll be quite good one day if only she'd stop all this scheming behind my back.' They could recognise Stephanie's game plan, to imply that because of Joanna's pregnancy she was paying less attention to the magazine these days. She, Stephanie, was having to plug the gaps.

157

'She's dumb,' said Liz. 'You could teach her such a lot.'

'I know. I'm worried about what's going to happen to the mag on my maternity leave,' admitted Joanna. 'You know how desperate she is for me to go off so she can take over. Well, I've no intention of going until the last minute. By then hopefully I'll have got the okay for all next year's promotions from New York. They told me they'd make a decision soon.'

'Smart move,' said Katya, momentarily diverted from her own problems. 'Don't worry, what goes round, comes round. She'll find out the hard way.'

In Joanna's opinion shits often prospered but she did not contradict her friend.

Liz took advantage of a slight lull to tap the side of her glass with a teaspoon. She switched to chairman mode. 'We have to get some order in this. There's an awful lot to get through before Miss Cinderella here has to fly off. I've been quiet long enough. It's nearly eight and I haven't even given you a sniff of what happened at the lunch. I reckon it's an MPP of nine point five. No, dammit, a ten.'

That caught their attention.

'Why didn't you tell me when you phoned?' asked Joanna.

'This is too good for that. I wanted to see your faces.'

She sipped her drink, enjoying their impatience. Finally she said, 'You could be looking at the first woman editor of a daily.'

Katya and Joanna shouted almost in unison, 'Not the Sunday?'

'Watch my lips. The *Daily* Chronicle.'

Joanna leapt towards Liz, letting out a prolonged yell that would not have disgraced the terrace at Chelsea cheering one of the rare home goals. 'Congratulations. You really deserve it.'

'You're a great journalist, Liz, and you'll be a great editor, too. It's time those bloody Suits recognised it,' added Katya.

Ever mindful of finance, Joanna asked, 'Did he discuss anything squalid, like money?'

They all laughed but Katya was the one to voice what they all felt. 'Don't let them do you down. Don't be so grateful that you'll accept less than they'd offer a man.'

Liz gave a slow smile. 'I've already thought of that. Charlie's secretary does all his accounts and, from what I've picked up here and there, I could make an educated guess at his salary.'

'Another toast,' said Katya. 'Here's to the best woman editor – no, the best editor in Britain.'

Liz put down her glass. 'Of course,' she said slowly, 'it's not completely sewn up. I'm acting editor on the Sunday for the next couple of weeks and in the charming way he has, Fergus has made it clear that I'm very much on trial. He's not fully made up his mind, I don't think, about the daily. It's a long shot but I'm going to go for it. If I'm lucky enough to get it, he'll be the first proprietor to appoint a woman for a daily. I bet he'll take some flak from the investors.'

'Why should he?' Katya was indignant. 'You're far and away the best man he's got.'

'Damn right,' added Joanna. 'Now, you'll need a few exclusives to show him what you can do. We've got to have a good trawl of the memory bank.'

'Thanks. I've got a sniff of something which could be good. Dirty tricks in the House of Commons. No, don't ask, I haven't all the details yet and I'm sworn to secrecy. If it firms up, it could make a splash and I'll do a deal with your lot, Katya, to get it on the news. Fergus is always impressed with any telly publicity we can get.'

The other two demanded to know every detail of the important lunch and Liz needed no more encouragement. She embellished the story, making the time she spent with Fergus seem far more relaxing and amusing than she had found it, though she was honest enough to include her visit to the sandwich bar.

Katya swivelled her champagne glass reflectively. 'Who'd have thought back in Mallorca that we'd be sitting here with Joanna as a famous magazine editor, me with my BAFTA and you just about to make history. My God, it's fantastic.'

'Not bad,' said Liz, 'for three gross – '

'Speak for yourself,' laughed Katya.

' – under-educated over-achievers.'

'And to think I didn't wear shoes until I was twenty-three,' said Joanna, who used to run around barefoot when she was a child and was known to make this remark in moments of triumph.

'There's only one straggly storm cloud on the horizon,' said Liz, 'and it's over six foot, with black shaggy hair and an even bigger ego.'

She looked at them expectantly and they all shouted together: 'That shit Tony.'

Liz sighed. 'He'll go ape over this. You know, I have the strangest feeling he has sussed out what happened to me in Mallorca. Perhaps I'm imagining it, but just lately I've noticed he lets certain words slip deliberately into conversations, like "beating your brains out" and charming references to "minds". The other day he said something about loopy women, "you know the type, Liz" – things like that.'

'Perhaps you're being over-sensitive,' said Joanna. 'There's no possible way he could find out.'

'Hope you're right, only when he gets his teeth into anything he's like a Dobermann with a rag doll.'

Everyone in the business knew about the editor of a national newspaper who'd had a nervous breakdown *in situ*. He was not even allowed to finish that week. There was no discussion about him continuing with his editorship. His career was kaput. Now Liz wondered whether she was being paranoid, but why did Tony keep harping on about brains, mental health and breakdowns?

Katya felt her stomach constrict, as if she was in an out-of-control lift. Even now some picture editor with the same characteristics as Tony might be peering through his magnifying glass to scrutinise that damn picture taken by the scum pap in the mews. Perhaps the picture was unusable. But Katya knew she was grasping at straws. What on earth had possessed her to go there when she knew Davina would be at the hospital?

Joanna saw Katya's troubled face and wondered why she was looking so fearful. What were the demons that had suddenly made her so full of dread?

Liz, seemingly unaware of the mood, was in full flood. 'You know what happened the other day at morning news conference? We were talking about Angie Smith making a film comeback and after Tony made that "loopy" crack he said, "I don't want to seem anti-women, Liz, but don't you all go funny from time to time? If it isn't that time of the month it's the menopause." See what I mean about his cracks?'

Her friends nodded.

'What did you say?' asked Katya.

'Well, as you can imagine, that was war. I slapped him down so hard the chief sub's mouth actually dropped open.'

Katya and Joanna were reminded that this was the tough side of Liz they did not often see.

Liz, smiling at the memory, carried on, 'I leaned back coolly, looked straight at him and let him have it. "Are we talking about your mother, Tony, your wife or someone even closer?" That sent him scampering back into his fox hole,' and she let out a mischievous chuckle.

'I can just picture his self-satisfied face, all crumpled up,' Joanna chortled.

'Katya,' said Liz. 'Remember that time you... What's the matter? Are you feeling all right?'

Katya was gazing at her hands.

'It's that bloody bloke you're involved with, isn't it?' Liz couldn't help getting angry. 'I hate to see you in this state. I mean, you've just got the biggest award of your life and you look as though you've been to a funeral. He can't be worth it.'

'And,' added Joanna, 'how many articles have Liz and I run where married men go back to their wives? I presume there are children involved – are they young?'

Katya nodded miserably.

'I rest my case.'

Liz put her hand on Katya's shoulder sympathetically. 'And don't we know from bitter experience how hypocritical the Great British Public can be. There's one law for them and another for their heroes. You'll be slaughtered if they find out, Katie, and you won't be able to keep it secret for ever unless you're very lucky.'

Katya smiled ruefully. 'I know you're right. I've got to sort something out. And I will, I promise. But you know I didn't plan this. It's so difficult for women like us to find someone who doesn't feel threatened or intimidated or who doesn't just want to go out with the image. I've longed for someone who cares for the real me.'

'But you've found him and he can't be yours, not properly yours?' questioned Liz.

Katya was silent.

'I suppose,' said Joanna hopefully, and not for the first time, 'it wouldn't help to . . .'

And she and Liz trumpeted, 'Share the burden.'

They looked at each other and even Katya was forced to smile.

'Also, we might be able to give you some useful advice,' Liz concluded.

They'd freak out if they knew the truth, thought Katya, and she shook her head. 'I wish I could tell you, honestly, and when I do you'll understand why it had to be such a secret even from you two.'

Liz smiled at Katya. 'Okay, the offer's always open.'

'Only if you think it'll help,' added Joanna, anxious that Katya should not feel pressured.

'Great salad, Jo,' said Liz. 'Any more left? Actually, the splash sub on the back bench told me a really good headline on Saturday night when we were waiting for the first edition to come up. He said no reader could resist buying the paper if it had this splash: DOCTOR IN MERCY DASH TO PALACE FOR SEX-SWAP OP.'

Katya smiled, grateful that her friends had the good manners to change the subject. The phone rang. Katya's driver was on his mobile to say he was waiting downstairs. Morning TV would have loved to insert a 'bed by 9 p.m.' clause into her contract but even they did not have the effrontery to do that. So they were generous with their car pool, keen to ensure Katya could face the relentless discipline of that 4 a.m. alarm call.

It had been a good evening, but there was still much unfinished business. They did not feel talked out. But then, they never did.

Chapter Ten

The phone rang in one of Britain's most expensive pieces of real estate. Twenty-eight by twenty-five feet of bedroom in Belgravia, London SW1, could cost a quarter of a million pounds on its own. Fergus Canefield had another seven of them. Once the dining room of Lord Villiers, for the last seven years it had been witness to the many and various sexual activities of Fergus.

The man himself was instantly awake to take the regular call from his broker in Tokyo. Nicola, lying by his side between monogrammed linen sheets, was also awake. And plotting. What could a girl do to keep this man's mind on her?

They had had dinner, four perfect courses, with three bankers. Then they had made love, including foreplay, for precisely fourteen and a half minutes before the first business phone call had come through.

At dinner, she had been dismayed by the escorts of the bankers. She had thought now that their affair was seven months old she would, at last, be mixing with wives but the dream died the moment these women came through the door. Her status had been clearly delineated. The women were at least twenty years younger than Fergus and quite obviously did not know much about their escorts or banking. They had bodies perfected for arching in beds but not for conferring with brains. One of them, a rather exotic dusky beauty, had after being silent all evening made the men laugh. When asked where she came from, she replied, 'Lahore.'

Nicola, a fully paid-up member of the National Union of Journalists, was secretly upset at being grouped with babes, nightclub groupies and the rest.

Later in bed, Nicola decided she would have to take matters into her own hands. Tomorrow she would get hold of every sex manual she could. Now she would do the best under the circumstances. So when Fergus leaned over and, muffling the receiver, said, 'I'm sorry for these calls,' she was not listening. By then, she had her mouth full.

Only four hours later, Nicola went to the office with new determination. Last night Fergus had been thrilled with the dress and the sex but, best of all, at last he had taken on board that he was going out with a girl with a job. This woman could not only gratify him in bed but was going to make him money the following day.

It was a good feeling for Fergus. And for Nicola. She was keen to impress Fergus. If anybody could help get the paper a scoop it would be her. She was in the office and on the case by 10 a.m. – for Nicola, a first.

Through the magnifying glass she scrutinised the print again and now saw there was a centimetre of lining showing. She decided to have the print blown up even bigger. When that version came down from the darkroom, she made out a fleur-de-lys scroll. After a few more calls, she had eliminated the cloaks from both Usher and Versace from her search. The Frank Usher version had a similar deep hood but no embroidery while the Versace one had shell buttons, no frogging and, again, no embroidery.

Eye perched over her magnifying glass, looking at prints of the last collections, she suddenly saw it.

'That's Bruce Oldfield's, I'd swear it,' she crowed to her secretary. 'Usually designers like to use their initials on the lining but unfortunately dear Brucie has never been able to do that. He started using the fleur-de-lys last season.'

As soon as he heard the description, the press officer at Oldfield accepted it was one of their garments. 'We've done lots of things with that embroidery. Tell me, does this cloak have a hood?'

'Yes, definitely a big hood.'

'Any frogging on the front? Or does it have a toggle fastening?'

'Hang on.' Nicola was peering through the magnifying glass. 'Yes, I can just make out some frogging, and there might be toggles, but it's difficult to see on this pic.'

The Oldfield man became suspicious. 'What do you mean it's difficult to see? Isn't it one of our catwalk pictures?'

'Er, not exactly. It's a pap picture, someone going into a party. You know the kind of thing.'

'It still looks good though, doesn't it?' he asked anxiously.

'Lovely, darling. I'd like to borrow one ...'

'Okay, let me look into it. I'll come back to you probably tomorrow.'

'Oh, can't you do it now?'

'Sorry, the order book's being updated on the computer and I dare not interrupt them. But it won't be a problem. None of the cloaks has gone out into the shops yet.'

By 12.30 p.m. Nicola felt she had done a good morning's work. And so did Tony. Since Oldfield had not gone into full production yet, the owner of the cloak would be easy to track down.

'My guess is it's probably a model,' Nicola shrugged.

Tony salivated. He could already see the headline: 'SUPER-MODEL AND FAMOUS STAR IN LOVE TRYST'.

Liz, walking by, saw Tony and Nicola in a huddle. That was an unusually dangerous pairing, she thought. Tony, the hard news man, was always dismissive of anyone in the features department – the shallow end, as he usually called it. What could they have in common? She dismissed the obvious as she knew Nicola was still playing doctors and nurses with Fergus and Tony's dalliance with Belinda was too useful for him to muddy the waters with another female in the office. But they seemed extremely pleased with each other. She would make it her business to find out.

As the closing music signalled the end of the programme, Katya thought, for the millionth time, how inane it looked to stay there sitting on the sofa appearing for all the world as if you had nothing better to do than to sit and chat with your co-host and the guests and sip the leftover orange juice.

If I had a dirty house and some kids, I'd be resentful, she thought.

The trick, as ever, was to look completely natural while acting in a totally unnatural way. These two sofas had never been relaxed into or reclined on. No one had ever put their feet up on them or had forty winks while lying on their pale apricot-coloured cushions.

Katya herself always sat bolt upright when interviewing the full panoply of political, showbiz and literary stars. Top PR people cursed when they knew she was away for Katya could make sawdust look like glowing mahogany. The dullest writer, the most tongue-tied actor sparkled in her capable hands.

Viewers felt the same about their Katya. One wrote to ask for her holiday dates, 'So I can be away the same time as you.'

'Imagine having such an empty life,' sneered her first co-host, secretly disappointed that no one had written to him in the same vein.

After the programme was over, there was always a ten-minute break for coffee so that the daily postmortem after the show would not be over-filled with the sound of fury and with the egos of 'the talent' still high on adrenaline. That break gave them all a chance to calm down. Some mornings Katya felt the adrenaline ebbing away so fast that although she would still be in her full regalia, with coiffed hair and make-up, she would be close to nodding off in the middle of the meeting. Other mornings she stayed so high that she knew she made her points too emphatically.

It was all so much physical and mental effort. You could not do a live show like Morning TV without reaching this high; the concentration was too intense.

Often Katya wished she could miss the meeting afterwards, but you were excused only if you could produce a death certificate. Postmortems in TV were taken inordinately seriously by those not in front of the cameras. It gave them their only real chance to manipulate programmes, for better or worse.

Katya wondered if her time clock would ever get back to normal. Here she was, basically with her best work of the day behind her, and yet for most people the day had only just begun.

But this day was different. In forty minutes' time Katya was due to leave for 10 Downing Street for her first-ever set-piece interview with Her Majesty's Prime Minster, the Right Honourable Edward Saunders MP PC QC, the Old Etonian who had confounded the critics by being elected eighteen months earlier though he was shorter, tubbier and greyer than his more photogenic opponent.

He had been nicknamed 'Steady Eddie' by the press because he was against radical change, feeling the country would be better for a period of quiet. Judging by the latest opinion polls, he was right. But Katya knew there were impending storms ahead, notably the latest economic figures. The series of sex scandals, albeit minor ones, was adding to a public perception of sleaze. Because of this, it had been strongly rumoured that the Prime Minister was in the process of reshuffling a cabinet he felt had had rather a lacklustre start.

Katya had met him several times before, at various receptions, on the election trail and in the House of Commons, but this was the first time the PM had granted Morning TV a solo audience. This had less to do with Katya than his press adviser's high regard for viewing figures in excess of two million and the demographics of the viewers. Targeting the unemployed and housewives was just what the party needed now.

Alex Kyle, the station's political editor, let everyone in the station and at the House of Commons know just how he felt about Katya doing this prize job. He regarded an interview with the Prime Minister as rightfully his and he felt resentful, particularly as the controller, trying to mollify him, had asked him to cast an eye over Katya's questions.

Katya knew that her questioning must not be average or soft. Another year of mornings on the sofa and its lunatic hours would kill her. Or at least put so many lines on her face that even the best Polyfilla the cosmetic companies could come up with would be useless. She had a good reputation within the industry but so far no woman had been allowed to become a Dimbleby, a Paxman or, best of them all, a Ted Koppel in the States. Katya was hoping this interview would help change that. She had to get out of the Morning TV studio more often and get a life. That was her most important reason, followed closely by a more personal one. With a politician lover, this was an area in which Katya wanted to show her mettle.

The final briefing was to be in the programme controller's office. Katya grew nervous when she realised her questions to the PM were being scrutinised by Alex Kyle. She was reminded of his bad reputation as a team player when he nonchalantly dropped her list into her lap, saying, 'Sweetie, do you really think you're asking anything difficult?'

Fight aggression with aggression, she told herself, and replied sharply, 'I'm questioning his handling of the economy, the peace talks and the European Parliament, the sort of subjects anyone would concentrate on. But I don't remember Walden, Dimbleby or any of them ever asking anything personal. The answers can tell you a lot more about the politician.'

'Y-e-s, I can see what you're aiming for but I'd be more aggressive than that if I were you,' he replied patronisingly.

Katya's questions were in fact an intriguing mix. Tough ones on the economy which any journalist would have asked were spiced with the sort of feminine nosiness which the programme controller knew the tabloids would love. Publicity for the station was meat and drink to him and Katya knew it.

'Anyway,' Katya went on, looking at the controller and for once biting back at her sniper, 'do you want this interview to reflect Alex's feelings following the usual lobby trail? Or do you want to find out the current state of the Prime Minister's mind?'

'Well, we can't dismiss Alex's experience entirely,' said the news editor. 'After all, this is his beat.'

Katya appreciated that news editors always had to champion their people in public, whatever they thought in private. Alex Kyle had often saved his bacon on a dull news day. He had an encyclopedic mind when it came to film footage which could be resurrected from the archives to emphasise and illustrate a fresh or even an old political angle. But the main man, the controller, was aware of the kudos that Katya brought to Morning TV. Also the publicity angle of a woman interviewing the PM, which was rare, was not lost on him. He privately thought it was half the reason they had been granted the interview. He was pleased they would get the film turned round and on screen by tomorrow morning. It might even influence Thursday's Question Time in the House and, hopefully, still leave something for the Sundays to chew over.

'You have to play these things as they roll,' he said. 'Katya will use her intuition and she'll push him as hard as she can, Alex.'

'If Katya can get a bloody word in,' retorted Alex.

'If you're worried that a mere woman interviewer will be steam-rollered, don't fret, I'll do as well as the men.' Katya was beginning to seethe.

'You don't understand, lovey,' replied Alex, now trying to be helpful. 'He's been taught well. It means he takes breaths when you least expect it. So when you think he's about to slow down and give you a break to put in a question, he's actually taken a breath already and is gearing up for the next rush of facts and figures. He's hell to interview.'

'I'll just have to do my best,' replied Katya with a sweet smile.

The controller, keen to placate her, said, 'You'll do fine.'

It did not do to be late for prime ministers and they still hadn't resolved the problem of the make-up girl. They had phoned time after time to ask Downing Street whether the PM wanted professional TV make-up. Obviously nobody there dared ask him and nobody would make the decision for him.

Katya put an end to the dallying and decided that Brenda Hart, the head make-up supervisor, would accompany her, complete with the fishing-tackle box full of cosmetics, in case Mr Saunders wanted to use her services.

'I thought it would look more workman-like,' added Katya, 'if I wore the same clothes for the interview as I had on for this morning's show.'

'Yeah,' said the news editor dismissively, 'you look fine. Serious but not dull.'

In her next life, thought Katya, slightly fractiously, she wanted to come back as a man. All they had to do was put on a navy suit.

'You're using God's car,' he told her, which is what they had nicknamed the chairman's black custom-built Daimler. 'We've given Downing Street the number so there won't be any problem with security,' he added. 'The crew's already gone in because you know how much trouble there is getting that electronic stuff into No. 10. Right, have fun and good luck.'

Katya thought she would need it.

The policeman in Downing Street peered into the back of the Daimler and recognised Katya immediately. He gave her a friendly smile and opened the heavy wrought-iron gates which screened No.10 from the rest of Whitehall. The gates had originally been erected because of the then constant threats from the IRA, amidst much muttering that the PM was giving in to terrorists and that Downing Street should not be cut off from the people, although the great British public seemed remarkably indifferent to this threat to their democracy.

The Daimler slid forward to the ramp in the middle of the short road and four security men came forward and asked the driver to open the boot and the bonnet. The driver opened the boot with alacrity but after a few moments it became clear he had no idea how to open the bonnet. 'Sorry, miss, I'm temporary,' he explained to Katya. 'Only on for the week and I don't know how this thing operates.'

Katya was embarrassed and irritated; this nonsense was taking her mind off the main game, not to mention using up valuable time, but there was no point in letting it show. If it had not been pouring with rain, she would have jumped out and walked but she had no intention of interviewing the Prime Minister with damp, frizzy hair.

Finally, after a search through the car's warranty instructions, the bonnet was opened, the inside inspected, the underside of the car X-rayed and Katya and Brenda were finally ushered into the geranium-red hallway of No. 10.

A smiling, black-haired Parliamentary Private Secretary greeted her and a lackey spirited their coats away.

'You'll see on the list of names we sent to your office that I've included our chief make-up artist, Brenda Hart, in case Mr Saunders has a moment,' Katya told him.

He looked flummoxed and Katya knew the PM had never been asked about the face fixer.

The cameras, miles of wire, lights and other equipment were being set up in the first-floor study, a favourite room of the PM's, being small and more intimate than the Cabinet Office or the ground-floor office. The crew were busy lighting the interview area. They would never be satisfied and would carry on all day if unchecked.

For interviews of such importance two cameras were used. Well, you could hardly ask the Prime Minister to do 'noddies and winkies'. These were necessary when there was only one camera, very much the modern, budget-conscious TV usage, saving as it did a second cameraman's salary, mileage and food allowance. With one camera trained on the interviewee's face, this meant never seeing the expression of the questioner. But one person's expression on screen for the entire interview made for a visually boring programme. To avoid this heinous televisual crime, 'noddies and winkies' were invented. It meant after even the most acrimonious of interviews, instead of picking up the equipment and leaving quickly, the camera was moved and focused on the interviewer. Prompted by a production assistant, the same questions were once more put to the now non-existent subject, in the same order and in an identical tone and the interviewer would have to pretend to respond, in the silence which followed, with either a small smile, a grave nod, a frown or perhaps the head slightly to one side as if listening intently. Later, in an edit suite, these two halves of the interview would be married together with no viewer ever seeing the join.

Katya was quite good at her noddies but it was a rare treat to know she would not have to bother with them. With the luxury of two cameras, one trained on her and the other on the Prime Minister, the tape editor could later intercut the chosen shots from the two video tapes.

There was a feeling of tense anticipation until the Prime Minister at last appeared. Like most world leaders, he was a quick glider and moved swiftly round the room, meeting all the crew.

When Katya introduced the make-up supervisor, Edward Saunders seemed relieved. 'I'd definitely like to take advantage of your services,' he told Brenda and leaned forward conspiratorially. 'The last time I did one of these interviews I was abroad and was too busy to be made up. When the interview appeared I looked so pale the pound dropped.'

He disappeared with the make-up artist into an ante-room for ten minutes. During the short wait, Katya was not made more tranquil by the mutterings of her director, Paul Hayes, who came over and stage-whispered, 'This place needs a change of ownership. I'd bet anything he'll lose the next election, whenever it comes.'

'I wouldn't place the bet,' said Katya. 'I'm with Enoch Powell, who thinks only fools and amateurs forecast results of general elections.'

Before the cameras turned over and while the lighting engineer perfected his art – he would never be satisfied – Katya was rather flattered by the Prime Minister's seeming interest in her views and opinions. She thought this was clever of him, to try to get her on his side before the tough questioning started. Then a tiny sliver of unease crept into her mind. Davina had used exactly the same methods, appearing to take notice of what she thought. Was this something they all learned? How real were any of these politicians? The thought hardened her resolve not to let him off the hook when she questioned him.

Because of Davina, Katya had made it her business to know as much about the political scene as a specialist commentator, not just the news that everyone was privy to but the behind-the-scenes lobby talk as well, including rumours that the party machine was waging a war on damaging leaks against prominent MPs. Davina had mentioned this to Katya but the information was still too vague to provide information for a penetrating question to the PM. Nevertheless, this background knowledge stood her in good stead now.

On the personal questions, the PM shrewdly opened up more than he ever had before. Katya realised he was well aware that his answers would make headlines the following day. Also his avuncular act would go down particularly well with the C1 and C2 social groups which his party needed to target.

On the political front, she continued to press him and eventually the PM categorically denied planning a reshuffle.

'Right, then there's definitely going to be one,' muttered the experienced cameraman.

The Home Secretary?

'Unassailable,' said the PM firmly.

'Goodbye to him,' was the cameraman's next aside as he zoomed in to do an extreme close-up of the Prime Minister's craggy face.

'It's a wrap,' said the director at last and everyone visibly relaxed, including the PM himself. Katya was pleased to find she had been

172

given an extra half-hour above the allotted time.

Edward Saunders allowed himself a full stretch, arms over his head, thirty seconds of relaxation before a private secretary came in, chivvying him, explaining they had to catch up on their schedule. The helicopter was waiting at RAF Brize Norton to take him north to make a major speech and his meeting with the Minister for Broadcasting was already thirty minutes late.

'She's waiting outside,' the secretary whispered into the ear of the Prime Minister.

He looked up and said to Katya, 'We're really finished then, are we?'

'Yes, of course.' Katya leaned over, unclipped the microphone from his tie and then her own mike. 'Thank you, sir. It was good of you to spare the time. I'm afraid the crew will be a little time longer taking out all the gear.'

'That's all right, I'll use the drawing room upstairs.'

The Prime Minister held open the door for Katya and she heard the click of high heels on the parquet floor before she spun round to see her lover, the Right Honourable Davina Thomas MP, advancing towards them.

The private secretary again whispered into his boss's ear and the Prime Minister clucked in annoyance. 'Davina, give me two minutes, will you?'

She nodded graciously and, seeing the PM in deep conversation, moved across to Katya.

'Good morning, Minister,' Katya said, hoping her voice was suitably neutral. 'How is your husband after the accident?'

'Thank you for asking.' Davina's detached tone matched Katya's. 'I think he's over the worst. At any rate his doctors expect him to make a full recovery though he'll be in hospital for another couple of weeks or so.'

'I'm so glad.'

Davina kept up the small talk. Katya was relieved. She did not want any awkward silences developing.

'Yes, my main problem is trying to cope with newspaper interest. The Sundays are the worst. I wish I knew how to get them off my back but it's—'

'I know how you feel,' Katya interrupted. This was her chance to warn Davina about the photograph. 'I've had flashbulbs popping in my face in the most unexpected places.'

'What? You mean the press are after you, too?' said Davina casually. 'Oh, of course, that BAFTA award, congratulations.'

'Thanks,' replied Katya trying to keep an urgent note from her voice. 'It's nothing to do with that. Just after I received it I was visiting a mews house and a photographer appeared right out of the blue. It was very alarming.'

Davina's face hardened. She understood what Katya was trying to tell her and what this could mean for both of them. In a low voice, she said, 'Well, you must never let that happen again.'

The Prime Minister finished his conversation and, without another word to Katya, Davina moved swiftly to join her leader. The ease with which she was able to switch her attention made Katya feel forlorn.

Many politicians had the mindset which rang bells when there was even a hint of personal danger. Davina had taken some risks to pursue her love life, but this was an especially bad time to cope with an impending exposé, with her husband in hospital, her boss warning against any further scandals and, even more important, a reshuffle in the wind.

Few newspapers would dare say two women together were more than ordinary friends unless they had a confession or photographic evidence, and they were unlikely to have either of those. Nevertheless Davina decided then and there she could only manage the problem of Katya by burying herself in a heavy work schedule, interspersed with regular visits to the hospital.

Davina concluded with a certain reluctance that the younger woman would have to become a non-person in her life.

The editing of the PM's interview took far too long. In addition to the friction between Katya and her producer Paul Hayes over almost every frame, the news editor kept butting in to insist he needed all the best bits for the news.

Katya felt Paul had a hidden agenda fuelled by his political views, while he accused her of wanting to edit out each offguard shot that made the Prime Minister look tired.

'You just want to keep in with those bloodsuckers in Downing Street,' he sneered. 'Isn't it a bit early to be going for a damehood?'

Katya was equally heated. 'I just object to you trying to twist the mood of the interview. Go back to time code 66:42:09 . . . there. You have the shot of him smiling after that answer. You left in the frown, then cut out the smile. That's bad journalism and also stupid. We're up for the franchise review soon and Downing Street will use examples like that to show how manipulative we are.'

She had to squash him once and for all.

'And remember, the Central Office of Information always tapes Prime Ministerial interviews. If they didn't think we were being fair, they might just take this chance to compare. How could that help either of us? The Prime Minister would end up getting the sympathy vote and we'd never get him for an exclusive interview again.'

Katya and the PM had talked frankly about the sex scandals that were bedevilling his government. She had dealt with this honestly, as had the PM. There was no need for Paul to suspect a whitewash. She had been tenacious but fair in her questioning.

In the end the news editor ended up being the referee and finally Paul grudgingly gave way, but it had been a draining business and Katya went back to her flat in Cale Street, Chelsea, mentally and physically exhausted and wishing Davina was waiting for her.

At least she had not had time to worry about the implications of the photograph or Davina's cool tone . . .

At the top of the long list of messages on Joanna's desk, including a contact helping her with the assaulted children refuge campaign, the Henley Centre who wanted her to make a speech, and a show-business agent anxious to get her client on the cover, was one timed at 1.35 p.m. from the MD.

Messages from him always meant trouble and now she was an hour late in responding.

She dialled his direct line. It was engaged. Good. No use trying to tell him she had started work at 8 a.m., as she had for the past two days. Damn, she shouldn't have had a manicure as well as the cut and blow-dry, but it was the one thing her mother-in-law – she with the perfect nails – always remarked on: 'Hands are so important, Joanna, don't you agree? I cream mine every night, then I encase them in cotton mittens. Look, you really can see the difference between mine and yours.'

When Joanna had reported this tip to Liz, there was a guffaw.

'Cotton mittens? She's heard that old joke about the woman who wore gloves to bed and confided to her friend it was because she understood she had to "actually handle the beastly thing".'

For weeks afterwards, Joanna couldn't help smiling each time she thought of Catherine Langford in bed.

Miss Angus came through the glass divider in the open-plan office. 'That freelance has been on again about the Greek article. That's the fifth call. She insists on talking to you.'

'I'm damned if I'm going to be bullied, Angus. The stuff stinks. Get her after I've spoken to the MD. She won't bother me again in a hurry.' Joanna had the reputation of being polite with writers but no push-over. She rarely lost her temper but this particular freelance was becoming a pest.

'And there was a call from Lady Langford.'

Joanna, minus George, was seeing her mother-in-law that evening, her personal idea of an evening in hell.

'She says please not to be late, this time – she stressed the "this time". You're going to have champagne in the Crush Bar with the trustees, before the performance.'

They looked at each other with raised eyebrows. Miss Angus would never say anything personal. But with little else in her life except her British Blue and her work at Amalgamated House, she worried more about Joanna's tense relationship with her mother-in-law than she did about her pedigree cat.

Joanna sank down on the sofa. 'Oh, I'm bone weary.'

'You shouldn't overdo it, you know. Not at the moment.'

Miss Angus's view, as Joanna was aware, was that she should give the baby priority. They had discussed the difficulties facing women like Joanna who were really the first generation of female high-achievers trying to fit in the demands of a career, friendships and family commitments. They had never been able to agree on the perfect solution.

The phone rang and the MD's slight nasal inflection echoed down the line. Miss Angus, standing at the other side of the desk, could not hear the words clearly but she gathered the tone.

'I've been waiting to see you, Jo,' he barked. 'Where the hell have you been?'

'I'm afraid Tom Hanks was giving me such a good interview I didn't notice the time, sorry.'

Miss Angus nodded approvingly.

'Miss Angus didn't mention any interview to me.'

'She didn't know. In fact, I shouldn't have told you. I'm slipping.'

Another nod from Miss Angus.

'Well, get up here right away,' he commanded.

Joanna crashed the phone down. 'Rightaway, massa, I'm a'coming,' she mimicked. She gave a wry smile as Miss Angus passed her a notepad and pen in preparation for her confrontation.

The MD, or 'Upstairs', as he was known, operated through anxiety and enjoyed the cut and thrust of dealing with what he described as his 'cabs in the taxi rank'. This was not learned at Harvard but refined on Wall Street, where he had started as a jobber. When he switched to publishing and went to work for Amalgamated, he gave himself five years to get the number one spot in the American HQ.

This year it was Britain, the outpost, but he hoped – and the staff fervently hoped along with him – that he would soon make it to the main board back home.

'You've got trouble,' he warned as Joanna came into his rather spartan office, devoid of any personal touches except his much mentioned Harvard degree certificates. 'I've been looking at this month's issue and you're missing the readership profile targets by a mile.'

You charmless, patronising shit, Joanna seethed silently. The baby let her know with a tiny kick that she was irritated by the relentless stomach-churning. Joanna's smile never wavered. In her pleasant South African-tinged accent she said, 'Come on now, last week you thought the balance was about right. What's changed?'

She never let him know how much his words disconcerted her, which was why he tended not to bully her quite as much as the other editors, a few of whom had been known to burst into tears in front of him.

'Nobody's got time to wade through all those words – it's supposed to be a *People*-type magazine, for Christ's sake. I've told you again and again, newspapers are dead. D-E-A-D. The way forward is the way we do it in the States with mags like *Time* and *Newsweek*, and you're not doing that.' He stood up, looking down at her in a fairly contemptuous manner.

Joanna's eyes never left his and she was gratified to note his gaze wavered. The prat.

'If we're up against what you call the best television in the world but what I think is boring, turgid British crap, the magazine has to have pace, something to excite readers. And this issue,' he threw the carefully prepared layouts of *Women's View* across the desk, 'will miss the readership we're aiming for.'

This was the most damaging criticism an editor could hear and Joanna was mentally boiling with rage. Who's he been talking to now? was her first thought.

This man was infamous for provoking his editors into justifying their editorial stance by goading them with ideas picked up at dinner tables. The sad thing was that it occasionally worked. One or two editors who were bullied into rethinking their strategy and redefining their editorial philosophy sometimes, in desperation, came up with a different package.

But this approach did not work well with most of his highly individualistic editors, Joanna among them. By antagonising his staff he built up deliberate barriers, a tactic which he found worked well with men but did not achieve the same results with these damned female Brits. Even with his IQ of 167, he hadn't yet worked out why, but he was confident he would.

Joanna tapped the desk with her newly tipped nails, mentally pushed back the jacket of her Donna Karan suit to reveal two imaginary guns in their holsters and let off her first volley.

'It may interest you to know that our market research on that same magazine gave us the best rating on target readership and seventy per cent said they would buy the magazine. They loved the Sellotape babies story. Over sixty-five per cent told us they found the contents different and would buy the next issue.'

He grunted. 'What's a Sellotape baby, for God's sake?'

'Babies conceived by wives who hope they will stick their marriages together,' said Joanna tartly. It was obvious he did not read the magazine. 'That particular cover line had a ninety per cent notice rating from readers.'

Then she aimed her second gun – straight at his profit-and-loss account, the only thing he truly loved.

'And because we held back on making deals on our advertising rates, the sales team has sold, as of yesterday, ninety-eight full-colour pages and fifteen half-pages for next issue. And the yields are the highest they've been on any woman's monthly magazine. That's because we're right *on* target.'

She allowed a silence to develop then mentally blew on the gun.

The game was over and he gave a rare smile. 'Just checking.' Then he countered with, 'But don't forget, excitement is what we need.'

She left then, her heart pounding. The bastard had not won – this time. And 'excitement'? What could he be getting at? It was a strange expression for him to use.

She was still angry when she walked into her office and saw Stephanie Ross, her deputy, sitting waiting for her. This did not improve her mood.

Stephanie was showing her even, white teeth in the sort of smile Joanna had learned to mistrust. Usually it meant she thought she knew something to Joanna's disadvantage.

'We've finished subbing the Blenheim spread and I'd like you to come and have a look at it.' She noticed Joanna's strained features. 'What's up?'

Before she could check herself, Joanna, who always acted on instinct and regretted it later, said, 'I've just had a session with the MD and he's managed to boost my morale, as usual.' And she clenched and unclenched her fists.

Stephanie put on her most innocent look. 'Oh? Daddy and I had drinks with him last night and he was so nice about you.'

So that was where he got the crap about 'excitement' from. The self-satisfied bitch. Stephanie would never be happy until she had the top job.

The rivalry that had been created was all the more galling for Joanna because Stephanie was her appointment. Until recently, she had been an eager, willing protégée, consulting Joanna on every detail. But lately there had been a notable change of attitude which had put Joanna on her guard. Stephanie had switched sides.

Knowing Stephanie was a dab hand at cover lines, Joanna looked intently at her. 'I'm glad you had a pleasant time with him. Actually, he did ask me who was responsible for the cover lines. I told him they were mostly yours. Well, I thought I was doing you a favour. Unfortunately, he hated the cover lines above anything else. Sorry.'

Stephanie was speechless.

The direct line rang. 'New York on three for you,' called Miss Angus.

More trouble.

Before she could pick up the receiver, the art editor came in clutching a sheaf of new layouts. 'I've had another go on the lines suggested,' he said, 'but I think the first lot were better.'

Joanna held up her palms to him, indicating she had to take the New York call. Hovering outside her office she saw her fashion editor and the chief sub waiting for their turn.

More problems, by the serious look on their faces.

Sitting opposite her was Stephanie, her expression mutinous.

Joanna sighed and picked up the phone. She should probably speak in private, but what the hell. If you could not be yourself, what was the point?

Another glorious day in Paradise.

Bruce Oldfield's press officer, Jeremy, informed Nicola that they had, so far, made only two cloaks with that particular embroidery, for customers who wanted them urgently.

Begging did not come easily to Nicola but she knew she had to find out who these customers were. Jeremy, who had only been working for the designer for two months, was not yet experienced

in the wiles of the fashion press. Although he quite properly refused
to divulge the identity of their clients, she was able to deduce that
one of the cloaks had been ferried out of the country by private jet
and another was for one of their 'regular royal clients'. But not
even Nicola could persuade him to reveal which one.

Two hours of intense phoning round her contacts in the society
magazines elicited the information that the Duchess of Kent had
missed all the Oldfield shows because of a charity trip abroad. But
the *Chronicle* photographer on the royal rota that day had taken a
shot of another VIP client coming out of the show. The Princess
of Wales.

Nicola gulped. The Princess of Wales? Why would she be visiting
Roland Mews in the middle of the night? And without her
detectives?

Another call was to a fashion public relations expert who made
it her business to know who was wearing what and where. She knew
about Diana's visit, of course, and that one of the cloaks had been
despatched to Kensington Palace.

'But I haven't seen her wear it yet in public,' she said. 'Don't
know about privately, of course.'

Nicola fought to sound casual.

'Of course,' she drawled, 'she always looks so good in Bruce's
clothes.'

She had been well trained. Never let civilians realise how much
they had told you.

Nicola's first instinct was to race across the newsroom and tell
Tony. This was a story of great potential and she was damned if
anyone else was going to take the credit for it. But she had to be
careful how to handle it, otherwise she was sure Tony would pass
it off as his at the afternoon news conference. More important, she
must find a way to let Fergus know of her clever detective work.

With her complete disregard for the achievements of other
females, Nicola dismissed the idea that it might be as important to
please Liz. Liz was only acting editor. Out of habit, Nicola decided
to stick with the men. She marched over to the crowded news desk.
'Can we go somewhere private?' she asked Tony. 'I think you'll
be interested.'

He looked up, annoyed by her imperious tone. Too often in the past her stories had fizzled out. 'Anything you found out, you can tell me here.'

'Not here.' And she walked off in the direction of his office.

When Nicola finally told him she had information that the cloak lady might be the Princess of Wales, Tony looked as if he was about to have an orgasm.

It would be the splash of his career if he could stand it up. It took only a second to decide that he definitely would not tell that pushy mare Liz yet. He would leave it as long as he dared. He would hand over the story as a *fait accompli*, which would leave no one under any illusions as to who had masterminded it. Nicola was junior enough to be accorded some credit. A small credit.

After a major tip-off like this, the news desk went to work like a machine. It behaved the same way as a detective agency, throwing several bodies on to the case. For this story Tony pulled all the good hands on board. He risked weakening other stories by such a full commitment to this one, but he reckoned it was worth it.

At some stage Liz would have to be told, he reasoned, but it was still only Wednesday.

'This news list hasn't got any better since yesterday.'

Liz's tone to the five editorial executives round the conference table was uneasy. She had hoped that something more inspiring would have materialised in the last twenty-four hours and her conviction deepened that some of her senior colleagues, many of whom had been Charlie's henchmen for years, were not exactly exerting themselves to cover her in glory.

The stories on the news list were dull and predictable – a rumoured rise in electricity prices; illegal arms deals to a foreign war; an election in France; the hunt for the mole who had been leaking political scandals to the press; a pop star up on a drugs charge; alleged insider dealings on the Stock Exchange by a pillar of the Church of England; a war veteran not getting his pension; and the now common court battle over money between the first and second families of the same man, in this instance a world-famous designer. There was a potentially explosive Washington story, but it would have to be worked on.

Yesterday's brainstorming session where ideas had been batted around had not brought forth obvious fruit. The political staff were still trying to firm up details on the mole inside the government but so far they had nothing concrete to show.

As they were about to file out, Geoff Wilson, the picture editor, who thought he'd do better if Liz was promoted, blurted out, 'I didn't put it on the list but Roddy's brought in what could be quite an interesting picture and Bob thinks it's got legs.' Bob Howard was ex-*Daily Telegraph* with two editorships behind him. A gentleman of the old school of journalism, he was number three in the *Sunday Chronicle* hierarchy. Liz had come to rely on him because he gave advice without fear or favour.

'Well, you're usually right, Bob,' smiled Liz. 'What picture's that?'

'Some mystery woman, taken after midnight outside Tom Reeves's house. Roddy said she was fishing for a key in her handbag and scarpered pretty sharply when he let off his flash. Why should she have a key? There's obviously something going on between her and Reeves, otherwise why would she nearly break her neck running off?'

'Tony, you didn't mention anything about this.'

Tony looked slightly uncomfortable. 'We don't even know who it is,' he said. 'It's a bad picture, a side view, taken late at night, and she's wearing some kind of cloak that hides her hair, her face and everything else really. I was trying to stand it up before bothering you with it.'

Warning bells rang in Liz's mind. If Tony was trying to stop her seeing the picture, it was probably for a good reason – to make trouble for her.

'It's the best bloody thing I've heard this week. Where is it?'

Geoff went to get the print. While he was gone, an embarrassed silence filled the room.

'I wanted to be sure of my facts,' Tony repeated quickly. 'I don't want this newspaper to be conned. We'd be out of our tiny minds if we didn't check. Don't you agree, Liz?'

That familiar barb again. How much did he know? The thought that he might have discovered her secret was alarming. If Fergus Canefield had knowledge of this, it could ruin her career. It was a standard joke that editors were halfway mad but the truth was, no proprietor would ever take the chance if a question mark even hovered above an editor's mental stability. An editorship endowed the recipient with total authority. Legal niceties and proprietor's interests took second place to the tyranny of urgent deadlines. He or she could override any advice. Complaints came afterwards. Newspapers worked just like the army. If the editor cried 'attack', the troops had to follow. A rumour that a potential editor had suffered a mental breakdown would rule out any chance to run a paper. A mistake could cost the company millions in a libel suit.

When Geoff handed the picture over, Liz felt a pang of recognition. With mounting fear she scrutinised the print. The shape and the blur of the cloak looked familiar. Was it the one she had borrowed from Oldfield, the one she had lent Katya? The woman was of similar height but it was hard to tell. The face was obscured by the deep hood.

'The only thing we do know,' said Geoff, 'is that the thing she's wearing is from Bruce Oldfield.'

Liz felt her stomach slowly reacting. 'Ah huh.'

'Tom Reeves has rented the house at the end of the mews,' Tony went on. 'We don't know who lives next door, but our woman was going into one of those two houses.'

Liz silently prayed that Katya, if it was her, had a bloody good reason to be there. Tom Reeves her mystery lover? Ridiculous.

'Anything the matter, boss?' asked Geoff.

'I thought he was the only Hollywood star who kept his hands to himself.' Her mind was racing. Katya had told them her lover was married but it couldn't be Reeves, it couldn't possibly. All eyes in the room were staring at her, waiting for her reaction.

'Got any ideas?' Geoff asked at last.

Liz looked up to see his shrewd eyes watching her. 'No.' She thought, I'm going to protect her for a day at least, until I can find out what's going on. Anyway, what would Katya have in common with Tom Reeves? He would only come up to her knees. She could not help smiling to herself.

'I'm afraid we can't mess around with this,' said Geoff, misreading her expression. 'Roddy's already rung twice. We're going to have to make him an offer soon.'

'Just stall him for the moment,' said Liz. 'Until we find out what it's worth.'

'We're on to something though,' said Tony. 'Nicola has found out only two cloaks were made.'

'What do you mean, only two? Bruce'll have dozens for all his franchises, apart from the ones for his boutique in Beauchamp Place.'

'Well, not like this one apparently. Not yet. Something to do with samples and them being from his latest collection. See those markings there?' He pointed out the fleur-de-lys on the cloak lining. 'Nicola's been told this type hasn't gone into production yet.'

At least Oldfield had made more than one version of the cloak. Thank God for that. Then it might not be Katya after all, thought Liz. Now she understood why Tony and Nicola had been closeted together.

'But listen to this,' butted in Geoff. 'One was picked up by jet to go to some millionaire's wife in America and the other's gone to – you'll never guess this one, boss, never in a million years.'

Her heart spent a nanosecond wondering whether it would work again. 'Stop messing about, cough it out,' she said quietly.

Geoff paused for dramatic effect. 'Tony's found out it's already gone round to Kensington Palace. To Diana.'

Liz could not believe it, much as she wanted to. Diana in a midnight rendezvous with a famous star? Nothing in Liz's career so far had been that easy. But she went through the motions. 'I'd like to believe this one. Ever since the scandals about Hewitt, Hoare and Gilbey, she's been worried about being reported back to the Big House. So maybe she went out to the man instead of him coming to see her at Kensington Palace. But where were her detectives? Was she even in London?' She turned to Tony, eyes blazing. 'Look, Tony, where royal stories are concerned, I want to hear about them as soon as you do. You know I have some extremely good contacts and I could save the paper a lot of time and money.'

She turned to the news editor. 'Let's get cracking. Make all the usual calls, to the equerry, the detective, that former lady-in-waiting who's been so helpful in the past. Why not send Gregg? He looks pretty, and he's the only one on the staff who can scout round those bars that the Buck House footmen use. See what he can ferret out. We'll only bring out the money when we have to. The budget could do with a rest.' She turned to Tony. 'That reminds me. We can't send anyone to Washington to cover the love-child story. I've worked out that the US per diem costs will break the budget. We'll have to use someone over there.'

'But that means we'll be at a total disadvantage. Everyone else has sent,' Tony objected.

'Well, you didn't spend hours yesterday with the bean counters. They say that we have to produce this paper to the budget. Our trouble is they've allowed no leeway for another Gulf War, another royal wedding. We couldn't afford them.' She began gathering up her papers. 'And when you're looking for the cloak owner, remember to check Princess Diana's movements in the Court Circular. It could be as simple as that.'

The *Chronicle*'s royal rat pack went into action.

Chapter Eleven

The red fluorescent light on the answering machine showed there were five messages waiting but Katya had no interest in playing them back. She knew Davina would not be one of her callers.

As she began to remove her studio make-up, she allowed herself to think about the encounter with Davina in No. 10. How was it that Davina could look and be so detached and calm? And, dear God, so cold? She seemed unaffected by the turmoil that was dominating Katya's life.

Could Davina have switched off that completely? Could she, Katya, have been mistaken about her involvement? She had had enough relationships with men to know that the feelings she had for this woman were quite different. They were overwhelming and, until today, she was sure they were reciprocated, however secretive they had to be.

Katya wiped off the layers of Dior Visiora, the special non-shiny matt foundation Dior made solely for TV and film work. Her face started to emerge, naked, in the bathroom mirror and she had a sudden flash of awareness. Of course! In Downing Street, Davina would have been confronted by a distant and professional TV interviewer, who would have appeared just as cool and detached, not as the Katya who responded so instantly to her intimate kisses and caresses.

But still Katya could not reconcile herself to that uneasy feeling that Davina had completely shut her out and was closing down all communication, just when she needed reassurance.

No matter how pressured, how wary of security, they had always found a way, until now, to keep in touch. They had even evolved a

187

simple phone code in which they pretended to be stockbrokers giving information about share dealings. Prices were used to arrange times and movements of the stocks to indicate whether it was going to be possible to meet. If the shares were up, the meeting was on. In this way messages could be left with Davina's housekeeper, driver, secretary and PA as well as Katya's office and on her answering machine. It also helped when communicating in public.

(Unluckily for them, the boys at Cheltenham GCHQ had instantly identified the two women, using their voice-detector equipment, and had then, almost as quickly, deciphered the simple code they used.

From then on, the operators had had hours of innocent, but uneasy, pleasure listening to the purrings of the two women, enjoying the frisson of knowing what a furore it would cause if Joe Public ever found out. But, they would argue to themselves, they were doing it all in the name of security. They knew lots of secrets. It made up for the hours of endless, turgid tapes they had to listen to and for the low pay.)

These days, Katya lived in a constant state of trepidation, as though she was about to make a parachute jump. And when the phone shrilled, her stomach went into what was now a familiar somersault routine.

As she leaned over the bath ready to grab the handset, the machine clicked into action and she heard Liz leaving yet another message saying she needed to talk to her urgently.

Katya could have cut in, but for the first time in their friendship she pretended she was not at home.

More and more, Joanna found herself grateful that another day had passed safely for the baby, and she found herself praying, 'If I can just get through today, I'll be all right.'

This pregnancy was like all the others. She was feeling terrible. And nervous.

She would have given a hundred pounds not to have to go to Covent Garden that night to attend one of her mother-in-law's charity functions. If I had the sort of mother-in-law I could talk to, she would have told me to stay at home for the sake of the baby, Joanna thought. But since she's convinced I spend all day having fun at the magazine, she sees no reason why I shouldn't be at her charity shindig.

George so wanted them to be friends that Joanna was always making an effort. If only her mother-in-law did.

As usual the page proofs for the next issue of the magazine were late. And as usual Joanna found herself racing to the taxi still unmade-up and fastening the last buttons on her little black Jean Muir dress, bought for a third of the original price at the designer's twice-yearly sale for fortunate insiders.

By the time she reached the Opera House, it was already crowded with hundreds of elegant women who looked as if they had done nothing else that day but prepare their appearance for the event.

She would be in bad odour with her mother-in-law who had stressed repeatedly how important it was to arrive well before the royal guest – the Duchess of Kent this evening.

Catherine Langford would not have been at all interested in the reason Joanna was late. Her cover lines had had to be changed again, just eight hours before going to the printers. Her MD did not understand some of the witty lines on the front of the magazine.

In an effort to win him round, she had tried to raise a smile by recounting the famous story about one of the glossy magazines a few months ago. It had featured a supermodel wearing a large straw hat with upturned brim bearing the cover line 'Spend This Summer Underneath A Black Sailor'. The entire run had had to be pulped. Instead of laughing, the MD had groaned, thinking of the expense of it all.

She was proud of the line she herself had written along the spine of that week's magazine: 'Stories to make your spine tingle'. But he didn't get that either. He did not understand most British wit, he took everything literally.

Nor would Joanna's mother-in-law have cared that a double-page advertisement had been cancelled at the last minute and Joanna had had to find something to take its place that would balance with the rest of the magazine's contents. Or that there was a complication in the contract she was organising for the cover story in the following issue.

No, Catherine Langford was not a compassionate woman.

Across the squash of the foyer of the Royal Opera House Joanna caught Catherine's eye. Her mother-in-law was standing at the foot of the staircase rather crossly waving the ticket counterfoils in the air. Joanna started weaving her way through the crush of people when she felt an insistent tap on her shoulder.

'Hi, Jo, how are you?' It was Mark Forster, the respected political editor of the *Sunday Times*. They kissed cheeks warmly. 'Haven't seen you for ages.'

'No, not since that night at Liz's place. Wasn't it fun? And what great gossip.'

'How are Liz and the beautiful Katya? Actually, I saw Katya lunching at Locketts last week. She was having a heavy-duty conversation with that new bright spark from the Home Office, Davina Thomas.'

Joanna took this on board, thinking it was part of Katya's plan to get off the early morning television treadmill and into the broader-based political arena.

From the corner of her eye, Joanna saw the furious fluttering of the tickets at the top of the stairs. 'Sorry, Mark, my mother-in-law's freaking out, have to dash. Let's meet for lunch, give me a ring.'

Joanna just made it to the top of the stairs before a fanfare from the red-liveried trumpeters announced the arrival of the royal party and the ushers repeated their insistent call: 'My lords, ladies and gentlemen, would the last guests kindly please take their seats now.'

Catherine was barely polite. 'Do hurry up. My other guests have been waiting inside for ten minutes.'

Joanna had learned to cope with her mother-in-law's imperious manner by never complaining and never explaining.

Aida was one of Joanna's favourite operas, but she found it difficult to concentrate on the music. She and George would never have been able to afford the £200 tickets, including the meagre buffet, but Catherine had kindly paid for her seat. It was Catherine's pet charity, the proceeds going to the Royal Society for the Prevention of Cruelty to Animals, and it was the one time in the year when she shelled out, even though by most people's standards she was a wealthy woman.

George once explained that 'Mummy's really worried about

money now because she is having to live off the interest'. Joanna
was baffled by this until he revealed that 'Mummy was used to
living off the interest on the interest'.

Money and security, or the lack of them, were the only real causes
of friction between her and George and it was just as well he did
not know about her secret bank account, started specifically to fund
a Norland-trained nanny.

She eased herself into a more comfortable position and caught
someone looking at her. To her surprise, it was her deputy, Stephanie, sitting across the aisle.

Why hadn't she mentioned she would be here? thought Joanna.
Stephanie knew Joanna was coming to the opera. Perhaps she had
been given a ticket at the last minute, but why hadn't she been
straightforward about it?

When they met in the interval, Stephanie was standing on the
curved staircase overlooking the Crush Bar, glass of champagne in
hand, talking to a tall, intense man whom Joanna recognised as
chairman of a large mail-order-catalogue company, one of the magazine's major advertisers. She smiled as they exchanged pleasantries.
When he went to get another drink, she turned to her deputy.

'This is a surprise, Stephanie. What are you doing here?'

Stephanie wore her irritating half-smile.

'I could have given you a lift. Why didn't you tell me you were
coming?'

'Oh, I thought you'd be too busy,' Stephanie paused, 'and tired,
what with the baby and everything. I didn't want to bother you.'

'Pregnancy doesn't mean that you fall apart after six o'clock,'
replied Joanna tartly, though thinking it often meant just that as far
as she was concerned.

'Of course not,' Stephanie said in a soothing 'let's calm down'
tone. 'But I'm glad I've seen you, Joanna,' she continued. 'After
you left the office, a call came through from the chairman's office
in New York but, don't worry, I've dealt with it. I'll fill you in
tomorrow.'

'Tell me now, it may not be able to wait that long,' said Joanna
through clenched teeth.

She was seething. She could just imagine the way her deputy had answered the phone to the Suits from New York – 'Oh, she's been gone some time, off to the opera, but I'm sure I'll be able to help you.'

'Right, what did New York want?'

'Really, Joanna, can't it keep till morning? I am a guest of one of our best advertisers, after all.'

'Tell me now.'

Stephanie let out a heavy sigh, another of her less endearing characteristics. 'The chairman just wanted a copy of the contract changes faxed over.'

'And the chairman rang about that himself?'

Stephanie looked guilty. 'Er, no. I didn't mean to give you that impression. It was his PA.'

That was the kind of twist she put on events to impress her audience. The MD would be encouraging her to be more upfront about what was really happening in the office. It was his usual trick of divide and rule. But right now Stephanie had an audience of only one.

'Look, Stephanie,' said Joanna, giving her an unblinking stare, 'I'd appreciate it if you wouldn't make things more complex than they already are. I need to be able to rely on you, but sometimes you make that really hard.' Stephanie's eyes were slightly downcast but she did not interrupt. 'You know, I think you may have the potential to be a good editor one day.' Joanna softened her tone. 'If you'll take my advice, you won't regard every woman in your way as your enemy. That'd be a big mistake and one you might come to regret.' Joanna hoped Stephanie would respond but the younger woman stayed silent. 'There are so many people who are out to get us. Can't you see the advantage of trusting women, particularly someone older who can be your mentor, who wants to see that you succeed?' she urged. 'Enough women's magazines are edited by men. I want you to get on, I really do.'

Stephanie was listening intently but it was impossible to read her expression. Joanna decided to be even franker. 'If women don't stick together, what hope is there? We might just as well stay at home and sew quilts. When women like us are out in the market-place, there's no one who'll look after us except ourselves. My philosophy is, until I'm bitten, I'll trust.'

Although she was not sure how Stephanie would respond to this, Joanna felt it was time to clear the air. 'I think you'll agree that so far I've done nothing but look after you and encourage you, Stephanie. Please, don't let your head be turned by someone who's using you for his own ends.' By the younger woman's intake of breath, she felt she might have made some impression at last. 'Yes, the MD likes to play his little games with us. It makes him feel powerful and confident. But I can help you more. If you'll listen to me, you'll go a lot further, Stephanie. I want to help you. Please remember that.'

'I'll think about it,' Stephanie responded, smiling and looking directly into Joanna's eyes.

Big mistake.

Joanna had the instinctive feeling that Stephanie was going to ignore everything she had just said.

Open war had been declared.

Aida's plight of being entombed with her lover seemed tame after that.

The digital clock glowed 4.10 a.m. in the darkness. Liz wondered why she felt panicky. It was the same feeling she had had before her breakdown.

'Oh God, not again.'

The doctor had told her it was highly unlikely she would suffer in the same way again; her breakdown had been caused by a unique set of circumstances. Then she remembered the photograph and realised the panic was not about the job. She was enjoying that challenge. No, it was the photograph that was disturbing her. She had been trying to deny all night her gut feeling that the woman in the cloak was Katya.

Tony's muck-raking mind had suggested the woman was there for, as he called it, 'bonking purposes'. How irritating that this time the bastard could be right. And if the woman was Katya, how should she handle it as acting editor of the newspaper? What do I do? Ask Katya if she knows him? Do I involve Katya at all?

Even if it was a man no one had ever heard of, it would still be news. Newspapers speculated endlessly about Katya's love life. She only had to turn up at a premiere on the arm of a man for rumours to start. What the media did not pick up was that Katya usually left halfway through any function to get home to bed. On her own.

If it was Katya, she was obviously in the mews to see her bloody lover. Liz could not believe it was Tom Reeves but she knew it would not take long for Tony to find out who lived in the house next door. Supposing that man was also famous?

Liz groaned. That would complicate everything. Tony would feel their newspaper had hit the jackpot. So, under normal circumstances, would she. And Tony did not even know the awful extra complication, that there was bound to be a scandal because Katya had already admitted to them there was a wife around. The panic feeling started again. What was she going to do?

Liz analysed her choices. If her newspaper did not identify Katya, someone else might. She could not control Roddy Hamlyn, the paparazzo; he was not on the *Chronicle* payroll and would sell his picture to a rival if her paper would not use it. He was becoming aggressive with the picture desk, constantly asking why they had not yet made him an offer. He was getting to be a real pest.

She could not divert Tony from the story. For a start it would be a highly unusual thing for an editor to do and if he had an inkling it involved a friend of hers, he could accuse her, justifiably, of behaving unprofessionally. Anyway, her analysis was irrelevant and she knew it. Like an inexorable machine, the news desk was already quietly and methodically going about its business, trying to stand up the story. They would be searching through voters' rolls, estate agents' lettings and the Land Registry, finding out who owned the house next door to Tom Reeves's.

By anyone's standards, the story was a circulation-builder. It would not change the world but it would attract the dilettante Sunday audience who loved tittle-tattle. Although the *Chronicle* would dress up the story in a serious way with many references to Katya's interviews with heavyweight politicians and world leaders, it was still, in the jargon of the business, the bonk of the week. And Liz knew nothing sold newspapers better than sex on Sundays.

But how could she do this to Katya? She had tried to phone her several times, without success. The clock now showed 5 a.m. Her friend would be at the studio already; Liz couldn't ring her just before a programme.

Although there had been times in her career when she had to make a decision about embarrassing someone she knew, there had always been a news editor or editor above her who could be blamed. Until now, she had never been the ultimate authority. And it had never before involved anyone nearly so close. This was why she had the feeling of panic, the sensation that she had just been jogging – sweaty palms, quick heartbeat and fast breathing. She could not fudge the issue nor could she blame anyone else if the *Chronicle* ran it. The buck stopped with her.

She knew it was a handicap in journalism to be this vulnerable. After countless conversations with Charlie and male colleagues on the *Chronicle* and other nationals, Liz was certain they did not suffer from any such pangs of conscience. Or if they did, they hid it behind a wall of Fleet Street cynicism.

She, Joanna and Katya had often noted, and most men admitted, that men simply did not have the same kind of close friendships women enjoyed. When they had to rat on someone they knew it would seldom occur to them to allow loyalty to stand in the way of their ascent up the greasy pole. Liz had become inured to the fact that one moment editors would be having friendly tête-à-têtes, private lunches and suppers with cabinet ministers and then, a few days later, would write a viciously critical leader about them or publish a damaging article.

'That's the game, old boy,' Charlie would say when they rang up to complain.

Not for the first time, Liz wished she had the emotions, attitudes and outlook of a man. Then came a horrifying thought. Maybe Tony was right. Maybe a woman could never be a successful editor.

Chapter Twelve

It was midway through Katya's Thursday stint on the Morning TV sofa. During the commercial break the make-up girl came on to the studio floor and deftly brushed in camouflage to conceal the nervous blotches on Katya's neck. At the same time the autocue operator stepped up the size of the type because Katya had been complaining she had trouble seeing the letters clearly.

While Katya's face was dusted with powder to dim the gleam on her nose and cheeks, she listened intently to the news from the next studio. Hugo Thomas's accident had been relegated to a tiny paragraph in the broadsheets where his condition was reported as 'stable'. That could mean anything. He rated no mention on the TV news.

Katya shook her buzzing head fiercely, interrupting the make-up girl's work.

Upstairs in the gallery the director muttered to his assistant, 'Hangover, do you think?' Then he swivelled in his chair and gave a wicked grin. 'Nah, on second thoughts not her. Probably that time of the month.' He took a swill of coffee. 'Let's not upset her. She could kill one of us and get off the murder charge by weeping in court and explaining it was all because of her periods.'

The rest of the crew in the gallery, even the feminist vision mixer, shared the joke.

Joanna was lying in bed hoping the nauseous feeling would go away. Like a child she could not project her mind into the past or the future and now could not remember ever waking up and not feeling sick.

197

In desperation her fingers felt across the bedside table, searching for the dry cracker kept there for emergencies, nibbling it while still supine. It tasted awful and she knew with a terrible certainty that whatever she did she would have to get up and be sick. But she would try anything to calm the queasiness which flooded her body each morning and which lasted for much of the day.

'Radiant pregnancy, huh,' she muttered to herself.

Crumbs in the bed, bile in the mouth and hours spent retching over the loo had been her experience of pregnancy so far but at least, apart from her stomach, she had never been thinner and her breasts were beginning to develop into a C cup. Bits from the biscuit dropped on to her newly formed cleavage. 'It won't be my stomach that'll be the giveaway, it'll be these,' she reflected, looking down on them and wondering how long she could keep looking her normal self.

George loved her bump. It was hardly visible except to a keen student of her anatomy, which her husband was, and before he left he would stroke it gently every day. 'Good morning, baby. How are you? Don't you go giving your mother a hard time, do you hear?'

Joanna's managing director, however, was not so enamoured of babies, at least other people's. He did not have a great reputation for being sympathetic to the concept of maternity leave. He had got over the shock of her pregnancy but not the thought of the six months' paid time off that accompanied it. But Joanna was already determined to be back in harness long before that.

That same determination drove her out of bed to put on a specially bought Belville Sassoon Empire-line dress and jacket for a board meeting of the magazine division. This was not the holding board of Amalgamated Magazines, which had no women members, but Joanna was still pleased to be on it and took her duties seriously.

She was gathering up her papers when the phone rang. It was Liz from the editor's Daimler. 'Jo, that cloak I borrowed from Bruce Oldfield for Sunday, the one I lent to our joint best friend, what exactly did it look like? You know how hopeless I am at this fashion stuff.'

Although Joanna was in a hurry and feeling grisly, she recognised Liz's urgent tone. This was no small talk. 'Well, it was heavy, good-quality stuff, black of course and, oh yes, it had a really unusual lining. Probably from France, with some wonderfully lush frogging and toggles. Looked a bit like the curtain tie-backs my mother-in-law would have.'

Oh God, Liz thought. The lining, the toggles. It all added up.

'Why do you ask?' continued Joanna. 'Are you thinking of buying it? If you are, that's good. I can share it. You'll never get the wear out of it and it'd be great to hide the bump.'

'No, it's not for me. I just need to know for the paper.'

Okay, she doesn't want to tell me now, thought Joanna, remembering how wary Liz, along with many others, had become of talking on cellular phones.

Still hoping her intuition was wrong, Liz asked, 'What was that you said about the lining?'

'It looked very rich,' answered Joanna. 'Some kind of embossed pattern, flowery, very French, the kind you see everywhere on plates and wallpapers. I can't remember the name of it. Oh, this pregnancy's given me brain rot . . . Fleur-de-lys, that's it. Hey, she hasn't lost it, has she? It'd just be like our friend, you know telly people, they're all waited on hand and foot.'

There was a slight hesitation.

'No-o-o, but there is a problem. Some woman's been spotted wearing a cloak just like that, late Sunday night right outside Tom Reeves's house, holding a front door key.'

Joanna dissected this for a moment. 'Tom Reeves? And our friend?' Her tone was incredulous. 'Do you think that's who she's been seeing?'

'It doesn't matter what I think. But there's a pap picture sitting on the news editor's desk showing just that.'

'But it couldn't be her, we were all together at BAFTA.'

'Not after midnight, we weren't,' Liz pointed out.

Silence.

'But hang on. Tom Reeves has only been in the country two weeks making this film. And our friend hasn't ever been to Hollywood, so how have they been screwing these last few months? By mail?' As always, Joanna was the logical one, but Liz still felt anxious.

'Okay, not Tom Reeves. I've a real feeling this is her although no one at the office has a clue who it is. Yet. And if it is her, what other reason could she have for being there?'

'I've absolutely no idea,' replied Joanna. 'There may be quite a simple explanation. Give me some time and I'll bend my mighty mind to it.'

'Great, because people in the office are trying to add two and two to make five. Anyway, I don't think we should carry on discussing our friend right now.'

'All right,' said Joanna. 'So how soon can we meet?'

'I'm off to Oxford tonight, you know, that Union thing.'

'If you get back early enough, I'll wait up.'

'You mean come back to London after the debate? That's an idea.' Liz gave a sideways look at Alan, her driver, who adopted the set face that telegraphed, *Don't you dare change your plans again*. 'I think it'll be too late for you, Jo.' Alan's face relaxed.

'Can you be free for lunch tomorrow?' asked Joanna.

'I could be. I'm sure I can postpone Lord Piccott. He's one of the few people who'll understand an errand for a friend.'

'I'll ask Miss Angus to phone the Ivy. Meet you there at one.' Joanna replaced the receiver. Talking to Liz had almost made her stop feeling sick for a moment.

The second assistant press officer at Buckingham Palace did his best to keep reasonable relationships with the nationals, so he was pleased he could 'give guidance', for once, and not fob them off with 'We are not commenting at all on this story. It is a private matter'.

As the Princess of Wales had already returned from Edinburgh, where she had been seeing friends, he could see no harm in telling the *Chronicle*'s royal reporter that Diana had indeed been on a private visit there and did not get back to Kensington Palace until Monday morning.

He was not told the context of the story but he was an old hand at managing the press, so he told the reporter the name of the Princess's host, who would confirm her visit.

'So the POW can't be the woman in Roland Mews,' Liz told her news conference.

It was common to give the royals nicknames. 'POW' was the

Princess of Wales; and her father-in-law, the Duke of Edinburgh, was 'Zorba' because of his Greek origins.

'We're not getting anywhere with this story,' Liz summed up. 'All we have is a bad print of a woman we can't see, let alone recognise. We'll have to come up with something stronger than that.'

In the newsroom a few minutes later, Tony, ever suspicious, told Belinda, 'I'm not falling for the usual palace cover-up. It's all too quick and easy. Phone our bloke in Edinburgh and get him to sniff around and see what he comes up with. You talk to the royal cops. They'll know where she's been.'

When half an hour later it was confirmed that the POW had not been in London, Tony began to lose interest, even though he had invested so much time and effort in the story.

A reporter phoned Tom Reeves's London PR yet again and this time managed to get an answer to his query. After consulting his client, the PR reported that Mr Reeves had not been expecting a guest in the early hours of Monday but that if she had come in, she would have found him in bed with his wife. This was confirmed by the head waiter of the Mansion House in Berkeley Square, the secluded and favourite eating place of visiting celebrities. The head waiter was one of the regular informants paid by the *Chronicle*'s gossip columnist. The reporter came into Tony's office and told him that Reeves and his wife had enjoyed a quiet and rather boozy dinner until the early hours when they were poured into their limo.

Tony picked up the print again. 'Another no-no. Unless something falls into our laps, let's not waste any more time on this.' He threw the print into the bin.

As Liz left her office for Oxford, where she was to oppose the motion in the Oxford Union debate that 'This house believes modern woman has lost her femininity', she was feeling happier, knowing that Katya had escaped the *Chronicle*'s net.

On the M40, she took a call from her political editor. There were some interesting developments in the mole story, he told her, fixing up a meeting for the next day. In quick succession she took calls from other of the newspaper's specialists, foreign, sport and health. All male. Some of the calls were useful, some plain boastful.

As always, Liz was amused by what good public relations these men gave themselves. She never had women reporters ringing her up to brag about how their stories were going or about what a great reaction there had been to them. Maybe that was one of the reasons why women did not do so well in this game as men, she thought wryly. Where did men learn their self-confidence? In the womb? Maybe it was all to do with gender. Did it take a great deal of confidence for a man to get his prick up?

Nicola was busy. Another date with her boss, Fergus Canefield, meant a worrying round of phone calls to obliging PRs in the search for a magical Chanel, Armani, Ralph Lauren or Lindka Cierach number.

The smooth flow of arranging for the delivering and collecting of the glamorous outfits for the evening was interrupted by the features desk secretary. 'Nicola, call for you on line six, Bruce Oldfield's office. They're hanging on.'

Nicola's brow furrowed. Had she asked them if she could borrow clothes? And if so, what story had she pretended she was doing? 'Hell-o, Jeremy.' Nicola put on the special husky tone she used for men, even gay ones. 'What have you got for me?' She was playing for time, hoping he would give a hint.

'That cloak you were on about.'

Ah, it was work, for once. 'Yes?'

'I told you we'd only made two so far, but I forgot there was another one floating around which we used for the shows, which presumably you know about . . .'

Nicola crouched over the receiver. The catwalk samples usually never left the premises; they normally stayed on the rails in the order they appeared in the fashion show.

'Yes?'

'I take it you were referring to the one Bruce lent personally to a friend by the name of Miss Elizabeth Waterhouse.'

Nicola betrayed no hint of her astonishment. Mindful of the ears all round her open-plan office, she said, 'Of course, silly of me to forget.'

Fergus would have liked to have brought such a huge, satisfied

smile to Nicola's lips. She contemplated the implications of this truly
scrumptious fact. When should she share this? And with whom?

For the second time Nicola, mindful of her relatively minor position on the paper, tried to work out how best to use this information.
Getting a major clue on a news story was such a rarity for her that
her mind skittered around like a butterfly on a bed of agapanthus.
She could tell Fergus, but that might be dangerous and could have
repercussions that she could not control. She could tell Liz, who
would then owe her one. But who knew if Liz would last? She
could tell Tony. After all, when the smoke cleared over the next
few weeks, he would still be there. Much as he resented it, he was
not in the direct line of fire.

From Tony's point of view, the name Nicola whispered to him
was even better than that of the Princess.

All right, Liz was single, free to do what she wanted. But the star
wasn't. And Liz was in the forefront of those females who kept
banging on about women and how they should be supportive of one
another – the sisterhood. This hardly showed support for Mrs Star.

Even more damning, Liz had obviously been trying to keep a
good story out of the newspaper. No wonder she looked so unsettled
when she first saw the photograph. This was something both Fergus
and Charlie would be really interested in. Of course proprietors and
editors liked to keep things out of the papers from time to time but
he did not think it right, this time.

'It's only Thursday, keep this to yourself.' Tony gave Nicola a
wink. 'I don't want it getting out to anybody.'

When Nicola had left, Tony told his secretary he was not to be
disturbed under any circumstances. Then he shook his waste paper
bin upside down and scrabbled around the cigarette stubs and torn
betting slips till he found the mews house print. This could be
dynamite. And blow up Liz Waterhouse.

Rummaging through his bin had given Tony an idea. 'Get
Debbie,' he bellowed.

He ordered her back round to Roland Mews. 'I want you to
go through the dustbins at Number Sixteen, Tom Reeves' next-
door neighbours.'

She pulled a face.

'Oh, for Christ's sake, it'll all be in a black plastic bag. Just bung it in your boot and bring it back here. There's bound to be something in there that'll give us a clue.'

Debbie went out and bought two pairs of heavy-duty Marigolds. She was not going to do this on her own.

Right in front of Liz's car were three young undergraduates on bicycles. The girl was laughing at her two attractive companions. The basket in front of her bike was stuffed with books, flowers and a tube of spaghetti. Her taut, size eight, denim-covered buttocks filled Liz with dismay.

Depression, no bigger than a frond, slid into her mind. It was definitely time to take the suit jackets off the exercise bike. She could watch Breakfast News and pedal off the pounds. Educate her mind and her rear simultaneously. Liz had already knocked five minutes off her rather cursory morning fitness routine by following Katya's example and doing her vaginal exercises during the dull bits at morning conference. If only those men sitting around her knew what was going on.

The three friends had often discussed what would have happened to them if they had spent three years up here in Oxford training their minds. On balance, they decided they might not have striven so hard but secretly Liz always felt people thought she was inadequate because she did not have a university degree. Maybe when she was an old lady she would come back here as a very mature student.

She smiled to herself, remembering Joanna's meeting with Prince Charles when he was guest of honour at the British Society of Magazine Editors' annual awards.

'I'm just off to Cambridge, to collect my MA. I've not had time to do it before now,' the Prince remarked to Joanna, who thought his photographs did not do him justice; she rated him highly fanciable, especially his clear blue eyes.

Joanna replied brightly. 'If I had an MA from Cambridge, I would have collected it the same afternoon.'

'But it's not too late,' the Prince came back at her. 'You could always register as one of those *mature* students.'

At the Randolph Hotel Liz sank into a foam-filled bath. What makes me so discontented? she wondered. I am about to go to one of the most prestigious places in Britain, wearing an outfit which would have cost anyone else thousands of pounds but which I borrowed from the designer for free. Every strand of my hair, the creation of an expensive Mayfair stylist, has been protected from the weather by a luxury car and matching driver. Looking at me, most women would wonder what the hell I had to whinge about. Why am I dissatisfied? Because I want to have it all. Career, fame, love, babies, money – but in what order? And what do I have to sacrifice?

She sighed. There were no easy answers and she decided she ought to run through the main points she wanted to make in the debate. It was going to be quite a tussle to convince the audience that 'modern woman had not lost her femininity'. Most of the students strolling around the streets, by the looks of them, were genderless. As a career woman of the nineties, she did not think she had become any less feminine. Didn't she shave her armpits, wear a Wonderbra from time to time and use her time on the loo to apply make-up? What more did they want?

Liz sank deeper into the hot water. The frond of dejection had become as big as a palm tree. Why did I agree to do this? It's not going to help my career so why do I constantly set up tests for myself?

She had been flattered by the invitation three months before from the President of the Union, even though she knew it would be an ordeal. Standing up in front of an audience, especially a young, bright one, was always traumatic, but she could not resist the challenge.

Liz had a sudden resolve. As she felt so inadequate on so many levels, in front of this Oxford audience she was determined to look what she was. In charge, well paid and confident in her role. It did not matter a toss but she wanted to win.

As usual she had packed two changes of clothes. Normally, she would wait to see what kind of mood she was in before deciding which one to wear, in this case either the red Catherine Walker, just bought after admiring a similar design in *Women's Wear Daily*, or the more sober black Tomasz Starwecski with its cross-over lapels. Liz had never worn red before but it was a formal dinner and perhaps this was the night to stand out amidst the black penguins of the student officers of the Union. Besides, red suited her feisty mood.

Away from the intense pressure of the office it was a pleasure to have uncomplicated admiration from a group of flirty under-graduates clustered round her at the end of supper.

Before they were called in to the chamber, she became aware of a tall, rangy man in his middle thirties lounging against a doorway, watching her. He had been introduced to her earlier as David Linden, a lecturer in modern history at Keble. Not conventionally good-looking, he had caught her attention because he looked so typically donnish. Brown hair flopped over his forehead, he wore a dinner jacket which he must have inherited from his grandfather, and he had an unworldly air, such a contrast to the kind of men who usually crossed her path.

As she was rising from the dinner table, he walked up to her and, leaning towards her, gave her a hard stare. 'Don't go too far,' he said slowly. 'I'd like to debate with you later.'

She had no time to reply as she was ushered into the chamber.

Liz's seconder in the debate was an eminent, young-looking fifty-seven-year-old professor of modern history, recently remarried and keen to show off his New Man credentials. What the professor conveniently overlooked was that wife number one had lost a great deal of her femininity struggling to bring up a family on an academic pittance, before television and wife number two found him.

The author and the industrialist debating against them had so many academic achievements after their names that the letters read like a Chinese alphabet.

The Union debate was good humoured, noisy and well argued. Liz was exultant when they trounced the opposition. Cheeks flushed, on an adrenaline high, she became aware of a pair of broad shoulders efficiently edging her away from the circle round her.

The walk from the Union through the muted streets of Oxford past high-walled gardens and silent college quadrangles took on a magic of its own. Liz and David walked side by side and she shifted her shoulder bag, subconsciously removing an obstacle. Consciously, he thought it was a good sign.

She found his candour refreshing even when he breezily confessed that weeks went by without him ever looking at a popular newspaper. He did not ask one question about her work and did not appear to think it was unusual for a young woman to be in charge of a national. As he expressed it, in his world, gender did not matter; brains did.

He was, however, extremely curious about her private life and she had to think hard about her responses. It had been a long time since anyone had talked about what she was feeling rather than what she was doing.

He was erudite and well read and he quoted poetry as effortlessly as she could remember headlines. It had been months since Liz had read anything that was not strictly necessary for her job and he sympathised with her lack of free time. He admitted that it was a danger in his world, too, that he mixed with only a small, like-minded academic circle.

They talked about personal matters with an ease that surprised them both. She discovered that he had been living alone since a long-lasting affair which had ended the year before. But she had the impression that since then he had not exactly been celibate. Liz was intrigued at his subtle probing into the state of her love life but was too wise to be candid. She did, however, let him understand that she had no serious involvement.

It was seamless the way he managed to persuade her to have 'another glass of wine' in her hotel, even though it was after midnight. To her great surprise, for Liz never made love to strangers, she found herself in bed with him only two hours later.

He was clean and fresh, gloriously perfect everywhere. She found she loved running her tongue all over him, the inside of his ears, his eyelids, his neck, on the bone of his shoulder blades, everywhere.

Later on he laughingly boasted that he was 'so scrupulously well washed you could eat your dinner off me. I'm not like your average Anglo-Saxon male who thinks pheromones are yesterday's curry smells. You're so beautiful. Every bit of you is delicious. So why shouldn't a man be? Particularly if he wants to be touched and stroked and licked the way you do . . . Oh, oh, oh,' he said as she proved it to him yet again. The second time in an hour.

Whether or not he could manage it again, he loved the feeling that she aroused in him. She was as provocative and active and lust-filled as he was. He found himself lingering and touching and speaking to her more lovingly than he could remember.

It was obvious to Liz that David had made love to many women. He was, after all, an unmarried, very heterosexual English don of good-looking height and mien and working in exactly the right place, and had been for several years. Students, his peer group, visitors, other dons' bored wives and the middle-class jetsam of Oxford and London were his to pick from.

But this sex was so good because it was so equal. They both had nothing to lose and everything to gain.

They had made love on the floor as soon as they came in. Then in the bedroom. He had watched her in the mirror on her knees in front of him. The rhythmic movements of that wild long hair had stirred him so much he had hardly been able to wait until he entered her.

They were irresistible to each other. Even now she was delicately stroking the inside of his thighs with long red nails in the same way his large, sensitive hands had got the measure of her body.

He liked Liz a bit too much. He must be careful.

Her last act when she extricated herself from David's arms was to creep into the sitting room of the suite to place an alarm call for 7 a.m. Drat, it was Friday. Damn Katya and damn all her work.

But she knew she had to go back early. She had already started to worry about seeing him again, even before she had gone away.

As she climbed into bed she slid her breasts against his back. As if on automatic pilot he turned and pulled her to him, kissed her hair and went to sleep.

In the morning she lay beside him, riddled with insecurities about herself, and not just because of her less-than-perfect body. Had he done this many times before with strangers? What had been his motive? Did he make love to her because he wanted to write for her paper? A step on the way to becoming a media star? She hated herself for the lack of confidence that made her ask these questions and regretted having asked her driver, Alan, to arrive so early. He was already waiting in the foyer as David busied himself offering to take her suitcases downstairs.

She was reluctant to say goodbye especially in front of Alan, who might report back to the office. There was a short awkward pause as he kissed her cheek.

'Well,' he said in what she thought too hearty a tone, 'I certainly know where to find you.'

'Night and day at the moment,' she said, hoping her tone was as light as his.

Then David added that most dreaded of all male phrases: 'I'll be in touch.'

Liz replayed those words in her head most of the way back to London and the office. Would he be in touch? And when? If it was today, it might show he was perhaps too keen. Leaving it a day or two indicated he was in the driving seat. She really did fancy him. Perhaps it had all been so good because she was sex-starved. Hardly anyone she met lately had stopped her in her tracks. Was it really eight months since the affair with the *Time* bureau chief had ended?

Should she take the initiative? Of course, she could give David a feature to write. No, no. Not cool. Liz cursed the fact that although she was in line to get a plum job, she was still stuck in the terrible female trap of waiting for a man to phone.

She was beginning to despair of ever finding a man she liked who liked her. This was the story of her life.

Liz had always envied the ability of men to compartmentalise their emotions. It was what she and her friends described as spaghetti versus steel.

Women interwove all aspects of their lives, unable and often unwilling to separate each strand. In the middle of a highly complex business discussion, unwanted thoughts would sidle up, ranging from what to make for dinner to what men really liked during oral sex, whereas many men seemed to be able to switch off completely and laser in on only one thing at a time.

It was the spatial quality of a woman's mind, the ability to do several unrelated things at once – talk on the phone, paint their nails, flick their eyes over newspaper headlines while keeping rough track of what was happening on TV – that made women 'different but superior', as they used to joke.

In the *Chronicle* there was always a mini-blurb conference between editor, art editor and deputy editor on Friday mornings. Promotions on newspapers mattered more and more and the blurb at the top of page one telling readers what was inside the paper had to do more work per square inch than any other part of the paper, except for the splash itself. While trying to decide whether it was worth saying they had a free bulb offer for every reader, Liz's mind was overtaken not by tulips but by Bosnia – and she fantasised that David might write a piece for the paper about it. She could possibly ask her secretary to see if there were any cuttings on David Linden. The fact that the *Chronicle* already had an academic under contract cast a tiny shadow across her thoughts, but somehow she would have to overcome this problem.

She was certain that David, deep into research at his college for a lecture at Berkeley, California, had not given her another thought. However hard she tried, she found it difficult to put his last words out of her mind.

Her secretary read out an endless list of phone messages. His name was, of course, not among them. She must take the time to teach the girl the difference between what was urgent and what was important.

Tony barged through the door in a peremptory manner to interrupt her thoughts. Had he ever done this to Charlie? She did not think so.

'Liz, I've got to speak to you right now,' he barked and, turning to her secretary, 'alone.'

Liz tried to hide her irritation. 'Helen, what was that message?'

Flustered, Helen looked down her notes. 'Sir Andrew Lloyd Webber phoned from the South of France – for the second time. He's agreed to be a judge for the book competition but wants to switch the date. And the political editor is trying to get hold of you.'

Tony grabbed one of the phones on Liz's desk and dialled an internal number. 'If that call comes through from Washington, I'm in with Liz.'

'Right, Helen,' said Liz evenly. 'This meeting won't take long. Buzz me in five minutes, okay? And if the Washington call comes through, I'll take it.' She looked down at her letters for a second longer than was polite, then said, 'What's up?'

'Why didn't you tell me it was you in that mews picture?'

Now he had her attention but he was not going to play all his cards at once and reveal that Debbie was even now combing through the dustbins at Roland Mews.

'What on earth are you talking about?'

'The Oldfield lot have tracked down every one of those cloaks. Only three of that type were made, and Bruce lent one of them to you last weekend.'

Oh shit, she thought, then a split second later, I've got to keep him off Katya's trail.

'Why the hell did you let me waste so much time, Liz? I've had reporters all over the place and Nicola's been tied up for two days trying to track it down. And then I find out it's you all along. What are you playing at?'

Liz was icy. She leaned back in her chair twirling her pencil in her fingers, trying to appear cool. 'My, you are in a sweat about this, aren't you? I'm surprised you've put so many resources into this trivial story – which I thought we'd binned yesterday – especially when you should be tying up the mole enquiry. And you're quite wrong, you know. I assure you, it was not me in that picture. I did not wear the cloak on Sunday night. Is that clear enough for you?'

'But you knew we were trying to track down that cloak. Why didn't you mention you had it then?'

'Because, Tony, everyone's making cloaks these days. There were dozens at BAFTA. I had no idea this one was it.'

'So what do you want me to do?' he asked sulkily.

She longed to say, 'Get a job on another paper.'

'It is the Oldfield cloak, Nicola's sure of that,' he added.

'Well, I'm telling you it wasn't me. I'll look into it in my own good time. But so what? A fuzzy picture of an unknown woman we can barely see. There's no story yet, and I'd prefer you to concentrate on the mole investigation. I want a full run down by conference time.'

Tony was seething. I'll sort you out, he thought. He had never really known but he had been suspicious that something had

211

happened to upset Liz's mental stability just before he met her on that story in Mallorca. He would bide his time until the stringer had reported from the clinic there. He would see what he could get on this bitch. What he needed was proof that she had been treated there in the specialist centre for mental illnesses.

Liz stood up slowly and walked to the door. 'I'm a little concerned that I have an assistant editor who makes such accusations, especially against his own acting editor, without checking his facts,' she said quietly. She knew she was blustering but it seemed to be working.

'Look, I'm just quoting the fashion people,' Tony said in a more conciliatory tone.

'Well, I'll talk to them and sort it out.' She opened the door. 'Now may I suggest you divert your energies to the other stories on the list? And on your way out, ask Helen to come in, will you?' From the expression on his face, she knew that now he had a sniff of a story involving her, he would never give up. She had bought time, but how much?

Tony was in a fury. He was positive Liz knew more about all this than she was admitting, but he would bide his time. As far as she was concerned the story was a non-runner. He could not appear to spend any more time on it without arousing her suspicions.

But Debbie Luckhurst changed everything when five minutes later she pushed her way into the newsroom and handed him a piece of yellow paper. It was made up of several torn scraps, smoothed out and Sellotaped together, and, apart from a slight tea stain at the edge, was perfectly legible. It was part of a scrawled note and it read: ' . . . night was better than ever. I've stopped worrying . . . what we're doing feels right. I love you so much.' It was signed 'Me', followed by several kiss marks, some of which had been torn in two.

'This was in Number Sixteen's dustbin?' asked Tony.

'Yes. Nothing much in Number Fourteen's except for empty orange juice packets.'

So it wasn't Tom Reeves the cloaked woman was visiting, it was his neighbour, Tony thought. Where the hell was Alec Preston? He'd had since Tuesday to find out who owned No. 16.

Debbie tapped the yellow paper. 'Look at the other side.'

The back of the note seemed to come from a TV script, with the running order down the left-hand side. Tony recognised exactly which programme it referred to and who was in it.

'Good work!' he told Debbie delightedly.

'There's more,' she answered. 'I found out that this programme script was used last Friday on Morning Television. Jimmy Carter was interviewed then and yellow is the colour they use for Friday's scripts.'

'Tony made a detour to the picture desk and roared at Geoff, 'Get me the BAFTA pictures out of the library and on to my desk now. I mean everything, the prints and all the contacts. And not just ours, everyone's.'

It was a good picture of Liz, Tony had to admit as he inspected the BAFTA photos. The teeth, the cleavage, that irritating superiority, but she had been telling the truth, damn it, there was no cloak in sight.

Shit, what a great pity. He had the story all worked out; he would anonymously tip off Nigel Dempster about how Liz Waterhouse, champion of the new feminists, found herself facing a tussle with her principles. 'Is this the same Liz Waterhouse' – he could picture the caption – 'who was seen in the early hours of the morning about to sneak into a London mews love nest? Being companionable, Liz, or just doing a very early interview? And with whom?'

Tony's spy glass was moving slowly along the contact prints. Row upon row of magnified stars were showing expensively capped teeth to the camera. Somewhere in these prints he was going to find a picture of that damn cloak, he was sure of it.

He leaned over to peer more closely. He let out a howl of triumph. He had almost missed it. There it was, tucked over the arm of one of Britain's most famous TV stars. It must be the cloak. God Almighty. Liz's reluctance about this story now made sense. It all fitted into place. What a story, what a week. And he would make sure Liz could not spike this one. All he had to do now was find out who owned No. 16 Roland Mews. No need to tell Liz that Tom Reeves was out of the picture until he knew what he had instead.

213

Tony rushed back to confront Liz with this latest information – too late. She was already in conference with the other executives. He slid in just before the door closed.

Liz indicated that conference should start, and the news editor was about to take his customary first slot on the agenda when Tony interrupted.

'Before news starts, I'd like to bring you up to date on the cloak story.'

'I thought we'd dropped that,' said Liz tersely.

'Item number one,' said Tony, relishing his conjuring trick, 'this photograph of Miss Katya Croft walking along the red carpet to BAFTA. On her arm what appears to me to be a long, black cloak.'

Liz was about to speak when he produced item number two.

'I'll read you this scrap of paper.' He recited the scrawl to an attentive audience. 'This on its own would be quite interesting but when I tell you it is written on the back of last Friday's running order for Morning TV, you'll understand the significance.' And he added, 'We must be grateful to Debbie Luckhurst for her detective work in fishing it out of the dustbin.'

Tony passed the note to Liz who, dismayed, recognised Katya's handwriting.

'Surely what we should do now,' said Tony, 'is to send Debbie back to Roland Mews, this time with pictures of Katya Croft. And shouldn't we send someone to interview her boy friends – there're dozens of them in the file – and let's not forget her parents.'

'Just a minute,' said Liz. 'Let's try and abide by some of the rules of the Press Complaints Commission, shall we? Before you go and upset Mr and Mrs Croft, let's just examine what we've actually got here. A muzzy picture which may or may not be Katya Croft—'

'Wearing the Bruce Oldfield cloak you lent her,' intervened Tony.

'I couldn't swear it was the same one,' retorted Liz. 'The top of the note is missing so we don't know who it was sent to, and there's no signature. Everybody involved in the programmes gets a copy of the script. That note could have been written by anybody working there.'

Tony longed to implicate her in a cover-up. He wanted to ask her if she recognised the handwriting, but even his senior position on the newspaper decreed that he could not speak to his editor, even an acting editor, in such a direct way, certainly not in public. 'Someone at Morning TV will identify the writing,' he said, looking straight at Liz.

'All right, supposing it is Katya Croft. We have no proof of who she's in a leg-over situation with and I hate doing riddle or innuendo headlines. Can I remind you we only do this type of story if we get a confession from one or the other of the parties involved. We're not an irresponsible rag like the *Gazette*. Think back, when was the last time we had a sexual scandal without one or other of the partners owning up? That's what we need.'

Tony knew the rules as well as any of them but he was taking great delight in pushing her to use the story. He enjoyed her discomfort. 'But I do have your permission,' he said with overt politeness, 'to go ahead and restart work on the story?'

Liz had no alternative but to agree.

As he walked away from conference, he thought, she knows exactly who that woman is. Before long I'll force her to admit it. He knew how close she was to Katya and the third member of the coven, Joanna Glaister. She never seemed to move a step without the other two. He was certain Katya would have told Liz all about the paparazzo.

His reverie was interrupted when Liz tapped him on the shoulder. 'Don't forget the other stories, will you?'

Tony bit back a retort and hurried to the newsroom where he immediately ordered Debbie Luckhurst to return to the mews with clear pictures of Katya Croft.

'I want to know what you find out as fast as possible,' he instructed. 'Geoff, dig out those pictures of Katya and that documentary maker. We want a Life and Good Times of Katya Croft feature. And ring round the agencies. I want to see everything you can get. But be careful what you tell them, we don't want them to click.'

Geoff nodded and went to work.

Tony looked round the newsroom. He couldn't see Alec Preston. He told another reporter, 'Find Croft, try the TV station first, then stake out her flat. It's in Chelsea somewhere. We've got her address but you don't want her to see you yet. That's vital because we don't want her vanishing off for the weekend. We may need to front her up, but not yet.'

Chapter Thirteen

Katya had enjoyed a long spell as Morning TV's Golden Girl. It was rare for her to be criticised inside the station, more so since the award. So she was unprepared for the programme controller's bluntness.

'Katya, you haven't had a very happy morning, have you? You missed two cues and you fluffed the intro on the Afghanistan story.'

'I'm sorry, Martin, I didn't sleep well last night.'

Martin Pickard did not return her apologetic smile.

'But it isn't just this one morning, Katya. You've not been what I call up to your usual excellent standard all this week. What's the problem?'

'No problem. Really. I'm sorry, I'll try harder.'

He got up. 'In this business, even award-winners are only as good as their last programmes, Katya. You'd do well to remember that.' He put an avuncular arm round her and smiled the grin of a bored alligator. 'You're normally first-rate and we can't have you below par, can we? Anything we can do to help you, just you mention it. If you need a few days off, just say. Okay?'

Katya knew Martin would not have talked in this way if there had not been some serious discussion among the station's senior executives. Since she had met Davina she had put the programme second and with so much praise and encouragement from her peers, as well as the BAFTA award, she had felt inviolate. But since the events of Sunday night, she had found the gruelling three-hour live sessions starting with a programme meeting at 4.30 a.m., more of a strain.

Normally the hyper-critical eyes of her colleagues in the viewing gallery monitoring her questions and keeping a close watch on her appearance did not perturb her. But she realised that make-up artists, however skilled at disguising blotches and bags, could not hide tension and strain. And she kept losing things, then forgetting them, then finding them, then dropping them . . .

She could not go on like this. Katya was as selfish as most people but, so far, her motives had been unselfish. It had been Davina she had been trying to protect. But what about her own career? She tried to imagine Martin's shock if he had realised that the missed cues and the grey bags under her eyes had not only been caused by lack of sleep because of a passionate new lover, but that the lover was a woman.

How would the British populace, who saw her as the girl next door, react to that? It would mean demotion to boring late-night slots for an audience of under a million, if she was lucky. The British public would never accept someone who came into their homes so often being so out of the ordinary. Homosexual men, yes, perhaps, but not lesbians. She had a regular postbag from viewers asking when they were going to see her married and then have babies as pretty as herself.

Katya left the building, resolving to sort out her life one way or the other. As she drove out of the station's underground car park she saw a cameraman on the ramp waving at her. A bit slow off the mark if it was about the award. Unless . . .

She pressed the button to lower the window. 'Where are you from?'

'*Sunday Chronicle.*'

She relaxed. Only Liz trying to be helpful, she guessed. 'There's no need to snatch a picture. Why didn't you just ask the station PR?'

'Dunno, just following orders.'

Katya flashed the kind of smile that still put up her viewing figures. 'Sorry, have to dive. Talk to my agent.' And she revved up the navy-blue BMW convertible and shot off in third gear, intent on getting home as fast as possible so she could phone Liz.

Liz left yet another message on Katya's answering machine and tried not to sound exasperated.

Only a minute later she answered her private line hoping it was

David. It was not but it was the next best thing. Katya had been on her mind almost as often.

Liz decided to go in slowly and leave Tony's allegations till later. How did you tell one of your best friends that your paper had been sifting through dustbins and that a love note in her handwriting had been read out to a roomful of strangers? And that journalists were now poring over the secrets of her private life?

Liz did what she thought she would never do with her friends. She procrastinated. 'Where are you when I need you?' she asked lightly.

Katya nerved herself for what was to come, but Liz went on, 'Guess what I was doing last night?'

'I remember. Debating at Oxford,' answered Katya. 'What else would a girl be doing on a Thursday night? Washing her hair? How did it go?'

'If by debating you mean a meeting of minds, you would be correct. But you might like to know, if you ever bothered to return my calls, that there was a further meeting, later on in my hotel, this time of bodies. I've been locked in physical passion with Oxford High Table.'

'How high?' Katya felt a heady sense of relief. So this was about Liz, not her.

'Modern history, very modern but hopefully not history just yet. Rather special, though.'

'He'd have to be, you were only in Oxford for five minutes. What came over you?'

'He did,' laughed Liz.

'We take that as read,' Katya retorted. 'What's his name?'

The next few minutes were taken up with pleasurable reminiscences from Liz, about the way his hair curled, what they talked about, what he said and, more importantly, what he did not say. Like when he was going to contact her again. They discussed what his tactics might be, what Liz could do if he didn't phone.

Katya was in as relaxed a state as she had been for days, her own worries far away. This was what friendship was all about, shared problems of daily life. So she was unprepared for Liz's change of subject. 'By the way, Katya, tell me, how well do you know Tom Reeves?'

The star who had moved next door to Davina. Fear began to

course through her but she tried to sound casual. 'Tom Reeves? I think I did meet him, once, at one of those polo charity bashes. Why?'

'Because a pap's come in here with a photograph he snatched after midnight on Sunday of a woman wearing a cloak just like the Oldfield one I lent you. She was in Roland Mews in front of the house Tom Reeves is renting.'

Oh my God. Here it was. 'Come on, Liz, there must be dozens of black cloaks around London.'

'Not three and a half thousand quids' worth of black velvet, there aren't. It's a sample from Oldfield's autumn collection and only three have been made so far. One's in New York on the back of a millionaire's wife, the Princess of Wales has one but she was in Scotland until Monday lunchtime and then there's the catwalk sample you borrowed.'

Silence.

'Katya? What have you got to say?' Liz felt she must have an answer before tackling Katya with the note on the torn-up script. 'What you can clearly see on the picture,' she said carefully, 'is that the woman has a front-door key in her hand. Which means they're on pretty good terms. If indeed she was going into Reeves's house.'

Katya stalled for time. 'Liz, it's impossible that there are only three of those cloaks in the world. Why can't Nicola come out of Fergus's shower long enough to do some accurate research?'

Liz knew Katya was lying but made one last attempt. 'I've got far more gruesome things in your past to blackmail you with,' she tried to josh her. 'Just tip me the wink about this one and I'll try and get the hounds to back off.'

'I promise you, Liz, that I do not know Tom Reeves in any sense, including the biblical one. Look, I must go. Speak to you later, okay? 'Bye.'

As Liz put down the receiver, she chastised herself for not pushing Katya harder. All the newscraft she had learned over the years seemed to fly out of the window when it came to tackling a friend. She re-ran the phone call through her head. She could not have been gentler. What on earth did Katya have to hide?

Bob Howard came in to congratulate her on having such a good potential splash. She trusted him enough to voice her fears that she would rather have an exclusive on something harder and more serious than a puzzle about a mysterious woman in a cloak.

'So would we all,' he said, 'but we take what the Lord provides and he's not suited you on this one. Have faith. He might turn up the goods yet.'

She worked out some rules in her mind. If Katya did admit anything to her, she would oversee the story personally and put the best twist on it from Katya's point of view. But how to persuade her to talk?

Alec Preston, the *Sunday Chronicle*'s junior reporter, was on his way up the ladder, like his father and uncle before him. So getting a story was for him more than another good day at the office. It was a tribal blooding.

And the phones ran red between *The Times*, his uncle, and the Newspaper Press Fund's home where his father was seeing out a pleasant retirement.

He was triumphant as he faced his boss, though he was careful not to show it. Even though he had been on the paper for only three months, he had absorbed the newsroom code of never over-selling a story, never explaining and never revealing your source. Even if sent to jail.

'Had a lot of trouble tracking down the owners of that mews house next door to Tom Reeves,' he told Tony. 'Contact of mine, very reliable, says it was bought some years ago by a most interesting couple.'

'How interesting?' asked Tony.

'Well, I've seen the lease. It's to a company called Orchard Properties which leased to another company but the contract was signed by a Hugo Thomas, of Symington in Warwickshire. At Companies House I found he's the sole owner of Orchard. He's married to—'

Tony held up a hand, knowing there were casual freelancers around.

'I know who you mean. Good work. Ask Barry Donlan to come over here. I'll send him down to the hospital.'

'I can do this on my own, boss.'

'No, I need you here.' Barry appeared and Tony gave him succinct instructions. 'Tell Geoff you'll need one of his best men. I want an interview with Hugo Thomas and a pic if at all possible. If they are having it off, you could make the front page splash, Barry, but you'll have to tread carefully. Go through the procedures with the hospital authorities of course.'

Tony picked up the phone that linked him with the political editor, Andrew Cahill, at the House of Commons. After several minutes of careful briefing, he sat back with a satisfied smile.

Now let Liz try and stop this one.

As Liz left the *Chronicle* office to go to the Ivy for lunch with Joanna, Alan, the driver, was waiting. So, unfortunately, was Tony, leaning casually against the bonnet. 'Any chance of a lift to the West End?'

It was too curmudgeonly to refuse; after all, Charlie had given her enough lifts in the past. But she sat in the front to avoid having to talk to Tony. To be even more sure of silence, she made phone calls to the office checking on some of the other stories on the news list.

Tony and the driver kept up a barrage of male-bonding chatter, analysing details of that Sunday's televised football match. For no reason at all, it irritated Liz. It was during a short hiatus between calls that Tony dropped his bombshell.

'I tried to come and see you ten minutes ago but you had your door closed.'

When her door was shut, Liz knew that Tony tried to intimate to the rest of the staff that she was doing her nails or making up her face rather than discussing private matters vital to the newspaper, such as editorial salaries, expenses and budgets, or phoning a cabinet minister.

'By the way, the Washington story's coming on a treat and of course it has my full attention. I forgot to mention earlier that that love letter Debbie found came out of Number Sixteen's bin, the house next door to Tom Reeves's. You might like to know who owns it.'

Involuntarily, Liz turned to face him. He was pleased to get a reaction. 'It's the London pad of no less than Mr and Mrs Hugo Thomas, also known as Mr and Minister Lovey-Dovey.'

Liz turned her face away before he could see her startled expression.

Hugo Thomas. So that was why Katya had been so nervy and strange at BAFTA, especially after the announcement about Hugo's car accident. And that was why she had reacted in the cloakroom to the sight of that chic woman with the blonde bob. From the back, Katya had obviously thought it was his wife, Davina.

Liz pulled down the sun-visor flap to check her make-up in the mirror and saw Tony's watchful eyes on her from the back seat. God damn the man. Why couldn't he have told her it wasn't Tom Reeves's bin before she spoke to Katya? Forgot to mention it, indeed. This news made the story much more plausible. She had to be very, very careful.

'I spoke to Bruce this morning,' she said, 'and he's not entirely sure that there were only three copies of that cloak. He's finding out and coming back to me later.'

They both knew she was lying. Tony even felt a flash of rare compassion. How would he feel if it was a mate of his? But then he remembered he had sensibly never formed any friendships as close as that, especially with celebrities. At least not unless they were newspaper editors or proprietors.

The car drew up outside The Ivy, the restaurant patronised by theatre people, publishing tycoons, the media and worthies listed in *Who's Who*.

'What a coincidence,' said Tony. 'I'm having lunch here too, with our MI5 contact.'

'Oh, great.' She smiled unenthusiastically. 'I'm meeting Joanna Glaister and her MD. They want to do some joint promotions and, sorry, I won't be able to give you a lift after lunch as I'm not going straight back.'

Tony was well aware that Joanna was one of Liz's closest friends and that the talk about joint promotions was meant to fool him into thinking their lunch was purely business.

Liz prayed Joanna would not be sitting there, on time as always,

223

at a table set only for two. Luckily, Joanna had been delayed by a problem with her page proofs and by the time she arrived, Mitch, the jovial maître d', had at Liz's request swiftly set a place for three at her regular table. He was fond of Liz and needed no long explanation.

When Joanna arrived, Liz quickly put her in the picture. 'Don't look now but that S-H-ONE-T Tony is over there in the corner watching us. This place here is supposed to be for your MD.'

'Ah. Unfortunately,' Joanna was always quick to catch on, 'he can't make it and sends his apologies. Slight attack of cholera – I wish.'

'No jokes. Tony will be watching us and even if he can't lip read, we don't want him to guess what we're talking about, which is supposed to be joint promotions, by the way. Look at your watch now and then and act as if you're waiting for someone. You look terrific, incidentally. How are you feeling?'

Joanna did not tell her about the pain she had been having all morning. 'Fine ... really. But I'll be glad when George gets home next week.'

When the MD failed to turn up, they made a great show of asking the waiter to remove the third place setting, then ordered their meal. Liz manoeuvred herself so she was not in Tony's eye-line.

'I'm extremely worried about this business about Katya and Tom Reeves,' Joanna said when they had settled down. 'It's absurd, don't you think?'

Liz smiled for Tony's benefit. 'You're absolutely right but how does Katya and Hugo Thomas grab you?'

There was a pause while Joanna struggled to control her shock. Like everyone else in the media, her magazine had written pieces about the golden marriage of the city high flier and one of the few women in the present cabinet. Despite the pressures, theirs was said to be a genuinely happy partnership.

'The Thomases own Sixteen Roland Mews, right next door to the house Tom Reeves is renting,' Liz told Joanna. 'It makes some kind of sense of her behaviour at BAFTA. Remember all those neck blotches that came up when she saw that blonde woman in the loo? And that explains why she looked so upset when Attenborough broke the news about Hugo's accident.'

'He's supposed to be happily married, isn't he? Katya must have been beside herself. How is he, by the way? There's been nothing on the news.'

'You know how it is,' said Liz. 'If there's no news, he's getting better.'

'Boy, she can pick 'em.'

'Yeah. I've never really heard anything about Hugo Thomas and bad behaviour but I've seen his pictures – very twinkly eyes, I thought. And just like all MPs' spouses, he spends a lot of nights alone.'

'Not completely alone, apparently.'

Liz leaned forward. 'Keep smiling. If that bastard scents we're worried, he'll smell it from right across the room.'

'Have you spoken to Katya?'

'Yes, but I didn't know about Hugo Thomas then. Now I see why she was so convincing that there was nothing going on between her and Tom Reeves.'

'You believe this Hugo Thomas stuff, don't you?'

'I've seen the picture outside his house,' said Liz. 'And Tony has other evidence.' She then told Joanna about the note.

'That all seems pretty conclusive,' Joanna said anxiously.

'I'm as sure as I can be it's Katya,' Liz went on. 'The nightmare is, this thing's got tentacles. If I distance myself from Katya, it's a brilliant story. Okay, it won't win a Pulitzer Prize but it sells Sunday newspapers. And you know how men would revel in the idea of a successful woman minister having a husband who screws around. They hardly love women at the top. They'll say it serves her right.' Liz crumbled a bread stick thoughtfully. 'Not only that,' she went on. 'Katya's a star, a BAFTA winner and seen on television daily. Put that little lot together and it could fill *Hello* magazine for ever. Then I have this added complication that Fergus would love any scandal to drop on the government even if it's the husband of a Minister, and Tony over there,' she waved across the room at him and, surprised, he acknowledged it, 'knows I borrowed that bloody cloak and has already accused me of wasting valuable office time in some elaborate cover-up.'

Joanna poured some more Highland Spring into their glasses.

'What a mess. On Thursday I went to Oxford hoping we'd buried the bloody story,' added Liz, 'but it keeps coming back and, believe me, Tony will be doing his damnedest to prove who the woman is. It's only a matter of time.'

Their spinach salad arrived. They both took the opportunity, when they were lunching together, to eat healthy food. So they were having a starter to begin with, followed by another dish from the appetiser menu, a small tuna collation. They would both be ravenous by mid-afternoon but their intentions, as always, were good.

'Maybe Tony won't be able to stand it up,' said Joanna, exuding more hope than she felt.

They painstakingly worked out how Tony would set about proving it was Katya in the mews. The photographer had not recognised her, but if she was having an affair, she must presumably have been a fairly frequent visitor to the house. Apart from anything else, Liz told Joanna, if the pap had any inkling of who might be in his picture, he wouldn't pass up the chance of selling it to another paper if the *Chronicle* did not want to publish. The story would surface, with or without her. Liz was starting to think the unthinkable.

'Okay,' said Joanna, 'so the story's going to come out anyway. Maybe it's better some other newspaper does it. Then Katya can hate them, not you.'

Liz understood why Joanna was arguing this way and chose her words carefully. 'This is make-my-mind-up time, Jo,' she said. 'We have this story exclusively. If I publish it, it will put on sales. If we put on sales, not only will Fergus Canefield like the fact I've taken a swipe at the government he hates, but I will have shown I can produce the goods. That means, Joanna, I could clinch the job and leapfrog to become editor of the *Daily Chronicle*. The first woman to edit a national daily.'

Liz tried to keep her pride under control. 'And, Jo, think how useful it would be to have a woman at the helm of a daily, able to put her views across every day on the government's actions and on what life's doing particularly to women. To be pro-active and not just pick up the pieces and comment at the weekend.'

'It'd be great, Liz, and so good for you.'

Liz attacked another bread stick. 'Yes, but on the downside, if I don't use the story, Tony will accuse me of a serious cover-up and he'd be right. And Fergus would most likely give me the bullet. Now do you see what I'm up against?'

Joanna was about to reply when the programme controller of BBC1 television leaned over their table.

'If I send over a couple of glasses of wine, would you regard it as sexual harassment?'

'Hopefully,' said Joanna, smiling.

'But, sorry, we don't drink on Fridays, Alan,' added Liz. 'Another day perhaps?'

Joanna was grateful Liz did not give her pregnancy as an excuse for their alcohol-free lunch. At present, it was better if outsiders thought she was growing memorable mammaries rather than that she was having a baby, although the news would soon filter out.

'You can't be the first editor to have faced this kind of dilemma,' said Joanna, returning to the subject. 'What would the others do?'

'Well, editors do say you can't ever be friendly with anyone famous because just this kind of thing may crop up.'

'But you knew Katya long before she became famous.'

'Exactly, and that's why it's so bloody difficult. And the other thing of course is that virtually all the other editors have been men and we know they don't have the same kind of friendships.'

'But it strikes me, Liz, that if you can only get the job on their terms, maybe it's not worth having.'

Liz sighed. They had discussed this many times. 'Jo, women can't avoid these problems for ever. We have to make a stand and without power we can't change anything. If we have to get our hands dirty in the meantime and play their silly little games, so be it.'

Joanna could not help but show how shocked she was. Liz seemed to be shattering the theories they had talked about so often. And the first time they were being tested, she seemed to be bending her principles.

'You just can't do this to Katya.'

'Look, if Katya's happy with Hugo Thomas, I'm happy for her,

227

whatever the complications. But, Jo, the story's going to come out anyway. Wouldn't it be better if I handled it? At least I'd make sure it was done sensitively.'

'How can you even consider that option? Think what it would do to her career! How could you do that to her?'

Liz felt a spark of anger. 'You live in the soft world of women's magazines. Don't tell me you wouldn't have done anything for your launch cover story. You've been sheltered from really difficult decisions in journalism, but this is the real world. You can't hush up the news. Remember when the *Post* sat on the story of Princess Di and the harassing phone calls? It surfaced in another paper later. You think the *Sunday Gazette* wouldn't do this story? Or any other Sunday paper? I keep on telling you, Tony is on to it. What's he going to spread around if the *Chronicle* doesn't go with this? I'll lose credibility with the staff as well as displaying unprofessional behaviour. And all those Fleet Street guys who say women can't hack it? I'll have proved them dead right.'

'Is that what we're all about? Using the same methods as men?' Joanna would not give way. 'If so, why bother coming to work at all? Why not just go back to cooking and cleaning?' When she was stressed, Joanna's South African accent became more pronounced. 'So you'll destroy Katya with something which is wrapped round fish and chips the day after?' she asked caustically.

'Better me than a stranger, Joanna. Believe me, the red-tops won't be satisfied with just Hugo Thomas. They'll put a microscope on Katya's life – her background, her romances,' she paused, 'her time in Mallorca. Would that be better for her? And incidentally, we may not come out smelling of roses either.'

'I understand that, Liz.'

'If it's going to come out that she's having a fling with that particular married man, isn't it better if I handle it?'

Tony passed their table. 'Hello, Joanna. Not many promotions going on then?' he said, pointing to the virtually blank page of Liz's Filofax which was lying on the table, ignored.

Joanna was not to be outsmarted. 'I've written reams,' she smiled sweetly. 'Some pretty good ideas, too. I'm sure Liz will tell you about them – eventually.'

Liz snapped shut her Filofax and Tony moved towards the door.
'What happens now?' Joanna asked.

'I'll have to speak to Katya as soon as possible. Maybe there's
some damage limitation we can try. But I have to do this myself.
Please, don't tip her off, and I promise I'll handle the story
myself. But just be around, will you? I'm sure we're both going to
need you.'

Andrew Cahill hated doing these kinds of stories but on a Friday
it did not do to argue with your news editor. He was keen to get it
over with; he had promised Liz yesterday that he would see her
with some new information on the molehunt.

Andrew prided himself on being a good political reporter, a
member of that tightly closed circle of political journalists from all
leading papers who were based at Westminster. The lobby
correspondent.

They spent as much time in the House as the Members themselves
and it was their daily briefings from No. 10 or the office of the leader
of the opposition which led to front-page stories with the words:
'Sources close to so-and-so said today . . .'

Andrew was wary of using telephones, for it was a mistake on
this kind of scandal story to alert your quarry in advance. So he
hurried across one of the busiest thoroughfares in Britain, the Central Lobby of the House of Commons, towards the policemen on
duty at their unimposing desk.

To the left was the carpeted corridor leading to the visitors'
galleries. On the other side of the desk was the broad, tiled corridor
to the Members' Lobby and, beyond, to the Chamber itself, its
doors guarded by bronze statues of Winston Churchill and Lloyd
George. One plinth was still empty, waiting, so the rumours said,
for the statue of Margaret Thatcher. It was a convention of the
House that no member's likeness, in oil or marble, could be dis-
played until twenty-five years after their death.

Andrew had often speculated how much it would take to bribe
a House policeman or barrier attendant to talk about what they
really knew. There was a rumour that one of his colleagues had
given a policeman a set of Cup Final tickets. They were gratefully

received and used but he did not get even one small tidbit in exchange. Nothing was ever said on either side.

There was the usual gaggle of eager tourists filling in the detailed questionnaire security demanded before their admittance to the Strangers' Gallery to watch a somnambulant House finishing off the week's business.

Andrew was pleased to see Kevin Hart on duty. He had been in the House for years and knew every single face and usually what they were up to.

'I need a quote from Davina Thomas. Have you seen her around?'

The other barrier attendant answered. 'You'll be lucky. She usually goes off to her constituency on Friday afternoons like the rest of them.'

Kevin intervened. 'Well, actually, there's a Private Member's Bill she's involved in. She's still in the Chamber.'

Andrew quickly filled in the green card requesting an audience with the Broadcasting Minister, glanced at his watch and jotted down the time at the top. Kevin took it into the Members' Lobby and handed it to the Serjeant-at-Arms, resplendent in his eighteenth-century costume with black long-tailed coat, ruffled cravat, black leggings and silver-buckled shoes.

He walked majestically through the Aye Lobby to the back of the Speaker's chair and handed the card to the government whip on duty who was sitting at the end of the front bench with his legs outstretched so he could get his heels on the table as tradition decreed.

The whip passed the card to his neighbour and, like the children's game of pass the parcel, it finally ended up with Davina who was to the right of the Despatch Box, where a minister was sending members to sleep with his lacklustre speech about a minor amendment to the Charity Law. It was one of 392 amendments the government had slapped down after the bill had completed its committee stage upstairs – a hallmark of inadequate drafting by parliamentary counsel, and a too trusting Secretary of State.

Shortly afterwards, Andrew Cahill was pleased to see Davina striding across the lobby towards him, facing the banner of St George, patron saint of England, perched above the corridor leading to the House of Lords. As always, she looked as though she was charging into battle against the proverbial dragon. On the stone floor her high-heeled shoes sounded like a drummer leading the charge.

Unlike other ministers who would fob off journalists with their press officers, Davina usually tried to deal with the lobby reporters herself. Not surprising, Andrew thought cynically, while she was jockeying into position to be promoted from number two at the Home Office. At her stage, the right kind of exposure would do her career no harm.

He felt a momentary qualm of conscience when she smiled at him in a pleasant manner. His paper might not be government-friendly but on a personal level the two of them maintained a mutual respect. 'Thanks for seeing me, Minister. I'll keep it short. I'm afraid it's not the sort of thing we usually discuss and I'm a bit embarrassed about it.'

'Come on, Andy, you don't usually mess about, let's have it.'

'Well, we've several people willing to testify that Katya Croft has been seen in and out of your house in Roland Mews at odd hours. Did you know about this?'

Davina looked at him sharply. 'Go on.'

'We also have a photograph taken in the early hours of Sunday morning showing her about to open the front door with her own key. What does this mean?'

'I have no idea.'

'I'm sorry, I have to ask for your reaction to what's fairly apparent, that your husband has been seeing Katya Croft.'

'I've had enough of this. My husband is certainly not having an affair and you can quote me. I have nothing else to add.'

'Look, we sympathise with you. You'll just be like a lot of people in this place. They say the wife's always the last to know.'

But Davina had already turned on her heel and was disappearing into a Members Only area where she knew he could not follow. She had already made the decision not to contact Katya again. Now she would have to think this through carefully.

Tony's undercover reporter, Barry Donlan, had persuaded one of the nurses on Hugo's hospital ward to go for a lunchtime drink with him after her spell of duty. In the Hare and Hounds pub an hour's pure flattery and several unaccustomed tequila sunrises persuaded her to tell him the latest hospital gossip.

He heard stories about heart by-passes, anaesthetics that would not take and the shocking truth about some nurses giving relief massage to boost their meagre salaries. He filed it in his memory bank for another week. Finally his patience was rewarded. He asked her about Hugo Thomas.

'You'd think he'd be interested in posh television, wouldn't you? But as soon as he began to get better, he insisted on being woken up at six thirty in the morning. And you'll never guess why?'

The reporter pushed another cocktail her way.

'It was to watch Katya Croft. He just loves her – when she's not on he doesn't bother with telly at all.'

'You sure about that?' asked the reporter casually.

'Oh, he made such a fuss this morning when his telly was switched to the BBC. Kept ringing his bell. He'd dropped the remote control and just wouldn't settle. I had to leave everything and change channels. You'd think a man like that would prefer the BBC, wouldn't you?'

It did not mean he could write the story without contacting Katya but it gave useful colour. In this simple way the reporter got his facts. Eighteen months later, he also got a wife. And former nurse Teresa Mary Kelly then spent the rest of her life frustratedly never knowing when to expect her successful journalist husband home. But they always made a point of following Hugo Thomas's career in the City. Everyone has to find their Cupid somewhere.

Chapter Fourteen

The Prime Minister's private secretary received a request from the head of security for a meeting with the PM on Monday morning.

'Please tell him there's something he needs to know about one of his ministers,' was the message.

Debbie Luckhurst wished she had worn flat pumps. Her stiletto-heeled shoes were being ruined on the cobbles of Roland Mews and her feet were pulsating.

She was posing as the property correspondent of the *Sunday Chronicle* and was enquiring of residents if they had heard that a few other well-known people were buying property in the area, and she mentioned a few international authors and some TV stars like Katya Croft. In fact, had they seen any of these prospective buyers around? she asked innocently, showing them pictures of Katya.

Unfortunately for Debbie, the kind of people who lived in the mews were more sophisticated than that. 'Well, why don't you phone their agents?' suggested one disgruntled resident, irritated at being brought to the door by an unexpected caller.

Know-all, thought Debbie. 'I tried that,' she said, giving him her most charming smile. 'But this is just the sort of information they don't like talking about.'

'Then neither shall I,' said the man, slamming his front door.

Debbie had a few more doors shut in her face before the nannies came home after the school round.

'Oh yes,' said one young girl, when shown the pictures. In an accent that showed she was obviously new to London, she went on, 'That's Katya Croft, isn't it, the one on telly in the mornings? I've seen her here lots of times – always in a hurry and doesn't seem half as nice as she looks on the screen.'

Debbie made her next question seem casual. 'And which house did she come out of?'

'That one, with the white door.'

'Number Sixteen, you mean?'

The girl nodded.

'Sure about that?'

'Yes. Well, I think so.'

That was enough for Debbie, who took down her name, age and address, after assuring her the details would not be printed. With a sigh of relief Debbie left the mews and went back to the office.

Tony was pleased with her news. He was even more satisfied when Barry reported the information he had gleaned from the nurse. 'Is she on duty tomorrow?'

'Yes, I've checked.'

'Good lad. We might need her to do something else for us. How much money would it take for her to deliver a letter to Hugo Thomas?'

'Nothing,' grinned Barry. 'The old baby blues seem to have worked so far,' he laughed, crinkling them up.

Andrew Cahill phoned from the House of Commons. 'Davina knows something,' he told his news editor. 'I'm sure of it, but she's not talking.'

'Okay, find out where she's going to be tomorrow, we'll definitely need to talk to her then.'

'You'd better get a news hound,' Andrew said. 'I don't think I'm going to get anything out of her, personal or political, for a long time. They say don't shoot the messenger, but she walked off in such a way I thought she'd like me hung, drawn and quartered as well.'

'I could talk to her tomorrow,' volunteered a keen Barry. 'She'll be at the hospital with her husband and, boy, would I like to be a fly on the wall when she tells him we know about Katya Croft.'

Tony smiled in satisfaction. 'Well, we might just have that fly – in a starched blue and white uniform.' What a great story, he thought. And he was going to have to hand it to Liz on a plate. It was hard. It would make her look really good. What a pity it would not keep until Charlie came back. There must be a way for him to get the credit for the disclosures. In newspapers, stories were occasionally held over but only if there was a really good reason, such as the paper being promoted on TV or if a cover price rise was imminent. And, of course, only if the paper remained positive that the story would remain exclusive to them.

Tony knew that the pap, Roddy Hamlyn, had been prowling around the picture desk, irritated at the stop-go tactics of the *Chronicle*. To keep him quiet till next week, he would have to pay him a lot of money. For that, he would have to get the okay from Liz who still knew nothing about today's brilliant finds. He had to weigh up whether to tell Liz at once or reveal the story at conference so he would get full credit in front of his colleagues and risk Liz exploding that he had done so much without discussion, though she might suspect that he had been on the phone to Charlie – and she would be right.

He still was not sure which of his colleagues were on 'his' side and who saw him as Charlie's successor. If there was just a whisper that he had been wasting reporters' valuable time, they would use it as a stick to beat him with for weeks. Newspapers only had a finite number of reporters and photographers. Careers rose and fell on how well they were husbanded and which stories were seen as priority. Perhaps to discuss it at conference was the safest option although it meant he risked Liz being able to stop the story behind closed doors.

Tony was still making up his mind when the decision was taken out of his hands.

On her way back to the office, Liz tried to phone Katya from the car. The line was engaged and for a second she toyed with the idea of going round to Katya's flat. But then no one would understand why she was not there for Friday's conference. Anyway, the engaged tone did not necessarily mean Katya was in. Maybe someone else was trying her number. She kept pressing re-dial and the phone was still busy as they drew up outside the *Chronicle* building.

The normally crowded newsroom was empty. Most of the

reporters were out gleaning facts and the only people remaining were sub-editors honing features and features people checking to make sure that everything in the early colour pages was perfect. But even some of these were being deployed on the Katya story, which Tony thought would be so big he planned to ask Liz to allocate pages one, eleven, twelve and thirteen to it.

'Where is everybody, Geoff?' Liz asked, surveying the almost empty newsroom.

'Well, we've got half the world out trying to confirm that this cloak woman is Katya Croft. I keep telling them you're the best person to ask her. Why don't you?'

'I plan to do just that.'

She was alarmed to think that her reporters were doorstepping Katya but, try though she might, she could not get her friend to return her calls. It was more important than ever that she got to her first, but it was only ten minutes before the Friday afternoon story-positioning conference. She could not miss that, especially on her first week as acting editor. Many stories would be allocated pages so that layouts and headlines could be done. They could be unscrambled on Saturday but as so little news broke on most weekends, for production reasons Liz liked to get early news pages ready.

She had to act quickly. 'Helen, come in a minute – and shut the door, please.' It was not often Liz asked her to do this and her secretary looked alarmed.

'Don't look so worried. I just want you to do me an errand. I've been phoning Katya Croft this last half-hour and her line's been solidly engaged. I've checked with the operator and it's engaged speaking, so she must be at home.' Liz's tone was urgent. 'I need to speak to Katya as soon as possible. It's very serious, newspaper business. I have to take conference soon and the only way I can think of getting to Katya is to send you to fetch her. You know I can't send Alan.' The unspoken implication, Liz's lack of trust in Charlie's driver, was understood between them. 'In fact, he mustn't even see you get a taxi, otherwise he'll be suspicious, he'll wonder why you aren't using him, so make sure you walk down the road away from the office before you grab one. When you get to Katya, tell her I'm in trouble and I need her help. Say it's too important to discuss on the phone, I've got to see her face to face.' She paused. 'But where?'

'How about the usual place, the American Bar at the Savoy?' suggested Helen.

'On a Friday afternoon? Much too public. Half of Fleet Street wanders through there just to see who they can spot.' It could look as if the acting editor of the *Chronicle* was having a girlie-tea on her busiest day of the week. 'Be resourceful, Helen. Find somewhere halfway between her flat and the office, somewhere near Victoria Station, I would think, and book it in your name.'

Liz gave Helen £100 from the bundles of notes in her bag. She always tried to have a stash of money around, particularly on a Friday and Saturday, just in case it was needed. Every now and again it came in useful if an informant demanded cash.

This was not like the old days when she first started in journalism. Then the cashiers were available seven days a week and every news desk had a float. The tenth floor had been a convenient 'bank'. Now journalists had to assess in advance how much money they would need after the bean counters shut up shop at 5.30 p.m. on Fridays. Liz had heard of some journalists who never drew cash from their own banks. They were always drawing money from the 'bank upstairs', even when their expense sheets had not been submitted for months. One old-timer boasted that he used his expenses to pay his mortgage. They were a masterpiece of creativity as he never left the office to interview or entertain.

'Don't worry, Liz,' said Helen. 'I'll find somewhere.'

'Good. Here, take my mobile. I'll be out of conference at half past four. I'll call you then and come to wherever you are.'

At the conference, Liz listened with increasing alarm as the news editor outlined how much the staff had found out about the Croft story.

Geoff's man was watching Katya's flat. Andrew Cahill had been talking to Davina Thomas at the House of Commons. Barry had some lovely quotes from the nurse at Hugo Thomas's hospital. And Debbie Luckhurst had come up with real gold from a nanny in Roland Mews.

Tony sat back, enjoying Liz's discomfiture.

Liz was torn. What a story. What a nightmare.

'Boss, have you managed to get hold of Katya Croft yet?' asked Geoff.

'If you see me disappearing out of the door, that's where I'm going,' said Liz.

'Shouldn't we have someone follow you so we can take today's picture of her?' suggested the women's editor.

'And we could wire you up, boss,' said an enthusiastic news editor.

Liz made a moue of distaste. 'If my word isn't good enough, we'll just have to busk it.'

'Well, if you won't be wired, you'd better take a witness,' said Tony.

'Don't be so naive. It's going to be hard enough getting her to talk to me. There's no way she'll do that if someone else is there.'

'But you've got to take a tape recorder.'

Liz glared. 'Tony, I'm handling this my way. She's one of my bloody best friends and I'll let you know when I need a photographer. Or a tape.'

Katya Croft should have thought about it before jumping into the sack with a married man, Tony thought angrily. If Liz tries to sit on this one, I'll go to Fergus. Well, I'll ring Charlie again.

Liz switched on her computer. It was a real struggle to focus on the spread and the front of the Arts and Entertainment section while she waited for Helen to tell her whether or not she had been successful in persuading Katya to meet her. She thought about David. When would she see him again? And when would the bloody man phone?

What was this? She peered more closely at the message relayed across the top of the monitor. 'Urgent!' it read. 'Can anyone speak Spanish to a photographer from Mallorca right now? Phone Phil on ext. 3476.'

Normally these messages were eminently ignorable and were used to fix up leaving parties, organise book sales or to offer freebie travel trips to the staff. But Mallorca? Liz's alarm bells started ringing.

She dialled the extension, heart beating a little faster. 'I can speak

Spanish,' she volunteered to Phil. 'How can I help?'

With relief he switched her to the Spanish photographer, who was delighted to hear his language spoken so fluently. 'I need to talk to Tony Burns but he is out and I am having trouble with the satellite. I have a picture to send and the people in your office do not understand me.'

Liz's scalp prickled. '*Me gustaria mucho de ayudarle*,' she said. 'I will pass on your message.'

The Spaniard carefully explained his problem. It was far worse than she could have imagined. This photographer had been working with a stringer to dig out the admission records of a British woman who had had treatment at the clinic for nervous diseases in Porto Colom, Mallorca, ten years before. The records had eventually been tracked down and the photographer had been able to sneak a picture of the relevant page of the entry book at the clinic. Could she help to sort out the transmission problem?

Liz thought rapidly. Tony would obviously use this information in his campaign to stop her getting the editorship. But she could not interfere with the picture because it would alert Tony to the fact that she was on to him. She would have to think of a better plan. 'I will tell them your problem. Wait a few minutes then try again,' she suggested to the photographer.

Liz contacted the darkroom, explained the situation and said casually, 'By the way, send a duplicate of the print to me, will you?'

When she saw the evidence Tony would be using, she made up her mind about what she was going to do. And soon.

Helen was amazed at how easy it was to persuade Katya to come with her. She did not appreciate that the friends always understood an emergency was just that and they responded fast with no questions asked.

They booked a room in the Royal Imperial Hotel, an immense glass and marble building in Victoria built to mop up the tourist trade. For some reason, it was full of Norwegians, fresh from the fjords, and Texans eager to explore Fortnum and Mason, the upmarket grocers who were holders of a royal warrant to serve the Queen.

Katya had not completely accepted the story about Liz being in trouble. She thought she had convinced Liz that Tom Reeves was not in the frame, but she knew it was just a matter of time before the *Chronicle* discovered that Hugo and Davina Thomas had the lease of the house next door.

She and Davina had been careful never to leave or enter the house together, but Katya realised there was a good possibility that she had been spotted by neighbours. She decided that either Liz really was in trouble or she herself was.

She reassured Helen that she would wait for Liz and, after the secretary was safely on her way back to the office, she phoned her solicitor. 'Where will you be tomorrow? I might be needing you. Something important has come up.'

'Important as in serious?'

'Important as in career-termination.'

'Ah. I'll be riding with the Beaufort Hunt, so take my unlisted mobile number.'

In the taxi en route to Victoria Liz reflected that she had never before deceived Katya. Their conversations were always direct, spontaneous and often in shorthand since they understood each other so well. She could not recall telling Katya even a social lie. Their relationship was founded on trust. If they could not tell each other the truth they avoided saying anything. She regretted asking her secretary to tell Katya that she needed her, that she was in trouble. Still, she justified herself, in a way she was. The editor's job looked as if it was flying out of the window. But if a job could depend on one story, how worthwhile was it?

For a second she considered asking the taxi driver to turn back to the office and letting Katya off the hook. No, that was unwise. And anyway, she rationalised, talking to Katya did not necessarily mean she would sanction the story. This was self-delusion but it was enough to make her sink back in the seat and rehearse what she would say and how she would approach it.

Liz felt more nervous than she could ever remember. She had done showdown interviews with people before of course, in her earlier years as a reporter. Fronting up the potential 'victim' with their so-called misdeeds took courage. But no responsible newspaper would ever publish allegations without giving the person involved the chance to put their point of view, even if it was 'no comment'. The last thing the reporter did when fronting up was mention the real reason for the meeting. They waited until some kind of relationship had been established, however tenuous, or until they had assessed the mood and circumstances of the quarry.

But this was different. Liz knew her subject well. And, worse, her 'quarry' knew her. If the Hugo Thomas story was true, it would eventually come out and tarnish Katya's professional image. It would make working in political circles just that much more difficult. It was unfair, thought Liz, that Hugo Thomas would not have the same career problems, although she did not speculate on what would happen with his wife and family.

But should the story come out now? Through her? And in her newspaper? The story in itself was not so damaging to the government, but it was one more scandal to add to the list. It was a pity that her best friend was caught in the centre of it. And a greater pity that Tony, with his other agenda, would not let her give it up.

The friends had in the past discussed how history would have been changed if ex-President Nixon had had the guts to admit he knew about the Watergate break-in, instead of covering up. There was a good chance, had he done so, that he would have survived and remained President.

The British MP, Winston Churchill Junior, had learned this lesson. When journalists quizzed him about his lover, Soraya Khasoggi, he had immediately admitted his affair with her and survived to keep his marriage intact and his historically important parliamentary presence. And so had the Liberal leader, Paddy Ashdown, nick-named 'Paddy Pantsdown' by the *Sun* newspaper. He had owned up to a brief affair with his secretary after incriminating papers were stolen from his solicitor's office. His speedy confession meant he survived to enjoy a happy marriage and continue to be leader of his party.

Perhaps this would be the best course for Katya.

In the hotel room, Katya was in an anxious mood. She well knew the penalty of having a famous face. Having been shielded into the bedroom by Liz's secretary, she did not want to jeopardise her anonymity now by ordering tea. Hotel staff were paid generous tips to inform newspapers of the whereabouts of celebrities.

There was a knock on the door. It was with relief she opened it to find Liz, breathless from running upstairs.

'Liz, what's the matter? Helen said you were in trouble.'

Liz looked steadily at her. 'Yes, I am in a bit of trouble, and so are you, I think.'

Katya dreaded what she thought she knew was coming next.

'I've something serious to talk about and I wanted to discuss it with you myself. It's about that picture in the mews.'

'Oh, you're not still going on about that?' Katya cut in. 'I told you, I don't know Tom Reeves.'

All ideas of a subtle approach vanished. 'But what about Hugo Thomas?'

'What about him?' Katya stalled a moment. Was it possible Davina was implicating her husband? If only she had returned the calls, they might have been able to work it out.

'Are you and Hugo Thomas having a relationship . . . something, anyway?' Liz burbled nervously.

To Katya's surprise and relief it seemed that Liz still had not guessed the real identity of her lover. Maybe she should let Liz believe it was Hugo? That would be infinitely less damaging than the truth. For all of them, her, Davina and Hugo. She was silent, trying to assess how much Liz really knew.

'Look, Tony Burns has had almost the entire staff working on this story.' Liz was clenching and unclenching her hands. 'He has a signed statement from someone in Roland Mews who has seen you coming out of Number Sixteen, which our reporters say was bought by Hugo Thomas's company. And there's a *Chronicle* reporter at the hospital right now, talking to him. Tony thinks the story will make a great splash for Sunday, the love nest of the TV star and the minister's husband.'

'And what do you think?' Katya was icy.

'Katya, you know that this isn't easy for me either. If it's all going to come out, I can't stop it, even for you. I'm here now because I didn't want to hand it over to that shit. At least let me try to do some damage limitation.'

Katya walked to the window and looked down over the sea of fast-moving heads, all making for Victoria Station. She turned round, eyes fiery. 'How dare you! How dare you presume on our friendship to trick me into coming here so you could stand up your tawdry little story. All that talk about a signed statement and what Tony's found out – you have no real proof of anything and I deeply resent you trying to worm information out of me.' She hated doing this to Liz but she felt totally unprotected. No Davina, no press office or television station to hide behind.

'Worm information out of you? Katya, haven't you understood what I'm trying to say?'

'Leave Hugo Thomas alone.' Katya's voice rose almost to a sob. 'And stop hounding me, do you hear?' For days she had not slept, she was raw, her emotions were on edge. This was all too much. She could not, would not, explain. She grabbed her handbag and rushed from the room.

Outside the hotel, she was uncertain what to do. Passers-by were beginning to stare at the well-known face, trying to place her. It was vital to tell Davina how much the *Chronicle* knew. Where would she be at this time? Katya, distraught, looked at her watch. There was a vague chance that she might still be at her office. In any case, her PA would know where she was.

Katya hailed a black cab and gave the address of the Home Office in Queen Anne's Gate. A few yards away, a man in a black Ford Escort nudged his companion. It was Steve West from the *Chronicle*, sent by his defiant news editor to keep an eye on his editor's movements. He fancied himself as a poor man's Carl Bernstein, the investigative newsman of Watergate fame. 'There she goes,' he told his photographer. 'For God's sake, don't lose that taxi.'

The capital was gridlocked with commuters anxious to get the 6.32 p.m. back to the suburbs. The journey from Victoria to Davina's office could be done in under five minutes in normal conditions but now Katya stared anxiously at the time as they crawled from red light to red light. Reliving the conversation with Liz she was filled with dread. She knew what tabloid newspapers could do with one tiny kernel of information. Even if the *Chronicle* printed nothing more than the picture with a riddle asking why a top TV star was visiting the mews home of Hugo Thomas at that time of night, it would be taken up by every other national newspaper. They would comb over every facet of her life and Hugo's. Their lives would be dredged out, dug into, commented on to find any fact that fitted their version of the story. She, Hugo and Davina would all be under siege. At home, at the television studios, in Whitehall, the House of Commons and Hugo's City office.

Her taxi accelerated through an amber light in front of the forecourt at Buckingham Palace. A policeman stepped into the road, hand aloft, and waved over the pedestrians.

The photographer cursed as a party of Japanese schoolchildren crossed over to stare through the black railings and point at the fluttering flag that indicated the Queen was in residence.

'Fuck it, can you see where her taxi went to?' asked Steve.

'Dunno,' sighed the snapper. 'It didn't go up the Mall, I'm sure of that. We could have a look next left.'

But by then Katya's taxi had disappeared past the bulk of Queen Victoria's statue and into Birdcage Walk. Dispirited, they had to report a failed mission to a furious Tony.

As her taxi swerved into Tothill Street, Katya felt another surge of terror. What if Hugo denied everything and the *Chronicle* found out about her and Davina? The repercussions of that were enormous. Davina was high-profile and therefore a much bigger fish than Hugo. She had real prospects of being promoted into the Cabinet. It was common knowledge that Liz's proprietor was hostile to the government. Liz might want to shield her but Tony would never resist this opportunity to curry favour with his boss who would be delighted to embarrass a prime minister he thought was wrecking the country.

For the hundredth time, Katya chastised herself for going to Roland Mews on an emotional impulse. She had not stuck to their strict secrecy rules and she knew Davina would blame her for this, and here she was planning yet another unexpected meeting.

Although it was a risk, Katya could think of no other way to contact Davina. Like most ministers, she was slightly paranoid about being spied on and believed her calls were monitored by MI5, Special Branch, someone. That was why she had called only twice since the accident and then only for seconds and using a public phone box, so she could not easily be traced.

Katya forced herself to stop thinking of her lover and gave herself a moment to think about her own career. The TV station would hardly be thrilled that their Queen Bee was embroiled in a messy love triangle. But how much worse would it be if the real facts were to emerge?

The homophobia of Britain's media was one of its many hypocritical aspects. A homosexual prospective parliamentary candidate had recently been exposed by one of the red-top tabloids and pilloried in many subsequent stories for his sexual proclivities. He lost the by-election but the irony of it was that Katya and other insiders knew that the man who won the seat was also a homosexual. How the victorious candidate had managed to maintain his secret could be explained quite simply. The loser had been honest about his sexuality. The winner had a wife.

Katya shuddered at the thought of what the papers would do to a pair of such high-profile lesbian lovers. What damage limitation would Liz be able to effect then?

She knew she was taking a great chance coming to Davina's office, but Davina would understand once she knew the danger they were facing. They had to co-ordinate their stories and Davina would have to brief her husband on the line to take.

Her taxi pulled up outside the Home Office. The staff on the evening shift of the twenty-four-hour surveillance team on the reception desk was bored. Friday afternoon was the dregs. The 'Thank God It's Friday' mentality started early in the Civil Service. Few mandarins stayed in their office much after 4.15, apart from a duty office which was staffed round the clock.

The security guard's usual hostile, suspicious demeanour dissolved at the sight of the television star he fantasised over at breakfast each morning. 'Ha-llo, Miss Croft, how very nice to see you. I watch you every morning. I'd never miss any of your programmes. To what do we owe this honour?'

She needed him on her side and flashed him the famous smile. 'Well, I'd like to see Mrs Thomas if she's still here, please. It's for a story.' Don't explain, you fool, she thought.

'I'm not sure, miss. Is she expecting you?'

'No, but she knows what this is about and if you tell her who it is, I'm sure she'll see me.'

Davina was coldly furious when she learned Katya had dared to break all their rules and was waiting in reception without prior warning. It underlined her determination to stick by her decision not to have anything to do with her again. Since Katya had told her about the photograph, Davina had closed off her emotions as easily as putting sticky tape over a shower head.

How had she ever thought they could get away with it? For a few unforgettable months, she and Katya had deluded themselves into thinking they could be different. There was even a short time when she had thought there was a chance they could spend more time together instead of the odd snatched hour. She had believed herself to be in love with Katya, but now her antennae reinforced the sense of danger always present in their relationship. If only she had paid greater heed to it before. But then the danger had been half the excitement.

Well, it was not too late.

At her last meeting with the Prime Minister on Wednesday, he had hinted that the changes he was planning in the forthcoming reshuffle could be to her advantage. Davina's imagination had taken flight. A promotion now could mean she could be Home Secretary if the government won the next election, or Chancellor of the Exchequer or even, why not, Prime Minister one day? Margaret Thatcher had done it from a lesser ministry.

For years, Davina had endured a loveless marriage, getting her satisfaction from her career and her children. She had never really enjoyed lovemaking with men but, discussing this with her university contemporaries from Girton, she learned this was not unusual. Indeed, the only time she had felt real sexual arousal was at a post-exam party at Cambridge, when she danced all night with a mini-skirted history graduate. On the walk back to their rooms, the long-limbed student had cradled her chin and tried to kiss her on the lips. Davina, alarmed by how excited she'd felt, had twisted away and run off, making sure they were never alone again.

Even when she found herself, a virgin, engaged to Hugo, she felt she was playing games, doing what her parents and his expected of her. And he was a great help to her career, a useful adjunct in her climb up the political ladder.

It was three years after the birth of her second child that Davina again felt a sexual urge for another woman which, for the first time, she did not ignore. As a prominent politician she received many invitations to address out-of-town pressure groups and it was when talking to them that she made her sexual contacts. Her affairs were infrequent, discreet and usually short-lived.

When she met Katya she knew it would be different. During the first weeks of their affair neither of them discussed past, present or future. It was the only carefree time Davina had ever known. Always she had conformed to other people's expectations – the exams, the successful husband, the two perfect children, the superbly run house in the constituency. And she was the admired hostess of a distinguished political and business salon blending the best of America, Europe and Westminster.

So why had she been prepared to risk it all for a future with Katya? Why had she thought it would be different with her? She had watched this self-delusion so often in her colleagues and had been surprised to find herself falling willingly into the same trap. One explanation was that the other women had all been less clever, less rich or less well educated. Or all three. Katya was far more her equal. Although not an intellectual she was street smart and gossipy – and very sexy.

Politics and fame were a heady mixture. Top politicians seemed to lose their sense of reality, to fall victim to what her driver called, disparagingly, the 'kitchen foil syndrome'. Cabinet stars, he maintained, could only see their own reflections in each face they met. It was this self-obsession which led them into dangerous waters and she had been about to succumb to the same weakness.

She packed her briefcase and walked into reception, determined and resolute in what she had to do.

'It's a surprise to see you here, Miss Croft,' said Davina formally. 'I'm just off to see my husband in hospital. Suppose you walk with me to the Commons to get my car.'

As they walked towards a near-deserted Parliament Square, Katya almost had to run to keep up with Davina, who was renowned for her half-running gait, a legacy from always trying to be in two places at the same time.

'This is an emergency,' Katya said. 'You know I wouldn't have come here otherwise.'

Davina nodded.

'That picture I told you about, in the mews. Well, Liz Waterhouse has just told me her news desk has identified it as me. But what's worse is they've tracked down the ownership of the house and now they think I'm having an affair with Hugo. And that's what's going to be on the front page in Sunday's paper.'

Davina slowed perceptibly. 'I know.'

'What?' Katya was shaken.

'A *Chronicle* reporter spoke to me about it in the House this afternoon. I denied it, of course.' Davina was at her most icy. Turning on Katya, she asked sharply, 'And what have you told them?'

'I didn't say anything, I didn't confirm or deny it.'

Davina halted abruptly. 'That might turn out to be a great mistake. Surely you know that it would have been far better to have denied everything at once?'

'I couldn't deny it. Liz told me they have a statement from someone in the mews who's seen me coming out of the house.'

'So?' Davina's voice sounded as hostile as if she was addressing an enemy. This was a Davina Katya had only read about in newspaper profiles, the minister who was said to be capable of reducing her senior civil servants to stuttering impotence. 'You must realise that they wouldn't dare print a story like that if you had denied it immediately. If my stint as a newspaper barrister taught me one thing, it's that you can't make allegations like that without foolproof evidence. And they haven't got that, have they?'

'I wish you were right, but newspapers don't bother too much with legal niceties these days. Whatever you think, they've got my name, Hugo's name and the address in the mews, which they can stick together to make up some kind of story.'

'Isn't Liz Waterhouse one of your closest friends? Couldn't you ask her to kill the story?'

'It's not as simple as that. She's not the only one involved.'

Davina waved her pass at the House of Commons policeman. She was such a familiar figure that he gave them just a cursory glance and a half-salute. They took the lift to the underground car park, probably the most expensive garage in the world, where Davina's car was one of only a handful waiting to be collected that Friday evening.

As they climbed into her navy-blue Audi Quattro, Davina took the ignition keys from her bag and started fiddling with them. Her voice rasped in a hoarse whisper. 'Katya, I think you've handled this extremely badly. From now on, I suggest we deal through our solicitors and have no direct contact with the newspapers.'

'That's fine by me,' replied Katya, stung. 'You don't think this is the kind of publicity that's good for my career, do you?'

Davina gripped the leather-bound steering wheel and turned to look at Katya's strained face. 'Your career? A fairly egotistical view, if I may say so. Can I remind you that I might be in line for one of the great offices of State? That's just a little more important, don't you think, than sitting on a sofa in a television studio in the mornings?'

Katya closed her eyes in pain. She was aghast at the apparent ease with which Davina was dismissing their relationship and her problems. She can't really mean what she says, Katya thought desperately, perhaps I'm taking this the wrong way. But she knew she was avoiding reality.

'You don't need to worry about Hugo.' Davina's tone was so curt she could have been addressing a stranger. 'I'll see to it that he denies it in the right way to avoid any further speculation.'

'What do you mean, "the right way"?'

'If he has to decide whether he would prefer to be branded as an adulterer or cuckolded by a woman, I think it's fairly obvious which he would choose, don't you?' Davina reasoned that if it was thought her husband was having an affair, she would get the sympathy vote. If she preyed on Hugo's protective feelings towards their children, he might just see the sense in it. But she would only confess her sexual proclivities to him as a last resort, to avoid the worst publicity – the truth.

'Would he do that for you?'

'No.' Davina gave a wintry smile. 'Not for me, but for the power it will give him, any time he likes to switch it on. And to protect the children.' She was watching Katya's stricken face. 'And think of your part in all this. The public could cope if they thought you had a short-lived affair with a man, now over of course, and that I had generously forgiven you. But I want you to understand that I must never be dragged into this, except as the injured third party. If you ever give any hint of our relationship to your friends, I shall deny knowing you.'

She paused for effect. 'And I shall make sure we never meet or speak again. It will all be over between us.'

'Isn't it over now?' asked Katya softly.

Davina hesitated for a moment. It would be dangerous to alienate Katya totally. At present. She put the key into the ignition. 'Well, it would be foolish for us to meet in the short term but when all this has blown over there's no reason why we shouldn't continue to see each other.' She reached out for Katya's hand. 'Just let's get through all this.'

Katya knew she was lying.

Chapter Fifteen

Katya was pacing up and down Joanna's kitchen. Joanna had never seen her so agitated and was puzzled by the vehemence of her tirade against Liz.

'. . . and I said I deeply resented her trying to trap me into a confession and then I walked out.'

'Trap you? Liz?'

'Yes. She's not even aware she's using that technique, but when you pretend to know more than you do to try to get someone to admit the facts, you're setting a trap.'

As she listened, appalled, Joanna had visions of their friendship disintegrating. 'I can't believe that, Katya. I can't believe she would try to trick you. About what?'

'About my so-called affair with Hugo Thomas. They've got this picture—'

'Liz told me about it. She thinks the woman is you and so do others on the paper.'

Katya hesitated for a moment. 'Well, I didn't tell Liz but, yes, it is me in that photograph.'

'It is? So what were you doing there?'

Katya hesitated for only a few seconds. Was it only a week ago that she was planning a future, albeit secret, with someone she loved? Now she was completely adrift and miserable. She needed to talk. 'I was trying to pick up a message, to get some news. The house does belong to Hugo Thomas but I swear I was not going to see him.'

'Well, who were you going to see?' Joanna confronted her as Katya was about to take her fourth walk round the table.

'Jo, I hate having secrets from you both but don't press me on this.' Her voice rose emotionally. 'I just can't tell you. I can't.'

Joanna held up her palms. 'All right, but if Hugo isn't your lover, just tell Liz and she'll be able to call Tony off the story.'

'Why should I have to convince Liz of anything? She should be on my side.'

'She is, Katya. I had lunch with her today and, believe me, she's torturing herself. She's not trying to trap you at all. She's been wrestling with this for days. And she had nothing to do with the original story. In fact, Tony Burns kept it to himself until it was well on the way.'

'But she's the editor this week. She could have squashed it any time she liked.'

'You know better than that. Once a news desk swings into action, too many people know about it anyway. You can't keep it secret, and even if Liz does stop it at the *Chronicle*, some other paper will pick it up. Try to see it from Liz's angle,' she urged Katya. 'She's within a whisker of getting to the very pinnacle of her profession and Tony's watching everything she says or does. He'd just love an excuse like this, Liz dropping a story for the sake of a friendship – that's not very professional, is it?'

'No, but I wouldn't have done that to her. You wouldn't do that to me . . . to anyone.'

'But TV and mags are softer, Kat. You and I don't often have the problem.' She scratched her hair ruminatively. 'Why on earth didn't you make it clear to Liz immediately that Hugo Thomas wasn't the man?'

'I was too angry.'

'Well, I'll say it again. I think you should tell her. Be logical. If Liz knows, she can call off Tony's hounds.'

'And have them try and find out who I really was seeing? I couldn't bear that. They can't print a story just about me visiting a house late at night, can they?'

'No – but they could do it as a "fancy that" front page splash.' Joanna filled the kettle. She felt exhausted. Maybe some herb tea would revive her and calm Katya. 'Liz is under tremendous pressure with all this but there's also another thing on her mind. Tony's actually got somebody sniffing around the clinic in Mallorca.'

'Oh God!'

'If he finds out about her breakdown, he'll be on the phone to the proprietor before you can cough and Fergus is hardly likely to hand his precious paper over to someone with that in their closet.'

Joanna poured boiling water to make a rosehip infusion and gave a mug of it to Katya. 'Katya, even if your lover is a man we've never heard of, you're still a star. There's still some kind of story, isn't there? Anyway, whoever it is, it can't be that bad, surely?'

Her friend sipped the hot drink gratefully. 'I haven't been thinking straight lately,' she said wearily, pushing her hand through her hair. 'There's such a lot going on and it's beginning to affect my work. Martin's already called me in and given me a warning. They've noticed I've not been concentrating.' She saw compassion, warmth and affection on Joanna's face.

'Come on, Katya, it can't be that difficult. The three of us have been through so much together. I can't believe we can't sort this out.'

'Whatever you say, Jo, I still feel Liz was prepared to use me to get her bloody job.'

'Then tell her that. We've always been completely frank with each other. She needs to know how you feel.'

'I'm not sure I'm ready to talk to her yet.'

'Well, the longer you leave it, the worse it'll fester. We've always tackled our problems at once. Please don't let this blow us apart.'

Katya gave her a cool look. 'Now stop and analyse what you've just said, Jo. Why is this friendship so important? Liz doesn't seem to think so, she's tried to steamroller me to get a lousy story.'

'No, she hasn't. It's not as simple as that. There're a lot of other people involved. If she could have binned the picture, she would have – she is your friend, remember.'

Katya started pacing again. 'I'm not so sure about that, not when her career's involved. Okay, I can see that we've needed one another in the past. When we started out, we didn't know anybody, we didn't know anything.' She wheeled round to face Joanna. 'It's all too complex now, Jo. We've all got these jobs, they've all got their different problems ... Let's face it, it's changing. We're changing.

It's harder to find time to meet and, realistically, once you've had the baby, we'll see each other even less.'

'What are you trying to say, Katya?'

'Perhaps women like us can't really maintain this closeness and we ought to be honest with one another now. Maybe a row like this was inevitable. Perhaps our friendship has reached its sell-by date.'

Joanna put her hand to her forehead and rubbed her temples to try and ease the tension. 'So the first time there's a big problem, you're saying you don't need friends? You think this secret lover of yours is more important than your friendship with Liz and, I've got to say it, with me? You sound so hard, Katya. I don't recognise you.'

Katya did not answer.

'I've told you that Liz has been doing everything she can to protect you and that's the measure of friendship. It's not important how often you see each other or even speak on the phone. It's knowing that when you need someone they're there for you. No ifs or buts. No "sorry I'm just going out". Real friends drop everything to help. Are you saying you don't need this in your life? Is that what you really want?'

The sound of the phone made them both start. Joanna automatically picked it up. It might be George. 'Hello, Liz,' she said and gave a questioning look to Katya, who shook her head vigorously.

'Jo, I've had the most terrible row with Katya and she's rushed out. I don't know where she's gone and I don't know what to do now. Do you know where she is? I'm worried about her and I desperately need to find her.'

Joanna again looked over at Katya enquiringly. Another fierce shake of the blonde head, then Katya slipped out of the room.

'No, I don't know where Katya is.' Jo was not used to lying to Liz. The cracks were widening.

She put down the phone and heard the sound of sobbing coming from the utility room. Katya was weeping like a lost child, sitting on the floor wedged between the washing machine and a basket of freshly laundered clothes.

Joanna pulled her to her feet and cradled her. 'Oh, Kat, don't get upset. I'm sure Liz won't really do anything to harm you. You know that, don't you?'

Katya tried to catch her breath. 'It's not about Liz. Not any more. My affair's over, we're finished. It's all over, Jo, it's all over.' Her sobbing became uncontrollable.

In situations like this, Joanna had learned to be briskly practical. She had spent a week inside a women's refuge for a magazine story and the helpers told her it was the kindest way to force someone on the borders of hysteria to concentrate on what had to be done rather than how they were feeling.

She tore off a couple of sheets of kitchen roll and handed them to Katya. 'Come on, you can cry all you want later. You'll have plenty of time for it. Right now, I need you to tell me what's upsetting you if I'm going to be able to help.'

Katya was trying to gain control of herself. She had been struggling with her emotions for the last eight months, muddled, anxious, excited and joyous in turn, a confusing cocktail which had left her drained and deeply in need of Joanna's calm counselling.

Davina's only thoughts had been for herself and her own career, Katya now realised. She had not once expressed any interest in how Katya was coping. She had offered no words of comfort or support and had shown no concern whatsoever about either her career or her emotional wellbeing. In fact Davina had sneered at her career and called her egotistical for suggesting she was under as much threat from publicity as Davina was. Katya felt badly betrayed. It was hard to accept how little she had meant to Davina.

She turned to Joanna and with a feeling of immense relief she haltingly began to confide in her.

She found it difficult and evaded what was uppermost in her mind. Instead she told Joanna about her past sexual encounters and how hard it had been to maintain any relationship. This was history but Joanna listened patiently. Gradually, what emerged was that Katya put the blame for all her short-lived romances on her own sexual inadequacy. And because of this self-perceived failing none of her relationships had had much of a chance to develop. And frankly, she now told Joanna, she had never been that interested in trying.

'Even with Mike Stanway?'

'I was more in love with the idea of leaving home and going to live in Mallorca than with him.'

'But you've had quite a number of affairs since him, haven't you?'

'Yes, but I never really enjoyed the sex. I know that to people who don't know me I look sexy. But how could I explain that I never felt sexy?'

Until eight months ago. That had been so different. There was no feeling of strangeness. No inhibitions. More important, she had felt sexually at ease, something she had never experienced before.

Joanna listened intently, now and then encouraging her to carry on. 'It sounds like me with George. You've met the right guy,' she said finally. 'What's gone wrong?'

Katya walked to the window. 'It's not that simple,' she said softly.

Her back was silhouetted against the small, square Georgian window, between the white antique lace curtains. She pulled them round her, almost like a shroud.

'You told us he was married. Has he decided to go back to his wife?' asked Joanna.

'No, he's not going back to his wife because . . . my lover is not a he.'

Joanna stared at her back. A *woman*. Katya is in love with a woman? The phrase went round and round in Joanna's mind.

Katya waited for her to speak. In any case, she did not know what to say.

Until then, Joanna had thought she and Liz had been told every aspect of each of Katya's new romances. She recalled vividly her friend's agitation when the new man in her life had not phoned as promised. She could remember shared weekends when all three had gone away with their man of the moment. Like most women, they rarely discussed the details of what happened in bed but certainly Katya gave every impression of enjoying men. And now she had fallen in love, she said, for the first time. With a woman.

Joanna could never imagine this happening to herself or to the friend she thought she knew almost as well as herself. She was taken aback that such an important part of Katya's life should have been kept secret from them. Perhaps Katya was right. Perhaps they had outgrown this friendship.

Joanna felt that some of the foundations of her life were being pushed aside brutally by a large JCB digger. It seemed like for ever before she said, feebly, 'I had no idea.'

'Neither had I. You don't have to say a word. You think I'm appalling, don't you?'

'Of course not. But it's hard for me to take in because you've had so many boy friends.'

'That was what I was trying to explain to you. I always pretended it was fun to go out with them but it meant less than nothing.'

'Even Alain, the one you flew to Paris to try and keep?'

'Easy. I wanted romance, I always liked the theatrical bit, the chat-ups and the talking. I suppose I went out with so many men because I was waiting for someone to turn the magic key. But no one ever did. I always thought I was frigid, asexual. Well, I've found out that I'm not.'

Joanna slid away from the thought of Katya making love with a woman.

Katya was warming to her theme, glad that the dam had burst. 'Apparently Marilyn Monroe couldn't see what all the fuss was about either,' she said. 'A lot of men believe that good-looking women aren't particularly sexy because they're so used to being adored, so busy looking pretty, they barely feel they have to join in. I thought I was like them. But what I could never face up to, or admit to, was that many men actually dropped me rather than the other way round.'

Joanna tried to contain her surprise. She did not fool Katya.

'Yes, I know. I often told you and Liz that I had bust up with someone. It was easier and you believed it anyway. I didn't ever care and I can honestly say I never spent a sleepless second thinking about any of them.'

More deception. Joanna felt she did not know Katya at all. It was almost like listening to a stranger.

'Joanna, does any of this make sense to you?'

'I'm trying to understand, but even if you had no regrets about the men, didn't you feel guilty about putting up such a false front to Liz and me?'

Katya at last turned from the window and sat down opposite Joanna. 'If you think about it, I didn't often have to fib. All I had to say was I wasn't seeing Mike or Richard or Guy any more and you two would just assume that because I joked about them, it was my decision.'

Katya was right. That was exactly what they had thought. There was a time when she had been the slightly wild one of the group, especially in Mallorca. More conventionally attractive than the other two and later on a TV star as well, she seemed to drop into the role effortlessly. In retrospect Joanna felt they had not paid enough attention to Katya's activities. She had been preoccupied with a country wedding to George and then had had two miscarriages in fairly quick succession while Liz had been consumed by her career in Fleet Street. They had thought Katya was behaving like the archetypal liberated woman.

'I didn't understand myself so how could you have done?' Katya went on. 'And I was quite content to let people think I was living a life of sex, TV and rock 'n' roll. I thought this was normal.' She sighed. 'I discussed our friendship with my lover, wondering if I would ever tell you about it.'

Her lover? Joanna sat up with a start. She had a good idea who it was now. Liz had told her that the mews house belonged to Hugo and Davina Thomas. If it was not Hugo, it must be his wife.

'It's Davina Thomas, isn't it?' Katya stiffened. 'I've just worked it out.'

'Well, if I wasn't going to the house to meet Hugo, I suppose it's fairly obvious who I was going to see. But it doesn't matter now. It's finished.' Close to tears, she went on to tell Joanna how she had looked into Davina's eyes and known this was going to be an important person in her life. It had nothing to do with gender and all to do with the individual.

For the first time a sexual relationship had heightened all aspects of her life, giving her the confidence of a woman who was appreciated and loved.

Joanna felt a sadness. Katya was describing exactly how she felt about George. What a pity it had taken Katya so long for such a deep emotion to come into her life. And with such complications.

Katya was describing some of the elaborate arrangements she and Davina had been forced to make to maintain their secrecy, still so necessary in their world. They had to be careful never to be seen together in public, apart from carefully chosen lunch venues. Not so careful, thought Joanna, recalling the journalist at Covent Garden who had mentioned spotting them.

Also, Davina's late-night sittings at the House and Katya's early morning job meant their schedules made it difficult to meet. That was why Roland Mews had been so important to them.

'Katya, I just don't understand how you could've thought that two such high-profile people could have kept their affair under wraps.'

'Well, Davina's managed it before. She had an affair with a writer and a radio presenter, both pretty well-known. Anyway, Davina's in the past. And, Jo, it was all my fault. After I told Davina the photographer had snatched that picture in the mews, she changed totally.'

Joanna was confused. 'It's hardly my place to defend Davina but she must've been petrified of losing her job – or, even worse, losing her children – if people found out about you. Does her husband know about her?'

'I'm pretty sure he doesn't. They lead very separate lives, you know, whatever their newspaper publicity.'

The phone interrupted them. Liz was more desperate this time. 'Jo, I have to speak to Katya, urgently. I've tried everywhere. Can you remember that bloke, Oliver something, the one who came with her to the Magazine Editors' bash? It's a long shot but maybe she's gone to ground with him. Can you remember his surname?'

Again, Joanna looked at Katya to see if she wanted to talk. The head shake warned her off. Joanna told Liz she would persuade Katya to phone if she contacted her.

By now it had grown dark. 'I've got to lie down,' said Joanna, aware that her heart seemed to be beating rather fast.

'Oh God, Jo, there I go again, thinking only about myself. I'm sorry you've got mixed up in all this. Go and lie down and I'll make you another cup of herb tea.' She hesitated. 'Jo, I've been up since four this morning and I'm really tired. I'm sure the reptiles will be doorstepping my place tonight. I'd love to stay here, but perhaps you don't want me to.'

Joanna felt a wave of pity for her friend. She stood up and cradled Katya in her arms. 'Don't be daft. Of course you can stay.'

'Thank you. Oh, Jo, I'm so unhappy. What am I going to do?'

'You're going to do absolutely nothing right now. Go upstairs, you know where everything is,' said Joanna. 'But don't creep away in the morning. Stay here. We need to talk some more.' Somehow she would have to convince Katya to meet Liz and try and heal the rift between them. Why was George away when she needed him to share this emotional burden?

'Joanna?' Katya turned at the top of the stairs and leaned over the banister. 'Thanks. You're right, you know. Everyone does need friends, especially me right now.'

Joanna felt the baby turn in her womb. Oh, thank God. It was the first movement for two days and though this brought her relief she vowed she would definitely arrange to see her doctor again. Tomorrow.

Liz had gone back to the *Chronicle* coldly determined. She had given Katya every chance to tell her the truth, to help her get out of this terrible jam.

Tony was not going to give up and Katya had given her nothing she could use. Though not exactly denying she was in the mews, she had refused to say anything. It would be difficult to resist pressure to go ahead with the story.

Liz asked Tony to come to her office. 'What more have you got on the Katya Croft story?' she asked.

He looked confident. 'Basically we reckon the public image of that pushy politician always accompanied by an adoring husband is way off-beam. The word from those in the know is they're a couple only for photo opportunities. There's not much togetherness after the cameras stop clicking, according to gossip around the House. And with her job, he's had plenty of time to play away.' His eyes narrowed. 'What did *you* find out?' he asked suspiciously.

Liz decided to be economical with the truth. 'I asked Katya outright if she was the woman in the photograph, but she wouldn't either confirm or deny it. And if she's smart, and she is, I reckon she'll be talking to her lawyer by now.'

Which way is the bitch going to jump? thought Tony, studying Liz's expression. She was giving nothing away.

A knock on the door made her pull an irritated face. But she relaxed when she saw it was Bob Howard, who had knock-and-enter status. With two editorships behind him he was one of the few on the staff who brought her solutions not problems. 'Thought you'd like to see this, boss,' he said, slapping down a faxed copy of a phone bill. He allowed himself a rare smile.

It was a British Telecom print-out of an itemised phone bill from an 0171 930 number, the Buckingham Palace area code. 'This is the mews number,' said Bob, pointing to the top of the bill. 'And those calls I've highlighted are all to the same number and it's one you'll recognise even though you usually press a memory button to get it.'

The bill was a recent one over a three-week period. The highlighted number she knew all too well. It was Katya's direct line at Morning TV. Someone at 16 Roland Mews was regularly phoning Katya at work.

Proof. In black and white.

This was the most unsettling part of the jigsaw yet. It confirmed all that the news desk had found out so far and it made it almost impossible for Liz to protect Katya. If only she could show her this evidence Katya might begin to understand why it would be so difficult to kill the story now.

When people referred to Liz as powerful, she shrugged it off. It was not something that occurred to her as she went through her day-to-day existence. But the power was hers. She had the choice whether to publish and possibly destroy people's lives or to hold back and see someone else do it. She now realised what power meant.

'Right, let's get it all written up and show it to the lawyer.'

Tony was amazed. Good God, she was going with it.

'And meanwhile,' continued Liz, 'get all the pictures and we'll do a spread on pages twelve and thirteen as well if the story works.'

She turned to leave, then swung round again. 'At the moment it's a riddle story, isn't it? I think we'll have to go with a denial from her, though it could be superseded if we get a statement from her lawyer. And we'll have to front up Hugo. That's essential. What I'd like to know is why he would choose to have an affair in a house owned by himself and his wife. Find out who pays the council tax.'

The newsroom was frantic. The picture desk had brought in every print of Hugo and his family, Hugo when single, Hugo out with the hunting and shooting set, and bulging files of pictures of Katya.

When they were all collated, the art editor started on a layout, knowing that the picture editor, whose brain worked like an encyclopedic picture library, would be bound to have suggestions of his own. Not to mention Liz's ideas, particularly with this story.

The reporters, Debbie, Mac, Alec and Andrew, the political editor, were tapping out their information as fast as they could on their computers. This would all be drawn into one main story. The *Chronicle* star reporter, Barry Donlan, would 'put it through his machine' to give it his special gloss.

In her office Liz was keeping tabs on their work through her computer, as well as checking up on the other stories for the news sections. The urgent feature proofs were waiting on her desk. Helen appeared at the door. 'It's a David Linden. He says you know him.'

Liz smiled. 'Get a number and I'll phone him in five minutes.' But when she did, two hours later, there was no reply.

At 7.30 p.m. she had another positioning conference. This was when the paper's top executives worked out what would go where. The first nine pages were always left till last but promotional blurbs for page one and stories for pages eleven to nineteen were given a rough position. This was so that the sub-editors could get working on the stories, making sure the facts were correct and the lengths were what the layout demanded. At the moment the best candidate for the splash on the front page was the Croft story.

After conference Liz again phoned David. Still no reply. Bastard. Why hadn't he waited? She tried Katya again and left a message for her to call urgently. Where was everybody? She then rang Joanna.

Success. A real person. 'Joanna, this place is buzzing with that story about our mutual friend. It's got a momentum behind it that I'm going to find difficult to stop. I have to speak to her now. Do you know where she is? Have you heard from her?'

'Yes,' said Joanna slowly. 'Actually she's upstairs, fast asleep. And whatever you say, I'm not going to wake her up.'

'Jo, do you realise how urgent this is? At the moment it's our splash and I need to talk to her about it, *now*.'

'Well, I'm sorry but it will have to wait till morning. She's tired out and if you force the issue now, I'm telling you she won't say anything.'

'All I want is for Katya to explain it to me.'

'Liz, can't you ever take no for an answer?'

'God, Jo. I'm trying to protect her and it's very difficult, I can tell you.'

'Well, I'm sorry. Look, she's not going anywhere so why don't you come round here first thing in the morning? It's been a tense evening,' continued Joanna, 'and I don't feel one hundred per cent.'

Liz felt remorse. This was all such a strain on Jo too. 'I'm sorry, Jo. Fine, I'll come round early on the way to the office.'

By 9 p.m. the editor's office was filled with various executives who came in to talk and have a glass of wine. They all discussed the possible splash they had and started a book about how many extra copies the *Chronicle* would sell. If they could prove a love affair, the consensus was it would be between 35,000 and 50,000.

'Better check with production that we've enough supplements to go round,' Liz instructed Bob Howard.

'Charlie'll have a heart attack out there in Palm Beach,' laughed Geoff. 'He hates holidays and this'll prove to him he was right never to leave the office.'

'I reckon Charlie'll be having a really long holiday from now on,' said Andrew Cahill. 'The *Chronicle*'s due for a new broom.' He was addressing someone else but looked straight at Liz.

She raised her glass and smiled back at him. What would they say if they knew Fergus was considering her not for the *Sunday* but for the *Daily Chronicle*?

Chapter Sixteen

When Joanna woke she could hear creaks coming from the hundred-year-old pine floorboards as Katya tried to move quietly around the kitchen.

The kettle was boiling and there were sounds of cupboards gently opening and closing. Joanna made a supreme effort to pull herself out of bed. She had slept very little and longed to turn over and go back to forgetfulness. But without her, Liz and Katya's quarrel might fester on.

Of the three women, Joanna was by far the most temperate. Over the years she had often found herself having to calm the more extravagant natures of her friends. Her parents had had such ear-splitting, violent arguments that in adult life she would do anything to keep the peace. Raised voices distressed her. It was no accident she had married a mild-tempered man.

The other two had been brought up in a far more competitive, pressured atmosphere. In Liz's case she had a father who constantly exhorted her to try harder, get further. Her experiences at the sharp end of a relentless parent inured her to explosive sounds of rows and a barrage of bitter accusations. Once, after she had achieved ninety per cent in an English exam, her father had shouted at her, 'What was it that you did wrong?' When she was chosen from 600 girls to play the second female lead in a major school play, his only comment was: 'It's no good if you're not number one.' Not surprisingly Liz always reacted badly against sarcasm and irony.

Katya meanwhile had been stifled by her parents' possessiveness. They stuck together mainly because of her and she thought that at least the high level of decibels and the multiplicity of languages (at least three) during rows gave it a certain honesty.

Consequently they or anyone else could shout and scream at Katya as much as they liked and she rarely reacted. It had been good training for television directors who yelled down her earpieces.

The noises in the kitchen continued. Joanna wrapped herself in the thick towelling robe George had given her for Christmas and went slowly down the narrow winding staircase.

She was pleasantly surprised to hear Katya quietly talking to Liz on the phone. She must have made the call as there had been no sound of ringing. That was a good sign.

She heard them arranging to meet here in half an hour. Perhaps the chasm between them could be bridged after all.

Katya put down the phone and turned a pale, anxious face towards Joanna. 'I decided during the night that I needed to sort this thing out now,' she said softly. 'I hope I'm doing the right thing.'

Joanna was not certain exactly what the right thing was. She tried to put herself in Katya's place. The temptation to try and bluff things out was enormous. At least if they were all together, face to face, they might be able to talk over the problem sensibly and, hopefully, without rancour. However, when thirty minutes later she looked out of the window and saw Liz's unusually worried expression, she wondered if it was wise for them to get together so soon. Perhaps Liz and Katya, like friends who know each other too well, were too close to discuss some emotional things rationally.

Liz wasted no time on preliminaries. 'I'm really sorry all this has happened. Believe me, it's the last thing I wanted. I'm not going to try and divert blame but as I said yesterday, the news desk had gone a long way down the road on this story before I became involved. And they're still working on it.'

Katya snorted. 'Who's the bloody editor, Liz?'

'Yes, technically I could order them back to the office,' Liz admitted. 'The reporters in Roland Mews. The people outside Hugo's hospital. The ones trying for a quote from Davina. But what excuse could I give them?'

'I know, I know,' interrupted Katya, an impatient edge to her voice. 'I can give you the excuse. Here it is.' She took a deep breath. 'I am not now having, nor have I ever had, or ever will have, an affair with Hugo Thomas.' She paused, wanting the words to sink in fully. Then she added, 'I give you my solemn word on that.'

Liz was silent for only seconds, then some of the tension in her face dissolved. She was relieved, but her voice was still puzzled as she said, 'Oh, thank God. That's the best news I could've had, even though it leaves a helluva hole in the paper. But,' and her strong features crumpled into a frown, 'that shit Tony won't let it rest there. I won't be able to stop him ferreting around until he finds out who it is you *are* having an affair with. He's got hold of an itemised phone bill from the mews house, for God's sake.'

Katya knew Liz was right. She had done a great deal of thinking throughout her sleepless night and had come to the same conclusion. Tony would get all the resources he needed, with or without Liz's approval. Liz had told her how keen Fergus was to produce some fresh scandal about the government, and though they thought this story did not directly affect an MP, he would see its potential for harm.

She had a choice. Bluff it out. Take the risk that the reporters would not uncover the truth, although the longer the papers had to chase up the story, the more likely it was that they would find people who had seen her at the mews. But that proved nothing, did it? She could not be sure. She could get the TV station's best lawyers to try and stifle the case. Or she could test a twelve-year loyalty and tell Liz the whole truth and hope that her friend would suggest a way for the real story to be buried, for ever.

She reminded herself of the countless occasions when Liz had been her firm and unswerving protector, overseeing the publicity so necessary to her career. She remembered how Liz had saved her from embarrassing revelations when she was to be the subject of the popular TV programme *This Is Your Life*; Liz had diverted one of the programme's more zealous researchers away from the details of her promiscuous time in Mallorca. As Liz later laughed with Katya, the stage would have been too small to hold all the 'very close friends' she had made out there.

And now, the way Liz had responded so far helped to make up her mind. Katya pushed herself up from the kitchen chair. 'I know you can find out who I was going to see,' she started, sounding calmer than she felt. 'I'll be taking a great risk if I tell you the name of my lover but you and I have helped each other avoid so many problems in our lives . . .' her voice trailed away and Joanna thought she was about to cry again, 'that I wanted to ask you if you could help me, as a friend. Not an editor.'

Joanna winced, knowing this would put any editor in an awkward position. She was not surprised when Liz sounded a little hostile. 'Look, Katya, I'll do what I can and I want to help. But you're putting me on the spot.' Liz paused to marshal her thoughts. 'I will give you this promise. Although I can't – and won't – hinder any investigations, whatever you tell *me*,' and she emphasised the word, 'will be confidential. But I can't absolutely guarantee that we won't get the story from another source. You know how this business operates.'

Katya nodded. 'I do,' she answered. 'It's why I'm prepared to take an enormous gamble with my life and career because,' she sighed, 'it's far more serious than you think.'

Before she could continue, Joanna broke in. 'Liz, I know what Katya has to tell you. This is the time when you have to decide what your priorities are.' Knowing what Katya's bombshell was, she felt a growing alarm. She had barely been able to stop thinking about it. 'Is today's headline, however big the story, worth sacrificing your friendship for? Not only with Katya, because anything you do will affect all of us. You know how important loyalty is to us.'

Liz put her hands over her ears. 'For Christ's sake, Katya, don't tell me another word, then if your story comes out, I can't be blamed.'

Despite the tension, Joanna and Katya gave a tentative smile. This was Liz's stock remark when facing trouble. All three knew that she only half meant it.

Katya made a decision. Now that the moment had come, she felt it was not going to be as difficult as she had feared. She did not feel the need for any build-up or elaborate background. Encouraged by Joanna's sympathetic reaction the night before, she hoped Liz would respond in the same non-judgemental way.

'The reason I've been so secretive is that . . .' she hesitated and Joanna glanced at her encouragingly, 'I've been having an affair not with a man but with a woman.'

The proverbial pin would have sounded like a cannonball. Liz was incredulous. 'You? Having an affair with a woman? Come on, be serious.'

It must have been the strain of the last few days but Katya found herself laughing helplessly, which set off Joanna, who started giggling hysterically.

'What's so funny?' Watching them, Liz began to have a horrible feeling that the joke was on her.

Gulping air, Katya explained the background, carefully leaving out the identity of her lover.

Despite herself, Liz felt a thrill of excitement. The hair at the nape of her neck seemed literally to tingle. The part of her brain that was the journalist thought, what a great splash! Think what a paper, nowadays any paper, tabloid or broadsheet, would do with the story of British TV's favourite sweetheart having a lesbian affair.

Katya gave her the central details of the affair and Liz, a life of interviews behind her, did not interrupt once until her friend faltered at the end and then she put in just one word.

'Who?'

'Davina Thomas,' replied Katya, without hesitation.

Liz could not help it. Her mouth dropped open. 'I can't believe it. It can't be.' She looked slowly from Katya to Joanna who nodded soberly. My God, the story got better and better. 'But I don't understand, Kat,' Liz found herself saying. 'You've had so many men.'

'I think that was part of the problem.' Katya smiled ruefully.

'But we've shared bedrooms, beds even, and lived together for months on end.' Liz still couldn't believe what she was hearing. 'You've never given even a hint of this.'

'You don't understand, Liz.' Now that she had told her secret, Katya was quite calm. 'I can't blame you, how could you understand? I didn't, at first. It's really quite simple, I suppose. I fell in love. It was a chemical reaction to a particular person who just happened to be a woman.' Her voice was soft. 'She's one of the most exciting, dynamic and vibrant people I've ever met. I loved being with her and we were serious about each other. We were trying to plan some kind of life together.'

'What?' Liz had not meant to shout.

'Oh yes, we knew how difficult it would be,' Katya continued, 'but Davina and Hugo have lived pretty separate lives for years, despite the happy minister and devoted hubbie façade. They live in a large place in Lord North Street but both of them own that little house in the mews and Davina uses it as her bolt hole. She and I have been meeting there since the spring.'

'And you kept it a secret all that time, even from us?' Liz could not help sounding hurt.

'What else could I do? Davina was paranoid about anyone knowing about us. I would have told you both eventually, I promise, when things were settled.' Katya paused and tears welled up. 'As they are now.'

'What do you mean?' asked Liz.

'As soon as Davina heard about the photographer taking my picture outside the mews house, she broke it all off. Ended it. *Pointe finale.*' Katya's face showed her pain. 'And in the most ruthless way. She didn't give a stuff about what I was going through and how it might affect me or my career. Oh God. She was so callous, so detached. It was a side of her I'd never seen before.' She shivered at the memory.

Liz put an arm round her shoulders. 'She's certainly tough when she's interviewed.'

'But that's her professional face.' Katya was fighting to keep her voice even. Tears were close. 'We used to laugh about it. In private she was never like that with me, until yesterday. At first I thought it was Hugo's accident that had changed her feelings. But now I'm certain it's more to do with her career. She has huge ambitions, you know.'

'Come on.' Joanna was sceptical. 'Everybody in politics thinks they should be prime minister. Getting there is a different matter.'

'She may not be totally singing in the moonlight,' objected Katya. 'The word is she's in line to be promoted in a cabinet reshuffle next week. And she thinks that's just the beginning.' She drained her coffee even though it had gone cold. 'She's only forty-two and if she's lucky and as ruthless as I know she can be, I can't see anything stopping her becoming our second woman prime minister.'

Liz stood up. She had just noticed the time on Joanna's prized old school clock hanging on the wall behind her. 'We've so much to discuss and I hate to go but I must get back to the office and pull Tony off the Hugo story.' There was no hint on her face of how difficult that was going to be.

'So what will you do about all this?' Joanna was looking anxiously at her.

Liz gave her a quick hug. 'Nothing. Absolutely nothing.'

Katya went limp with the relief of it all.

'Look, I must warn you,' Liz said gently, 'we might not do the story, but people in newspaper offices talk. Somebody's seen you in the mews, many people have seen that photograph, so they're bound to speculate about your love life.'

Katya was on firmer ground. 'The last thing Davina said to me was that if all else failed she thought she could persuade Hugo to say that he and I are having an affair.'

'So he knows his wife's a lesbian?' asked Liz.

'No, no. But if the story does surface and she has to tell him, she's banking on the fact that he'll want to protect the children. And his own reputation, of course.'

'I suppose it's preferable to be known as an adulterer than as a man whose wife prefers women,' interjected Joanna. 'If this ever came out, Davina's career would be over, wouldn't it?' she added.

Katya was thoughtful. 'She doesn't think it will come out through Hugo. He's far too traditional and worried about the City and his Club. No, she's always been petrified about some woman she suspects knows the truth about her. That was why she was always so neurotic about security.'

'What woman?' Liz's instincts were to shake every last detail out of Katya but she forced herself to sound calm.

'She would never tell me, but it was connected with those leaks behind the political resignations about the sex scandals. Davina thinks it's the same woman, and she thinks she knows who it is.'

Liz sat down again. 'Knows who it is? Well, who?'

'She'd never tell me. All she would say is that the woman works in the House as secretary to her husband.'

'You mean she's the wife of an MP?' Joanna exclaimed.

271

'Yes. Davina hinted he's in a neighbouring constituency in Warwickshire.'

'Which one?' Liz could feel the excitement build. If she could track down the mole . . .

'I don't know. She trusted me on most things but on this she said the less I knew, the better.'

Liz thought furiously. 'It shouldn't be too difficult to narrow it down. Rack your memory,' she implored, 'and tell me every single thing you can.' She looked at her watch. 'There isn't much time but if I can stand it up, it'll make a good splash, a great splash. And for HMG reasons, better than you and your girl friend.'

'HMG?'

'High Moral Ground.'

But try as she might Katya was not able to help much more. All she knew was that this woman had worked with one of Davina's past lovers and Davina was not sure how much she had been told about their relationship.

'One thing I am certain about, nothing unnerved Davina quite like this woman did. She was terrified of her. She said the woman was ruthless and if she ever knew about us, she wouldn't hesitate to use the information against her.'

'You mean there's someone who knows enough to bring Davina down?' Liz was surprised.

'Well, Davina mentioned her every time there was a scandal in the press. Only last month she became jittery when you did that three-in-a-bed defence story.'

Joanna asked, 'If you can stand this up as a splash, Liz, do you think this woman would talk about Davina? And would that lead to Katya?'

Liz jumped up. 'I doubt it. Once she'd been rumbled she wouldn't dare. Whichever party she's in, their machine would really have it in for her. Neither party wants personal crap all over them. They're all frightened, so many of them have something personal to hide in the cupboard. Anyway, it takes weeks to stand these stories up. And I still have to get Tony away from Katya, Hugo and the so-called mews love nest.'

Before Liz went back to the office, she gave them some serious advice. 'Katya, you know what'll happen now, and, Joanna, you'll be involved too because they know you're our friend. Sit tight, don't speak to anyone. They will ring and say it's an emergency or your mother or your father. They'll even try and pretend it's me on the phone. The only person to speak to is me. And George – you'd better warn him this is going on. Warn your parents too, Katya. They're a soft target, someone is bound to go for them. We need a code word so nobody can pretend they're phoning on my behalf, something only we will know.'

'Constantia,' said Joanna. 'You've heard so much about my delightful home town, let's make use of it.'

Liz nodded. 'If you leave here, please let me know where you will be. I'll have to go now but I'll get back to you as soon as I can.'

On her car phone, Liz contacted Andrew Cahill, as well as Stacey's, a Midlands news agency covering the Warwickshire area. Let the game begin, she thought.

After Liz left, Katya put her head in her hands. 'I'm so lucky to have you two as my friends,' she said.

Joanna put her hand on Katya's shoulder. Why did she still feel uneasy?

Chapter Seventeen

Fergus was entertaining twenty carefully chosen house guests at his pale pink turn-of-the-century villa at Cap Ferrat. It was set on the Côte d'Azur's most expensive promontory, where no property with more than two bedrooms was worth less than £2 million.

It was Fergus's weekend way of mixing business prospects with pleasure. His guests thought they had gone to heaven. After a journey to Nice in Fergus's private jet, they were taken by boat to a jetty below the house.

The villa looked out over the sea: on the left, in the distance, the skyscrapers of Monte Carlo were just visible, and on the right it had a view of the cupolas and terracotta-tiled roofs of the *belle époque* skyline of Villefranche.

The hot sun warmed the narrow lap pool, suitable for just one serious swimmer to swim stamina-building lengths. Of the three pools, this one was nearest to the house. Alone, Fergus was doing his morning work-out. The children's pool and the family pool next to the gymnasium with its adjustable table left pre-set for his daily massage were all designed to blend with the architecture of the house.

Guests were impressed by the grandeur and elegance of every detail of their surroundings, from the iroko wood chaises longues outside the huge house, strategically laid out on stone-flagged terraces, to pool boys, and manicured lawns kept green with sprinkling systems which automatically switched on at 8 p.m. each evening.

His wife had imported a pair of peacocks when they first acquired the villa. Now every summer she and the children would spend an edgy month with Fergus. Guests rarely mentioned to their hosts that the shrieks of the birds awoke them at dawn. They did not need to.

The following year when his family returned, the peacocks were still there, but silent. His wife suffered that way too.

In such a glamorous, meticulously run household, guests were at first puzzled by the array of bottles and canisters of insect repellent of every shape and size ranged on a silver salver alongside the exquisitely cut-glass flutes set out for the pre-dinner champagne. It was only the next day they learned how necessary the insect repellents were when they discovered dozens of mosquitoes had given them pink, itchy bumps everywhere from their calves to their necks.

Fergus completed his daily thirty lengths in the fifty-metre lap pool that he reserved solely for himself. He could hear the sound of laughter and happy shouts in three languages from his guests in the family pool but before he allowed himself to join them, he went to what he called his South of France office. Here in a corner of his private terrace by his own special pool was all he needed: a mobile phone and a fax. What made it even more perfect was that most of it was tax deductible.

He pressed the recall button on his telephone. It was picked up instantly under the grey skies of London in the *Chronicle* newsroom.

On Saturdays, it was the custom for the Sunday paper to move down a floor to the *Daily Chronicle*. More space, extra terminals and an electronic picture desk meant a quicker turnaround of proofs, pages and copy, so vital on press day. Here the banks of desks were arranged so everyone was within shouting distance, absolutely essential because decisions had to be made fast and senior executives on news needed to know simultaneously what was going on.

The line of command was clear. Power focused on the back-bench row of desks, parallel and directly in front of the news editor. At the far left sat the chief sub. Next to him – or, very occasionally, her – sat the production editor, in charge of the sub-editors who ensured that articles would fit into the page layouts.

Centre stage sat the day's editor. On her, or usually his, right was the deputy editor, and next to him the copy taster who constantly

checked the wires of Press Association, Reuters and other international news-gathering organisations.

Liz usually liked getting in early on Saturdays and had an elaborate Saturday morning ritual which gave her a relaxing start and at
the same time enabled her to read all the overnight proofs, listen
to the *Today* programme on BBC Radio Four and read through all
the Saturday papers thoroughly before leaving home. These days
she also kept an eye on Sky TV News and CNN. Her aromatherapy
bath was a mixture of essential oils of lavender and grapefruit,
supposed to produce a calming beginning to the day. When the
newsroom was in full swing at 3 in the afternoon, the bath was just
a distant memory but it usually got Liz off to a good start.

This was the first Saturday she had ever been in sole charge, so
Tony was amazed when she had not appeared by 10 a.m. Every
other Saturday she had beaten him to her desk.

Equally surprised was Fergus Canefield, who was in the habit of
phoning the editor first thing every day from wherever he was in
the world.

'No,' reported Tony, 'I'm afraid she's not here yet. But don't
worry, we already have a very good story for page one.' And he
outlined the Hugo Thomas/Katya Croft splash.

Fergus was happy. The story was a good seller and the ultimate
plus was that it sounded as if it would have strong reverberations
for the government. Hugo Thomas was only connected to the scandal by marriage but MPs' sex squalls muddied the water of public
opinion.

Fergus then rattled off a series of questions about other political
stories as well as asking for news of stories in the City section
before abruptly ringing off.

Tony was doubly pleased. Now the proprietor knew about the
Croft story it would be much harder for Liz to pull out. And he
felt the proprietor had liked the succinct way he had told him about
the splash.

Liz hurried into the lift ten minutes later. The doorman gave her
a special salute. This was the day. The first time she would edit
the newspaper.

Alone in the lift, she thought, this might have pleased even Dad.

From his point of view it would have been the wrong paper but she could just imagine the pride in her mother's face.

Then reality hit her. In a few minutes, she would have to dismantle half the paper and stand up the tip from Katya in spite of the fact that she already had a splash that would reverberate around the country. But she had given her word. Mentally she shook herself. Get thee behind me Satan.

Thank heavens she had caught Andrew Cahill at home and instructed him to brief Mac about what they were to do, and to stay out of Tony's way; he could send his junior, a young political reporter, in his place. And Stacey's were already in place. Thank heaven the *Chronicle* had a good relationship with the regular Midlands news agency they used in Warwickshire.

Walking briskly through the newsroom, she felt the familiar surge of excitement listening to the hum of computer terminals, people discussing page proofs over large cups of tea, the phones ringing incessantly. It was this extreme change of pace that made Saturdays on a Sunday newspaper the best day of the week. Other days were just a rehearsal. This was the day for decisions, right or wrong. You had to stop talking about stories and write them. Fast.

More than half of the *Sunday Chronicle*'s ninety-six pages had to go to press before 5.30 p.m. Liz thanked God that so many of them were sport. Even so, there was little time for tactful diplomacy and not much chance to deal with long, reasoned debates or irritating management memos. This was journalism at the coal face.

On the back bench, several executives were discussing the running order of 'the book'. By a Saturday, the book meant the dummy version of the newspaper. The proofs were made of much whiter, thicker and better quality paper than newsprint, which turned the dummy into a thick manual. Hence its name.

Fanned out across the desk Liz would use today were the *Chronicle*'s colour magazine, the Review, the London supplements, the Scottish and the finance sections, all pre-printed. They were there as an *aide mémoire*. If any of the subjects dealt with in those sections were going to be featured in the news pages, cross-references would be inserted in the paper. Making sure none of the articles clashed was becoming almost a full-time job.

Unaware that the splash was about to be killed, Tony, the art editor and one or two of his cronies on the sub-editor's bench were playing about with a headline that would fit across the front page. Few outsiders realised that many words still survived in the English language only because of their usefulness to headline writers. The average width of a tabloid headline was under thirty centimetres. It was impossible to get more than twelve letters across the front page in a size large enough to make an impact on the news stands. So words like 'slur' were used instead of 'incriminate' or 'blacken'; 'shun' instead of 'avoid' with its space-consuming 'D', and Maggie instead of Margaret, a diminutive that the former Prime Minister had never been called by colleagues or family.

It was always a matter of great pride to be the one who thought up the front-page headline. Bottles of champagne were often wagered on it.

As she reached the back-bench command centre, Liz realised how late she was and asked Tony to call conference at once. Behind her back, he muttered softly so she would not hear, 'What kept you? Your hair or your nails?' He exchanged smirks with the news editor, one of many diehards in the office who had great difficulty reporting to a woman. They both felt she had moved up the 'easy' way, through features and not hard news.

Liz felt how lonely the editor's job was as she walked up the long corridor to the conference room. Who could she confide in now? No one. Not even her experienced number three, Bob Howard. She entered the room to silence and looked round the crowded table at the greying masculine heads and vowed to promote more females into executive positions if she was confirmed as editor.

She would never be forced, as the *Independent* was at its launch, to 'rent a female' when the television companies asked to film their first news conference. Two women were pulled off the secretarial desks and 'promoted' for a couple of hours to give a better impression of equality.

In her conference room, Liz told her team, 'We'll talk about the splash in a minute. Let's go through the rest of the list.'

The news editor went painstakingly through his schedule and Liz commented on several items, suggesting different angles to the stories and also ideas for photographs. The foreign editor followed. The City editor had a tip-off which he suggested would feature better on the news pages. The sports editor gave a lengthy explanation as to why the front of the 'book' had to be on time because he had a batch of late match results. On a Saturday this was vital information, at least for male readers. If the news section missed their deadline by only a few minutes this would delay sport and could mean missing vital production schedules, essential for the complicated timetable used by the circulation department's fleet of vans and trains taking the papers to the far corners of the country. It was vital for circulation building that sports reports hit their target areas. Newcastle was not much interested in Manchester's matches and Birmingham did not care who won in Liverpool. For sport, even national newspapers needed to be local.

'That should be no problem,' asserted the news editor, 'because we already have a splash.' This was the moment, and Liz had been dreading it. She knew the effect her next words would have on the team.

'I'm afraid we don't have the splash,' she announced to the conference, sounding more confident than she felt. 'We have to kill the Hugo Thomas story.'

'What?' Tony jumped up, then quickly forced himself down again. He knew it. The bitch was going to protect her bloody friend. 'What lies has Katya Croft been telling you to persuade you to do that?' His tone was contemptuous. 'The whole thing holds together perfectly and even if she denies it when we front her up, you can't pretend that's not her in the picture.'

Liz stared at him with dislike. 'I have irrefutable proof,' she said, enunciating every word, 'that Katya Croft and Hugo Thomas are not, repeat *not* having an affair. And never have had.'

The executives shifted awkwardly in their seats.

'That's what Katya Croft says, I suppose,' Tony sneered. 'Well, she would, wouldn't she? We can't let that story go, Liz, it's the splash and a spread. And,' he was getting more and more excited, 'we've got a quote from someone in the mews and Barry's down at the hospital now trying to get to the husband. Also we've got that cloak she's wearing in the picture positively identified as the one,' he paused, 'you lent to your friend.'

Liz was icy. 'I'm well aware of all that. But I'm telling you we're on the wrong track.'

Tony's face reddened. 'Look, everyone round this table knows that Katya Croft is your best friend. But it's a bloody good story by anybody's standards and you should never let your personal feelings interfere with that.'

'I want you to get this straight, Tony. I'm killing the story for one reason and one reason only. It is not true. It would cost us a great deal of money in a libel suit if we were irresponsible enough to go with it. While I'm acting editor, that's the way it's going to be. Is that understood?'

In the embarrassing silence that followed her words, Tony stared sullenly at her. The rest of the staff looked none too happy either.

Liz went back to the news list. 'Let's look at this again. This story about the Home Secretary's wife.'

'We've been working on it all week.' The news editor broke the tension. 'And it's come good this morning. You were right, Liz. She is ill, she's in the early stages of Alzheimer's. The interview's coming in at the moment but I'm told she's been quite candid and we've also got quotes from her old man. I've asked the medical correspondent to do a piece as well.'

'But that isn't a splash,' Tony interjected quickly. He was not letting her off the hook.

'No,' agreed Liz, 'but it's an exclusive, and a good lead for page five.'

She went back to the news list. 'This arms story could make a splash, couldn't it? Or if you could harden up this one about the American presidential candidate's British love-child, that would certainly work. And what about you, Mike? How are we going with the money tussle between the millionaire designer's first family and his second?'

Liz listened, made some suggestions then told them, 'I have another idea for the splash. Andrew and Mac are working on it for me with Stacey's in Warwickshire. Tony, I'll tell you the details in my office in a minute.'

Now she had given the conference her decision, Liz pushed aside her personal dilemma and switched into professional mode.

Before she spoke to Tony, she wanted to contact Peter

MacLennan on his mobile in Warwickshire and Andrew Cahill down in the library where she had asked him to sift through old clippings about Midlands MPs and their wives.

Mac sounded pleased. 'We've done quite well. You'll never believe this. We thought it was an opposition dirty tricks campaign but it's beginning to look as if that doesn't add up.'

'What?'

'Well, it's like this. Andrew told me which four constituencies to concentrate on. Two are government, two are opposition. Okay. So I went for the opposition first. They were closest and seemed the obvious choices, especially Malcolm Pickett's wife. He hates the government. But I've confirmed that Mrs Pickett doesn't work for her husband any more. She's only been to the House twice in the last year. I get the impression the marriage is going a bit wrong. She's working locally now. So I don't think it's her. Then I tried Nigel Carter's wife, but she's a teacher at the nearby comprehensive. I've only ever seen her at election time. Couldn't be her.'

'So what are you saying, Andrew? That the leaks come from the government side?'

'Looks like it.'

'But why should a wife try to scupper her husband's own Party? It doesn't make sense.'

'I know, but both of these government wives really do work as their husbands' secretaries in the House of Commons so I should check them out, shouldn't I?'

'Yes, of course. That's dynamite if you can stand it up.'

'I won't have time to tackle both of them so I'll send Stacey's round to the Davidsons. I'm on my way to see the Burroughs now.'

'All right, ring me by one for sure.'

Andrew's time in the library tracking them down had been well spent.

Liz could not believe that any woman married to an MP in the government could be leaking stories about her husband's colleagues. What would be the point? She had heard of disgruntled spouses grumbling about Westminster's long hours and mediocre salaries but that seemed like paltry reason for such treachery. When she read the cuttings on the two suspects, she was even more doubtful. The two remaining wives were pillars of society, married to attractive backbenchers in their early fifties. Both MPs had entered the House three elections ago and were well regarded by their peers.

As a last throw she wondered if the three former cabinet ministers who had been so savagely exposed recently had any idea who might have done this to them. The usual suspects, the mistresses, had not pointed a finger. They had not even asked for money. It was going to be difficult to identify the mole in time for production deadlines and Liz began thinking the unthinkable.

In spite of her promise to Katya, she was still waging an inner battle. Katya's story was salacious, not Liz's favourite type at all; she preferred long investigations which exposed wrongdoing – but even so it was special.

Liz started to fidget with the ends of her fingers, a compulsive habit of hers when she was overwrought. It did not matter to her that one of her best friends was a lesbian but it was a very different proposition for her as a journalist.

Charlie Mays had once warned her that editors should never make friends or promises. 'It's very difficult if you get close to people and then have to shaft them,' he had told her.

How right he was. She hated herself for feeling like this, but what if nothing else came her way? Would it be worth sacrificing her friendship with Katya and Joanna? By even asking the question, she had not quite closed the door. She could publish the story quoting sources close to Davina Thomas without attributing the facts to Katya. But how to stand it up without writing the story herself?

She would go out on the floor, look at the paper's progress and then see Andrew and Tony.

She had given her word she would not publish. Was she strong enough to keep that promise?

Tony was venting his anger and frustration on the hapless hacks on the news desk. Only a minute after ordering a call to Washington, he screamed at one of them, 'I fucking told you it was urgent. Why haven't you got Gordon on the phone yet?' And without waiting for an explanation, he shouted, 'When I say now, I mean *now*, not next Wednesday fortnight.'

He was critical of the home lead stories, loudly sending reporters back to their sources, while making heavy weather of rewriting the intro on the rather dull tale filed by their royal correspondent.

On the picture desk, Geoff took yet another phone call from Roddy Hamlyn. The usual procedure in buying a picture was to discuss payment in private with the deputy editor or, if the figure justified it, with the editor as well. As Liz had just said at conference that she was not going to run the story, Geoff assumed she did not want the photograph. But, like any canny picture editor, he always liked to cover his back, particularly as the subject was one of his editor's best friends.

He saw Liz at the news desk. Putting his hand over the phone, he called over to her, 'It's Roddy. I can't put him off any longer. It's the third time he's phoned this morning. He's not daft. He's heard that we've been rushing around and thinks we've identified the woman.' Liz's secretary gave her a phone message slip. 'David Linden. It's the third time he's been on,' she said. Liz picked up the phone then saw Geoff waiting for her reply. She said quickly, 'I'll call you right back,' and put the receiver down, then turned her attention back to the current problem. 'How much does he want for it?'

'Hang on, Roddy. I'll call you right back.'

Geoff joined Liz at the news desk. 'He thinks it's worth a lot.'

Sometimes an editor bought a picture 'off the street', effectively removing it from the market so that no other paper would use it. Once they had even spent £500 for pictures of Hillary Clinton leaving their proprietor's home after a party because Fergus did not want them published in any paper, including both the *Sunday* and the *Daily Chronicle*.

Liz did some calculations in her head. Her budget was already close to its limit. If an editor failed to use a picture because it became out of date, it was understood. But if she bought a photograph of a friend to keep it off the market it would be dead money. It put her in a difficult position.

Over-buying was part of the business. Every day stories were killed for various reasons – because they had appeared somewhere else, would not stand up legally or just didn't balance with that issue's contents. Good newspapers might spend between fifteen and twenty-five per cent of their budget on stories that never saw the light of day. 'It's the ones we reject that make us a good newspaper', was a quote often heard on a news editor's lips if he was worth his salt.

Liz made her decision. 'It's taken us four days to get where we are on the Katya Croft story. I don't believe that from a standing start any other paper could get all the information we have together by tonight,' she said finally. 'But I'd still like to hang on to it. Offer him a grand.'

Roddy dismissed this offer contemptuously. Unless he was given at least three grand, he was determined to have his picture back.

That figure was out of the question, so Liz reluctantly agreed to give up the picture.

On the news desk, Belinda looked at Tony and whispered, 'You mean she's killed that great story? Just because it's her bloody friend?'

He nodded.

'But it's a tremendous story, and after all the work you've put into it, too.'

The way she looked at him, all wide-eyed and dewily sympathetic, was why Belinda was known as Tony's Bambi. 'I think it should reach a wider audience,' he told her, looking steadily into those doe eyes. And he smiled as Belinda walked upstairs to the now deserted *Sunday Chronicle* office to make a phone call to the paparazzo.

Twenty minutes later, Roddy Hamlyn was seen in the newsroom of the *Chronicle's* traditional rival, the *Sunday Gazette*, negotiating a fat fee for his photograph of the woman in Roland Mews.

The fee grew bigger when he was able to tell them the identity of the woman as well as the leaseholder of the house she was about to enter.

He unleashed a frenzy of activity with *Gazette* reporters and photographers being despatched to trawl through the mews for anyone who had seen sight or sound of either of the two parties. A girl reporter was sent to South London to Katya's parents. And the diary team phoned as many of Katya's escorts as they could find.

The chief reporter went on a fruitless visit to the hospital where Hugo Thomas was making a good recovery. And their political editor was briefed to contact Davina Thomas, but not until the *Gazette*'s seasoned news editor had given the all clear, which would be when all the other pieces were in place.

Tony was still seething when he received a summons to Liz's office. As he swung angrily through the door, he was wondering how long he could put up with all of this, how long Charlie was going to be away. Fergus had better let him come back soon if this is how the paper is going to be run, he thought.

Instead of confronting him behind the desk, Liz was perched on the end of the sofa.

'Tony, before you tell me just how angry you are, let me explain. First, I am absolutely sure that Katya is not having and never has had an affair with Hugo Thomas.'

'What about that letter in the dustbin? It's not old, that script was for Friday's programme. What about the phone calls? We've seen the bill. And what about the person who's seen her in the mews?'

'I found out about the phone bill,' Liz improvised. 'Morning TV are planning a documentary about Davina Thomas and Katya's fronting it. And the letter was probably written to someone else and left in the house after a script conference.' She could see he was not convinced. 'I know that a midnight assignation in that mews does make it look like she's having an affair with him. It's the obvious explanation, but it's not the right one.'

'So who *was* she going to see?' he demanded.

'I don't know,' she lied.

He was not remotely fooled. 'Well, I don't think we can give up on it now. She's a star and our readers would like to know who she's screwing. I've got Barry trying to get to Hugo Thomas now. Why don't we wait to see what he comes up with?'

The key to taking the heat off Katya was to get Tony's mind focused on making the new splash work. But they did not have much time.

'Tony, I've been given a tip-off that it is one person who's been leaking all these scandal stories about the government MPs. It's a woman. She's married to an MP and she works at the House as his secretary.'

This stopped his pacing. 'Opposition tactics, you mean? Dirty, desperate, but can we prove it?' he asked. 'What else have you got to go on?'

'Remember that woman who put us on to the minister and his pregnant researcher? We were a bit baffled that she never asked for money.'

'Yeah, and she phoned the news desk again to make sure it was going to be used,' Tony recalled.

'At the time we thought it could be some evangelical nutcase on a moral crusade but now it seems it's politically motivated,' Liz said.

'God, I've heard of playing dirty tricks but I always thought the oppo wouldn't do it because they've got as much to hide as the government.'

'Hold your breath. It looks as though it's someone on the government side.'

'Bloody hell!'

She had his undivided attention now. Tony's professional instincts took over, his resentment temporarily forgotten. Liz briefed him on what Andrew was up to and where Mac was.

'I'll bleep Mac,' said Tony. 'We have to get both wives on tape. We'll get someone to phone from here to speak to the two of them. They can pretend to be checking details of some story.' He had a flash of inspiration. 'I'll have a voice-print expert check whether the tape of the woman who gave us the tip-off on the minister matches either of their two voices. Lucky Vera kept it. And I'll get Geoff to dig out all the pictures on the two families just in case,' he added, with obvious excitement.

'Great. Thanks.' She decided to take him further into her confidence. 'Let me put a question to you. If you had just lost your reputation, cabinet position and salary, driver, car, almost your wife and family, wouldn't you spend a fair bit of time trying to work out who had fingered you?'

He followed her line of thinking. 'Yes, good thought. We did try and pump them at the time, the two that would talk to us anyway. The one we shafted put the phone down on us, naturally. But they had no ideas.'

'Supposing we go back to them with these two names,' said Liz. 'It might jog their memories.'

'Smart thinking, Liz.'

She felt better with Tony on her side. Like most women, she hated fights.

In Warwickshire the news-agency reporter eliminated one of the MPs' wives from the enquiry. Unknown to anyone except the Prime Minister, the MP had contracted motor neurone disease, a progessive illness that attacked the nervous system. He would not be returning to Westminster after the next election. It was most unlikely that the source of the leak could be his wife. But the *Chronicle* nevertheless phoned her from the office and recorded her voice.

Meanwhile Mac had made an appointment and was about to arrive at the home of the remaining suspect.

It was the weekend when Philip Burroughs, the constituency's popular Member and Private Parliamentary Secretary to the Minister for Health, was free from the fortnightly advice surgery. Pruning the roses with Rosemary, his hard-working wife, would take over from listening to complaints about blocked drains, housing transfers and noisy neighbours.

Why on earth did a reporter from the *Sunday Chronicle* want to see them in person and on a Saturday, the MP wondered.

The *Sunday Gazette* had now garnered as much of the jigsaw as their lawyer would need.

The reporter despatched to grill Katya's parents arrived to a warm welcome and a cup of tea. Mr and Mrs Croft were used to gentle feature interviewing which centred on Katya's swimming trophies and childhood pets. Though forewarned by their daughter, they were unprepared for and distressed by the aggressive hard news and sex-orientated questioning. The reporter was not offered a second cup.

But taped interviews with the neighbours in the mews had

produced proof that Katya had been seen coming out of the Thomases' front door on at least two occasions.

A diplomat's wife at the house opposite told a delighted *Gazette* reporter that she had seen Katya leave the mews house at 4 a.m., obviously on her way to the TV station. The breakthrough they were looking for came when the Thomases' Filipino daily allowed one of the *Gazette*'s charming girl reporters into the mews house, for a sum equal to a month's wages.

The reporter was shown the fridge containing bottles of champagne and mineral water. 'Empty, always it is empty of food,' said the daily.

In the sole bedroom, the reporter sifted through a cupboard which contained only a collection of filmy Janet Reger underwear and peignoirs.

And then she hit paydirt. Recessed into the ceiling rose was a minute video camera. Only someone looking for it would have found it. This was obviously no family pied-à-terre, although the reporter did not know that the camera had been installed by a private investigator on Hugo Thomas's instructions.

The video of Davina and Katya's passionate lovemaking had been the cause of Hugo's car accident.

'The two tapes have gone off to my voice man,' Tony informed Liz. 'He'll phone in an hour to tell us if the voice on our phone tape matches Rosemary Burroughs'. And reporters are doorstepping both the ex-ministers. It looks as though at least one of them is at home.'

It was the perennial nightmare of all Sunday newspaper journalists that, for the most innocent of reasons, people tended to go AWOL at weekends just when they were needed most. However great and grand the celebrities were, they had some strange habits on Saturdays, like going fishing in remote spots without – an even greater sin – taking a mobile telephone with them, or actually spending time with their families.

Reporters spent hours of valuable time each weekend tracking down their quarry and it was especially irritating when the usual haunts, where they could be found all week, offered up nothing but answerphones and foreign maids speaking bad English.

Tony took a call from Mac. The news was so good he thought Liz should talk to the reporter. At that moment she remembered how well she and Tony had worked together in Mallorca. If only it could be like that all the time.

Mac's voice sounded exultant. 'I think this is our woman. I knew we were getting desperate so I departed from the script. I said I wanted to talk not about MPs and their hobbies but to do a better story about those unsung heroes of the back benches who ought to be in office. Of course I had to reassure them that it was all non-attributable, no names mentioned, and once she felt free to speak, boy, I couldn't stop her.

'He's a nice modest chap, but she obviously feels extremely bitter about him being overlooked. He's been five years as a PPS and she thinks he ought to have been moved up, especially now that those philanderers, as she called them, have been discredited.'

'And you think that would make her squeal on her own party?' asked Liz. 'That takes a bit of believing.'

'I'm just reading my notes. She went on and on about these young, sexy researchers who were after the scalps of powerful politicians. Of course her husband resisted them, she said, but others did not. Why should they have the big jobs when they had no right to them?'

'Still too hit and miss,' said Liz. 'She couldn't have thought that sneaking on them would ensure him a job in government. The Prime Minister has four hundred backbenchers to choose from.'

'Well, you can cut down the odds by half if you take out the ones who're too young, too old, too loony, too thick or who've done the job already,' countered Mac. 'Anyway, you're not talking about someone rational,' he went on. 'He's in his early fifties and if he doesn't get preferment now, she obviously thinks he'll miss the boat.'

'Mac, it's hardly conclusive proof.' Liz was feeling deflated. 'But we'll see what the voice-tape man says. Stay there because you'll have to front her up if he says we have something.'

There was a short silence when she put down the phone. Andrew voiced her fears. 'What'll we do if the voice man says it's not her?' he asked.

'Then we'll have a lot of white space on the front.'

Liz tried to concentrate on all the other things that were going on in the newspaper, checking proofs and taking the leader conference early so that she could devote more time to the splash. The Katya colour spread was replaced with some dramatic overnight pictures of riots in Shanghai.

Page three had the picture of the six-month-old royal baby, and on page five was an interview with the Home Secretary and his ailing wife – how many male editors had thought of that one? They also had an exclusive interview with Nancy Reagan, who had met the Home Secretary on several occasions, and was now helping Ronald Reagan cope with the Alzheimer's he had contracted. Liz was still hopeful they could stand up the identity of the mole, which would make a great splash.

The *Sunday Chronicle* looked a lot more intelligent and interesting – at least it did in her biased judgement.

In the old days on a Saturday, Charlie and his cohorts could spend a couple of hours at El Vino's or even have a three course lunch at the Savoy. But better production techniques, especially with colour schedules, meant that Saturday lunchtime had to be spent at the desk. So the back bench sent out for toasted cheese sandwiches. It was only when the production team was left to push through the first edition, all editorial decisions made, that Liz and her back-bench team would have a substantial high tea in the conference room. This was one time in the week when Liz gave up all thought of diet. Once, in an effort to be calorie-conscious, she had ordered vegetarian tidbits but the canteen staff frustrated her efforts and put the vegetables inside slices of thickly buttered bread.

She was discussing with Geoff the merits and demerits of using a different picture of the royal baby when Tony's raised voice made her turn round.

'Bad news from the voice expert. There are enough parallells between our tape and the new one from Andrew to make him think it's sixty-five per cent certain it was Rosemary Burroughs. But he says his profession would frown on him making a conclusive judgement on this alone.'

'Fuck his profession,' retorted Geoff.

'He says we need a linguistic expert,' Tony went on.

'What's the difference?' Liz was impatient.

'He says the actual words and phrases used on the tape could identify the caller more positively. If they match up, we'll have better proof.'

'Why didn't he warn us of that this morning? It's all taking so much more time. Okay, get on with it,' said Liz, mentally crossing fingers and toes.

The toasted cheese sandwiches were forgotten.

Although Katya Croft seemed to have gone to ground, Hugo Thomas was uncontactable in hospital and nobody could get through to Davina, by 4 p.m. the editor of the *Gazette* decided he had enough substance to meet the deadline for his first edition.

The deputy editor suggested they hold over the Croft story for the main run on the third edition so that rival newspapers could not steal it.

'Nah, we're not going to get any of the principals involved now, so we may as well go with it,' was Robbo's reply. 'As it's a riddle, make sure we include the question mark on the headline.'

'All the way through.'

'And let the lawyer check every word.' And he let out a giant guffaw.

The art editor picked out the biggest type to fit across two decks of his front page: 'MP'S HUSBAND AND TV STAR'. The strap across the top read: 'Riddle of late-night visits to love nest'.

The circulation director ordered a five per cent increase in the print order and hundreds of extra display bills for distribution to the street sellers. Billboards were never subtle. But the circulation boys figured that 'KATYA IN MP LOVE RIDDLE?' would slaughter the opposition that Sunday.

The *Gazette* lawyer did not like it but the story would run.

The language expert's report was promising. The mole had used the word 'philanderer' in her original phone call to the *Chronicle* news desk. It was not repeated during her second call but Rosemary Burroughs had used it in her off-the-record interview with Mac. A few other signposts, such as use of the double negative and certain pauses in her speech patterns, made the linguistic guru as sure as she could be that the mole and Rosemary Burroughs were one and the same person.

'Eu-bloody-reka,' howled Tony.

Liz was delighted but she held her enthusiasm in check. The lawyers would never advise that such a speculative story be published without stronger evidence.

Then Mac reported back from Warwickshire. 'I don't know how you're going to break this to Liz,' he told Tony. 'The story's collapsing round my ears.' He had, as instructed, told Philip Burroughs the paper had scientific proof from top voice experts that his wife was responsible for leaking the sex stories. 'I asked him to put this to her and he did. Now either she's a magnificent actress or she's innocent. She denied it right away, strenuously, and says she'll sue if we publish. I don't feel there's much more I can do here.'

'Don't leave yet, I'll come back to you.'

When Tony relayed this information to Liz, she realised how much she had been relying on this story. She looked at the clock on the office wall. Colour for page one on the first edition would have to go soon. She had already approved the blurb stories and pictures to lure in the readers, to give everything else on that page more time. But within minutes some kind of splash had to be done if this one was not firmed up.

It was unbearable when all the while she had a far better splash in her head – the love affair between Katya and the government minister. That would need very little work doing to it. And, even more galling, it would almost certainly give a great surge to sales, perhaps even as much as 100,000 copies. And on her first week as editor.

As always, I want everything, she thought. To keep my friendship, have a luscious affair with David and get a great front page.

It was all so easy in theory.

'Bingo!'

However many times he did it, Andrew always loved it when he cracked a story. He had just come from seeing the former Minister for Health who had been forced to resign when news of his love-child was leaked to the public. Andrew, as a leading member of the parliamentary political lobby, had shared many a bottle of Chablis with the former minister. Over the years, they had become friends. As much as anyone, Andrew had been responsible for promoting the minister's good-guy image. Now all those convivial talks over glasses in Annie's Bar at the House of Commons bore fruit.

'He was still a bit shirty with me until I told him I had some information he might find useful,' Andrew told Tony. 'He didn't react at all to Mrs Carter but the second name made an impact.'

'You sure?'

'Definitely. I then told him that the voice experts were fairly certain she was behind the leaks. Well, that did it. You see, his secretary had already mentioned she was suspicious of Mrs Burroughs.'

'Great God,' exclaimed Tony.

The secretary to the former Minister for Health was a member of the House of Commons fitness club. This gymnasium, in the Norman Shaw south building, was open to all staff working at the Palace of Westminster. Few MPs took advantage of it. Instead, the joke went, they would send their secretaries to do the exercises for them. Rosemary Burroughs was part of a group of Commons PAs who worked out twice a week. These secretaries became quite friendly and, the former minister's PA had to admit, most of them did gossip about their bosses.

After the minister had to resign, boss and secretary had tried to work out who had passed on the damaging information about him. The distressed secretary confessed to having told Mrs Burroughs, in confidence, of her suspicions that her boss was having an affair. But Rosemary Burroughs had been acquitted because she was, after all, 'family'. In any case, other indiscretions among the same group had never seen the light of day. But the information from the *Chronicle*'s voice expert reactivated the former minister's suspicions. 'I've let my Prime Minister and my party down. But if she's the sneak, the one thing I can do is help them nail the vindictive bitch. I'll go and brief the Chief Whip on all this first thing on Monday morning,' he told Andrew.

Liz was impressed with Andrew's work. But it was not over yet.

The Burroughses still had to be confronted with this new information.

'Somehow Mac's got to get in there and tell the Burroughses that an ex-Cabinet minister is going to inform the Chief Whip that he thinks she is the mole. What do they say to this?' But the Burroughses had slipped out by the gate at the back of the garden, roses left only half pruned. Unaware of this, Mac still sat patiently outside their front door. When asked later, neighbours said they had no idea where they had gone. Calls to relatives, friends and constituency officials brought nothing.

Liz was distraught. She blamed herself for not sending more reporters up there to help Mac. 'We can't waste any more time on this,' she told Tony, who slammed a pencil down in frustration.

'I know we're on to something,' he said.

'Yes, but unless a miracle happens and we track down the Burroughses and get them to admit something, we can't use it. We should have sent more people up there. Mac couldn't do everything on his own. What else have we got for the splash?'

'The Croft story – all the layouts are done.' Tony had not given up.

'We can't do that one. What else?'

'I want a real inquest on all of this once we've gone to press. I'm not letting it go,' he warned her.

She glared at him.

The war had restarted.

Chapter Eighteen

Davina's PA had been contacted by the duty officer at the Home Office to warn the Minister of State that there was likely to be some trouble at the hospital. The young civil servant knew that today was the children's first visit to their father. The minister would be grateful that she had been tipped off about the press interest.

'There have been three phone calls from the *Gazette* this morning,' he told Davina over the mobile phone in her car. 'They say it's personal and I thought I'd better warn you, they'll be trying to get you at home or at St Theresa's. I told them there was no possibility of getting hold of you today.'

Davina was grateful. 'Thank you for the warning. Perhaps you'd better send another policeman down to the hospital.' First the *Chronicle*, now the *Gazette* as well. How many bloody pictures were there? For a shocked moment, Davina thought that they must know about Katya and her. Then she shook herself. No, of course not. It was that silly story involving Hugo. How fortuitous that she could get rid of it with a firm denial. And with a bit of luck Hugo would not have to be bothered at all.

The fear that her husband might think to ask why Katya was photographed at the mews house, a place he had rarely visited, was too difficult to think about. If he knew the truth, it could pull down the careful edifice she had built round herself and her career. She had boasted to Katya that if there was no escape from the story about an affair, she would persuade Hugo to lie about his involvement with Katya. The truth was, she did not dare.

Davina swore to herself that if she could just get through this, she would have no more adventures. She would re-evaluate her priorities. Her career, naturally, had always come first but lately her little escapades had taken precedence over Hugo and her family. It was far too risky.

She and Hugo would just have to rub along as they had for so long with no passion but also no hate. Sex was just a ritual, like Christmas dinner, and done about as often. The only exceptions were the times when Hugo, turned on by nubile bodies at hunt balls and the like, would mutter drunkenly, '*Vite, vite au lit que je profite.*' 'Quick, quick, to bed so I can profit.'

She despised him and herself for submitting but it was part of the sacrifice she made to preserve their public image. For her the prize of political success was worth any humiliation.

Her next call was from the hospital. The agitated sister in charge of Hugo's floor had caught a *Gazette* reporter, tricked out in a white coat and stethoscope, trying to enter his room. An extra policeman was going to be too late.

'That's outrageous,' responded Davina. 'I shall report the newspaper to the Press Complaints Commission. Is the reporter still there? I'd like to have a word with him.' In truth, she was bluffing and the last thing she wanted to do was talk to any reporter. She was immensely relieved to find he had been ejected at once.

Davina looked in the rearview mirror at her two young daughters sitting quietly behind her. They held drawings and small presents they had made for the father they adored.

'Darlings, remember what I've always told you, to smile at photographers? Well, there might be some not such nice ones around today, but I still want you to smile. After all, Daddy's getting a lot better. And if any of them shouts at us, just ignore them and anything they say. All right?'

The girls did not totally understand what their mother was saying but they nodded, wanting to please her. Mummy could be frightfully angry sometimes.

As Davina swung the car towards the hospital car park, the porter, recognising her, lifted the barrier and waved her through. At the same moment, a *Gazette* cameraman appeared from his hiding place and placed his Leica up against the car window. Davina could vaguely hear shouts as she accelerated into the car park and anxiously looked in the mirror at her daughters.

They seemed fine. Quite composed.

Fergus was, as usual, faxed the front page of the paper's first edition to his villa. As he sat on the huge white sofa in his study, he was concerned.

The *Chronicle* splash, 'CABINET RESHUFFLE IMMINENT', was not entirely original or new. It was unexciting and not, he felt, up to Charlie Mays's standard. Had he made a mistake about Liz?

His call to the editor was, as usual on a Saturday evening, directed to the back bench where Liz was still sitting. Once again, it was Tony who picked up the receiver. Watching Liz's back hunched over the art desk, he lied easily. 'No, can't see her at the moment. Tony Burns here. Can I help?'

'What's happened to that Croft splash you told me about this morning?'

'The editor killed it, I'm afraid. Well, it was about one of her best friends. But we've heard rumours that the *Gazette* is splashing on it. They're very pleased with themselves.'

Fergus made no comment. 'Ask Liz to phone me, will you? At once.'

Tony took great pleasure in giving Liz the message five minutes later. 'Fergus is blowing his top about the Croft story.'

'How does he know about that?'

'Oh, I mentioned it to him this morning when he called at ten o'clock. If you remember, you hadn't arrived then. He's just phoned again. He wants you to call immediately.'

Liz was in no mood to be conciliatory when she spoke to her proprietor. 'Fergus, I'd rather, if you have a problem with the paper, that you talk to me first and not to my staff.'

Fergus let out a guffaw. 'My God, you've got balls. Well, I suppose if you missed out on the story of the night, your best bet is to attack.'

'What do you mean?'

'Tony told me this morning we had the Croft story in the bag and now he says it's the splash in the *Gazette*. What's going on?'

What a duplicitous bastard Tony was.

Fergus was in full flow. 'Liz, I believe the woman involved is one

299

of your best friends and I suppose this does put you in a difficult spot. You know, running newspapers is a difficult job. I've been doing it now for over fifteen years but you can't ever let friendship interfere.'

'I didn't, Fergus. The story is not true. The *Gazette* has no proof. It's the usual heap of kite-flying and it's going to cost them a lot of money. That's the reason, and the only reason, we didn't go with it.'

'Well, all right. I'll have to accept what you say,' said Fergus curtly. 'But I don't think much of our splash. It's dull.'

'It may be dull but at least it's real news, not sucked out of the air.' She paused for a second. 'More importantly, it's a spoof splash. The presses should be changed up by eight thirty. We'll let the foreigns go so they catch their planes and then we'll do a new front. If I had had a chance to speak to you, I could have told you all this but Tony didn't tell me you had phoned. And naturally I didn't want to bother you.'

'Bother me any time.' She was aware that though he said this, like many proprietors he did not always mean it. 'So what's the new story?'

Liz carefully explained the new splash to her proprietor. She omitted nothing. She heard him grunt in a highly satisfied way. He apologised for not speaking to her direct, then he was gone.

Liz slammed down the receiver and walked quickly to the Ladies. Inside a cubicle she put her head in her hands. Charlie had published many dull splashes. It was just how it happened sometimes. But, and she groaned to herself, not for his first ever issue.

She got up and walked one floor upstairs to her own office. She would not let Tony see her tears. It was all so desperate. If they could not prove that Rosemary Burroughs was the leak, the new splash was pretty tame too.

Almost involuntarily she found her finger hovering over the button on the console that linked her to the paper's in-house lawyer. She took her finger away. What would she say to him? 'The splash may collapse and I want to bounce something off you. It's a little sensitive, about a woman politician and her lesbian lover . . .'

Liz hesitated. Consulting the office lawyer was similar to broadcasting it over the intercom. His loyalty was to the company, not its editors. It would take her one more step down the wrong path.

She had sworn not to tell anyone about it.

She left her office to join the staff on the floor below.

One of the things Hugo had given Davina when they married was the freedom to operate without the need to earn real money. He had made several fortunes in his lifetime and he knew this financial security enabled her to concentrate on her political career. Not for her the worry of having to have a family member as a secretary to boost the expenses, or eking out an MP's salary by organising phantom trips to the constituency to bump up the car mileage expenses.

Hugo was under no illusion when they married that, although Davina was fond of him, his main attraction was his bank account. He had married for the first time at the age of thirty-five, having never been in love. He was infatuated rather than in love with Davina but he decided when he met her that it was time for him to settle down and have children.

Lying in the hospital bed with his right knee strapped to a pulley, Hugo's mind was fully alert. He had spent his conscious hours trying to plan his next moves. Everything had to be in place before he confronted Davina. The video images of the lesbian lovers ricocheted across his eyelids whenever he drifted into sleep . . . twisting, turning bodies, Davina's blonde head bending over Katya's nipple, deep, deep, interminable kisses . . . Like many men, Hugo had fantasised about watching two women making love. But not when one of them was his wife.

By Tuesday Hugo had analysed all his options and made up his mind. He was, above all, a pragmatist. As with all the major decisions of his life, from the subjects he read at Cambridge to his choice of career, marriage partner and even down to the sports he took up, emotion played no part in this one.

It was emotion caused by viewing the video of his wife in bed with another woman that had made him crash the car. He would never again make the mistake of allowing his feelings to consume him. It did not matter a shit about Davina's career. He would make decisions coldly, practically and in the best interests of himself and his children.

There would be no divorce. Not yet. His conclusion was based as much on the importance of protecting his children from possible taunts from their schoolfriends as to safeguard his own reputation. In Hugo's world, adultery was commonplace. A wife who preferred another woman was not. He could imagine the gossip – oh God, the laughter – at Lloyd's or, worse, the golf club.

He would not have his children branded as the daughters of a lesbian. Hugo was no aristocratic libertine. His values were firmly rooted in Middle England. He had read about the antics of lesbians like Vita Sackville-West and Violet Trefusis and despised the corrosive influence of these decadent writers, as he described them. Hugo might educate his children alongside similar upper-class people but he would be horrified if they acquired what he considered their perverted values.

The first time Davina visited him in hospital, he had wanted to hit her. But he controlled his anger. He had to get well, get out of hospital before he confronted her. On subsequent visits, he would turn his head away from her, his thick shock of greying hair concealing his expression. He could not bear to look at her. She thought that the crash and the painkillers had made him drowsy and bad-tempered.

His first thought when he had regained consciousness was the video the private investigator had made in Roland Mews. Had it survived the crash? He asked the nurse about the blue canvas sports bag he had had in the car with him.

'It's quite safe. The police delivered it here on Monday afternoon,' she said. 'Shall I give it to your wife to take home?' 'No, no,' he answered quickly, using his most authoritative tone. 'There's stuff in there that I need. Just put it in the locker down here. Please make absolutely sure it does not get moved. Can we lock it? Marvellous.'

He wanted complete care and control of the children, and the incriminating video would give it to him. Blackmail was not a word he used to himself, but that was what he intended.

Hugo adored his daughters and when their mother turned up with them both in tow it was the first time she had seen him heave his lanky frame to sit up. It was the first smile she had seen, too. The two girls were delighted when their father cuddled them and bombarded them with questions.

Davina allowed them ten minutes of this before she decided to drop her bombshell. 'Daddy and I have some business to talk about,' she pronounced, shepherding the children to the door. 'Just play in the corridor for a while, we won't be long.'

'What did you do that for?' demanded Hugo querulously.

'Sorry, but I've got to talk to you. The press have got this strange idea that you and Katya Croft have been having some sort of fling. Ridiculous of course and I told them so.'

Katya Croft? The vein in his temple pulsated. Weeks of pent-up rage and pain burst out, all his plans to wait for the right moment forgotten.

'That filthy bitch?' His usually tranquil features were contorted. 'You know a lot more about her than I do, you dirty lesbian cow.'

Davina stared at him, her mouth sagging. Hugo had never, ever used such an expression. In fact, he rarely cared enough about anything to lose his temper.

'You've got a fucking nerve accusing me,' he went on, almost spitting with rage. 'Just what are you playing at?' His voice was close to screaming and it scared Davina. She began shaking. He knows, she thought. He knows. Oh Christ. I must lie. Lie.

'I don't know what you're talking about.' Her voice wobbled as she fought to keep control. 'I think your medication must have affected your brain, Hugo. Stop making such a noise. The children will hear.'

'You weren't thinking about the children when you were rolling around the bed in the mews with that tart from television, were you?'

After a barely perceptible pause, she said quietly, 'Hugo, what are you going on about? Have you gone mad?'

His voice suddenly dropped. It became measured and quiet. 'I know all about your grubby little secret.' He stared at her with such distaste, she shrank back. 'And don't try and deny it. I've seen you both with my own eyes.'

His words frightened Davina but she made herself sound exasperated. 'I don't know what you're talking about. Seen what with your own eyes?'

'Never mind that now,' he told her, with real loathing, 'but I have all the evidence I need to destroy your career and if you give me any trouble, any trouble whatsoever, I won't hesitate to use it, even though it could drag us all down to your level.'

Davina slumped. She could see he was not bluffing. Had Katya phoned him? If so, she still had a chance to convince him it was all lies. 'Did Katya Croft tell you that? Surely you don't believe a word she says. She's lying.'

Hugo's voice rose again in cold fury. 'You're the fucking liar. I have a video of you and Katya in bed. And don't try to find it, either. I have several copies.' He surprised himself at how easy it was to lie to his wife. He had only one copy. He must arrange for his lawyers to have another made.

Davina, normally so confident, so in control, shrank back, as Hugo carried on. He seemed quite calm now. 'Listen and listen carefully. I'm going to tell you your future. From now on, you can forget about raising the children. I don't want you to be a major influence in their lives, God knows where that would lead. I don't want you with us in either the house in Warwickshire or the one in London. You can have that place in Roland Mews, I never want to see it again. My sister and the rest of the family will come and help me and you will have to make an appointment through them to see the girls.'

'Hugo,' Davina felt panic rising, 'you can't do that, you don't have any right.'

'You're absolutely correct, my dear wife,' he spat, 'I don't have the legal right. I have something better. The video.'

Davina was silent.

'I haven't finished,' Hugo went on. 'In two years, I will arrange a no-blame divorce and you can live on your MP's salary. See how you and your little tart will like that. In the meantime, if any newspaper prints this stupid story about me and her, I expect you to act like the outraged wife of a decent husband. Then I shall sue them for every penny they have.'

Davina was thoughtful. One part of her brain was scheming. Surely there was something she could rescue from this mess? 'Hugo, I love my children. Whatever's happened between us, you can't deny that. Supposing I don't agree to all this?'

'If you love them as you say, then you won't want this story to come out, will you?' Hugo was scornful. 'Because if you give me any trouble, I'll see to it that your political career dives into the gutter, which is where you belong.'

For a second she stared straight at him and saw the enmity in his face. 'So you're prepared to sacrifice the children to get your revenge against me?'

'No. I don't want them to suffer. You may have given birth to the girls but you're not a normal mother, as I'm sure the courts will agree. You hardly see them, even in the holidays. The nanny and I put them to bed most nights. And another thing. One hint that you've been trying to poison the girls against me, and I swear I'll release the video.' His head was aching but he would not let her see any signs of weakening. 'I'll get Ginny down in the morning and you can move your stuff out as soon as the girls go back to school.'

'You can't do this to me.'

'Can't I? Don't take the chance, Davina. I've backed you, supported you, done everything a man could to help a wife. Did you think I didn't know your affections were elsewhere? This thing has been with me for months. I prepared myself for another man. It would have been upsetting, we would have had to split, but at least that would have been normal.'

Hugo slumped back on his pillow. Davina sat silent, thinking. Then, after what seemed an age, she whispered, 'I'm sorry, Hugo. I never meant you to find out.' Her voice was low but the words were heartfelt.

They had no effect on her husband. 'I suppose you're worried about your lousy career and your all-important image,' he sneered. 'Well, you'll be glad to know I've thought of that, too. Until the divorce, you can visit the house at weekends but there'll be a locked door between you and us.'

'Hugo, I'll change. I'll give it all up.'

'Really? For how long? This one's obviously not the first, is she? I wonder what would happen if I had a frank chat with that little researcher you were so pally with, or the French nanny who left so suddenly.' He looked at her with contempt. 'You can't change.'

Davina rarely cried. She was shocked to find the tears pouring down her cheeks.

'Pull yourself together,' Hugo snapped. 'The children will be wondering what's going on. Send them in and you wait in the car till they come out. Remember, if they suspect one word about what's going to happen, that's it. No second chances.' Hugo looked weary. 'Get out of my sight. I just want to see my daughters.'

Now was the time for the traditional exchange of calls between news desks from Wapping to Canary Wharf, from Blackfriars to Kensington.

This had developed over the years as a way of saving time when following up rivals' stories. In the sixties and seventies members of the National Graphical Association in the packing department had earned as much as a week's wages by making sure that one of the first copies of a newspaper off the press went 'missing'. It would be slipped to a boy on a motorbike who would rush it round to the competition. Now things were not so dramatic.

Seven o'clock was late enough to ensure your rivals did not get the story in their first edition. If the scoop was so good it would walk off the news stands, a paper might not swap it by phone but instead give their contact on the other newspaper a tidbit from the second lead story. A wily editor might even do a spoof first edition, putting a lesser story on the front page and printing it only in the first few hundred copies. These were distributed to the competition and by the time the real story came out, most of the other editors were tucked up in bed.

The City editor stuck his head round the door of Liz's office.

'You won't forget that you're coming to that lunch with Lord Rushington next week, will you?'

'Oh yes, James reminded me about it. That'll be fine, it's in the diary.'

'By the way, boss, I've got an interesting one I'm working on. I'm not sure what you'll do with it. Remember that City firm that had the bother with the client who disputed an order to buy? Well, they started to tape all the transactions but they didn't tell the staff because they didn't want to inhibit them. The very first dispute they had, they checked through the relevant tape and guess what they heard? One of their top women dealers, a real, cool, Armani-suited, butter-wouldn't-melt-in-the-mouth type, was telling her client, "Buy a million Fowler plc shares and I'll give you another blow job." '

Liz raised her eyebrows.

'Apparently, the partners were so outraged she was frogmarched out of the building within the hour,' continued the City man.

'Blimey, and I thought things were tough in newspapers,' commented Liz.

'Good way of getting her target quotas up, I suppose,' grinned the City editor.

'What will happen to her?'

'Don't know. Perhaps one of her clients will set her up in business. Anyway, do you want to go ahead on this one?'

'Sex in the City . . . hmmn, could be good although we'd have to handle it with care.'

'Like she did?'

They both laughed. It was the first light-hearted moment in Liz's tense day and she still had no idea if she could use the Burroughs story.

'We'll have to get the Good Taste Committee in on it. I don't know how much we can use.' So not only newspapers tape-recorded their 'clients', she thought.

Tony interrupted them. He was in a wild mood. 'Guess what the *Gazette* is splashing on?'

Liz was wary. Tony quoted the *Gazette* headline, 'MP's Husband and TV Star'.

She raised her eyebrows. 'We knew Roddy would rush round there with the photograph.' Liz chose her words carefully. 'But they must have some real whizz kids over there to catch up so fast they could get it into their first edition. I mean, to have identified Katya Croft and Hugo Thomas, and then to get the statement from people in the mews so fast, that's impressive.' She walked round the desk. 'I wonder who they've got over there? Who's written the story, do we know yet?'

'Phil Wallace, apparently,' Tony replied. 'He came from the *Daily Express*. Young chap.'

Liz was heavily sarcastic. 'Perhaps we should have him and their news editor in and have a look at them. They're certainly fast workers. Ask Bob to fix it, please.

'Okay,' she went on, 'can we clear the room, please. I have some calls to make.'

Katya was under siege, a prisoner in her own flat.

True, she could eat and drink what she liked and watch whatever she chose on television. But she could not leave the flat without being followed by a swarming horde of cameramen and reporters sent round by every Sunday paper news editor in London.

She saw the first hint of what was in store on her return from Joanna's house at lunchtime. A young couple was parked at the entrance to her block of flats. They could have been lovers except for the gleam of a telephoto lens resting on the dashboard of their Ford Escort.

It was unsophisticated thinking for the *Gazette* to send a photographer. A girl reporter on her own, armed with nothing more aggressive than a Biro, was more likely to get a reasonable response from someone like Katya than a photographer who clicked away frenziedly in her face. The newspapers had hundreds of pictures of her in their photo library. But they always wanted that day's photograph and every now and again sending someone out yielded great results. Tearful and famous, angry and famous. The papers loved it. This usually produced hideous, un-retouched pictures and the celebrities could do nothing about it.

Katya debated whether or not to return to Joanna's. But Jo had looked worn out and could probably do without her dramas. Anyway, Katya was desperate to get back to her own flat, her own things. She could handle a couple of newspaper journalists. She put on huge sunglasses and signed the mini-cab driver's chit as the photographer started his clicking. Katya lowered her head. She was in no mood for this now. It had been a tough twenty-four hours.

'Excuse me, Miss Croft.' The girl reporter was nervous. 'We're from the *Sunday Gazette*. I'd like to talk to you about . . .'

The *Gazette*? How had they got on to the story? Liz's words echoed in her ears: 'If we don't do this story, somebody else will.'

Katya walked past the reporter and began to key in her front door security number.

Desperate now, the journalist shouted out, 'What about you and Hugo Thomas?'

Katya hunched her shoulders and was relieved to see the bulk of the doorman striding across the foyer to open the front door.

'Thanks, Arthur. Tell these people I don't want to be disturbed, will you?'

'Quite understand, Miss Croft. Leave it to me.'

How the hell did the *Gazette* know about Hugo? And how did they get to her so fast?

Liz had no answers when she phoned. 'I've been asking myself those same questions,' she said.

'It could have been Davina,' Katya said slowly. 'Remember, she told me she would persuade Hugo to admit to an affair with me if the story came out, to divert the press from the truth.'

'God, if she's done that, what am I going to tell my staff?' said Liz. 'Not to mention Fergus. I've told them all it's not true.'

'Would it get you off the hook if I gave you a denial story?'

'Yes, it would, and you'll have to threaten to sue the *Gazette* so Davina will know she can't get away with it. I'll put it on page one, column one. That should worry the *Gazette*. But we're running away with ourselves,' Liz went on. 'Maybe Davina's had nothing to do with this. I mean, why would she volunteer any information to the *Gazette* or anyone else? We'll have to wait until we see the paper. I have a nasty feeling the information may have come from somewhere closer to home, mine rather than yours. If I can prove it, it's a firing offence.'

'What am I going to do now, Liz, after the *Gazette* comes out? All Fleet Street will be round my door.'

'I'd get out. It's going to be nasty.'

'Where can I go? Joanna had enough of me yesterday and I wouldn't want to wish this swarm of locusts on anyone.'

'You could stay with me, but in the circumstances it's probably better to phone your TV station. They could sort you out a hotel – and a lawyer.'

Liz was right. Katya needed some legal advice fast. Her solicitor

309

was surprisingly bullish when she assured him that there was no truth to the allegations. 'Don't issue a denial just yet. It won't stop them printing in the first edition and four million copies of the *Gazette* will get you far more damages than a hundred thousand.'

'Well, I've already promised a denial to my friend, Liz Waterhouse. She's acting editor of the *Sunday Chronicle*.'

'It would be better not to do it until tomorrow.'

She could not explain why she could not wait because of the debt she owed Liz and that if Davina was behind the *Gazette* story, she had no choice. 'Can't I issue an injunction to stop the *Gazette*?'

'Too late now. We'd never get a judge in time. The *Gazette* will claim it's true and say they'll see you in court. I'm sorry, but by the time we get all that sorted out, it'll be too late. Look, if the reporters are driving you mad, do you want to come round here?'

'Thanks, but at the moment I think I can handle it.'

'I'll sort out the station. See if they have any thoughts. And phone any time, I'm used to it. I'll come to the office on Monday and we'll have a meeting. I don't have to tell you that these guys are clever. They'll think of ways to trick you into talking to them. Don't.'

Katya's neighbours had been used to a few of her fans hanging around the entrance but normally they would disappear once she had given them her autograph. Nothing had prepared them for armed invasion later that evening. The decorative hydrangea bushes in front of the block were slowly being trampled underfoot by photographers, rushing to capture anyone who went in or out of the flats.

Arthur, the doorman, was shown pictures of Hugo and promised vast sums if he would tell them whether he had ever been there. To his credit, he just smiled and retreated to the security lodge inside.

The posse adopted the well-known tricks of doorstepping. They began pressing the buzzers of all the flats in turn, in search of information. Katya's neighbours turned down all the reporters' blandishments. Some felt secretly tempted but they knew nothing.

One paper ordered a pizza in Katya's name from the local takeaway so that when the delivery man pressed her bell they could insert cash for interviews, saying they would donate the money to her favourite charity. Katya was too wily for this scam.

The saddest aspect of all this was the jangled nerves of an elderly couple living only half a mile from Katya's parents. They could not understand why their phone rang all that night, asking questions about a Katya they had only ever seen in their front room, on television. The reason lay in the London phone book where the man had exactly the same initials and surname as Katya's father whose own number was unlisted.

Blood. Unnervingly bright red blood.

As Joanna looked down in horror, two globules splattered the pale beige carpet. For a second, half of her mind strayed to how she was going to get the stains out. Then total panic. Not again.

She shuffled gingerly to the phone, leaving a vivid jelly-like red trail, cautiously sat down and rang Dr Bischoff. Because of her gynaecological history, it was a number she knew by heart. She looked at her watch. It was 8.30.

Listening to the rings, she visualised the doctor's house in Notting Hill Gate where the phone would be shrilling in the hall, between the surgery and the living room. Please let her be there. Please God, let her be there.

Joanna counted the rings. The gynaecologist was over seventy. It would take her time to get to the phone. But after several minutes, hope subsided and she rang off.

As the blood started coursing down the inside of her thighs, Joanna dialled 999. She was told the ambulance could be ten minutes. Her terror was so great she felt that if she moved, her womb would open. She did not even dare take deep breaths. How was she going to move to the front door to let in the ambulance men?

It was hateful being alone again. She wanted George. Why hadn't she been honest with him yesterday? 'I'm fine, really, no problems at all,' she had reassured him when he called from Kinshasa. It never occurred to her to say, 'I've had twinges and pains since Thursday morning. I had an upsetting lunch with Liz. It's all been a terrible effort and it's taken all my strength.' It had always been so important for her to put up a good front, she did it without thinking.

Damn, damn.

He had been anxious about her and asked lovingly whether she was looking after herself and if she really, really felt all right. She, like her friends, had a visceral hatred of being boring so she diverted him to the story, so far, of Liz, Katya and the Thomases.

Once again she wondered how was she going to let in the ambulance people.

Of course. Katya had a spare key and she was only seven minutes away by car. She would be able to come round.

'Katie, I'm in trouble. It's the baby. I need my spare key. Now.'

Katya, picking up the fear in Joanna's voice, did not waste time with questions. 'Don't worry, I'm on the way.'

Katya ran to check Joanna's key was in her handbag, grabbed her coat and then stopped. She realised with horror that once she left through the front door she could not go anywhere alone.

She stared from behind her lace curtains out of the window. The press army was still there waiting for her to come out. They were well settled in their cars, mobile phones at the ready. They would certainly chase her to Joanna's house. She could not let Jo face that now.

It would cause fewer complications if Liz, who also had a key, went round to help Joanna. Katya could join them at the hospital. The journalists would not be allowed to follow her in there. As so many times in the past when she needed instant help, she dialled Liz's number.

At the *Chronicle* office, Liz was supervising the last details of the front page when the phone rang. All calls were banned at this vital time, but she looked at the news desk secretary who was dealing with it. Could it be David?

'Who is it?' Liz could not resist asking.

'A woman, says to mention the word "Constantia" to you. Says it's very urgent.'

'Okay,' said Liz, picking up the phone on her desk. 'Make sure this is faxed – ' and she indicated the paste-up – 'to Fergus Canefield at his South of France place right away, will you?'

The news was bad. She listened in silence as Katya outlined Joanna's predicament, all disagreements between them forgotten. This was Liz's first Saturday in charge of the paper, but there was no hesitation.

'Don't worry,' she told Katya reassuringly, 'I'm on my way round there now.'

In the car she made two calls. One to David, who was still not answering, and the other to Fergus Canefield to check his comments on the splash. It had all the ingredients he liked but she still wondered if she had made the right decision for the second edition.

Casualty staff did not like dealing with threatened miscarriages so they hurried Joanna to the ante-natal ward as soon as possible.

With a concerned Liz following on behind, Joanna was wheeled into a large ward, all pale green eggshell with toning floral curtains. Twelve beds were arranged along the walls in rows of six, all in good National Health Service taste but still heavy with that cloying hospital aroma, a mixture of sugar, soured milk, iodine and disinfectant.

Joanna wondered why all hospitals smelled the same, even the private ones with carpets instead of lino.

Settling Joanna into a bed, the sister bustled around her. After twenty-five years in England, Sister Mary Gallagher still talked as if she was in her village of Ballymaloe, County Cork, on the south-west coast of Ireland. 'The doctor will be along in a minute, dear. I don't want you to move out of this bed. Not for anything. Do you understand? This little baby will decide for itself if it's going to stay put or not.' She gazed down on Joanna's alarmed face. 'Now try not to worry, dear, you've come to the right place.'

Joanna wanted magic to happen. She did not want to hear the homilies she had heard twice before. She appreciated the kindness but she was desperate for more information. Liz sensed how she felt. 'Jo, I feel so guilty. Katya and I have been so selfish banging on about our problems. You should have kicked us out this morning.'

'Oh, don't flagellate yourself. Let's face it, it's not the first time. I'm just not very good at this.'

Sister Gallagher walked back after sending off a new, ecstatic father. 'Doctor's just on his way, dear.'

Joanna looked up at Liz miserably. 'I don't want a doctor to come and tell me I've lost the baby, that it was just one of those things and I can try again later.'

'Oh, Jo.' Liz took Joanna's hand. 'I'm sure he won't do that.'

'I can't help it ... and George isn't here ...' Joanna's voice trembled.

'Katya's trying to get through to him now before she comes over here.'

'Oh, I don't want him worried.'

'Joanna, you always try to shield people, too much sometimes, and George would want to know about this. Now just relax, we've got everything under control. Katya'll be here soon and she'll tell you what he said. Okay?' A slight nod encouraged her. She must try and deflect Joanna's morbid thoughts. 'I don't know about you but I hardly slept last night with the shock of Katya's news. Our Katie a lesbian. Unbelievable. Did you ever, ever suspect?'

'No, it never occurred to me. After all, she's been to bed with loads of blokes.'

'Maybe she's bisexual.'

Joanna gave her an old-fashioned look. 'Are you telling me that if your relationships with men went badly wrong, you'd end up fancying a woman?'

'Nah. Especially now I've met David.' She made a mental note to try his number again later. Liz thought back to the white-washed room above the harbour in Palma. 'In Mallorca I shared a double bed with her for months. I never got a hint of it, did you?'

'God, no. We've never been shy about getting dressed or having showers in front of each other.'

Liz leaned over the bed and whispered, 'Perhaps we're not very fanciable.'

It was the first time for hours that Joanna had laughed. 'Oh, don't make me laugh, I'm not supposed to move.'

Memories of their friendship came back to them like treasured snapshots – sunbathing in the nude on their private balcony, swapping party dresses before a special date, Saturday-night conversations making up at the washbasin while one of the others was in the bath.

'Do you think she's always been a lesbian?' Joanna asked.

'Dunno. I know so little about them.'

'Was she born like that or do you think it's because of that domineering father of hers?'

'Who knows? He was always a bastard. He still wants to dominate her and her mother.'

'But we had difficult fathers as well and it hasn't made us switch to women. And I haven't been approached by a woman, or at least if I have, I haven't noticed.'

Joanna became thoughtful. 'Do you think fathers really can affect one's sexuality?'

'Not sure,' said Liz. 'All I do know is that my father made me feel I had to get to the top of the tree and your father made you so insecure that you think if you don't have money behind you, you'll end up a bag lady. Who knows what happened with Katya.'

There was silence for a while.

'Jo,' said Liz carefully, 'has it changed the way you feel about her?'

'To be absolutely honest, I'm not sure,' answered Joanna slowly. 'I think I feel worse about the fact she couldn't trust us and wouldn't tell us about it than what she actually does in bed.'

At that, Liz moved her chair closer to Joanna. 'Yeah, and what do you think they do in bed?' she whispered.

'God knows. It can't be that different, can it?'

'Yes it can. One of them hasn't got the right equipment.'

'Exactly, that's the whole point of the exercise. They're supposed to be afraid of penises.' Joanna sighed. 'We all believe in individuality, don't we? Well, this is one aspect of it. It's the person who matters, not their sexuality. I read only the other week that today's woman thinks lesbianism can be chic.'

'So is juggling. Why didn't she try that?'

They traded mischievous looks.

'And why Davina Thomas?' added Joanna. 'She's so controlled, so hard-faced.'

'That's certainly how she appears in public but when I travelled on a train with her to Manchester once she was amazingly good fun.'

'Ah, but did she fancy you?'

Liz gave a shrug. 'Listen, Katya'll be here soon. Do we mention it?'

'Oh, I think we've got to. Now it's all out in the open, we have to accept it's part of her. She's still our friend, isn't she?'

Liz nodded slowly, remembering with a pang the conversation she had nearly had with the office lawyer. Thank heavens she had thought better of it.

'Has David phoned again?' Liz started. At a time like this, Joanna was thinking of her love problems.

She shrugged. 'We keep on missing each other but I have him in my sights, don't worry.'

Sister Gallagher came briskly over. 'I think it's time your visitor left. The doctor should be here any . . .' She trailed off as a famous face walked up the ward.

'Joanna, how are you?' Katya gave a tense smile. She was still trembling from trying to dodge the army of cars that had followed her to the hospital and the paparazzi lensmen. Luckily they had been halted at the hospital doors.

Sister Gallagher's stern features relaxed into a beam at Katya. 'You'll probably want a bit of privacy. I'll draw these curtains round the bed. And may I say how much I enjoy your programmes, Miss Croft.'

Once again, Katya's fame had been useful, this time to gain them extra time. All over the world, stars bemoaned their lack of anonymity, conveniently forgetting how fame could oil the wheels of life that often cranked to a standstill for the great unknown.

Katya was ill at ease and covered it by gabbling. She had never felt embarrassed with her friends before and was highly sensitive to any changes in their behaviour towards her. And she was feeling even more guilty about Joanna's condition than Liz was. Having tried to convince herself that friends were a luxury she did not need, she was the one who had kept Joanna up late on Friday night, using her as a confessor.

And earlier, when she had asked Liz for help, there had been no ifs or buts, no 'I'm editing for the first time' and no repercussions about Katya's recent behaviour. That was what friendship was about.

'I've been very efficient, Jo,' she said. 'I've left a message for George. He wasn't there when I phoned but they said we'll be able to get hold of him at six in the morning our time. And I bet you didn't remember your mobile. I'll leave you mine.'

The other two recognised that she was nervous. 'Katya. It's okay. Jo and I have talked about it,' said Liz, 'and we both agree. You're our friend and short of committing murder, and even then we're not sure, we're on your side.' Instinctively, they all reached out to each other and clasped hands.

It had been fifteen minutes and still the doctor had not appeared. Joanna had been instructed to stay absolutely still but during the conversation she had surreptitiously been moving her hips, which normally stimulated the baby to move. But nothing was stirring today.

Joanna felt the tears well up. 'Perhaps I'm never going to be a mother.'

Although the others had secretly thought this after her last miscarriage, they had never heard Joanna herself say it out loud, whatever she had been thinking.

'What rubbish,' pronounced Liz, hoping she sounded more convinced than she was. 'You're going to be all right.'

The curtains were parted by a young Asian doctor who looked so tired that Joanna nearly moved over to give him some space. In spite of his fatigue, his tone was solicitous.

Katya and Liz scuttled off to the deserted waiting room. While Katya organised two cups of tepid hospital coffee, Liz checked with the office. Bob Howard sounded elated. 'I phoned ITN as you suggested,' he reported, 'and they want the exclusive on our splash. They're sending a crew to get the paper coming off the presses.'

'Great,' said Liz. 'Any news from Warwickshire?'

'No, but Mac's still doorstepping the Burroughs home.'

'Okay, keep me posted.'

Katya had been listening to Liz and asked nervously, 'What did you do about denying the story about Hugo and me?'

'Page one, column one as promised,' said Liz as she fished out the photostat of the *Chronicle* front page. 'TRAITOR' screamed the banner headline. Underneath was the sub-deck '*Scandal sneak is party wife*'. On the left was the headline: 'TV STAR'S LOVE DENIAL'.

The story did not identify Rosemary Burroughs by name but gave all the details so carefully pieced together by Liz, Tony, Bob, Mac, Andrew, Stacey's News Agency and the language and linguistic experts.

'It looks dramatic,' said Katya, noting with gratitude that the mole story totally dominated the page. 'Thanks for helping me, Liz, you've been a real friend.'

For the first time that week they were at ease with each other.

'Well, there are a few questions I'd like to ask you as a friend,' said Liz mischievously. 'I'm curious to know if you've been been putting on an act all these years?'

'Not really,' said Katya, 'although now I come to think about it, I did have crushes on other girls.'

'Oh, everyone has school crushes, including me,' said Liz. 'Mine was on Lorraine Thompson, the first eleven's hockey captain. I thought she was wonderful.'

'My crushes didn't stop at sixteen,' admitted Katya. 'When my friends started getting interested in boys, I never understood it. The thought of kissing one of them was a real turn-off. I never wanted to go to parties or neck in the back row of the cinema and if ever I got dragged into a double date I used to make an excuse and go home early.'

'And you still didn't suspect anything?'

Katya gave a rueful smile. 'Absolutely not. My parents and teachers thought I was a late developer. So did I. Even when all my friends were sticking pictures of pop stars on their walls, I was pasting photographs of female sportswomen in my scrapbook. I thought it was because I was keen on sport. Ha.'

'When I met you, you had dozens of boy friends, especially in Mallorca. Didn't they mean anything to you?'

'One or two of the blokes were good fun to be with but I thought my experiences seemed very much like yours. When we used to discuss sex, you and Jo would say that most lovemaking wasn't very good for you and that you faked orgasms. So I always thought I was fairly typical. Until I found out how it could be.' She gave a heartfelt sigh. 'To think I don't ever have to have oral sex with a man again. Blissful.'

Liz smiled. 'A lot of married women would probably say that too, but they still wouldn't swap a bloke for a woman.'

'Then they don't know what they're missing,' said Katya firmly.

Liz thought of her night with David Linden. 'I don't agree with you. When it's good, oh boy.' She gave a pleasurable little groan.

'Don't knock what you haven't tried, Liz.'

Liz made a grimace. 'I mean, the very idea of French-kissing a woman.'

Katya smiled, finding it cathartic to talk about her secret love life at last. 'I'm telling you, I've found that sex with a woman is a lot more, well, intimate, I suppose. Let's face it, all you need do with a man is,' she gave Liz a wicked look, 'just lie there groaning and moaning at regular intervals. Fools them every time.'

Liz did not return her smile. 'You've just been unlucky. I've had some bloody wonderful times in bed with a man, as recently as Thursday night.'

Katya shook her head. 'I'm glad, but for me there's no contest. It's wonderful with a woman. Think about it. You're having the same things done to you as you're doing to your partner.'

'That happens in hetero sex, too.'

'Not in the same way. At least, not for me. Okay, the same places are kissed and touched, but when the lover is a woman the touches become different, the kisses are different, the whole aura is different.'

'How can they be? Not to be too crude, you're stimulating all the same areas, aren't you?'

Katya was staring into the middle distance. 'Yes, but the feel is softer, smoother. The lesbian writer Jeanette Winterson says that women, unlike men, do not appear to agree on the definition of what is sexy, and I think she's right. Lesbian lovemaking is more . . . unhurried. There's none of that quick tightening up into a ball of sweat and demanding the old in-and-out. I didn't lie awake while my partner fell asleep the moment he was satisfied.'

'Don't knock the panting and the sweat. Some of us like that kind of thing. I wouldn't mind having a bit more in-and-out with David.'

Liz needed more caffeine. The vending machine coffee was tasteless but it was hot and she hadn't eaten for hours.

Katya was intent on making her friend understand. 'Liz, the one thing I've found out about sex with a woman is that it's honest and giving. I felt cared about and I could say I love you and I want you without the other person feeling threatened. It was so ... freeing.'

Liz took a swallow of coffee and grimaced. She emptied most of it into the solitary potted plant and threw the empty carton into the bin. 'Okay, I'm happy for you,' she said. 'But, Katya, you kept it such a secret. You must have felt so alone not being able to talk to us about it. That's what we're feeling regretful about, that you felt we wouldn't understand.'

'Well, I didn't understand myself. For a long time. But loving Davina seemed the most natural thing in the world, that's the funny part of it. I knew what to do. I wasn't unsure, like with so many boy friends. In fact, I was desperate for it. You're horrified, aren't you?'

Liz examined her feelings. 'No, I'm not. After all, women get desperate for sex with men. I suppose I'm a bit surprised, that's all. And I'm curious. What do you actually do?'

'It's like a circle,' said Katya. 'It goes on and on. Lots of touching and affection and kissing, all over, and then oral sex, either mutual or one of us at a time. It's lovely.'

'Yeah,' Liz responded, 'but I still prefer men, rough beards, heavy bodies ... oh!' She shivered at the memory of Oxford. 'But if it was all so perfect, what went wrong with you and Davina?'

Katya's beautiful face clouded. 'I suppose we were at different stages. I felt as if my whole world had changed but obviously she didn't feel the same about me. Liz, I can't tell you how cold she was when she broke it off. Colder than any man I've known.'

'Has she always been a lesbian?' asked Liz.

'I think so.'

'So she's been through this before. I'm really sorry it all ended so badly for you, Katya.' When comforting a person hurt by a lover, Liz realised that gender was unimportant. 'Katya, can I ask you something really embarrassing?'

'After what we've been talking about? I can't wait.'

'Well,' Liz shuffled in her chair, 'if you've always secretly been drawn to women, you know, in the way you say, er, have you ever been attracted to Jo or me?'

Katya did not hesitate. 'Absolutely not. You and Jo are like sisters to me. And I'm not into incest.' She gave a slight smile. 'I'm exactly the same, you know, no less of a friend than I was before. I hope it won't make a difference.'

'Certainly not,' declared Liz. 'I'm not saying we weren't taken aback when you told us you were a lesbian but only because we had no hint of it.'

Katya started to speak, but Liz held up a hand. 'Yes, I know what you're going to say. Davina and the job she has complicated things. We appreciate now that it wasn't only your secret to keep. If you'd been with someone less newsworthy, I hope you might've told us. So, friendship intact. Okay?'

Katya gave a broad smile. 'Yes, very okay.'

Liz made another call to the office. The situation was the same. The Burroughses had still gone to ground and Andrew had added to the story that had appeared in the second edition the news that the former Minister for Health would see the Chief Whip on Monday morning to tell him the name of the traitor.

'It's not as good a splash as it could be,' she told Katya, 'but it's the best I can do in the time.'

She looked at her watch. Maybe David had come home. Liz had dialled the first digits of the number when Sister Gallagher's head appeared round the door. 'Doctor's finished but we don't want to tire Mrs Langford, do we? So why don't you go home now and come back tomorrow?'

'Can't we just say goodbye to her?' The Sister gently shook her head at Liz.

'Do you think the baby's going to be all right?' asked Katya.

As she ushered them to the door, Sister Gallagher's soft Irish brogue sounded weary. 'It'll be as God wills and in His own good time.'

They could see the press pack still hanging around outside the hospital gates. Liz had a brainwave. 'Let's ask an ambulance crew if they can take you out of here on their next call. Here's the key, stay with me tonight. I'm going back to the office.'

Two bottles of vintage champagne were waiting in ice buckets on Liz's desk with copies of second editions of all their rivals. 'Thank God you're back, boss, we're all dying of thirst here,' laughed Geoff. While Liz glanced at the front pages, the team, without Tony who was probably still at the office pub, congratulated each other on theirs. Apart from the *Gazette*'s story on Katya and Hugo, it had been a slow Saturday.

They were about to drink a toast when Bob Howard glanced at the mute television and pointed to the *Chronicle*'s front page, which filled the screen. Someone turned up the sound and they heard the newscaster give full credit to the *Chronicle* for its exclusive. The *Gazette* splash was not mentioned.

An impromptu cheer ricocheted around the room and Liz raised her glass, 'To the best splash in town', then made another silent toast to Joanna and George's baby.

As the staff left one by one, Liz picked up the phone. She tried the Oxford number. He was still out. Dejectedly she grabbed her handbag and went out on to the nearly deserted news floor. It had been an extraordinary and exhausting day. What a pity her parents were not here to share her triumph. Sitting next to the driver on her way home, Liz fell fast asleep.

Chapter Nineteen

Was Joanna's baby still alive?

The unspoken question hung between them as Liz and Katya walked as fast as they could towards Joanna's ward on Sunday afternoon.

The sister had refused to discuss Joanna's condition on the phone and they hurried anxiously across the green lino, ignoring the ripple effect among patients, visitors, nurses and doctors alike caused by Katya's presence.

Liz still felt guilty. How much had her paper, pursuing Katya for the splash, to do with Joanna's possible miscarriage? And who knew what the *Gazette* story would still do to Katya's career? The headline had been enough to make Katya phone her parents to warn them. The shock was lessened because she was able to direct them to the *Chronicle*'s front-page denial. And they were pleased to hear she was issuing a writ.

As Liz and Katya entered Joanna's ward, they heard the sound of stifled sobs. They looked at each other aghast. But they were relieved that it was not Joanna who was crying, although she was lying flat on her back staring into space looking miserable and alone.

One look at her pale face and they feared the worst.

'Oh, Jo,' said Liz, bending over to kiss her. 'I'm so very, very sorry.'

Katya, wordless, took her hand.

Joanna managed a weak smile. 'Don't worry, I think it's going to be all right. The doctors say if I don't move a muscle for the next three months the baby will probably be fine.'

'Oh, that's wonderful.'

323

'Fabulous.' Her friends were overjoyed.

'They want to put a stitch in my cervix later today,' Joanna went on, 'to strengthen the womb. But even with the stitch it's still going to be touch and go. The surgeon's coming to have a look in a minute.'

'That's great,' said Katya. 'Is this stitch thing difficult?'

'They think not and anyway Dr Bischoff warned me this might have to happen.'

'Well, you're certainly in the right place.'

Joanna sighed deeply. 'I've brought this on myself. I knew I shouldn't have gone to New York, I shouldn't have gone to BAFTA and I should have come home much earlier every day from the office. I feel so guilty and so stupid for letting myself get into this state.'

'Come on, don't be so hard on yourself. You've just been unlucky. You've got one of those bodies that can't cope. How are you feeling?' asked Katya.

'Well, the bleeding's stopped, stopped last night actually, and I'm feeling better in myself, but the really worrying thing is that I'm not allowed to move. I can't even get up for a pee. I'm going to have to stay like this until the baby is born. How on earth can I edit a magazine from here?'

'It's not impossible,' Liz replied slowly. 'Of course, you'd need to do it in a different way. You'd have to be sensible and delegate far more. You can't worry about every caption and every story.'

'Yes, but it's the big stories and the covers,' replied Joanna anxiously. 'I'd have to get involved in those, wouldn't I?'

In the silence the whirrings of three brains ticking away was almost audible. Then Katya theatrically fished in her handbag for her battered canvas-and-leather Filofax and held it up with a flourish. 'Look, between the three of us, we must be able to get to anyone you'll ever want or need, Jo. You'll have some of these numbers but we might have different ones. Take the As,' she went on, 'Andrew, Prince, home and ship numbers; Anne, Princess, London and Gatcombe; Aga Khan ... Albee, Edward ...'

Liz did not miss a beat. She, too, dug deep in her bag for her electronic organiser. 'Berlusconi, Silvio, all the numbers; Bardot,

Brigitte, both her numbers in St Tropez . . . C . . . Caine, Michael; Caroline, Princess, her Monaco and St Rémy de Provence numbers.'

They looked at their prostrate and still pregnant friend.

Joanna smiled.

They were back on course.

But a thought came unbidden to Liz. How had she ever come so near to ripping this closeness apart? Fears for Joanna and the baby certainly put journalism and its transient needs into perspective. She made a solemn vow. She would never again think of sacrificing everything and everybody for her career, would she?

A flustered nurse put her head round the floral curtain and asked shyly, 'Miss Croft, could you please sign this card for the children's ward? It's for the hospital raffle.'

'Certainly,' said Katya.

All three friends were still smiling when the curtains were pushed aside again. They stared in disbelief. A tall, lean, tanned figure was struggling to hold on to what looked like the entire contents of the ground-floor hospital flower shop.

'George.' Joanna fought back tears.

'My poor, darling Jo,' he said and throwing the roses on the counterpane he put his arms round her. 'What a fright you've given me.'

They held each other wordlessly and Joanna let out a sigh of pleasure as she rested her head in the curve of his neck. Neither noticed Liz and Katya tiptoeing away down the ward.

George cupped Joanna's face in his hands and kissed her eyes, then the tip of her nose. 'I'll tell you what, my love,' he said. 'I'm not ever leaving you again. From now on I'm going to look after you properly.'

Joanna nodded happily.

'Good.' He sat back. 'I've been travelling all night and I could kill for a cup of tea. What do you think of my chances?'

She laughed. It was good to have him home.

In front of the Prime Minister's official residence in Downing Street the Chief Whip's dark blue Jaguar stood parked, un-chauffeured.

The policeman outside No. 10, one of those who are on a twenty-four-hours-a-day, 365-days-a-year rota, shifted from foot to foot to keep himself awake. This Sunday had, as usual, been unrelieved boredom. At least it was not wet. And at least tonight there was some action.

The boss had arrived back from Chequers only an hour before, so the policeman was surprised when the Chief Whip's car had arrived and the man himself had emerged from the driver's seat. The policeman was an old hand. Driven himself, he thought. Wryly, he smiled to himself. Just like the royals, this lot, they've learned not to trust the telephone any more. As always, he marvelled that when something really important was being plotted the photographers were miles away and the press reptiles fast asleep in their beds. Or someone else's.

Fergus decided he had spent quite enough time grappling with the problem of Charlie Mays's successor as editor. Impatient, always on the go, for him business deals were done quickly or not at all.

It was just after 1 a.m. on Monday morning when he dialled the *Chronicle*'s switchboard on the freephone number from his villa in the South of France, giving instructions to wake his secretary at home so that she could arrange for Charlie to be on the first available plane out of Miami airport to Heathrow. Fergus wanted him to be in his office in the *Chronicle* building by 5 p.m.

He asked for Liz Waterhouse to be summoned to the penthouse at 6 p.m. Prompt.

And for Nicola Wellesley to be there at 8 p.m.

Over coffee and hot buttered toast, the disgraced former Minister for Health was voicing his suspicions about Rosemary Burroughs to the Chief Whip.

'You'll never keep this under wraps. It was the *Chronicle* that jogged my memory. They're nearly there.'

The mole hunt gathered speed.

Once the children had gone back to school on their special bus, Davina started packing her belongings into four large suitcases. She could not use the ministerial car to transport them from Warwickshire to Roland Mews. That was domestic use and not allowed. In any case, it would have been unwise. Gossip about her private affairs would be round the House of Commons by lunchtime. The cases would be brought up by the family gardener. Later.

After she had finished, she locked the cases and, looking every inch the minister, she stepped into her chauffeured car for London and the usual departmental meeting. As she disappeared down the drive, Hugo's architect arrived to make plans for the internal partitioning of the Manor House.

Once again Liz tried to phone David Linden. She was starting to believe that Thursday night had been a figment of her imagination. Including the messages from him on her memo pad on Saturday.

Still no reply from his number. Where the hell could he be this early in the morning?

The first edition of the *London Evening Herald* followed up the mole story, or tried to, but they also printed a front page blurb: 'The TV Star, the Journalist and the Minister's Husband.' Inside, they had a double-page article explaining the background to Katya's alleged affair.

This was the wonderful way in which other papers could repeat every sordid detail that had been alleged by the *Gazette* plus Katya's statement to Liz in the *Chronicle* without being sued themselves. Somehow they had obtained pictures of Katya with Liz and Jo taken in Mallorca and since then at BAFTA, as well as many details of their lives which they had forgotten.

Tony had given his family a miserable Sunday working himself into a fury. Not only had their rival printed the right and proper splash, but his so-called editor had allowed her friend page one, column one, to deny it. Okay, she had told him that Morning TV had been planning a documentary about Davina. That explained the calls itemised on the phone bill. Maybe.

But what about the most damning evidence of all, the letter? 'Left behind after a script conference' indeed. No, Tony did not believe Katya's denial story.

Attack was the best method of defence. He felt he had right on his side and decided to waylay Fergus on his return from France.

The news man pretended surprise when he bumped into the proprietor in the *Chronicle*'s marbled entrance hall but asked if he could take up a few minutes of Fergus's time.

Facing Fergus over the desk, Tony grudgingly conceded that the paper's splash on the party traitor had been quite good, though they had not been given the go-ahead soon enough to be able to publish the name.

'A pity because the story might not have held till next week.'

'What would you have done?' asked Fergus. Tony felt a surge of adrenaline. Now was his chance.

'I'd have gone with the splash on Katya Croft and Hugo Thomas,' he said. 'I know we printed that denial but I don't believe it, not with the evidence we had. I think Liz published it because Katya Croft is one of her best friends. In fact, I'd like your permission to pursue it for next week. The *Gazette* put on several thousands and ours will be a lot stronger than their story.'

'Those two are suing the *Gazette*,' said Fergus coolly. 'It's going to be messy. Drop it.'

Tony was not getting anywhere and because he knew of Fergus's legendary impatience, his words were more direct and clumsy than they otherwise might have been. 'Look, I hate to tell you what I'm about to but I feel it's my duty to the paper. Liz had a mental breakdown not too long ago.'

He handed over the photograph of the admissions register from the Mallorca clinic with Liz's name ringed in red.

As Fergus studied it, his face was impossible to read. Tony plunged on. 'She was an in-patient at a clinic for nervous diseases. Last week her mood swings caused real problems on the paper and her changes of mind lost us the time to front up Rosemary Burroughs so the dailies will cash in on the work we did on that story. I just wonder if Liz can handle the mental pressure of the job.'

Fergus leaned back, swivelling a pencil beween his fingers. There was a slight pause before he said, 'Oh, I think she can. It wasn't so much a mental breakdown as depression after her mother's suicide. And it was twelve years ago, after all. Liz told me all about it last week. I don't think it played any part in the problem of the splash and I don't believe it will in the future.'

He gave Tony a half-smile. 'I think the best duty you can give to this newspaper would be to give her your support and I know I can rely on you to do that.'

Afterwards, a worried Tony put through a call to Charlie. There was no reply from his suite. Tony was even more anxious when he was told that Charlie had already checked out.

A dark blue Rover carrying one of the senior partners from Farrar and Co., solicitors to the Queen, and his junior, swept past the photographers now standing by St Theresa's hospital gates in tiered platforms on aluminium ladders.

He had been summoned to see Hugo Thomas. The deposition from his client read, 'I have never once been in the company of the woman in question, nor have I met this woman, nor have I knowingly been in the same building with her.'

The grey-haired legal eagle who had been at school with Hugo allowed himself a rare chuckle. 'Sounds like a good, strong defence. I like it.'

He dialled his secretary and began to dictate: 'To the editor of the *Sunday Gazette*. Dear Sir, We act for Hugo Thomas who has consulted us in respect of an article published . . .'

The letter ended with the usual legal barb: 'We must ask for your immediate reply and wish to make it clear that Mr Thomas fully reserves all rights in this matter in any event.'

When he left, the boot of his car contained a blue canvas sports bag given to him by his client, to be placed in Farrar and Co.'s office safe.

Katya, her agent, the station's managing director and the company's solicitor met to discuss whether or not she would sue the *Sunday Gazette*.

The star convinced them that, because of her image, she would prefer not to take further legal action. The managing director disagreed. He thought it would maintain Katya's squeaky-clean family image both for the viewers and, even more important, for the

Independent Television Commission who were in charge of renewing franchise licences. He also did not discount the value of the attendant publicity.

Katya's agent was mystified by her reluctance to go to court.

The argument continued but came to no final conclusion that day.

The Thomas–Croft affair had lured the major media gossips into El Vino's wine bar from all over London.

Who had leaked the story from the *Chronicle* to the *Gazette?* And when? What was happening to the editorships at the *Chronicle?* Someone said that Charlie Mays had been spotted at Heathrow.

Would Hugo really sue? Would Katya? If they did, how much would they get?

And who was the mole in the government?

Except for those who worked for the *Gazette*, the journalists and newspaper managers were full of hypocritical smugness. It was great to see another newspaper under fire, getting a kick right where it really mattered. In its profit centre.

The *London Herald* had a new front page. The blurb had been swapped and incorporated into their splash. The headline read: 'WE'VE NEVER EVEN MET, SAYS MINISTER'S HUSBAND.'

The statement from Farrar and Co. made it clear that further legal action was intended after Mr Hugo Thomas was discharged from hospital. Katya, too, was expected to issue a writ.

The Prime Minister's Private Parliamentary Secretary was having a working lunch with his boss over a good bottle of claret and selected sandwiches of egg and cress, tuna and mayonnaise and ham and mustard.

The Chief Whip had passed on his information about the traitor in their midst and the PPS was shifting appointments so that Philip Burroughs could be fitted in at 2 p.m. to tender his resignation.

Their depression at the prospect of a by-election made them agree to delay the announcement until 4 p.m. when the PM would be safely on his way to Heathrow to greet the American President on his arrival for an official visit to Ireland.

Next on their agenda was a Note from the Foreign Office advising the security service that on this occasion it was not going to serve any useful purpose to claim that Hugo Thomas's car accident had been caused by a terrorist bomb.

The Prime Minister was aware that Hugo Thomas had retained Farrar and Co. and was saying that he had never even met the TV star he had been linked with and was planning legal action.

The PPS said, 'You remember that discussion with the Chief Whip last night?' For the first time, his boss smiled.

'Ah yes,' nodded the Prime Minister. 'Hugo Thomas's accident.'

'The security boys downstairs have a copy of that video.'

'That reminds me,' said the PM, 'make sure I see Davina tomorrow morning. Early.'

In the much-discussed government reshuffle that followed, the Minister of State at the Home Office was moved from the broadcasting portfolio. No official reason was ever given and Davina never found out how much about her private life was known and by whom. She had her suspicions.

It took her some time to reconcile herself to being a backbencher again. Permanently.

Hugo Thomas's canny lawyer, justifying a bill of thousands, demanded an apology from the *Gazette*. It was to have a prominent headline, be positioned above the fold, on a right-hand page, and to be published only on page three or page five.

The *Gazette* complied.

Hugo accepted a large out-of-court settlement which he publicly donated to the Red Cross, international division.

'Philip Burroughs, fifty-three-year-old MP for West Warwickshire, today tendered his resignation to the Prime Minister for personal reasons,' announced a Press Association news flash at 4 p.m.

The mole was not identified but many in the press added two and two together and for once made four, not five.

In the press coverage that followed, the Prime Minister thanked the resigning MP for his hard work and loyalty and the party looked forward nervously to a by-election within the next three months.

What happened between Philip Burroughs and his wife Rosemary was not made public. They never spoke to the media. Weeks later their full story emerged.

Liz was shocked. She had arrived early on the sixth floor and had glimpsed a tanned Charlie Mays emerging from Fergus's office looking very, very happy.

So that was it. By being loyal to Katya she had thrown away her chances. She was therefore amazed when Fergus offered her the editorship of the *Sunday Chronicle*. She was even more inspired when Fergus told her that Charlie had been appointed editor of the *Daily Chronicle* but only until his retirement in three years, seven months' time.

Fergus had winked. 'Not long at all.'

Over the remnants of the Krug that he had opened with Charlie, they discussed the *Gazette*'s legal problems and what they should do about Tony Burns.

No one ever suspected that the real lovers were Katya and Davina, mainly because both looked so feminine. However, a zealous reporter on the *Gazette* decided to keep watch intermittently on Davina's mews house. He was certain there was a story to be written, and he could wait.

The phone bill was explained away as connected to the documentary Katya and Davina were allegedly collaborating on, the letter from the dustbin was never discussed again. Liz lodged it in her safe.

The divided house meant that Hugo and Davina camouflaged their separation, which became permanent after a no-blame divorce two years later.

Immediately afterwards, Hugo married a woman fifteen years his junior who had no wish to pursue a career other than as her husband's hostess. Davina's daughters became happy half-siblings to two new half-sisters.

The next generation of high fliers, which included Stephanie Ross and Debbie Luckhurst, carefully observed their role models and wondered whether the sacrifices were worth making in order to win the top prizes in a man's world. Yes, they wanted to achieve the same rewards, but how much were they prepared to give up, both spiritually and emotionally? Although envying these women's success, they did not have unqualified admiration for them. To many outsiders, Katya, Liz and Joanna appeared tough and self-sufficient.

Later the younger women learned they would have to cut the same corners and restrict their lives to a narrow focus of work, work and more work with time for only the basic obligations of family life.

In fact, little had changed.

Epilogue: Six Months Later

Dr Bischoff's prediction was proved completely wrong. Luke George Glaister Langford was most definitely a boy. Six weeks after his birth he filled St Peter's church in Broad Chalke, Wiltshire with robust yells when the cold water from the 500-year-old font touched his forehead.

Dressed in the Langford christening robes, made of embroidered muslin and cotton with puffed, lace-trimmed sleeves and Peter Pan collar, Luke looked far from small and delicate. More like a junior version of Sir Winston Churchill. The baby's two godmothers stood in the small circle around the font and marvelled that a baby who had caused so much trouble in the womb could be so noisy out of it.

As they repeated the solemn words after the vicar, renouncing all evil, Liz and Katya both had the silent, identical thought: I haven't been so good at looking after myself, how the hell am I going to help this little mite?

Luke's grandmother stood in the front pew, stiff and proud, her eyes misted with sentiment that another generation of Langfords was in place, able to continue the line. That was all that mattered. The baby had, at last, earned Joanna a scintilla of approval from her mother-in-law.

Shoulder to shoulder with Joanna stood a proud George, who had cried with happiness when he witnessed the birth of his son. The morning afterwards he had gone job hunting for the first time in his life, his previous job having been 'offered' through his public-school network. He landed a position as the enthusiastic if modestly paid deputy director of a new international charity. Its headquarters were firmly based in Belgravia because of an endowment by a philanthropist who loved the world but London best. At last, George was able to stay close to his wife, and to his new son.

After more than three months lying in bed, Joanna had been desperate to rejoin the world outside the hospital ward. Money was not her prime motivation because George's slightly larger salary helped. Her return to work was more a matter of pride. She needed to prove to herself that her fierce drive had not been diminished by motherhood, as many had predicted. Like her son, the 'curse of ambition' was very much alive.

By the time of the christening, she was back in harness at *Women's View*, where thankfully Miss Angus had outstayed the MD who had been moved unexpectedly to the Sydney office.

It helped that since Joanna was back at the helm of the magazine the sales and advertising of *Women's View* had more than lived up to the forecasts. Joanna wondered if the magazine would have been as successful without her weekly conferences with her two friends. Even now she was up and about, they continued to feed her with ideas for features, contacts to interview and great pictures they had seen in foreign magazines for which she could buy second rights.

But, despite herself, motherhood had changed Joanna. The Fulham terraced cottage had been sold for enough money to buy a four-bedroomed Edwardian house in Chiswick, reasonably near the river and with a garden large by London standards. But it meant a longer journey to and from work and she now had to be far more calculating about how she spent her time out of the office.

Most nights she relieved her nanny at 7 p.m. but once or twice a week she would have to go to cocktail parties or receptions as a necessary part of her job. Occasionally she had a drink with Liz and Katya, but she had to admit that she felt guilty about being away from her baby.

She preferred to see them for supper every Monday night at her home when George was on baby patrol.

After the church service, the guests were entertained in the blue drawing room (slightly warmer than the yellow one but still with a temperature reminiscent of the Antarctic) at Catherine Langford's home.

As Joanna handed the sleeping baby over to his gratified grand-mother she looked fondly at her baby's two godmothers who were, with some surprise, taking a glass of champagne from a silver salver being proffered by Stephanie Ross.

Joanna hurried over. 'Look, here comes the lion-tamer,' said Liz, raising her glass.

Joanna lowered her voice. 'Quite a turn-around, isn't it? I think Stephanie feels lucky to have kept her job after the hash she made while I was away.'

'Yes, but inviting her here? To help? What's going on?' asked Katya.

'Well, since the MD disappeared she seems to be trying to join in, rather than feather her own nest. She's very pleased I persuaded the Suits not to sack her by saying she still had potential.' Joanna gave a wicked laugh. 'You can't imagine how useful it is to have a deputy who's grateful.'

'Yes I can,' retorted Liz. 'Bob Howard's turning out to be exactly what I need, steady, dependable and loyal.'

'Ah, but how does he get on with Tony?' enquired Katya.

'Amazingly enough, he's developed into quite a match for the creep, who's as sour as ever, by the way. I'd get rid of him in a minute but Fergus has asked me to try and work with him.'

'Why does he want to stay?' puzzled Joanna. 'I thought he'd be first out the door when you got the job.'

'Because Fergus finds him useful.' Liz emphasised each word. 'I always knew Tony told Charlie everything, but now he's got the boss's ear. Fergus encourages him. Apparently he has a nark in every one of his businesses, like most tycoons, I suppose. At least I know where most of the snide stories in the other papers come from.'

'I would hate that,' commented Joanna. 'I had a bit of it with Stephanie. I wouldn't recommend it for a happy environment.'

'How do you put up with it?' Katya asked Liz.

'It's not all roses being a newspaper editor, I can tell you,' she admitted, 'but I try to neutralise the bugger whenever I can and that new features exec I told you about is turning out to be a real asset. She's got great ideas and makes them happen without all the puffing and blowing that Tony comes out with. She makes him look really old-fashioned.'

'Ouch,' said Katya. 'And to think that on Mallorca we thought you fancied him.'

Liz smiled at this distant memory. She was looking lovely but tired. The responsibilities of being an editor had eaten further into her energy and leisure but the *Sunday Chronicle* was slowly building circulation and, more importantly to Fergus, was increasing its advertising revenue.

'Talking about fancying, how did Thursday go?' asked Katya, taking another glass of champagne from a passing tray. Liz looked rueful.

The affair between her and David Linden was still progressing well but Liz herself described it as 'G. I.' – Geographically Impossible.

Each time they met was an Occasion. These were extraordinary hours. Intense sex. Intense conversation. Intense fascination with one another. But they did not meet very often. It was wonderful, but it was not real life.

'Remember I told you last week that things were going too well? I was right. Now he's started grumbling about my job. Last night, he actually said he thought that I put it before him.'

The three exchanged glances, heavy with meaning. How often had they heard this before?

'What could I say to that?' said Liz. 'I had to lie. I said most of the problem was that we lived so far apart. And then what happens? When I am free, he isn't. I ask him to come with me today and he has to prepare for an important lecture. Or so he says.'

'Ah, do we detect a little lack of trust here?'

'Absolutely,' replied Liz. 'Well, he made the big mistake of telling me about his past. It doesn't make for security, I can tell you, especially with someone like me.'

'When will lovers learn to keep their mouths shut?' asked Joanna. 'Even though he knew I'd been married before, George somehow got the impression that I was a virgin when we met.'

They had laughed when Joanna told them she had managed to obliterate all memory of her sex life with her first husband, even

338

to the extent of forgetting whether or not he was circumcised.

They rarely discussed Katya's love life unless she raised the subject. Nobody close to her could be unaware how painful the break-up with Davina had been and that she was still suffering. Katya had bumped into Davina once or twice during the course of her job but nothing is so dead as the passion of two people who once loved so much. They had barely spoken.

Katya's television station had insisted on an immediate apology from the *Gazette* and the consequent out-of-court settlement led to the sacking of Stuart Roberts for his lack of judgement. Katya used the substantial damages to buy a hideaway cottage for her and her friends to retreat to from the madness of media life in London.

She had decided to keep her sexuality a secret from everyone except three people: Joanna, Liz – and her mother, who was not as shocked as Katya thought she would be. Out of habit they kept the information from her father who, the year before his death, decided that what he wanted most in life was a grandson. He had died never knowing his daughter was a lesbian, always feeling she had disappointed him.

Although she continued to be publicly linked romantically with every eligible man she met, Katya joked to her friends that celibacy was good for creativity. In the last couple of months she had had two television series ideas accepted and there was a strong possibility that she would get her own political discussion programme.

The friendship between the three women was as strong as ever, though now it took a different turn. The arrival of Joanna's baby had done more to disturb it than Katya's lesbianism. They had learned that the days of casually dropping everything to rush to the cinema or a new restaurant were over for good.

Katya still could not be phoned after 9.00 at night and as she was now trying to present a more mature image she was seen less often in the glitter spots.

Liz was in a total stew towards the end of the week and was usually exhausted on Sundays. And neither she nor Katya felt they could phone Joanna easily at weekends for fear it might disturb a much-needed nap or, worse, wake the baby.

But one of many enduring things about their friendship was that they could admit the problem without feeling as if they had let one another down, and the fact that they all doted on the baby increased their affection for each other.

Eating a tiny canapé to mop up the christening champagne, Joanna told them, 'I think I've got this marriage and baby lark licked. I now know exactly what not to do. I'll be the perfect wife and mother with my next husband.'

Liz dug her in the ribs. 'You can't get on to your third before I've had my first.' She sighed. 'Do you think I'll ever meet anybody that I'm attracted to who won't feel threatened by my job?'

Katya looked thoughtful. 'It won't be easy. It never is, especially with the sort of hours you work.'

'But surely things won't always be as bad as now,' Joanna chimed in. 'You'll become more experienced, more organised and, who knows, even learn to delegate.'

They all guffawed at this.

'But I can't ever see a time when any of us wouldn't want to be financially independent,' said Katya.

'And living in the manner to which we have, sadly, become accustomed,' added Joanna.

George, walking past, overheard Liz say, 'Thanks partly to your dabbling on the stock market, we've not done badly lately. When we grow up, let's do something completely different, form a company together. Why not?'

Joanna smiled at her husband. 'She's talking about Money Making Idea number nine thousand five hundred and two.'

George kissed the top of her head and stole the remains of her drink. 'Haven't you heard the phrase "if it ain't broke, don't fix it"?' he asked. 'I don't know why you lot keep on worrying about what you're going to do next.

'Men don't.' And he moved back across the room towards his son.

The women smiled at each other and Katya raised her glass. 'I have a toast. Here's to the worry, lack of confidence and insecurity that drives us on.'

'And to one thing more important than all that,' said Liz.

There was no hesitation. Their glasses and voices were raised in unison.

'To friendship.'